MW01128944

COME AND GET ME

MARISA RAE DONDLINGER

Black Rose Writing | Texas

ISBN: 978-1-68513-405-1
LIBRARY OF CONGRESS CONTROL NUMBER: 2023949042
PUBLISHED BY BLACK ROSE WRITING
www.blackrosewriting.com

Printed in the United States of America
Suggested Retail Price (SRP) $23.95

Come and Get Me is printed in Baskerville

*As a planet-friendly publisher, Black Rose Writing does its best to eliminate unnecessary waste to reduce paper usage and energy costs, while never compromising the reading experience. As a result, the final word count vs. page count may not meet common expectations.

To Lolita and Harlow. My angels, my loves.

"An edge-of-your seat thriller with an intimate look at marriage, *Come and Get Me* never lets up on the action. Heroes can have feet of clay and somehow the bad guy earns our sympathy. The writing is tight, the emotion raw, and the story so compelling I hated to finish it."
–Joyce Hurd, author of *Always Forward*

"*Come And Get Me* is a gripping domestic thriller that takes readers on a harrowing journey into the depths of obsession, desperation, and the destructive power of unrequited love. Perfect for fans of twisted narratives and complex characters driven to the edge."
–Gayle Brown, author of *A Deadly Game*

"*Come And Get Me* is a fast-moving, gripping, psychological thriller. The clever plot, short, propulsive chapters, flawed characters, severely damaged villain, and concern for Daisy, the sweet baby at the center, made it impossible to put down. I loved it."
–Karen E. Osborne, author of *Reckonings* and *True Grace*

"*Come And Get Me* is a tense, compelling novel that will shock you. Perfect for fans of Gillian Flynn and Laura Dave, as it explores themes like infidelity, desire, and the bonds of motherhood."
–Laurel Osterkamp, author of *Beautiful Little Furies*

ACKNOWLEDGEMENTS

Although writing is a solitary pursuit, the people listed below are invaluable in their commitment and enthusiasm to ensure *Come And Get Me* is the best book possible.

I'd like to thank Black Rose Writing, Reagan Rothe, and his team, for believing in my story, proactively communicating during the publishing process, lending a keen editing eye, and helping with promotion. I'm honored to be part of the Black Rose Writing family.

Kathie Giorgio at AllWriters Workplace and Workshop for her guidance in bringing this book to life. Your willingness to give your time to discuss plot lines and publicity, as well as be everyone's biggest cheerleader, is deeply appreciated. To my Tuesday night writing group. Thanks for all the insightful critiques and encouragement to keep pushing ahead.

Kathleen Eull at Pyxis Creative Solutions LLC for her stellar publicity work.

To my parents, the best unpaid publicists on the market! Thanks for promoting my work with friends and strangers alike, and encouraging me to never let go of my dreams.

Lolita and Harlow. You two are the best part of my day. I will always have time to listen, laugh, and give hugs.

Andy. You play so many roles in our lives; husband, father, tennis coach, and best friend. None of this success happens without you in my corner. Thanks for reminding me on tough days that I'm your favorite author. Believe it or not, you're my favorite tennis player.

COME
AND
GET
ME

PROLOGUE

VANESSA
FRIDAY, SEPTEMBER 1, 2023 9:55 A.M.

Parked on the street outside Cassidy's house, I watched through the floor to ceiling windows as she glided around the kitchen, putting away breakfast dishes, wiping counters, sipping coffee, all while wearing the Moby wrap like a girl scout's sash. Caffeine was horrible for breastfed babies. Led to irritability, inability to sleep, jitteriness—according to Google. I wouldn't know personally— fuck you, August. Yet, Cassidy refused to make this tiny sacrifice for her baby's health.

Not that it surprised me. I already knew she was selfish. A liar. Just like her husband.

I pulled off my binocular glasses and checked the notes app in my phone. If habit held, she would put the baby down for her morning nap in five minutes. *First piece of advice, new moms: get the baby on a schedule,* Cassidy instructed on her weekly podcast, *Lost in Babyland. When the baby sleeps, take a break. You earned it!* God, her voice grated. Girl-next-door vibes with her relatable confessions and a throaty laugh that said, *Hey, I used to be a good time, shooting whiskey and giving my boyfriend the occasional bathroom stall blow job, before pushing out a couple babies.* What a slut. And yet, Cassidy got to keep August's baby.

She was worthy. Not me.

Sure enough, five minutes on the dot, I watched Cassidy carry the baby upstairs. The back of the house spanned two floors, almost entirely windows, but once upstairs, the house provided cover until she emerged in the baby's—

Baby. I rolled my eyes. Stop being so impersonal. Her name was Daisy. Horrible choice. Daisies tried way too hard to be beautiful. And they never would be, not compared with the classic beauty of roses, the uniqueness of magnolias, or the brilliant colors of stargazer lilies. They were setting Daisy up for a lifetime of low self-esteem.

I would fix that. I would fix everything. Save her. Starting with a new name. Kiah. It meant "New beginning." I planned to name my baby Kiah. But I wasn't pregnant anymore, was I, August?

I lowered the window a couple of inches, inhaling deeply. Anger made it difficult to breathe. Think. Exist.

This will be over soon. I'll be a mother. Be happy again.

I pulled up the Sunshine Baby app, watching as Cassidy changed Kiah. The baby cam. What I first feared would be a roadblock quickly became a bonus. Cracking their Wi-Fi code was easy. The password was Piper, their elder daughter's birthday—a date Cassidy talked about on her podcast ad nauseam. It was also the garage code. Such naïve, unoriginal, lazy people. Better yet, Cassidy kept the remote access enabled on the app. She wanted to check up on Kiah when out—*Date nights are vital, ladies!*—but it gave me a front-row seat to watch Kiah from the comfort of my apartment. Again, trust. Had no one ever done Cassidy wrong?

Well, yes, in fact, August did her wrong hundreds of times. In dozens of ways. With me. And other women. But Cassidy didn't know that.

Yet.

While listening to August and Cassidy on the app, my emotions ranged from apoplectic with jealousy when he complimented her or shared an inside joke, hysterical tears when he said he loved her, to toasting their demise when they bickered. Some nights, I'd fall asleep with the app on, listening to my daughter sleeping, the gentle coos—

"Time to sleep, darling," Cassidy said now. I watched as she picked Kiah up and flipped off the light. The infrared LED on the app allowed me to see Kiah. "When you get up, we'll get Piper from school, have some lunch, and then go to the park. Can you take a good nap and let Mommy work?"

Cassidy was incorrigible. Bargaining with her infant daughter to work longer.

She flicked on the sound machine, kissed Kiah's head, and lay her in her crib. Like a robot. No smile. No "I love you." I bit my thumbnail, ripping it until the cuticle bled. Her selfishness made me rabid.

Did she get any joy from being a mother? Doubtful. Her podcast was one long bitch session. She was tired. Frazzled. Plagued with guilt. And the questions. So. Many. Questions! Who was she, other than a mother? What was her purpose? Did she have an identity of her own? How could she reclaim it? How would she ensure she didn't pass her "issues" onto her children?

I laughed. She'll get her answers soon.

Cassidy went to close the blinds. I looked up. She didn't bother to check her surroundings. And why would she? In her gilded world, nothing bad happened.

After Cassidy closed the bedroom door, I watched Kiah as she stretched her arms, wiggled her legs. Her eyes darted around the room, while rhythmically sucking on her pacifier. Adorable. Clearly, she wasn't tired. I shifted in my seat, wanting to march into the house, bring her home, tell her she'd never have to follow a stupid schedule with me. I had everything ready—

No. Be patient. Stick to the plan. If I go now, I'll make a mistake.

When Cassidy reemerged downstairs, she grabbed the baby monitor and her coffee cup—can't be without caffeine!—and headed toward her office. She didn't stop to set the house alarm.

I turned on my car, looping around the block for a better view of her office. Cassidy and August lived on a large corner lot, the front and left side of the house facing Sawnee Conservatory. Trees spanned toward the horizon. Trails. Ponds. Cars were parked along the street—hikers, fisherman, nature lovers—giving my car cover. It was a new bougie development, half-hour outside Milwaukee. A half-hour drive, every goddamn day, for my baby.

And August said I wasn't ready to make the sacrifices required of motherhood.

I looked in my rearview mirror, taking in the infant car seat I bought months ago. Back when the positive pregnancy test was my secret alone. Back before August ruined everything. It was detachable to work with the stroller. I got a great deal on Amazon and couldn't pass it up. I squeezed the wheel tighter as fresh rage thrust through my veins. Soon, soon, my baby would fill the car seat. Fill my life. Love me. As August promised.

As I turned back on their street, I drove slowly, inspecting the four houses on their block. This project required constant surveillance. Looking at faces. Documenting habits. Discrepancies. Finding DoorCams. Another reason I varied my parking spots and times.

One car was parked in front of August's house. I parked behind and shut off the engine. Unlike the nearly wall-to-wall windows that showcased the back and side of the house, the front was mainly brick. She kept the shutters on her office window permanently down, obstructing my view. Peering through the gaps felt like looking through the planks of a rickety bridge.

Parts of my plan would be left to chance. I'd never been inside their house—how could I when August lied to my face? Kept his wife and kid hidden? Lucky for me, Cassidy had no filter. Her podcast was a treasure chest of information. August tricked out her office with state-of-the-art recording equipment and her favorite furniture from Pinterest. Husband of the year! She never set the house alarm, because Piper often tripped it. Thanks, Piper! And the pièce de résistance? She told listeners she kept the monitor next to her while working, with the sound on low.

Liar.

I watched now as she closed her office door and set the monitor on the bookshelf across from her desk. Five feet away. Up high. Not in her eye-line. Why didn't she keep it close? Sleeping babies were the cutest. What kind of mother—ugh. Nope. I gnawed on the bloody stump of my thumbnail. Seeing her selfishness in action cemented my resolve. Cassidy deserved to lose Kiah. She'd have plenty of time to "find herself."

As Cassidy settled down to "important business," I traded the binoculars for sunglasses and slouched in my seat, watching to see how long she worked in her office. In the two weeks since Piper started school, Cassidy never diverted from her schedule. But I had to be certain. Meticulous with every detail. Careful not to leave evidence.

I would only get one chance.

My breath quickened as I thought about how it would feel to hold Kiah. Her heartbeat reverberating against mine. My lips pressed against her downy hair. Inhaling her powdery scent. How she'd gaze up at me with love and adoration, as if I set the sun and hung the moon.

I'd given up everything for her. Changed my last name. Got a new bartending job. As of last night, my apartment lease ended. Fell out of touch with friends so they wouldn't question my absence. Got a new phone. Closed my bank account. Bought prepaid Visa cards at different gas stations and groceries stores with cash, careful to never leave a trail. Eliminated all social media. Scored a fake ID. Bought formula, diapers, clothes, a bassinet! Prepared the lake house Mom left me after her death to be our new home. Lined up a job caretaking for seasonal houses this winter.

The list was endless. Exhausting. All so Kiah and I could be together—without August, Cassidy, or the police interrupting us.

For now, I stayed patient. It wasn't time to meet Kiah yet. But soon.

My baby was due Wednesday.

CHAPTER ONE

CASSIDY
WEDNESDAY, SEPTEMBER 6, 2023 8:10 A.M.

Cassidy was bleary-eyed and snappish by the time she dropped Piper off for kindergarten. She stood by the gates of the playground, pushing Daisy back and forth in her stroller, while watching Piper run to the slides to join the other kids. A rush of love, regret, and guilt filled Cassidy's heart, replacing her irritation, now that it was time to leave. Why couldn't she see Piper's decision to change her outfit five times this morning as a sign of creativity, her growing independence, instead of another obstacle toward getting her to school on time? Piper, as if sensing Cassidy's vulnerability, turned around and waved, the sky making her blue eyes shine brighter.

Forgiveness bestowed, relief seeped into Cassidy's veins, a steady drip-drip-drip that reminded her of coffee brewing. Everything reminded her of coffee. She was an addict. In three and a half hours, with copious amounts of caffeine, she'd accomplish her work and emerge at school pickup as the mom Piper deserved. Patient. Attentive. Loving.

Cassidy looked down at Daisy, happily gnawing on her hand. The saliva glistened in the sunlight. Last night, Daisy woke up crying three times, only to suck on Cassidy's nipple for a moment before spitting it out, stretching her neck back and wailing as if it was covered with anthrax. As if it wasn't the same meal she'd happily consumed the entire two months of her existence. After feeding failed, Cassidy tried changing her, rocking her, walking laps through the kitchen and living room. Nothing worked. Daisy's blood-curdling screams woke August around three. He stumbled out of the bedroom, clad in boxers and a t-shirt, hair tufted in all directions, voice gritty when he offered to take her for a few hours so Cassidy could rest. She declined. He needed to be energetic, charismatic, *lucid* to sell houses, while she, in theory, could sneak an afternoon nap by letting Piper watch *Encanto* for the thousandth time.

Unlike Cassidy, Daisy bore no ill effects from her sleepless night. Her crabbiness evaporated with the rising sun. The topsy-turvy sleep schedule had to change. Cassidy couldn't survive on three hours each night.

Cassidy pushed the stroller to her car, transported the infant seat into the car, then folded up the stroller and heaved it into the trunk. By the time she reached the driver's seat, sweat dampened her armpits. Nothing was easy with a baby. Nothing.

She drove in a fog, seeing the other cars as shadows, hearing the traffic noise as if from inside a tunnel. A horn blared. She looked to her left, realizing she drove through a stop sign. In a school zone. "Ahh!" She let out a strangled scream. Heat rose to her cheeks. Tears sprung in her eyes. She held up her hand to the driver before accelerating.

After making it safely home, she parked in the garage, took the stroller out of the trunk, and latched Daisy in. Since giving birth—who was she kidding, since the seventh month of pregnancy—she hadn't visited the gym. Walking was her exercise. She convinced herself that walking was the holistic way to energize, with fresh air and nature. Get some endorphins running through her blood instead of caffeine.

She pushed Daisy across the street and onto the dirt trail of the Sawnee Conservatory, a hundred and fifty-acres of interwoven trails, ponds, and wetlands. It was a peaceful morning. Warm with a light breeze. Enjoy the beauty, she admonished herself. Savor this time with your daughter.

Five minutes in, exhaustion took over and she wanted to turn around. Cuddle with Daisy on the couch. A half-hour, she told herself. Enough to get her heart moving, awaken her brain, strengthen her muscles, feel good about herself. Because, honestly, since having Daisy, she felt anything but beautiful. With Piper, she shed the baby weight in weeks. She didn't lose her hair or the shine of her skin like some of her friends. Then again, Piper slept like she was being paid for the hours logged. And with one child, Cassidy had more time for self-care. Cassidy actually gained weight since Daisy's birth. The blue-black bags under Cassidy's eyes made her look like an amateur boxer. And she got stretch marks. Cosmically unfair. Shouldn't it happen the first time the skin stretched?

Worst of all, August noticed. He didn't say anything—too much of a gentleman. But she knew her husband. He had a large sexual appetite. They'd have sex every night if it was up to him. But since her six-week appointment, giving them the green light, sexually speaking, they had sex twice. Twice in two weeks. An all-time low. Not that she wanted it. Far too tired. But she hated that *he* didn't want it.

Should she do a podcast on sex post-birth? How a woman's self-esteem played into the lack of intimacy? That could raise her streaming numbers. She'd run it by August first. He was her biggest supporter in getting the podcast off the ground, but he thought she shared too many private details. Discussing their sex life might push him too far.

She looked down at Daisy and smiled. "Should Mommy do a podcast on sex? Sex sells, right?" Daisy smiled. She was adorable. Cassidy stopped and pulled out her phone. "Smile, baby!" Daisy complied, her cheeks glowing pink as if embarrassed by the attention. Cassidy texted August the photo, writing, *Can she get any cuter?*

He immediately texted back, *Takes after her mom.*

Cassidy's cheeks wore a matching glow. Nice to be flirted with again. *Almost makes up for never sleeping!*

I'll take tonight's shift, he texted.

Let me nap for an hour when you get home and I'll be golden.

You got it.

She sent a kiss face emoji and started walking. After passing the pond, she cut over to the street, taking the shorter route home. She was on a schedule, after all.

Houses on the left, forest to the right, the neighborhood was serene. Large lots. Privacy. Nature. A cozy nook in suburbia. Expensive. Too expensive, she thought, but August insisted. She later learned his parents helped—a few glasses of wine and his mother lost all awareness of personal and spatial boundaries. But Cassidy let August have his secrets. Being a man, providing for their family, protecting Cassidy, was important to him.

She walked up the driveway, opened the garage using the key code, and left the car seat in the stroller—no point lugging it inside when she was using it again in a couple hours—next to the car. She grabbed Daisy and went into the house, debating whether to put her in the swing. While exhausted, she knew from Piper that this time of constantly holding Daisy was finite. Soon, Daisy would be crawling. Pulling up on things. Walking. Before Cassidy was ready, Daisy's breath painting her face would be a memory documented on her iPhone.

Instead, she put Daisy in the sling. Then tackled the chores. Dishes. Laundry. Rehanging the outfits Piper tossed on the floor. Finally, it was time for Daisy's nap. She changed Daisy's diaper, turned on the sound machine, gave her the pacifier, kissed her forehead, and lay her in her crib. For a few seconds, mother and daughter looked at each other. Smiled. Last night's antics were forgiven. Daisy's eyelids grew heavy. There would be no screams now.

Cassidy closed the drapes. As she softly pulled Daisy's door shut—no click, because she taped the latch—a familiar rush of anticipation filled her lungs, one that made her want to hold up a fist and run down the hallway, shouting, *They can take our lives, but they can never take our freedom!* She laughed. Maybe she should open the podcast with that quote. Would one line cost her money or was it part of the public domain?

So many questions for a silly joke.

With fresh coffee, she walked to her office, shut the door, and set the baby monitor on the bookshelf. Once in her chair, she rubbed her eyes, craving a nap. No time. She fired up her computer, ready to work, ready to leave behind her world outside these four walls.

CHAPTER TWO

VANESSA
WEDNESDAY, SEPTEMBER 6, 2023 10:10 A.M.

Today was my due date. The day I would meet my daughter.

I should've been numb up to my waist, wearing a cheap cotton hospital gown, grunting like a wounded animal, delirious tears running down my cheeks. Instead, I was white-knuckling the steering wheel as I drove toward August's house, dressed in black athleisure wear to mimic Cassidy's depressing wardrobe, mentally rehearsing last-minute details of how I would safely bring Kiah home.

Everything had to go perfect.

My track record for being perfect? Zero for roughly a gazillion.

I turned onto Swan Road, which wove through the middle of the Sawnee Conservatory. Flickers of sunlight pierced my eyes as it streamed through the leaves of the elm trees bracketing the road. I pulled over and parked past the trail. I was the only car parked here. Fingers crossed, if anyone took note, they would assume I was walking the trails.

My plan was to walk to August's house. Fifteen minutes. A necessary inconvenience. The path let out in front of his house, avoiding his neighbors' DoorCams. August didn't have any cameras installed. So trusting, those two.

I double-checked the contents of my backpack. Plastic gloves to not leave fingerprints. Benadryl; the dosage ready. A baby carrier to bring Kiah back to my car. The doll.

In the backseat, Kiah's car seat was rear-facing, like the manual instructed.

I was ready, right? *Right?*

On my phone, I pulled up the Sunshine Baby app. As I suspected, Kiah was asleep, one arm flung above her head, the other holding the pacifier near her mouth. Cassidy, presumably, was working, pretending what she said about motherhood mattered.

After shutting off my phone and shoving it in the glove compartment, I looked in the rearview mirror, jarred by the sight of the icy blonde wig. The blown-out tresses matched Cassidy's hair, but did my pale skin no favors. I pulled on a black cap—no logos, people remembered logos—and steeled my nerve with a pep talk.

You were born to be a mother. Kiah needs you. You cannot leave her with August. Or Cassidy. They are selfish, greedy, deceitful—

Stop it. I shook my head once. No time for anger.

Move! She's waiting!

I opened the car door, feeling like I was forgetting something. A-ha! I grabbed Cassidy's perfume from the middle console—Miss Dior, gag me, but she claimed August loved it—and stomached one quick spray so Kiah would take to my scent.

Every. Detail. Mattered.

I crossed the street and stepped onto the dirt path, alert for danger. In the woods, the smallest of noises were amplified. The inhale and exhale of my breath, the slap of my feet hitting the dirt, animals snapping stray branches, my backpack swishing against my sweat-wicking top, the song of birds. A woman ran past with headphones in—in the woods, alone; this one wasn't a genius— muttering a breathy hello. I held up my hand and kept my head down.

Fear made my saliva evaporate. I kept licking my lips, burning the chapped skin. I'd murder some water right now.

I veered off the trail and came out on the street, August's house standing before me. The sun glinted off the windows, the dark stone, the steel framing. My eyes immediately found Cassidy's office, to the left of the front door. From this angle, though, it was impossible to see inside.

I bit my fingernail and spat it out. Kiah is sleeping. Cassidy is working—

Fuck! Could the police get my DNA from the fingernail? I looked down at the dirt and pebbles, unable to find my nail.

But if I couldn't, the police couldn't either. I kicked the dirt for good measure, hopefully burying it.

Stupid. Stupid. Stupid.

I crossed the street and started up their driveway, freezing when I saw the garage door open. A change. What did it mean? Was Cassidy planning on leaving soon? A doctor's appointment? A friend coming over? Or did she forget?

I looked back at the woods. Should I turn around? Recalibrate for another day?

Then I saw the stroller with the infant car seat next to the car. My shoulders unhinged a fraction of an inch. She went for her walk and forgot to close the garage door. A gift. I wouldn't need to wear Kiah in the carrier, making the walk back easier. Cooler. And less conspicuous.

Before stepping inside their house, I grabbed plastic gloves from my backpack. My hands were sweaty, making it feel like each finger was coated in glue. Come-on!

Annnndddddd done.

I looked at the street, ensuring no one was walking past. All clear. I zeroed in on the doorknob, touching the cool metal, willing my hand to turn it, willing myself to be brave.

With a spastic jerk, I opened the door and stepped inside.

CHAPTER THREE

CASSIDY
WEDNESDAY, SEPTEMBER 6, 2023 10:25 A.M.

Cassidy sat at her desk, trying to stay awake, while brainstorming this week's podcast on potty-training. She pulled up an old picture of Piper in a t-shirt and her training underwear—her heart contracted, seeing Piper's ringlet curls and chubby thighs—and posted it on Instagram. The beast of social media required constant updates, inventiveness, and creativity. Kid pics upped engagement. *Potty training doesn't have to be hell—for long! New episode of* Lost in Babyland *drops Monday!* This would keep her accountable.

She rubbed her burning eyes. Sticker charts and candy prizes were overdone. And didn't work. How could her podcast stand out? First, she would sympathize. Share a few horror stories from potty-training Piper. The comments suggested her listeners loved her personal touch. The way she wasn't afraid to air dirty laundry, admit how confounded she was by motherhood. Then, she'd tackle the topic with a fresh, yet workable solution—as soon as she developed one.

Cassidy looked at the monitor on the bookshelf. Daisy was sleeping, making up for last night. Taking a cue from her daughter, Cassidy rested her head on the desk. Five minutes. Nothing more. Something to take the sting out of her eyes. The fog from her brain. The knots from her muscles. She closed her eyes, remembering how she started the blog during her pregnancy with Piper. Worries about motherhood kept her awake—along with a brutal case of sciatica. With her background in PR, writing a blog came naturally. When Piper was an infant, one reader suggested she start a podcast. That comment gained over a thousand likes.

August encouraged her too, but she was afraid. What if no one listened? What if she said the wrong thing? Got blacklisted? Publicly humiliated? In this era of woke-ism, it was easy to offend. She couldn't decide. Shortly thereafter, she went away for a girls' weekend. Spa and relaxation time. While gone, August renovated her office. Bought a new Apple computer with top recording features. Gray and white furniture, mimicking her dream office on Pinterest. August's faith propelled her to try.

As stated on her website, Cassidy strived to create a community, a safe place women could go for an empathetic ear, where their concerns were reflected and handled with respect, care, and humor. A place where they wouldn't feel guilty, less than, or ostracized for not abdicating their former lives and falling on their knees at the altar of motherhood. Life was an evolution, success comes in many formats, and it wasn't selfish to want more than motherhood.

Over the past fifteen months, she started making a little ad revenue. Local businesses. As Cassidy drifted to sleep, she dreamed of her podcast topping the charts, writing a book, making talk show appearances. With time and hard work, everything was possible.

CHAPTER FOUR

VANESSA
WEDNESDAY, SEPTEMBER 6, 2023 10:40 A.M.

Deep breath. Stop shaking. You're doing it. Just. Stay. Calm.

I gently closed the door to the garage. The house smelled of pancakes. The kitchen lay ahead, the stairs just before. Cassidy's office to the left. Laundry room to the right, a load in the dryer masking my footsteps. Still, each footfall felt like an elephant.

I crept up the stairs, refusing to be distracted by the family portraits on the wall. False images. Libelous. If I was a curator, I'd entitle the collection, Hypocrisy of a Happy Family.

First right. Then left. I pushed open the door, afraid of a screech, but the hinges were oiled, the latch kept flat with a piece of masking tape. I padded across the room and opened the drapes a few inches for light. Three steps later, I stood over Kiah's crib. I gasped. She was beautiful; the tiny bow of her lips, the snub nose, thick, dark eyelashes, adorable little breaths. The wave of emotion pummeled me. It felt like listening to a CD of my favorite band and then seeing them in concert. I could've wept.

Along with love, though, fresh rage burned. Kiah was two months old, not two seconds. I missed precious first moments. Pushing her out. Laying eyes on her. Hearing her wail. Holding her. Her weight insubstantial, but everything to me. The intimacy of her mouth on my breast, the high of nourishing her. First kisses. She would've been beautiful. An angel. Mother and daughter, but also best friends. Like Mom and me.

Instead, this. Kiah. Me. Thrown together two months too late. *Thelma & Louise* meets *Rosemary's Baby* meets *Baby Boom*. Mom loved old movies.

I unzipped my backpack a couple inches and pulled out the doll. Ever so gently, I rested her in the crib next to Kiah. An excellent match—pale skin, blonde hair, pink lips. The ultimate fuck-you to August. As much as I wanted my baby, I wanted to hurt him. Make him ache. Understand the pain of having his baby torn away. Not from his body, of course. Some pain you can't mimic. This doll was the angel standing guard as he entered hell.

I bit my lower lip.

Don't get distracted.

A pacifier rested next to Kiah's head. I shoved it in my pocket. Then I reached down, pressing the back of my hands into the mattress, one hand beneath Kiah's neck and the other beneath her butt, and pulled her toward me.

Not too fast. Not. Too. Fast.

Kiah burrowed her head to my chest, as if she knew I was her salvation. As if she had been waiting for me too.

No time to savor the moment. Go. Go. Go!

I walked out of the room, legs as taut as the tinman, not bothering to close the door. Down the stairs, which felt like descending Mount Everest, each stair steeper than the next. What if I stumbled? Missed a step? What if Cassidy came out of her office? What would I do? Run?

But Cassidy never appeared. And Kiah never stirred.

Taking my hand off of Kiah's back for a split-second, I opened the door and stepped into the garage. Then shut the door behind me. Kiah whimpered as I stretched her arms beneath the straps of her car seat. Beads of sweat dotted my hairline, making the wig itch like a thousand mosquito bites. Hurry! I drew the canopy over her body, pulled off the rubber gloves, stuffed them in my backpack, and pushed the stroller down the driveway.

Once inside the woods, the trees, thick with leaves, provided cover. The director appeared, assuring me we would get through this together. From a young age, I pretended I was in a movie whenever nervous or scared. It started when Dad was upset with me—almost every day. I'd act snarky or indifferent, so he couldn't see how much it hurt. She later came when I was crushing on guys, needing to act like I wasn't a toxic dump of insecurities.

Now, the director gave me a pep talk. You're a mom. Taking your daughter for a walk. Slow down! Relax your mouth! Stop strangling the handle bar! Look happy!

For the first time, possibly ever, the director didn't help. My panic increased with each step. My heart raced. Cold sweat trickled from my armpits.

I stopped and bent to a squat, resting my head between my knees. Breathe. Breathe. It's over. You did it. Now move. Get to the car. Drive. You'll get caught if you stay here.

The panic wouldn't ebb.

The director whispered in my ear, Kiah belongs with you. August and Cassidy don't love her. Not the way you will. Fight for your child.

I stood up. Without my phone, I didn't know the time. Based on practice runs, if Cassidy stuck to her schedule, she didn't know Kiah was gone.

But she would soon.

I pushed the stroller, too fast, over a rooted branch in the dirt path. Kiah wailed. Every nerve pinged to attention. I whipped off my backpack and searched for the Benadryl. By the time I found it, she already settled.

"Thank you." I tilted the baseball cap back and wiped my brow.

Keep walking. Not far now. One foot in front of the other. You got this.

I needed to protect Kiah—at any cost. Weren't mothers engineered to do that? Sense danger? Protect their young? Cassidy wasn't. Too egotistical. Selfish. Careless. And it caught up with her today.

Mothering Kiah was my destiny. Well…maybe not my destiny. Giving birth today was my destiny. But August played God, altered the course of fate.

Today, I evened things up. Took what was rightfully mine.

When I got to my car, I grabbed Kiah and transferred her into my car seat. I had to tighten the straps—she was smaller than I thought. After closing the door, I turned my attention back to the stroller, quickly seeing the problem. It wouldn't fit into the trunk of my Jetta. A couple suitcases, the final items from my apartment that I hadn't moved to the lake house, took up the space.

Hmm. I bent down, looking closer. There had to be a way to collapse it. I've seen mothers hit something, folding it in two like ninjas. I kicked several levers and bars, but nothing happened. It wouldn't budge. I took the car seat out, but that didn't make a damn difference.

I stomped my foot. I should've stuck with the baby carrier, as I planned. Why did I get greedy? Lazy? Stupid. Every time—

Stop it! No time for a meltdown.

Okay. I had to leave the stroller behind. Not ideal, but not a crisis. I clicked the car seat back inside the stroller. Then I grabbed bleach wipes from inside the car and cleaned the handle and the straps, the only places I touched. I worked quickly. Post-COVID, though, sanitizing was in vogue. No one would look twice.

Now, where to put the stroller? I couldn't leave it on the side of the road. The police would find that too quickly. I got another pair of rubber gloves from my backpack and pushed it straight into the woods. Plants brushed the nylon of my leggings. My feet sunk into the soggy, muddy ground. A Lyme disease diagnosis was surely in my future.

About fifty yards in, I dumped the stroller on its side. Far enough away that no one would discover it until I was long gone.

I ran back to the car, realizing I never locked it. What if someone stole Kiah? Ultimate irony! I had to get better at mom-things, like locking car doors.

Breathing hard, I opened the car and peeked over the seat, relieved to find Kiah sleeping. I sat in the driver's seat, catching my reflection in the rearview mirror. Disgusting. Puffy, dark bags under my eyes. Complexion? Vampire pale. Lips? Charred. A cold sore in the crease. Maybe if I was beautiful like Cassidy, August would've wanted me. I'd have my baby—

I felt the sting of the slap, saw the pink swell of my cheek, before I realized what I did. I stared at my hand, as if it had a mind of its own. The message was clear, do not think of August. He never deserved you.

Back in control, I grabbed the keys from my backpack and started the car. As I pulled onto the road, tears blossomed in my eyes, and not from the slap. All the planning, practicing, dreaming—I finally understood why athletes cried after winning a gold medal. So much work went into succeeding, heart and soul.

CHAPTER FIVE

CASSIDY
WEDNESDAY, SEPTEMBER 6, 2023 11:30 A.M.

Cassidy jerked awake. She wiped drool from her chin with the back of her hand. Eleven-thirty. Nooooo! She had ten minutes to wake Daisy, change her diaper, put her in the car, and drive to school for pickup. She bolted out of her chair, into the foyer and up the stairs, taking them two at a time. Nice work, Cassidy! You promised to be patient and cheerful when you picked up Piper and now look at you. Rushed. Annoyed. Did every mother self-inflict paper cut-sized insults all day? Guilt hovering like fog, making it difficult to enjoy the moment?

She ran down the hall and into Daisy room. "Alright, sleepyhead," she said, softening her voice and turning off the sound machine. Cassidy loved waking up Daisy. Watching as she rubbed her eyes, stretched her arms and legs. The moment she lit on Cassidy, a huge smile broke out, as if to say, *You came back.*

Standing over Daisy's crib, a silent scream formed in Cassidy's throat. A plastic doll, with features similar to Daisy—tufted blonde hair, dark eyelashes, ivory skin, eyes the color of the sky at dusk, pink onesie—lay in Daisy's place.

Cassidy slammed her eyes shut—please, please, please. She must be dreaming.

She opened her eyes. Daisy wasn't there. Cassidy looked under the crib, wondering if Daisy somehow pulled herself up and over, despite being unable to hold her head up longer than a few minutes. But then she'd be crying. Cassidy flung open the closet door. Nothing.

"Daisy! Daisy!" She sprinted down the hall. Perhaps she'd hear Cassidy's voice and call out.

At the top of the stairs, she turned back and looked at Daisy's bedroom door. Was that open when she came upstairs? It was! Someone was here. Took Daisy.

August.

Yes, August came home from work and got Daisy. He didn't tell Cassidy because she was sleeping. That must be it.

But what about the doll?

A present. Maybe from someone at his office. People liked to gift dolls that resembled the child.

She tore downstairs, running into her office and grabbing her phone. As she called August, she pinched her thigh, hoping against hope that she'd wake up.

CHAPTER SIX

AUGUST
WEDNESDAY, SEPTEMBER 6, 2023 11:33 A.M.

August silenced Cassidy's phone call for the third time. He was in the middle of a meeting with new, lucrative clients with a two-million-dollar budget. And while it was on Zoom, he couldn't answer the call. But three calls in a row meant it was more serious than Piper throwing a fit or Daisy not sleeping. Keeping his eyes locked on the computer screen, he texted Cassidy beneath his desk. *In a meeting.*

He nodded while Jennifer Stenson talked about a property a half-million over their budget. No matter the budget, everyone wanted more—

CALL ME! Cassidy texted. *EMERGENCY!*

Emergency? He stared at the words. With her? The kids?

"Thoughts on how much they'd be willing to reduce the price with an all-cash offer?" Jennifer's question cut through August's thoughts.

"I apologize." He smiled, the aw-shucks-don't-hate-me one he learned at a young age softened the features on Mom's face and thereafter employed it on every woman he met. "My wife texted me, saying there's an emergency—new baby at home. Can I call you back?"

His phone rang again and he held it up, pleading innocence. They replied with the obligatory congratulations and he promised to call them back this afternoon. Every business advertised putting the customer first, but his actions proved his dedication. Answering calls at any hour, working weekends, late nights, fighting to put in the best offers, driving the price up for sales. Hard-working, honest, and knew how to close a deal. It took years to build that reputation and he didn't want any cracks in the foundation.

He clicked out of Zoom and called Cassidy.

"Daisy!" Cassidy yelled. "Do you have her?"

"No." He hoped this was a postpartum freak out. Exhaustion making her delusional? "I'm at work."

She screamed, primal and high-pitched. "She's not here, August. I put her down for her nap and when I went to wake her—" A sob cut her off.

"What?" His muscles tightened. "You went to wake her and what?"

"There was a doll."

"A doll?" The crying jags made her impossible to understand.

"Yes!" She moaned. "A doll where Daisy should have been."

He bolted out of his chair. So many questions, but one overriding thought prevailed. "Did you call the police?"

Another sob. "I was hoping—"

"Now!" he interrupted. Despite his closed door, the entire office likely heard. "Call them now, Cass!"

"—you came home to get her and didn't want to bother me."

Why were they still talking? And in what world was that a plausible explanation? Had he ever done that? "I'm calling the police. Then I'm coming home, okay?"

Cassidy cried harder. "She's so little—"

"It'll be okay, babe." They didn't have time! "I'm calling the police." He ended the call, his finger fumbling as he dialed 9-1-1, three numbers he learned as a child, but never had occasion to use.

"911, what's your emergency?" the operator said.

"My daughter. She's missing. She was sleeping in her crib and someone took her." He pressed his thumb and index finger to his temple, trying to solve this puzzle. Like a Rubik's cube, it proved elusive.

"How old is your daughter?"

"Two months." He remembered kissing her forehead this morning as she rested on Cassidy's shoulder. The glint in Daisy's eyes. The gummy smile. The tongue poking through her lips. Cheeky. As if she knew she kept Mommy up all night, but, like August, she could employ that smile and get people to forgive anything.

"Address of the location she was last seen?"

He gave the operator his home address, while staring at the inside of his wrist. The ink fresh on the heart tattoo he got for Daisy's birth. He had one for the day he married Cassidy. Another for Piper's birth.

"How long ago did she go missing?"

He held out a hand, asking the air for answers. "My wife called me one minute ago. Presumably that's when she went to wake her up, but I have no idea when she went missing."

"What time did she start napping?"

"I don't know." He made a windmill gesture, wanting her to dispatch the police already. "I've been at work all morning. Again, my wife would have that information, but she's too panicked to speak right now."

"I'm sending officers to the house," she said. "In the meantime, answer some questions for me. Your daughter's race? Height? Weight? Hair color?"

August gripped the phone. "She's white. Blonde hair. She's—" How much did she weigh? Cassidy carted the children to doctor appointments. He got the highlights. "Maybe twelve, fifteen pounds. I'd have to ask my wife."

"Can you give me your wife's number?"

He rattled off the number. He had to get home. Get some answers. Find Daisy.

"We'll call her, sir. Please keep your phone on in case the police want to speak with you."

After ending the call, he grabbed his keys off the desk. As expected, the five employees working in the open space looked up as he walked out of his office. "Charlene?" He stopped by his office manager's desk. "I have two showings this afternoon. The Bookmans and Gellars. Cancel both. Reschedule my call with the Stenson's for tomorrow. There's an issue at home."

"Yes." She watched him carefully. Charlene had been with him since he opened a boutique real estate agency five years ago. He poached her from his last employer, promising better benefits. As a single mom, she needed it. "Everything okay? You look pale."

"I don't know." August felt like his limbs were disconnected from his body. His feet hovering over the floor. "I'll keep you updated."

Walking outside, questions plagued August. Daisy gone? Taken from her crib? A doll left in her place? A doll meant this was intentional. That someone took her. Who would take her? How could someone get into the house? Cassidy was home.

He started the car and hit the accelerator without buckling. Kidnapping. His baby. This was something you heard about on the news—murder, rape, school shootings. You felt horror, sympathy. But it always happened to someone else. The other guy.

Now, August was that guy. Today, his life changed forever.

CHAPTER SEVEN

CASSIDY
WEDNESDAY, SEPTEMBER 6, 2023 11:45 A.M.

Cassidy did not wait for the police to arrive to continue searching. After describing to the 911 operator how she came to find Daisy missing and giving her height and weight—eleven pounds, four ounces, twenty-two inches at her two-month check-up last week—she ran out the garage door. Remembering how small Daisy—

Wait a second. She turned around. The garage door was open. Did she leave it open? She remembered coming home, taking Daisy for a walk, bringing her inside… Fear trickled into Cassidy's belly. If she left the garage open, anyone could've taken Daisy. But who? Who would walk inside a stranger's house and steal a baby?

Someone unhinged.

She looked across the street at the woods. The trees towering, some thirty feet in the air, leaves as thick as knotted hair, stretching toward the horizon. Despite the hot sun, she shivered. The world was vast. How would they ever find Daisy?

Cutting across the grass, Cassidy ran up her neighbor's porch and rang the doorbell. Faith was a recent widow and retired elementary teacher. She often watched Piper, having endless patience to play games, color, and read—easier when handing back the child in a few hours.

Cassidy pressed the doorbell again while scouring the street. Nothing unusual. A couple cars. No people. Sunshine. Baby blue sky—

Baby.

She pressed her fists to her eyes, blocking the tears.

"Cassidy?" Faith stepped outside, holding Cassidy by the elbows. "What's wrong?"

"Did you—" Cassidy gulped, trying to speak through the tears. "I can't find Daisy. She was napping in her crib, but when I went to get her, she wasn't there." Faith's eyes widened. "Did you see anything?"

Faith shook her head before Cassidy finished. "No, I was at yoga and then went for coffee with friends. Oh, Cassidy..." Faith wrapped her arms around Cassidy, pulling back when Cassidy's phone buzzed.

A blocked number. Cassidy struggled to swallow; her mouth felt like sandpaper. Could it be the kidnapper, calling with a ransom demand? "Hello?"

"Ms. Chapman?"

It was a woman. Older. "Yes."

"This is Elaine at Maple Leaf Elementary," she said. "I have Piper here in the office. Are you on your way?"

Cassidy's knees buckled and she braced her hand against the house. Oh God! Piper. How could she forget? New to kindergarten, Piper must be terrified.

Cassidy couldn't leave now. "Faith Meister—she's on my list of emergency contacts—is coming." After ending the call, she turned to Faith. "Will you pick up Piper from school? The police are on their way."

"Of course." Faith rested a hand on Cassidy's back. "I'll bring her back to my house. You take care of this."

This. The kidnapping of her daughter. Cassidy briefly squeezed her eyes shut. How? Why? Make it stop.

"You'll need to take my car," Cassidy said. "It has her car seat."

As Faith grabbed her purse and locked the house, Cassidy heard sirens in the distance. She prayed somehow, someway they already had Daisy.

Impossible. But hope died last.

Cassidy jogged back to her house with Faith walking behind. Once inside, Cassidy handed her the car keys from the wall mounted key rack. "Tell Piper—"

The doorbell rang.

"Don't worry. I've got her." Faith hugged her and left through the garage door.

Cassidy ran to the front door and opened it. A man in a dark suit, along with two uniformed officers stood waiting. Three police cars were parked on the street. "Ms. Chapman? I'm Detective Lewis." He held up his badge. "Can we come inside?" He was tall with dark hair and eyes, a full beard, broad shoulders, and a baritone voice. Wall Street confidence with a linebacker's body.

She led them to the living room and sat in the armchair. Detective Lewis perched on the edge of the couch cushion across from her, elbows on his knees, the two officers flanking him.

"Is someone leaving the house?" he asked, turning toward the garage.

Cassidy heard the garage door closing. "My neighbor, Faith, is going to pick up my older daughter from school."

After asking a few questions about Piper, he quickly listed his credentials and then started in on the case. "We need more information before issuing an AMBER alert. Do you have a recent photo of Daisy?"

Cassidy located the photo she took this morning on her walk, unprepared for the murderous pain that ran through her chest upon looking at Daisy's bright blue eyes and apple-cheeked smile. "This is what she was wearing when she—" Cassidy swallowed a sob as she handed her phone to Detective Lewis.

He texted it to himself and handed it back. "Does she have any identifying features—birth marks, moles, freckles?"

"No." She was as unique as a snowflake.

"These first few hours are crucial," he said. "So, please, start at the beginning and don't leave anything out. The more you tell us, the better chance we have of bringing her home safe."

The officers pulled out their notepads, pens poised.

Cassidy held her body as tight as a fist. Not knowing where Daisy was, *how* she was, whether she was crying or hungry or scared, was a torture only a parent could understand. "I was in my office, working."

"What's your job?" Detective Lewis asked.

Cassidy's cheeks flushed. How does someone who offers themselves up as an expert on parenting let their child be kidnapped, while at home? She would lose all credibility—

She clutched her stomach, sickened by her selfishness. No time for a pity party though. "I write a parenting blog and have a podcast."

He blinked and then asked, "Did you notice anything unusual? Hear any strange noises?"

"No. My office door was closed. I had the baby monitor on, but I didn't see anything." She stopped, not wanting to admit she put the baby monitor on a shelf across the room. Not wanting to admit she fell asleep. *Sleep while the baby is sleeping!* Every doctor, magazine, and mother dispensed that advice. And yet, she couldn't force the words out of her mouth. Couldn't stand the scathing judgement. "When I went to wake her up—"

"What time was this?"

"Eleven-thirty. I remember because I had to hurry to pick up Piper from school." Cassidy ran to the kitchen island, grabbing the doll. "Daisy was gone. And this was left in her place."

One of the uniformed officers snapped on rubber gloves, pulling out a plastic bag from a suitcase. "I'll take that," he said, grabbing the doll with his pincher finger and thumb.

Detective Lewis inspected it through the plastic bag. "And this isn't your doll?"

Cassidy shook her head. It was cheap, probably toxic. "No. Definitely not."

"Your husband called 911 at 11:36 this morning," Detective Lewis said. His preciseness was a small comfort. "What happened during those six minutes?"

"I was looking for her." Cassidy tugged her hair, remembering those harrowing first moments when she registered the empty crib. "I called my husband, hoping he picked her up—"

August walked through the garage door. His dark hair was slicked back, his pants and polo pressed, but his eyes looked concave, as if someone sucked the soul out of them. She ran to him, drawn like a magnet, as she had since they met in college fifteen years ago. They wrapped their arms around each other, neither one strong enough to bear their fear alone.

He pressed his lips to her ear. "We'll find her. I promise. Everything will go back to normal."

August always knew exactly what she needed to hear. His confidence, his strength, would see her through.

CHAPTER EIGHT

VANESSA
AUGUST 2022

It was hot. Scorching. One of those blistering summer days that needed to be spent in a pool, drinking frozen alcoholic beverages. I was SOL, catering a wedding, shuffling between the tent, where the humidity hung in the air like exhaust, and the kitchen, which doubled as a sauna. The underwire of my bra chafed and my underwear was wet—and not in a good way. I could think of nothing else but ripping this horrible button-down white shirt off stripper style as soon as I got to my car.

I hated catering. A thankless, exhausting job. But I wasn't scheduled to tend bar at Top Shelf tonight. And money was money. Since graduating last spring, my humanities degree garnered me zero interviews.

The night turned as I carried two platters of pizza for the late-night snack out of the kitchen. A hot guy stood by the bar, talking with two other men, gesturing with his drink. Hello, you. I took a detour, walking close enough to him to breathe the same air. His blue eyes hit mine and I felt an electrical charge. A surge strong enough to make me stumble. I fell to one knee, holding out both platters of pizza like a Broadway performer, nailing the last beat.

He bent down, grasping my elbow to steady me. Heat radiated up my arm. "You okay?" he asked. His blue eyes were framed by long, dark eyelashes. A crease of worry between his eyebrows told me he was older. Stubble on his square jaw. He smelled of sandalwood and whiskey. I wanted to taste him.

"I'm good." I stood, carefully balancing the pizzas. "You hungry?"

A smile tugged at his lips. Nice teeth. Straight. Not too big. Not too small. Suddenly, I was the Goldilocks of teeth.

He patted his firm stomach. "I'm full from dinner."

"Your loss." I winked and walked away. OMFG. Why did I wink? Since when was winking cool? Why couldn't I act normal? At times, it hurt to be inside my skin. Dealing with my exhausting thoughts. Alcohol helped. It lowered the volume on my insecurities. Unlike bartending though, drinking while catering was a no-no.

I set the pizzas on the table and walked back to the kitchen. Back and forth. Back and forth. To the kitchen, I ran. A gofer. A food bitch. A servant. Three hundred dollars, I reminded myself when some guy brushed his hand against my ass. Three. Hundred. Dollars.

As the late-night crowd grew rowdier, I ached to be one of them. Free. Dancing. Laughing. Pounding shots. On the precipice of hooking up.

Soon.

One tedious hour later, I left. On my way out, I scanned the tent for Hot Guy before exhaustion, stickiness, and thirstiness outdueled my desire. In the parking lot, I untucked my white shirt, unbuttoning the top three buttons and fanning the hem to get air on my skin. I pulled out my phone. Sure enough, my friends were out. I needed a shower and food before joining—

"Hey!"

I turned around. Hot Guy was walking toward me, hands tucked in his pants pockets, looking one-hundred percent out of my league. He stopped a few feet away, the soft light of the lamppost flattering his gorgeous features.

This is it. Right now, the director said, sensing my anxiety. Be sexy. Confident. Do not act weird. Quirky only works in the movies.

"Hey." And because I was completely unoriginal, I asked, "Did you enjoy the wedding?"

He looked back at the tent. It was lit up against the inky sky like a flamethrower, all fiery oranges and yellows. "Yeah, it was good. Former clients, so we're not close, but—" He shrugged. "I enjoy weddings. They make me hopeful."

"Hopeful of what?"

He smiled. "You're going to make me say it?"

I wasn't sure what he was referring to, but his tone suggested I was in on the secret and torturing him. "Well, yeah."

I swear he blushed as he ran a hand through his hair. "That true love exists."

I never dated anyone who dared to think those words, let alone say them out loud. Maybe because standing before me was a man and I'd been dating boys. Fuck boys. "Aww. Look at you. A romantic."

"Oh, no." Hands on his hips. Mock anger. "Here I am, being vulnerable, and you're teasing me?"

"Sorry." I laughed. I wasn't acting. I repeat, I wasn't acting! This felt…comfortable. Realizing I was comfortable instantly made me fidget with the zipper of my bag. "Your answer; it surprised me."

"Weddings don't make you hopeful?"

A couple walked past, getting into a car near us. The interruption gave me time. A chance to think. Never a good thing.

"When I see a happy marriage, maybe I'll believe." Now, I was acting. Beneath the snark, the alcohol and pills that dulled the pain, the blasé girl that shrugged off rejection as a rite of passage, I believed in love. Finding the "one." My unicorn. The idea of someone understanding me—

"You're too young to be this jaded." He lightened his voice to a flirtatious tease.

I gave it right back. "And you're too old to be this naïve."

"Probably." He rubbed the scruff on his chin with the heel of his palm. He made the most innocuous gestures sexy.

"I'm not that young." Pause. "In case you were wondering." Ugh! Why did I add that last part? I sounded thirsty.

His eyes searched my face before drifting down my body. Why couldn't I have been wearing a low-cut tank? A tight dress? This sweat and food-stained white button-down held the sex appeal of a nun's habit.

"Twenty-five," he said. "Although age is hard to gauge with beautiful women."

Now, I blushed. I wasn't beautiful. Cute. Sure. Heard that. Interesting eyes. Good hair. Great breasts. Men's eyes always darted to those. Which this stupid white shirt didn't show off! Beyond that? My father, bound by genetics and blood to see me through rose-tinted glasses, never told me I was beautiful. It was a line. But Hot Guy found me worthy of using it.

Or maybe, it was the truth. Perhaps Hot Guy was my unicorn.

"I'm twenty-two," I said.

He grunted—the primal sound made my vagina stand at attention. "Ah! You're still in the good part."

"When does the bad part start?" I leaned forward to whisper, "Warn me so I never get there."

"You know what?" His lips curved into a closed-mouth smile. "I can't remember. You pulled me back into the good part."

"Whatever I can do to help." Maybe older men were the ticket. Honest. Vulnerable. They wouldn't play games.

"Actually, two things would help." The intensity of his gaze made me feel like his hands were exploring every dip and curve of my body.

If only.

"First, your name."

I forced myself not to look away. "Vanessa Prescott."

"Vanessa Prescott." I loved the way my name rolled off his tongue, elongating the vowels. A quick fantasy stirred in my brain: his arm around my waist, fingertips realizing that I wore no underwear, a secret smile only for me as he introduced me as his girlfriend.

"And your phone number," he said. "So, I can ask you out on a date."

I wanted to be a worthy sparring partner. Worthy of him. "On one condition."

Head cocked to one side. "I'm intrigued."

I stepped closer, daring to brush my finger against his wrist, a whisper of skin against skin. A current of electricity ran through my body, accelerating and multiplying as it penetrated each cell. Talking was a precursor. With one touch, I knew I would fuck him. His eyes said he knew it too. Sometimes that certainty kills a moment, drains all the tension about what was to come. Sex becomes rote, almost obligatory, like reading a book to the end simply because you started it. And on rare occasions, like right now, it jacks up the intensity, slows down time, each second toeing the line between the exquisite pleasure of what was to come and the pain of having to wait. "Tell me your name."

"August." His voice rough, like driving over freshly poured gravel. "Just like the month."

I grinned. "Yes, August, just like the month, I'll give you my number."

After inputting my digits in his phone, he kissed my cheek, his stubble rough against the velvet of mine, and whispered in my ear, "Goodnight, Vanessa."

Then he walked away.

He. Walked. Away.

I chewed on my thumbnail, tears threatening, as I watched him get in his car. We just met. His abrupt decision to leave should not hurt. It was romantic, right? A kiss on the cheek? A gentleman! And yet, if he was into me, why wouldn't he seize the moment? Start our date now?

Insecurity obliterated our connection, rising to the surface like an inflamed pimple. The urge to blame myself felt compulsive, my brain taking the familiar path through the prickly branches of self-loathing. I was ugly. Sweaty. Smelly. Not witty enough. Sophisticated enough. Smart enough. *Enough*. I would always fall short.

I texted my girls. *B there in 30*. I needed a man to blunt the pain, take the toxic sting out of this rejection.

CHAPTER NINE

AUGUST
WEDNESDAY, SEPTEMBER 6, 2023 12:15 P.M.

August stood in the kitchen holding Cassidy, inhaling the panic that wafted from her skin like perfume. Her shoulders rose and fell with each sob and he shushed her in the same way he did Piper when she skinned her knee. Everything would be okay. He would be strong for Cassidy, not give into his own escalating fears.

"Sorry to interrupt."

August turned and saw a tall man in a suit. He held out his hand and August shook it. "Detective Lewis," he said, releasing August's hand. "We'd like to ask you some questions."

August cut to the chase. "What are you doing to find my daughter?"

"We've sent an APB to surrounding police stations. The AMBER alert should go out soon," the detective said. "Twitter, Facebook will also blast the information. We're setting up a tip line. My team is searching the area, taking down license plates, talking to your neighbors, and obtaining video footage."

"Are you searching the woods?" August looked out the kitchen window, taking in the densely packed trees. Dozens of trails. A hundred and fifty acres. How would the police cover that much territory?

"Rest assured, my team is searching everywhere." He pointed down the hall leading to the garage. "I noticed you have a security system. Was it armed?"

August looked at Cassidy. Her chin fell to her chest like a stone. "No," she said. "I was home."

August inhaled his frustration. They'd argued about this before. Five buttons. Two seconds. Boom. Everyone was safe.

"I'm always running in and out of the house with the kids," she said, pleading her case. "And it's such a hassle. Especially when Piper opens the door and the alarm wakes Daisy…"

August ran a hand through his hair. Piper was at school this morning. It wouldn't help to point this out. No one liked a backseat driver.

"I'm sorry." A single tear clung to her lower lashes. She blinked and it disappeared. "I should've armed it."

He rubbed her back. "This is a safe neighborhood. No one should've come in."

"Any cameras around the house?" the detective asked. "Inside or out?"

August shook his head. "No—"

"Wait," Cassidy said. "Technically, the baby monitor is a camera." She paused, then added, "But it's a live feed."

"The doll strikes me as odd," the detective said. "August, do you recognize it?"

"It's not ours," Cassidy said. "And I'd never put a toy in her crib. She's too young. It's not safe."

"Can I see it?" The detective handed August a clear plastic bag with the doll inside. It was generic; a doll you could buy at Target. August trusted Cassidy on this front. She knew the minutia of the kids' lives. "It doesn't look familiar."

"Two options here." The detective held up his finger. "Option one. You know the kidnapper. This person knew when Daisy was napping, where to find Daisy's bedroom, and how to get in and out undetected. Leaving the doll behind was deliberate. A message." He let that thought sink in. "Is there anyone that holds a grudge? Angry with you?"

"No," Cassidy said. "Not with me."

August walked to the back windows, looking out. A uniformed officer was searching the jungle gym, as if Daisy secretly wanted to have some fun.

"Any ideas, August?"

August turned around. The detective watched him closely. His stare piercing. Something about him irked August, though he couldn't say what. Certain men rubbed him wrong, as if they knew something August didn't, as if they determined, on sight, they were better than him. But he had to set his feelings aside. This man was in charge of bringing Daisy home.

"I can't think of anyone," August said. Certain clients struck him as off, but he kept details about his family vague. No one had a grudge against them. Except—

"Your podcast." August snapped his fingers, willing the memory to come. "People leaving comments that you're selfish. A bad mom." *Look,* he remembered Cassidy saying, holding up her phone with the offending comments. *How can people be so hateful?* He reassured her she was an amazing mother; that these people were unhappy with their lives and needed someone to blame; that she should focus on the positive comments. But now? With Daisy missing? The comments felt ominous.

"When was this?" the detective asked.

Cassidy said, "Last winter—"

"Didn't one threaten to call CPS?" August asked. "Recently?"

She looked at August, her mouth dropping open. "Oh my god, oh my god." Her words tumbled over one another. "The day we brought Daisy home from the hospital."

Once again, August remembered telling her to ignore it. Part of doing business in the public sphere. They were both oblivious.

"Where can we find these comments?" the detective asked.

"My website," Cassidy said. August walked over and wrapped an arm around her. *"Lost in Babyland.* In the back matter. You can accept or deny a comment and I didn't post the mean ones."

The detective asked for Cassidy's password to the site and assigned an officer to investigate. Then he turned back to them. "Any other thoughts?"

"After I spoke with the police, I went outside and noticed our garage door was open. I—" Cassidy hesitated. "I'm not sure if I closed it when I got home this morning."

August pulled away from Cassidy, absorbing this news, only to realize a second later how that must look. Under the detective's scrupulous gaze, their marriage felt like a performance, one where he didn't have the lines or stage direction. He put his hand back on her shoulder and gave it a reassuring squeeze. He didn't want her to think he was abandoning her either.

"Would you have heard the garage door, from your office, if someone opened it?" the detective asked.

"No." Cassidy's cheeks flushed. "I closed my office door. I—I don't know why. I wasn't even recording today." Quietly, she added, "Habit, I guess."

August ground his teeth together, forcing himself not to look away, as he recounted her mistakes this morning. She didn't close the garage. Didn't lock the door. Didn't set the alarm. But she remembered to close her office door.

A sigh seeped through his nostrils. Cassidy looked up at him, her eyes sorrowful and, yes, frightened. "It's okay," he repeated. If he said it enough times he could will it into being. "We'll find her." To the detective he asked, "What do we do now?"

"Stay calm," the detective said.

"Calm." August wanted to calmly punch the detective in his face. Instead, he walked to the sink and filled a glass with water.

The understanding that he was helpless, at the mercy of the kidnapper, slowed his movements. Helplessness was the worst feeling in the world; one he sought to avoid at all costs. It reminded him of his childhood, where being at home felt like wearing clothes several sizes too small. Dad always broke promises, came home late, or some nights, not at all. August watched as Mom's smile became too wide, her movements manic, her voice piercing with its cheerfulness, only to hear her cry herself to sleep later that night.

"You'll remember more details if you don't panic," the detective said. "Focus your energy on providing us information. Be available by phone at all times." The detective recited his direct number, which both Cassidy and August put into their phones. He handed August and Cassidy each a sheet of paper from a leather binder with the heading, Informed Consent to Police Wire Tap.

August started reading, tuning out the detective as he explained the reasons for the phone tap. He wasn't a lawyer, but he was well-versed in real estate contracts. This looked broad. Too broad. It allowed the police to listen in on phone calls, read emails and text messages from the last 90 days, and track location data. Sweat prickled August's hairline. The date of the agreement extended until a week from today or until they found Daisy.

Bottom line, if there was anything on his phone to help find Daisy, he'd hand it over. Immediately. There was nothing. But. And this was a huge but. There was data—texts, emails, photos—that would cause severe damage to his marriage if Cassidy found out.

He couldn't let that happen.

He was about to tell Cassidy to hold off on signing when she leaned over the table, scribbling her signature. Obviously she wasn't hiding anything on her phone. Not that he suspected otherwise. She just had a baby. And, unlike him, didn't succumb easily to lust. Still, nice to know.

The detective collected Cassidy's sheet and turned to August. "I'd like to read it over first," August said, buying time.

"*August.*" Cassidy pressed down on his name like a car slamming on the brakes. She'd fight him, but he'd rather argue about the agreement than the information uncovered on his phone. What could he say, though, to put her off?

"I'll sign it," August said. "But I need to read it first. You know how I am."

She gave August a hard stare. Then opened her mouth to say something when a high-pitched pinging sounded throughout the house. August pulled his phone out of his pocket, finding the AMBER alert. "Delafield, Wisconsin. Female. 2 months. Caucasian. Blue eyes, blonde hair. Eleven pounds. Last seen in the 200th block of Rainer Parkway wearing a pink bodysuit. No known vehicle or suspect." It included a picture of Daisy smiling, her blue eyes dancing, along with a number to call or text with information.

August felt sick remembering how many times he read an AMBER alert only to immediately forget it. Were people dismissing this text? Not even reading the details?

"This goes to everyone?" Cassidy asked. The same horror August felt was written in the worry lines of her forehead.

"In Wisconsin," the detective said, walking to the stairs. "While August is reading the agreement, can you show me Daisy's room?"

"Wait," August said. "What's the second option?"

The detective faced August. "Second option?"

"Yeah, you said the first option was that Daisy was kidnapped by someone we know."

The detective pressed his lips together. "The second being that one or both of you is involved in her disappearance."

"That's cra—no. Absolutely not." Cassidy shook her head, sounding breathless. "We had nothing to do with this."

"Can anyone verify your whereabouts this morning?" the detective asked.

Cassidy splayed a hand against her heart. "I was here, with Daisy. Working."

"August?" the detective asked. "What about you? Where were you this morning?"

"Work." August forced an even tone. "I had a showing at nine and then went straight to the office afterwards."

"We'll verify—"

"So, that's why you want a phone tap?" August asked. "Because you think we're involved. You're investigating us."

Cassidy's eyes volleyed between them.

"That's one option, yes. But we'd also like to have a tap in case the kidnapper tries to make contact. That way, we can do an immediate trace."

August groaned inwardly. The detective's reasoning made sense. He couldn't risk Daisy's safety to cover his mistakes. "Let me read it."

The detective nodded and ushered Cassidy upstairs.

August would talk to the detective. Man to man. Without Cassidy around. Get a verbal promise that he wouldn't expose anything unrelated to the case. The detective wouldn't want to upset Cassidy more, right?

Or maybe a miracle would happen. The AMBER alert would work. They would find Daisy safe and the police wouldn't have to search his phone. The consent agreement would be a blip, a scare, a warning to stop taking stupid risks with his life.

He vowed to heed the warning this time.

CHAPTER TEN

CASSIDY
WEDNESDAY, SEPTEMBER 6, 2023 12:45 P.M.

Cassidy walked upstairs, her mind reeling from Detective Lewis's accusation that she and August might be involved with Daisy's disappearance. It was unthinkable. What kind of parent would hurt their child? What specifically about Cassidy and August set off alarms inside Detective Lewis' head?

"Do you notice anything amiss?" Detective Lewis asked once they stepped inside Daisy's room. He wore rubber gloves and was poking through drawers.

She looked around, feeling like something was off, but unable to say what. Detective Lewis needed her help, but her brain was paralyzed, stuck on the moment she peered down at Daisy's empty crib. Saw a doll where her daughter should have been.

She forced herself to focus. Clothes, sleep sacks, diapers, in the closet. White furniture. Gray painted walls. Daisy's name splashed across the wall in cotton-candy pink cursive. Canvas prints of Daisy as a newborn on the other wall. Only two months ago, but already, Daisy had grown. Her blue eyes now alert, observing, curious. Her full-bodied gummy smile. The color of her skin settled into a porcelain hue after being born with jaundice.

Everything was in place. Right? She didn't trust herself.

"Nothing obvious." Cassidy fell to the chair where she rocked Daisy to sleep each night. She pressed her fingers into her eyelids, digging in, begging her brain to work.

"My crew will test for fingerprints when we're done talking, particularly around the crib and the door handle." He looked beneath the crib, as she had earlier. "We're going to need yours and August's for exclusion purposes. Piper's too." He stood up. "Is there anyone else we should exclude?"

Cassidy didn't understand. "Exclude?"

"Yes. A nanny? A cleaner? Relatives? Friends?"

Cassidy shook her head. "We have people over, but no one comes into Daisy's room other than Faith. My neighbor."

Detective Lewis paused at each picture of Daisy on the wall. "Does Faith have a key for your house?"

"Yes." Cassidy's mind caught the insinuation a moment later. First her and August, now Faith. A veritable saint. "She's in her seventies. A former schoolteacher. She'd no more kidnap a child than rob a bank. In fact, she's watching Piper right now."

Looking far too big for the room, Detective Lewis leaned against Daisy's dresser. "And you don't remember if you locked the door today?"

"The front door was definitely locked. But the door leading to the garage? I doubt it." While Cassidy didn't have a clear memory either way, her habit wasn't to lock the door except at night. "You'd have to know the garage code to get inside the house. That's why I rarely lock it."

"But you're not sure you closed the garage door," he reminded her.

She bit her lip, suppressing a scream. "True."

"Does anyone other than August know the garage code?" Detective Lewis asked.

"Faith. She takes Piper to the park while I'm working. My mom might. I can't remember."

"We'll also fingerprint the key tab. What's the code?"

"Piper's birthday. Zero, five, twenty." Cassidy felt the sun on her cheeks as it streamed through the window, the heat irritating her. Again, she was missing something, but, like a fly she could not kill, the thought buzzed just outside her grasp.

He pointed toward the hamper. "These clothes are dirty, right?"

Was he piling on now? Pointing out her inability to keep up with the housework? "Yes."

"Good. I'll have my guys take something to get Daisy's smell for the K-9 team."

"K-9 team?" Wasn't the K-9 team used to track a body? "What-what for?"

"They'll track her scent. Give us a direction to look in. You'd be amazed how good they are."

Cassidy imagined Daisy's lifeless body being found by a dog. She looked at Daisy's pictures, healthy and alive, focusing on that image instead.

"Tell me more about your podcast," Detective Lewis said.

Cassidy pulled her legs to her chest and wrapped her arms around her knees, needing to fill the oppressive emptiness in her arms. "Before Piper was born, I had all these ideas about motherhood and the reality left me wanting. The monotony was tough and I felt a lot of guilt about that. So, I started blogging. At first, I put it on my Facebook page. That gained some traction and I started a website. Then a podcast. It's been—" The premise behind her podcast was that women were allowed to be successful *and* a mom, to pursue their ambitions without apologizing, and yet, she still had to tamp down the desire to justify her time. Something fathers never had to do. "It's a work in progress."

"And these messages," Detective Lewis said. "Tell me more about the CPS comment. What triggered it?"

"Honestly, I don't know. It upset me—I mean, the thought of someone taking away my kids. But I just gave birth and had too much stuff going on to dwell on it." Cassidy caught herself. Because, given their predicament, she should've done something. But what? Gone to the police? Was posting an upsetting comment on someone's website a crime? She doubted it.

MARISA RAE DONDLINGER 43

"Any other messages that threatened you or your family?"

"Umm…" Cassidy drummed her chin against her knee. "Stuff about my kids hating me, my husband leaving me. Nothing threatening, per se…"

"Have you talked to anyone about your…dissatisfaction?" He lowered his voice as if dissatisfaction was a dirty word.

"That's why I started the blog and podcast," she said. "To create a community for all new mothers, while giving me an outlet. If I'm struggling, I thought, why not help others?"

"I understand," he said. "But I meant your doctor. Perhaps a therapist."

The hairs on Cassidy's arms didn't actually stand up, but the sensation was the same. Some ancient survival gene kicked in, warning her to be on guard, that a predator was in the midst. "No." She swallowed. Her throat was bone dry. "I don't have a therapist."

"Are you breastfeeding Daisy?"

His eye contact was relentless. "Yes."

"Are you on an anti-depressant?" He quickly added, "I'm not judging you. The postpartum months are hard."

Anger ignited deep inside Cassidy, making it feel like her skin was engulfed in flames. Cassidy pulled her hair into a bun, taking a moment to steady herself. She would withstand any embarrassing, personal, offensive questions to get Daisy back. "I don't have postpartum depression," she said. "I have two small children, a house to run, a husband that works long hours, and a career I'm trying to grow. If I'm depressed, which I'd argue I'm not, just busy, that's the reason. Your regular, run of the mill, not enough hours in the day, frustrations."

He gestured toward the door. "Let's go downstairs. Give my team a chance to work in here."

Cassidy stood and looked around the room one last time. Something irked her, and it was more than Detective Lewis's line of questioning. She left the room before abruptly turning around, her face smashing into Detective Lewis's cement wall of a chest.

"The window!" She pushed past him, her brain zapping awake. "The shades are up halfway."

He bent down to look out the window, eyes lingering on the street before speaking again. "And that's unusual?"

"Yes. I always put them down during her nap. When I came to get her, I flipped on the lights, but I never got around to opening the shades because she wasn't there. Whoever took her opened them."

"On the baby monitor, would you have been able to see if someone switched the light on?"

Another wave of guilt took hold. On the off chance she was looking at the monitor when the light switched on, then yes, she would've noticed the brightness. Otherwise, no. "Yes."

"But not necessarily if someone opened the shades halfway?"

"It probably wouldn't have changed the lighting that much, especially with the sun not hitting the window at that hour."

"This person knew about the monitor." He crossed his arms, staring intently at the shades. Then he turned to Cassidy "Anything else strike you as unusual? I need your help, Cassidy. You know things I don't."

Cassidy stepped closer to Daisy's crib, aching to find something. "I'm sorry."

As they walked downstairs, Cassidy thought about who could've taken Daisy. This person knew the layout of their house, their schedule, the nuances of their life, something only family or a friend would know. Not an internet troll. Who? Who? Who? She held onto the banister, reciting this question.

No answers came.

CHAPTER ELEVEN

VANESSA
WEDNESDAY, SEPTEMBER 6, 2023 1:00 P.M.

Farm land. Main Street. Farm land. Main Street. To avoid detection, I took two-lane highways instead of the expressway, cutting through what felt like every small town in Wisconsin. They all looked the same: drug store, grocery store, bar, hair salon, maybe a fast-food chain if the town boasted a population over a thousand.

I drove the speed limit, despite my desire to push ninety. The AMBER alert went out a short while ago. They knew Kiah was gone. What else did they know?

Drive. Don't think.

In a little over three hours, we would be at my lake house in northern Wisconsin. The eastern tip of the state, close enough you could almost walk to Michigan. When Mom died of breast cancer three years ago, she gifted me the lake house, as her parents passed it down to her. She and Dad discussed it with me ahead of time, because she was worried it was too big of a responsibility at such a young age. Dad watched on, barely able to smother his skepticism. He thought I'd flake. Ultimately, she gifted the property to a trust to pay for the upkeep and expenses until I was thirty. Thirty and responsible, presumably.

Not that Dad wanted the house. While Mom and I would spend entire summers there, Dad came for one week. No more, no less. Many of my childhood memories, most of the good ones, took place there. Exploring the woods, reading in the hammock, swimming in the lake—escaping. Escaping Dad. The kids at school. My head. Things were less stressful there.

Now, more than ever, I needed a place to escape with Kiah. A place where I could raise her without prying eyes, in nature—

Kiah started fussing in the backseat. The whines quickly turned into a panicked screeching that sounded like a cat being murdered. The sound was piercing. Relentless. Enough to drive a sane person mad.

"Fine, fine." I pulled off on the side of the road. "You win." It wasn't a horrible place to stop. Isolated. Fields and trees without a house in sight.

I crawled into the backseat. Her mouth was open, mid howl. Her face was pink. Tears streamed down her cheeks. She wriggled her limbs like an overturned beetle. Up close, the noise was deafening. I reached inside my pocket, searching for the pacifier I took from her crib—anything for a few seconds of silence while I changed her diaper. But it wasn't there. I turned the pocket inside out and cursed. It probably slipped out, lodged between the front seat and the side of the car, never to be found again. Kiah's screams let me know I didn't have time to search.

After grabbing a diaper and wipes, I unstrapped her and rested her on the open seat. I pulled her onesie over her head, chucking it up front. I planned to cut it into little pieces and toss the evidence out my window like confetti. Erasing every tie to Cassidy and August.

Clothes off, I unfastened her diaper. As I went to grab a wipe, warm liquid splashed against my wrist. "Ugh!" I jerked away. Pee dripped onto my pants. I grabbed a wet wipe and toweled down my arm and pants. Kiah started gnawing on her wrist, making a frantic sucking sound that reminded me of my high school boyfriend going down on me.

After cleaning her and fastening a new diaper, I tugged a yellow bodysuit over her head. It said "Mommy's Miracle." I took a second to admire her. The yellow made her blue eyes pop. The bodysuit fit, but she would have room to grow. I smiled. Totally. Nailing. Motherhood.

Her cries interrupted my moment. I grabbed the formula and a bottled water, shaking the mixture like a martini. Once ready, Kiah latched onto the bottle with a ferocious tug, clutching it with both hands as if afraid I would take it away. As the food hit her stomach though, she relaxed. Her muscles loosened, while the wrinkle between her eyebrows smoothed.

I read that the transition from breast to bottle might be challenging, but Kiah was as opportunistic as an alcoholic at an open bar wedding. Maybe Kiah, already precocious, sensed that Cassidy's breastmilk was as poisonous as her words.

Spontaneous cooing noises emerged from my mouth, evidently a side-effect of holding the world's most beautiful baby—

Second most beautiful. My baby would've stopped a block. "Fuck you," I said through gritted teeth. A reflex any time I thought of August.

There was a time when love filled my heart at every thought of August. That love soared to infinity when I became pregnant with our baby. And dwindled to loathing when he took both away. Kiah would have to fill the gigantic hole her father carved in me, cutting me open as apathetically as a pathologist performing an autopsy.

She could do it, too. I pressed kisses to Kiah's cheek as I burped her, inhaling her warmth. With a full belly and fresh diaper, she was all smiles, acting like I did something miraculous. And maybe I did. I made her the center of my world—attention she never got at home with August cheating and Cassidy obsessed with her career.

August never thought I'd fight back. Take what he promised me. Rise.

I misjudged him from the start, but he misjudged me too.

CHAPTER TWELVE

VANESSA
AUGUST 2022

On my first date with August, I felt like the star of my own rom-com. August called—called, not texted—and asked me to meet him for a walk. I'd never been asked out on a walk before. The romance! We'd taste-test food. People watch. Stay sober. A first. Nature would provide our ambiance, not some thumping bass in a bar. Already, August put miles between himself and all the jerks littering my phone with DTF's and dick-pics.

We met at the Milwaukee RiverWalk. The sun beamed in the cloudless sky, sparkling glitter across the inky river, the steel buildings, and the pavement. I leaned with my elbows against the railing, the breeze drawing my jersey dress tight across my body, long hair fashioned in a fishtail braid. Be cute, the director said. But. Not. Too. Eager!

"Vanessa."

I turned. My breath got stuck in my throat as I took in the aviator sunglasses, lush lips, chiseled shoulders snug in his light gray polo, fitted jeans, and Nikes. He looked like a leading man. Cool. Confident. Crush-worthy.

I was an imposter. Never good enough.

"You look beautiful." He stepped forward to kiss me on the cheek. Lips soft, stubble rough. Over all too quickly.

I thanked him, dipping my toes into the compliment as one would test a warm bath. Maybe I would finally get my love story.

The way he complimented me, ninety percent conviction and ten percent awe, made me believe.

As we walked, I learned about him—thirty-four, real estate agent, Milwaukee native, loved sushi, hated horror films, and never missed a Packer game. I gave my story a finishing gloss—twenty-two, recent college grad, tending bar until I found my passion. The conversation flowed easily. No awkward pauses. No topic off-limits. He had depth, a level of sophistication missing from my usuals who rarely strayed from discussing fantasy football and video games.

August listened. Asked questions with depth. A fact he proved when he linked his fingers through mine and asked, "What makes you happy?" Warmth from his hand spread throughout my body. He didn't say the words, but the gesture said it all. *She's with me*.

"Simple things," I said, both of us sidestepping to the left as another couple approached opposite. Already in sync. "Hanging out with friends, good pizza, going for walks…" I smiled at him. He laughed, then leaned over and kissed my forehead. I was nailing the funny, easy-breezy girl. Me! "Honestly, though, I try not to spend too much time trying to solve the happiness equation."

Furrowed eyebrows replaced his laughter. "Why not?"

Defenses momentarily down, a hint of truth escaped. "I feel like everyone is posting every party, meal, relationship, and FOMO hits. Like, I'm not where I'm supposed to be."

"You're young." He stroked the inside of my palm, a rhythmic pressure that caused my clit to swell in anticipation. "You have plenty of time."

"Maybe."

"Definitely." He squeezed my hand. "Want to know a secret?"

"Sure."

He leaned in close, whispering in my ear, "No one shows their true self online."

"You're right. I know you're right. I try to enjoy the moment, but—" Suddenly, I felt near tears. This date, August, the support he was giving me—it was beautiful. Promising. Was he for real? The director walked beside me, shaking her head in disgust, muttering that I ditched the fun girl role too soon. Men liked fucking complicated girls. For a night. Maybe three. But they never became the girlfriend. And how I wanted to be August's girlfriend. "Too many people have disappointed me to expect happiness…like, long term."

He brought my hand up to his lips and kissed the inside of my wrist. "Men?"

The way he pulled me closer, instead of putting distance between us, emboldened me. "I'm hoping you won't be like the others."

He stopped walking and faced me, holding both my hands now. With the sun setting, his sunglasses were in the collar of his shirt and his blue eyes made fast work toying with my heart. "And what did the others do?"

Passion paralyzed time. Nothing, no one else existed. The director disappeared. A reminder that this wasn't a movie. To be present. Soak in every second of August's attention. "They saw what they wanted. They didn't see me."

He inhaled and said, "I see you."

"I think you do," I whispered.

He tugged me into the alleyway, pushing me up against the brick building, his face inches from mine, one hand cupped behind my neck, his eyes gazing, gazing, gazing. "You feel it, right?"

With each pulse. "Yes."

"It's real." His voice was gritty. Almost pained.

I hardly dared to breathe. "Yes."

Softer, he said, "It's not just me?"

His vulnerability made my knees weak. I shook my head, knowing I was about to experience a kiss that would change my life.

And it did. I think I levitated, floating above myself, watching us kiss, watching my life begin. Everything that came before, every shitty man, starting with Dad, every indignity I suffered, the indifference, the shame, the cruelty, was a prelude to this moment.

We went back to my apartment. I didn't care that you shouldn't fuck a guy on a first date because he'll never respect you or call again. His words, the underlying promise that he was falling in love, a promise his body confirmed, told me those rules didn't apply to us.

Fate drew us together. A chemical and emotional cocktail. Kissing, licking, grinding, moaning. Lust and love. Raw and deep. As we came together, I thought, yes. Finally. Thank you.

After, I rested my ear against his heart, listening to the beat slow, thinking, you, you, you. I waited years for you.

CHAPTER THIRTEEN

CASSIDY
WEDNESDAY, SEPTEMBER 6, 2023 1:45 P.M.

Soon after police sent the AMBER alert and the APB to police stations around the state, Cassidy noticed media vans arriving in front of their house. Reporters stood across the street, on the outskirts of the Sawnee Conservatory, speaking into cameras, hungry and clawing, eager for a story.

She retreated to the master bedroom, off the living room on the main floor. Close enough to hear any major happenings. She closed the door behind her before collapsing on the bed, hugging the body pillow she slept with even though no longer pregnant. Everything ached, her heart mostly, but also her breasts. She pressed them with her fingertips, unsurprised to find them hard and full.

Daisy skipped lunch. Because someone stole her. Not that nature gave a damn.

Cassidy went to the nightstand where she kept the materials for pumping. After screwing on the bottles and attaching the plastic cups, she pulled off her tank-top and bra and plopped down on the chair. With a sigh, she held the cups to her breasts with one hand and flicked on the machine with the other. She closed her eyes as a gentle whooshing noise filled the room. Pumping usually relaxed her. Not quite meditating, but the benefits similar. She emptied her body and filled her mind with peace.

Today, though, the task felt cruel. She would freeze this milk, as she did with all the milk she pumped, but would Daisy ever drink it? Cassidy bit her lip. Think positive. Daisy *will* drink this milk. She *will* come home. She *will* live a happy, long, fulfilling life.

Cassidy opened her eyes, instinctively seeking the photographs hanging on the wall opposite her. Candid shots of the girls, her and August. A beautiful family. A blessed life. Was that a motive? Was someone jealous of their good fortune?

Who?

The door opened and August stepped inside. She hunched her shoulders, wanting to hide, feeling more cow than woman. Her stomach spilled over her waistband. Her nipples suctioned and stretched like taffy. Blue veins crisscrossed her breasts like a city grid. No resemblance to the woman who used to sext August pictures of her breasts to spice up his work days.

August was also drawn to the pictures. With his back to her, she couldn't see his expression, but the way he leaned closer, brushing a picture of Daisy with his thumb, made her stomach ache. He must blame her. She blamed herself.

When he turned around, his eyes were glassy, but no tears fell. He was stronger than her. "I'm struggling, Cass." He sat on the edge of the bed, leaned forward, resting his elbows on his knees and tenting his hands in prayer. "How did this happen?"

"I fell asleep, okay?" The truth felt like being attacked by a hive of wasps. "I didn't mean to, it's just—I'm exhausted, August. I was up all night with Daisy, *again*, and I—" There was no excuse.

His cheeks colored, whether with rage or empathy, she couldn't tell. "You should nap," he said. "You need sleep. But why didn't you…" He stood up and walked back to the pictures, not finishing his sentence. She could finish it for him: Why didn't you lock the door? Set the alarm? Leave your office door open? Put the baby monitor next to you? Why? Why? Why?

"I miss her," he said, his voice low and thick.

Two knocks at the door. August turned around and looked at her, cleared his throat, and then opened the door a crack to protect her modesty. Even when upset, a gentleman. She turned off the pump, tipping her chest forward to get every drop into the bottles. She fastened her bra and pulled on her tank-top as August closed the door.

"The detective wants us to make a statement to the media," he said. "Are you ready for that?"

She nodded, but inside she felt queasy, her stomach flip-flopping like it did riding the teacups with Piper at Disney World last year. This person risked arrest several times over by breaking into Cassidy's house. After all that, what would convince them to bring Daisy home?

Before leaving, she grabbed a lightweight zip-up from her closet, not wanting to appear on TV with milk stains or too much cleavage.

Detective Lewis stood waiting in the foyer. "I'll give the background," he said, "then Cassidy will talk first and we'll end with August. Speak directly to the kidnapper. Humanize Daisy. Let this person see how much you love her."

"Okay." Cassidy's voice shook.

"Pretend you're talking to a friend." August pressed a kiss to her cheek and then whispered in her ear, "We're a team, okay? I love you. We'll get through this together."

As Cassidy stepped out the front door, a half-dozen or so cameras were pointed at them. The click of pictures sounded like a million flies buzzing in the air. Reporters stood with microphones and phones held out. If she wasn't holding August's hand, if she didn't have his strength keeping her upright, she probably would've run back inside. She squeezed August's hand, a thank you for his support. He squeezed back.

Detective Lewis explained the timeline of events. When it was Cassidy's turn to speak, she stepped up to the microphones, filled with terror, yes, but also determination, one borne of a primal need to protect her child.

"She just learned how to smile." Cassidy's voice broke and the tears came faster than she expected. "She smiles at everything now.

When you pick her up, when you make a silly face, when her older sister plays with her—she's such a happy baby." Cassidy struggled to swallow, to continue speaking. "Please. Please."

In the end that was all she had. A mother's plea.

CHAPTER FOURTEEN

VANESSA
WEDNESDAY, SEPTEMBER 6, 2023 1:55 P.M.

Each mile marker ticking past worked like a Xanax-tequila cocktail on my nerves. I sang along with Taylor Swift, basked in the warm sun, and relaxed into the drive. I would not get caught. No one was following me. No one knew Kiah was with me.

My thoughts drifted to August. Was he panicking? Comforting Cassidy? Or blaming her? I looked at my phone, mounted on the dashboard next to the steering wheel, tempted to check the Sunshine app. Did Cassidy leave it on? Would I be able to hear the police? Get inside info? I reached for my phone, fingers aching for a fix, only to jerk back.

Stupid girl. What if they already linked the baby monitor to Kiah's disappearance? I couldn't risk it.

Could I?

No.

But I could mess with August.

A few miles down the road, I came across an abandoned fruit stand. Stopping again wasn't smart, but I'd be quick. I pulled into the small dirt parking lot, taking in the peeling green paint on the sign, the dancing strawberry faded to pink from the sun. The air held a stench of manure.

This is where dreams came to die.

I grabbed my phone and got out of the car, wanting to stretch my legs and get some fresh air. Before closing the door, I checked on Kiah. She was sleeping, happily sucking on her thumb. I lowered her window an inch. I wasn't an idiot.

I leaned against the hood and navigated to ViperByte.com, an email and texting service that boasted, for a fee, untraceable communications. An IT guy who frequented my shifts at Top Shelf told me about it. I flirted shamelessly, asking him various tech questions. Back then, I didn't have a plan. But I was angry. And options were a girl's best friend.

Sure, I could tell myself I was being virtuous, rescuing Kiah from these selfish, horrible people. Fulfilling my dream of becoming a mother—like August promised. But I wasn't an angel. And I could multitask. My other goal? Torture the motherfucker. Make every minute of August's life feel like the drilling of a tooth without Novocain, wondering where Kiah was, whether she was safe, healthy, happy. Transform his mind into a prison, one where he stood gripping the bars, able to see his previous happy life, but unable to find the key to freedom.

Much like my life the past nine months.

How many scars have you left behind? I texted August. *How will you atone for them?* I attached a picture of him and Maxi kissing to ensure a full-blown anxiety attack. I wasn't the only woman he screwed and screwed over. There was bound to be dozens more. I was banking on that. Banking that my face wouldn't skirt across his mind. Banking on his narcissism, his inability to reflect on how his actions hurt others, his lack of emotional intelligence.

Would he show Cassidy the text? Or would he suffer alone? If he told Cassidy the truth, she'd turn on him. Any woman would, right? Losing Kiah would expose the messy, vile parts of their marriage, their blackened souls, for everyone to see. Family, friends—

Media. I navigated to a local news site. "Live: Parents of Missing Baby Daisy Hold Press Conference." A giggle emerged from deep inside my belly. Oh. My. God. It was happening. I nearly peaked with anticipation.

I clicked on the link, heart pounding as the video pixilated. I started walking, hoping to find a hotspot of satellite coverage in this Podunk town. When I reached the other side of the parking lot, it loaded.

Cassidy appeared on camera. Her makeup was smudged, her eyes swollen, her mouth quivering in a frown. "Please," Cassidy said. "Please."

Cassidy rejoined August, both standing in front of their house, holding hands, like two mannequins manipulated into contact. Please what? Damn. I missed something important.

A man in a dark blue suit and striped tie took center stage. A picture of Kiah was imposed on the left, with the details of her disappearance below. Her smile looked coaxed. Nothing like the love that radiated after I finished feeding her.

"Remember," the man said. "We need your help. Text, call us, at the number on your screen with actionable tips. No detail is too small. Now, August Chapman, Daisy's father, will speak."

I pulled the phone closer, nearly touching my nose, wanting to feast on every detail. August stepped forward, running a hand through his hair, exposing sweat stains under his arms. Disgusting. How was I ever attracted to him?

He looked directly at the camera. "Daisy turned two months last week."

His voice was raspy. Was this put on? A nice film-op of a grieving father? Or was he in real pain? Instead of bringing me pleasure, his pain sparked fury. I loved you. I would've been the perfect wife, the perfect mother, if you gave me the chance. Infuriating the way men decided for me what I was capable of.

"She's too young to know what's going on," August continued, "but she knows us. She knows her family. She knows she's loved. If you're trying to hurt us, then fine, hurt us, but don't hurt Daisy."

As he finished, fear stole the breath from my lungs. Hurt us? Why did he say that? Did he already suspect it was personal? Impossible. Unless he looked at the text during the press conference. I strained my eyes, recognizing the shape of a phone in his front pocket. He'd look like a jackass if he checked it during his daughter's press conference.

I put nothing past him.

I rocked back and forth on my toes and heels. What if Cassidy saw me spying on the house? Or August noticed me following him? Or Cassidy remembered me from the grocery store? Or, or, or…what if August told her the truth months ago? The affairs, the baby—everything? I only had access to their conversations in Kiah's bedroom. Maybe Cassidy chose not to share his cheating on her podcast because it was too humiliating, too damaging to her brand, too—

I smashed my phone against my forehead. Stop it! I was nothing to him. Nothing. He never checked on me after the breakup. Forgot me as soon as he hung up the phone.

Besides, he said hurt "us," not "me." He didn't realize he was to blame. Yet.

And I knew him. Knew he'd never tell Cassidy the truth. He was drowning in his lies, wouldn't grab onto the truth if it was a life raft.

Knee deep in my pep talk, I didn't notice the red pickup truck until its engine roared next to my ear. I looked up, watching as it slammed to a stop between me and my car, spraying dirt.

An icy fear trickled into my veins as I looked around, confirming there wasn't another car or building in sight. I was alone. On the side of the road. Unable to call 911 because I was traveling with a baby no one would understand was mine. With no weapon.

A man jumped down from the cabin, wearing ripped jeans, a threadbare gray shirt, and a blue trucker hat.

Fuck. Me. I was in trouble.

CHAPTER FIFTEEN

AUGUST
WEDNESDAY, SEPTEMBER 6, 2023 2:05 P.M.

August walked inside the house behind Cassidy, his hand resting on her lower back. This felt surreal. A press conference discussing his kidnapped daughter. The detective said to humanize her. Talk in the present tense, as if Daisy was alive, waiting to come home. Not get angry. Did he do that? He couldn't remember a single word he said.

Cassidy stepped into his arms once they were safely in the foyer. He held her, relieved he could momentarily help. "No one can disappear without a trace in today's world."

She pulled away. "I'm going to get some water."

His words served as a reminder that his secrets were under threat of exposure. He found the detective in the back hall, talking with one of the evidence guys taking prints around the house. Not wanting to interrupt, August decided to visit Piper before pulling the detective aside for a chat. One where August would sign the consent to tap his phone and the detective would promise August discretion in return.

Piper. His spunky, smart, silly girl. She redefined the meaning of love for him. Both his girls did. Their smiles, the downy softness of their skin, Piper's voice like honey, the smell of Daisy, which reminded him of rain, a fresh start, undid him. No matter how bad the day, and today would test this theory, his girls made it better.

He slipped out the patio door and walked next door, ignoring the media camped out front of his house. He knocked on the sliding door attached to Faith's deck. Faith answered, letting him inside. "How are you?" she asked, her face wrinkled with worry.

Before he could answer, Piper jumped up from the kitchen table and ran to him. "Daddy!"

He picked her up and swung her in the air. Sure enough, her infectious giggle filled the room. He flipped her over, holding her by the ankles, swinging her back and forth like a pendulum to keep the giggles coming. Medicine for his fear. When she claimed she couldn't breathe, he flipped her over and plopped her back in her seat.

"What 'cha coloring?" he asked, sitting next to her. Faith was at the stove, giving them time together. Or possibly feeling awkward, not knowing what to say. Unlike Cassidy, he didn't know Faith well. Certainly not enough to have an in-depth conversation about the kidnapping of his daughter.

"A unicorn." She picked up her marker. "Wanna color with me?"

"Yes." She climbed into his lap and they began coloring. He quickly switched it from a unicorn to a dragon with large teeth and fire coming out of its mouth.

"Daddy!" she screamed. "It's a unicorn, not a dragon."

This was a regular "argument" between them. "I can't help it. I love dragons."

She grabbed the black marker and made a gigantic heart over the dragon's face. He laughed. "We could draw a princess that defeats the dragon."

"No."

"A shark that comes up and eats the dragon?"

"No-o-o."

"A nice dragon like in *Shrek*?"

"No. Dragons. Daddy."

August switched the scenarios each time, pretending to love dragons because she was terrified ever since watching *Sleeping Beauty*. He wanted to tease the fear out of her. "How about—" His phone buzzed inside his pocket. A text from Charlene, his office manager. *Saw the press conference*, she wrote. *We're getting calls. What should I say?*

"Do you have to go to work, Daddy?" Piper asked.

"No, not yet." He typed a reply, telling Charlene to cancel his appointments tomorrow, not give away any personal information, and that he would update her. Then he went through his other texts, from family, friends, and clients, giving bare-boned replies. One sender he didn't recognize. A long string of numbers.

How many scars have you left behind? How will you atone for them?

"What the...?" When he clicked on the attached photo, however, his demeanor switched from confused to alarmed. He stood in profile on a street, pressing Maxi up against her car. Kissing her. Their first kiss. First kisses always did him in.

He slammed the phone against his chest, not wanting Piper to see. His heart accelerated to match the questions firing in his mind. Who sent this? Why? How did they get this picture?

"What's wrong?" Piper's eyes widened.

"Nothing." He pressed a kiss on her head and placed her on the seat next to him. "I need to use the bathroom." Faith eyed him as he stood up. He nodded. "Everything's fine."

Nothing was fine.

He locked himself inside the powder room located off the kitchen. He flipped on the fan and turned on the water, as if the sound could mask the panic of his thoughts. He bent over, resting his head against the cool sink. He knew he could get caught. The thought was an ulcer that grew and receded, depending on how risky his behavior. But if cheating was a skill, then August had a black belt, natural talent at passing off lies, courtesy of his father, combined with years of practice to avoid detection. Even so, he feared Cassidy uncovering the truth. Unlike his mom, a kind, forgiving, and ultimately defeated woman, Cassidy would eviscerate him. She had sweetness in her, but she also had fire.

Each time he ended an affair, he vowed to never cheat again. Devoted himself to Cassidy afresh, being affectionate, attentive, understanding, and most of all, present. He came home earlier from work. Took Piper on excursions to give Cassidy time to work. Worshiped her body, each kiss and touch a promise to never look elsewhere for pleasure. Bought little gifts to show he was listening. Held her as they slept. Became everything she wanted. Needed.

He was a good man. He was a flawed man.

Time would pass, weeks, months, but then a woman would snag his attention, monopolize his thoughts, muzzle his promises. He'd tell himself no. That Cassidy deserved the best. But fighting himself was part of the game too. He craved the chase. The thrill of the unknown. Pushing boundaries. The riskier the indiscretion, the more powerful the fuck.

By satisfying the parts of himself that were too kinky or low-brow elsewhere, he gave the best of himself to Cassidy.

He needed help. But also thought he had the willpower to stop.

He was on the right track, having ended his affair with Maxi before Daisy was born. Almost three months of fidelity.

But now this picture. His past haunting him. The phone tap made him fear this very situation—

Wait. Could it be connected to Daisy's disappearance? This text on the same day his daughter goes missing? When the police requested access to his phone? But how would this person know about the phone tap? Was it standard procedure? Or something they asked because the circumstances were suspicious with Cassidy being home?

Maxi. It didn't add up. She didn't know he was married, let alone had children. Still, it was his only lead. *Hope you're well,* he texted her, feeling like a jerk. They hadn't talked since the breakup.

A clean break, done over the phone, was rule number one. *Random question. Did you send me a picture of us today?*

Okay. Think. Who else, if not Maxi? He pulled up the picture again. From the grainy look, it was taken from a distance and then magnified. In a neighborhood half-hour away, where he knew no one. Perhaps Cassidy became suspicious and followed him? No. She'd confront him. She wasn't the type to store up her anger. Or send a cryptic text. And she'd never text him today. She was barely holding it together; she wouldn't drop a bomb in their marriage on top of it.

Given he was about to give the cops access to his phone, deleting the text wouldn't help. Instead, he addressed it head on. *Who is this?* His text did not change from "delivered" to "read."

He splashed cold water on his face. When he looked into the mirror, he saw pale skin, heavy eyes, a frown. His soul was being dragged through the gutter, his body showing the effects.

If this was connected to Daisy, he would never forgive himself. He knew cheating might have consequences for his marriage—truthfully, he thought he was stealth enough not to get caught. But he never considered his behavior put his kids at risk.

It wasn't connected. It couldn't be.

But what if?

He had to find the detective.

CHAPTER SIXTEEN

VANESSA
WEDNESDAY, SEPTEMBER 6, 2023 2:07 P.M.

I stood frozen, heartbeat in my throat, phone in my hand, debating whether I should walk the twenty or so yards past this strange man to my car, pretend it was normal for him to pull over at an abandoned fruit stand. But what if he grabbed me? Threw me to the ground? Or into his truck? Almost a foot taller and dozens of pounds heavier, he could easily overpower me. The moment I put my back to him, I became vulnerable. And what would happen to Kiah if he hurt me?

I couldn't let that happen.

A flash of inspiration hit. I couldn't call the police, but I could pretend he caught me in the middle of a conversation. Just as I was in the dark about his intentions, he didn't know mine either. I brought my phone to my ear and said, "Sorry, I got distracted. Some guy pulled into the lot." I kicked pebbles, pretending to hear the other person's reply, while keeping the guy in my peripheral vision. If he moved, I'd bolt. "I should be there in an hour," I said. "Send out a search party if I'm not." I laughed to make the last part a joke, but I wanted him to think I had people waiting for me.

As I ended the call, the director put her arm around me, telling me to feign bewilderment. Be polite, but not chatty. She would guide me through this. "Hi…" I waved as I moved toward my car.

"You're not from around here," he said.

I gestured at the empty fruit stand, the trees, fields spanning toward the horizon. "Doesn't appear too many people are."

He smirked. Honest question. When does a smirk not make you look like a dick? "What brings you to Mount Point?" he asked.

I passed him. The grill on the front of his truck looked like gnarly teeth wanting to chomp me. "Mount Point?"

A real laugh this time. "Are you lost? That's the town you're in, little lady."

Little? Lady? Was he trying to remind me of our size differential? "Not for long."

I heard the brush of his boots against the dirt, the scattering of pebbles, behind me. I didn't turn around. Didn't move faster. Showing fear would be worse, right?

"Hey." His breath felt like stray hairs tickling the back of my neck. "Wait."

As I reached the car door, he grabbed my shoulder. I spun around. "Don't touch me." My voice was low and fierce, but it also shook, betraying me.

He held up his hands and backed away a couple feet. Not far enough. "Whoa," he said. "Calm down."

He tucked his hands in his back pockets. A gesture to show he meant no harm? Unless he had something in his pockets? A gun? Didn't criminals hide guns in the waistband of their pants? A knife?

"Thought you might be lost," he said. "A gentleman always stops to help a lady."

Panic prevented me from getting an accurate gut check. Did he stop to help? Possible. We were in the middle of nowhere. Equally possible he meant to hurt me. Again, we were in the middle of nowhere. "I'm not lost." I waved at his truck. "So, you can go."

He didn't move. "You're scared of me." A smile grew to his ears. "Come on, now, I don't bite."

I touched the door handle, the metal slick against my fingers, debating whether I'd have time to pull the door open, jump inside, and close it before he got to me. Doubtful considering my legs were the consistency of Jell-O. "I don't know you. And I learned a long time ago not to talk to strangers."

He smirked again. "I'm Kent," he said with faux patience. "And you are?"

My mind blanked. "Cassidy." Why did I say that? Any other name would've worked.

"Cassidy." He spoke as if tasting the word. "Now we're not strangers."

"Great. I have to go." I opened the door and he stepped forward, resting his hands on the top of the door. He had letters tattooed above each knuckle. RIDE on one hand and HARD on the other. Words that didn't put me at ease.

"Why're you in such a hurry?" His words were innocent enough, but the way he kept closing the gap between us, making it so I couldn't leave without his permission, freaked me out. I felt naked under his gaze. Hated how men did that, their eyes an assault.

I opened my mouth to answer as a high-pitched scream filled the air. Both of us jumped.

Kiah.

"What the...you have a baby?" He walked past my door, shielding his eyes with his hands to peer through the back window.

With him distracted, I jumped into the car, slammed the door, and hit the automatic lock function. Kiah's screams became frantic with the bang of the door.

Kent knocked on my window.

Ignoring him, I turned the key, which I left in the ignition. Kent yelled something. Impossible to hear what over Kiah's screams.

Adrenaline rushed through me. Why wouldn't he leave? Who was he to question me? Terrorize me? Why did men always take control? Think they could do whatever they wanted to women without consequences?

Not anymore. Starting today, I made the rules.

I slammed on the gas. Seconds later, I was out of the parking lot and flying down the highway. I gripped the steering wheel to the point of pain, eyes alternating between the road and the rearview mirror, fearful he might follow me.

After a few miles, I lowered my speed to the limit. Hard to relax though, when Kiah was crying as if someone was prying off her fingernails, one by one. Was this normal post-nap crankiness? Was she scared? Or could she be hurt? Maybe the strap was too tight?

She had to deal. I'd stop when we—

Kiah. He saw Kiah. OMFG.

I squeezed the wheel tighter. Would he recognize Kiah if he saw her picture on the news? He didn't strike me as a guy to keep up with current events, but the story would soon be everywhere. And I said my name was Cassidy. What defunct part of my brain took control there? If he heard the name Cassidy, it would remind him of the girl that freaked out in the parking lot. And then he'd remember the baby.

He saw my car, too. Did he clock the license plate? Perhaps as he pulled into the lot?

My mistakes were piling up. I had to be careful. More importantly, I had to get Kiah out of sight. Only two hours until we arrived at my lake house.

If only Kiah would stop crying.

CHAPTER SEVENTEEN

CASSIDY
WEDNESDAY, SEPTEMBER 6, 2023 2:45 P.M.

After Cassidy finished giving her fingerprints, she waited outside on the patio while Officer Parks packed her gear. Cassidy stood beneath the pergola, breathing fresh air. The sun shone, birds sang, and bees feasted on the potted hibiscus she kept as a divider between the stone patio and the grass. Life continued after the kidnapping; a brutal, yet unavoidable truth.

Officer Parks stepped outside. She wore plain clothes, which Cassidy appreciated, not wanting to scare Piper or spark questions. Cassidy planned to introduce the fingerprints as an art project.

They walked across the yard toward Faith's house. Between their houses, Cassidy could hear the din of conversation from the reporters.

"Ignore them," Officer Parks said.

Easier said than done.

Cassidy took the steps up to Faith's deck and looked through the glass doors, seeing Faith and Piper at the kitchen table. Cassidy drank her daughter in; the long, sandy-blonde hair, the thick eyebrows, the way the tip of her tongue skirted out the corner of her mouth when concentrating. This was a moment. Right now. Piper's life would never be the same if Daisy—

No. Cassidy couldn't go there.

She knocked on the door and stepped inside. The kitchen smelled of chocolate chips cookies. Faith probably had the patience to let Piper collect the ingredients, mix the dough, scoop each cookie—things Cassidy was too hurried to let Piper do.

Piper looked up and ran over. "Mommy!" she squealed.

Cassidy squatted and threw her arms around Piper, needing the full weight and warmth of her daughter.

"Who's that?" Piper asked, tilting her head and staring at Officer Parks.

"This is my friend, Marie. Marie, this is my daughter, Piper, and my friend, Faith." She paused while Faith and Marie exchanged hellos. "Marie's going to help us do an art project."

Piper went back to her seat and resumed coloring. "When I finish my picture."

August stepped out of the bathroom, flinching when he saw her. "Did something happen?"

"No." Cassidy watched as he cracked his knuckles. A nervous habit. Then again, it'd be odd if he wasn't nervous. She gestured toward the fingerprinting materials Marie was unpacking on the table. "I'm doing a special project with Piper."

"Sounds like fun," August said.

"I need to get yours next," Marie said.

"Sure," August said. "I'm going back to the house. I want to see if there are any updates."

Cassidy said, "Nothing's happened—"

"I have a few questions." Curt, which wasn't like him. He tussled Piper's hair and brushed a kiss against Cassidy's cheek. She wanted to ask him if he was okay, but it was impossible with Piper, Faith, and Marie there.

When he left, she sat next to Piper. "How was school?"

"You forgot to pick me up. I had to wait in the office."

"I'm sorry, baby." Cassidy rubbed Piper's back, watching as she made a rainbow pattern inside some four-legged creature. "It won't happen again."

"Where's Daisy?" Piper asked.

Cassidy and Faith exchanged a look across the table. Marie paused her preparations. What should Cassidy say? Piper was a smart, curious girl, but she was only four. What could her mind digest? "She went to Grandma and Grandpa's."

She turned her big blue eyes on Cassidy. "I want to go."

Thankfully, Faith intervened. "I think those cookies are ready, Piper. Should we check?"

Piper followed Faith to the stove. The power of distraction. The power of sugar. If Cassidy's brain wasn't preoccupied with Daisy, she would've put those tools to good use. When Piper returned, cookie in hand, wearing melted chocolate like lipstick, she forgot the conversation. But more questions would come. And Cassidy had to be ready. Daisy was missing, but Piper needed her too.

"Okay, Pipes, listen up," Cassidy said. "I want to create something cool for Daddy's birthday. Do you remember when we did the hand print picture?" Piper nodded. "It's sort of like that, but with the tip of our fingers."

Piper stared blankly at Cassidy. "And you think Daddy wants this?"

The adults laughed. Piper could be very intense. "Yes," Cassidy said. "I do."

Marie sat on the other side of Piper. She held up the ink pad and showed Piper the sheet of paper that was sectioned off into smaller rectangles. "I'm going to press each of your fingers into this ink pad and then rub it against the paper. Sound good?"

"Remember, it's for Daddy," Cassidy added.

Piper studied the dark ink. "I'll try my best."

"Let's wash our hands first." Cassidy took Piper to the sink, holding her up so that she could scrub her hands. Back at the table, Marie took Piper's thumb and rubbed it from side to side on the paper, having to tell her more than once to not help. A better print came about when the person's hand played dead. Then she did the same with each finger.

When finished, Piper picked up a blue marker and said, "We need to add some color."

Cassidy grabbed her hand, while Marie yanked the paper away. "Daddy likes black and white pictures," Cassidy said.

"No," Piper said. "His favorite color is blue."

Because she was arguing with a four-year old who changed her favorite color almost daily, Cassidy said, "He changed his mind. Here, color a blue picture on this one." Cassidy handed her another piece of paper.

"I'll leave you to your coloring," Marie said. "Nice to meet you, Piper."

This time, Piper smiled.

After Marie left, Cassidy gave Piper another cookie and went with Faith into the dining room to talk privately. With dozens of generational family pictures on the wall, the dining room was normally full of love and light. Today, the shades were drawn over the two windows that faced the street, dimming the light.

"Daisy must be terrified," Cassidy said, tears falling before she finished her sentence. "She's waiting for me to find her, hold her, make it all better. And I never show up." Cassidy's breath shuddered. "I'm her mother. My job is to protect her. And I let someone take her."

Faith pulled Cassidy close. "You didn't *let* anyone take her."

Faith's floral perfume was familiar, her arms around Cassidy strong, yet soft. If Cassidy could stay here, safe and warm and comforted—

Cassidy jerked back. How dare she think about herself when Daisy was not safe nor warm nor comforted. "I was asleep. I forgot to set the alarm. Forgot to lock the door. Perhaps even forgot to close the garage. I was careless. Unforgivably so." Cassidy looked at Faith, afraid she would see horror, judgment, disappointment, but Faith's eyes welled up.

"My dear girl," Faith said. "You're going to drive yourself mad. Are there things you'd change if you could? Yes. But you're not responsible for someone breaking the law."

Cassidy pressed her palms to her eyes. "Maybe people are right. Maybe I don't deserve to be a mom."

"Who's saying that?"

Cassidy was about to tell her about the comments on her website. That the police considered her a suspect. Instead, she shook her head.

"You're a wonderful mother." Faith took a step back, looking through the doorway. "Are you perfect? No. But no parent is. Right now, you need to be strong for Piper."

Cassidy clenched her jaw, trying to stop the tears. "Can Piper stay here tonight? The police—it would terrify her."

"Of course." She cupped Cassidy's chin. "I'm praying for Daisy. She'll come home soon."

Cassidy wanted to believe, too. But each minute that passed without word, without any meaningful update from the police, without a single clue who took her or where she was, Cassidy's faith weakened.

She walked back in the kitchen to hold Piper. Because she could.

CHAPTER EIGHTEEN

VANESSA
OCTOBER 2022

After our first date, our relationship progressed fast. Yes, fucking played a huge part. He would come inside of me, his breath heating my mouth, tongues, bodies, one, and instead of whispering my name, he would say, "More." With me, he always wanted more. I was a drug that intoxicated his mind, captured his heart, freed his body.

Not that our entire relationship was sex. We talked for hours. With me working nights, he'd reschedule showings to spend afternoons in bed with me. Those gestures worked like a wrecking ball to my walls, leaving me with rubble to guard my heart. I told him about my domineering father, my mother whom I grabbed my phone to call even though it'd been months since her death. He'd stroke my hair while listening, lips mumbling promises against my skin of how I was safe now.

Even as a few red flags crept in—Why wouldn't he sleep over? Why did he delete texts on his phone? Why hadn't I met his friends? Or vice versa?—I ignored them, wanting, needing, to believe this time was different. That August didn't see a girl he could fuck and ghost, cheat on, humiliate, treat as a receptacle for his desires, never once considering mine. I needed to believe August saw the real me. Loved me. That I was enough.

You have a choice in life, trust or not. I trusted August.

Until I didn't.

Thursday night. Happy hour with the girls. He promised to be there. Us. A real couple. Six o'clock. The girls giggled and awed as I gushed about August. Seven o'clock. Jokes about how men were always late. Quick text, *Are you okay?* No answer. Eight o'clock. Pitying glances. Excuses about getting up early. Nine o'clock. Everyone left.

Already lit from drinking to lessen my embarrassment, I called him on the walk home. Voicemail. Every. Fucking. Time. Once inside my apartment, I poured tequila into a coffee mug. How much did I drink? No idea. A melody awoke me. I was lying face-down in bed, the phone stuck to my hand like honey, the coffee mug having tipped over, tequila dampening the mattress.

12:27 a.m. *Sorry*, August texted. *Last minute closing. Will make it up to you.*

You can't. Fuck him. Fuck every single man who used and abused women.

I feel horrible.

Good. *Who has a closing until after midnight?*

Those goddamn bubbles appeared and disappeared. Appeared and disappeared. Was I drunk enough to hallucinate?

Finally, he texted, *We went for drinks to celebrate.*

You embarrassed me in front of my friends. Images of earlier tonight flit through my mind, the girls avoiding my eyes, trying to distract me with silly stories.

Give me another chance, he texted. *Please.* Heart emoji.

I loved him. Goddamn it. And he apologized. *Don't do it again.*

Late the next morning, however, my pounding head made me irritable. He chose clients over me? I knew he was insecure about our age gap, worried about what my friends thought, but to stand me up? Not cool.

I wanted to see him. Tell him how much he hurt me. See if his apology was genuine.

I got in my car and drove west to his office. I'd never been to Sweet Home Realty before. It was located in "downtown" suburbia, where the clapboard houses were converted into businesses, salons, coffeehouses, and Pilates studios. Old, yet trendy.

As I parked on the street across from his office, he came out the front door. He carried a blonde girl in pigtails to a nearby SUV while talking with a woman.

Was she a client? Relative? Friend? Who was this child? After putting the kid in the car, he walked to the driver's side, cupped the woman's chin with both hands, and pulled her close. Closer. Closer. Kissing! Nausea swept through me, shock, horror, rage, making it impossible to move. Drive away.

He was just like the rest. Selfish. Narcissistic. Egotistical. Only older.

I rested my head against the steering wheel, dug my nails into my thighs, and screamed. This wasn't happening.

I looked back up.

It was happening.

I hated him.

Hated her more.

Finally, they separated. She got into the car, while he went back inside, leaving me with a decision. Stay and confront him or follow her.

I pressed the gas, needing to know more about this woman. For fifteen minutes, I followed her, spitting a litany of curses. She pulled into the driveway of an ultra-modern house that nestled the perimeter of the Sawnee Conservatory. Huge windows. Dark brick. Flat roof. Slick and expensive, a real fuck-me house. This from a guy who'd rather cook than go to restaurants. Drink at my apartment instead of a noisy bar. I thought he was romantic, possibly a little cheap; turned out he was hiding.

Here I was, imagining a ring. A future. I was his dirty little secret and didn't know it.

I parked on the side of her house, facing the garage, watching as she carried the girl inside. Was August dating both of us? Or...I ripped off my thumb nail, watching as the blood bubbled, barely registering the sting. Was she his wife? This his child?

I grabbed my cell phone and called his office.

"Sweet Home Realty, how can I help you?"

"Can I speak with August?"

"He's in a meeting. Can I send you to his voicemail?"

A meeting. He didn't make time for me last night and he wasn't making time for me now. But he'd make time for his wife, right?

My entire chest vibrated with anxiety. "This is his wife."

"Cassidy!" The woman's voice rose in pleasure.

I ended the call, staring in disbelief at my phone.

He was married. Her name was Cassidy. They shared a child. A house. A life.

I started the car, tires screeching as I sped away. He lied. Why tell me he wanted more when he had nothing to give?

I couldn't take my foot off the gas pedal. Twenty over in a residential. Who cared? Thirty. I had to get away. Away. Away.

By the time I hit the freeway, insecurity replaced my anger, warnings running like fault lines beneath my thoughts. He didn't love me. Probably saw me as an easy lay. I was in a cycle of worthlessness that I knew from the past took days to recover.

Once home, I lay in bed, consuming a medicinal dose of tequila and family-sized bag of spicy ranch Doritos, staring at pictures of us on my phone. All taken in my bed. Another sign I missed. Stupid girl. FWIW, he looked happy. Smiles. Seductive looks. Post-cum haze in his eyes. Lots of kisses. Burying his face in my neck. Playfully biting my ear. Sleeping with his arms wrapped around me.

I banged the phone against my head, willing an explanation for his deception. I wasn't crazy. The pictures proved what I felt deep inside. We were happy together. The start of something real. A lifetime connection.

Love. That was the only answer. He truly loved me. He married the wrong woman. He must be terrified if he told me the truth, I'd dump him.

A different woman would've ghosted him, at least confronted him. But I wasn't that woman. I loved August. I had faith in us. We were end game. And so, I would do the unthinkable and be patient. Give him the support he needed, ultimately the courage, to leave his wife.

CHAPTER NINETEEN

AUGUST
WEDNESDAY, SEPTEMBER 6, 2023 3:00 P.M.

August jogged home from Faith's house, holding his phone like a grenade. He needed to talk to the detective. Get the wiretap going. Find out who sent this anonymous text and whether it had any connection to Daisy's kidnapping.

He opened the patio door and found the detective in the kitchen speaking with two officers. Sweat ran down August's back, making his shirt cling to him. He took a deep breath. "Sorry to interrupt, but can we talk?"

The detective spread his hands wide. "I'm all ears."

August clocked the other officers. "Let's go in Cassidy's office."

August closed the office door behind the detective, watching as he picked up a notebook from Cassidy's desk and flipped through.

"Initially, I was skeptical about signing the consent to tap my phone," August said. The detective set down the notebook and straightened up. Shoulders back, head high, tree-trunk legs spread, arms crossed. Casual intimidation. "I thought the parameters were too broad and there's some information on my phone, not related to this case, that I'd like to keep private. But I received an odd text…" August stepped forward, lowering his voice despite knowing Cassidy was at Faith's. "I need your word you won't discuss this with my wife."

The detective's expression did not change. "If it's related to the investigation, I'll have to tell her."

"The stuff that's not related?"

"If there's no chance it's related, I won't share it."

They didn't shake, but August considered it a deal. He pulled up the text and handed the detective his phone. He watched as the detective's eyes scanned the text and then the picture. "That's not your wife."

"No. It's Maxi Rogers." August tugged at the collar of his shirt, feeling like he was being strangled. He didn't talk about his affairs. Not a single friend knew. It was his problem to solve and his alone. "She was a client of mine. We had a short affair this past spring. Cassidy was pregnant and not very…" August struggled to find the right word, a reason to explain cheating on Cassidy. There was an undercurrent of embarrassment, which slowed his thoughts. "Available. It was a horrible choice and one I regret very much."

The detective looked at August. "Cassidy doesn't know about this affair?"

"No." August's gaze lit on a framed picture of the two of them at the beach. Cassidy glowing in the sun, her body ripe and luscious. One woman. One love. Why wasn't that enough? "I'd like to keep it that way."

"*How many scars have you left behind? How will you atone for them?*" The detective rubbed his chin. "Scars. This woman one of many you left brokenhearted?"

August looked around the office he custom-built for Cassidy. He painted it; bought furniture she pinned on Pinterest. An idea that took weeks of planning and one weekend to accomplish. He made mistakes, but he also did good. If she found out, would cheating tip the scales so far that it couldn't be evened out by his good deeds?

That wasn't a conversation he wanted to have. "No. I made one mistake—"

Before August could finish, his phone buzzed. The detective read it and then held it up. Maxi. *No. I didn't send you a picture. Forget me. Forget my number. I've already forgotten you.*

He doubted she forgot the fun they had. A bit dramatic, though, to be upset with him months later. August pushed those thoughts aside. "I knew it wasn't Maxi," August said. "The text didn't sound like her."

"Even so, she'll need to be questioned." The detective copied Maxi's information into his phone. "If not Maxi, then who sent the text? Why today? For what purpose?"

August cracked his knuckles. "That's what tripping me up, too."

"I can't investigate this until you sign the waiver." The detective's voice was hard.

Time to man up for Daisy, bear the consequences. "Get the agreement."

The detective nodded. "Good choice."

After the detective left, August squeezed his phone, wanting to smash it against the wall. Problem was, it wouldn't solve anything. Everything was stored in the cloud. Minutia of his business. His marriage. Evidence of his mistakes. Possibly Daisy's salvation. All he could do was sit back and watch as his life imploded, picking up the pieces wherever they fell.

Maybe it would lead to Daisy. Hope buried in the wreckage.

CHAPTER TWENTY

CASSIDY
WEDNESDAY, SEPTEMBER 6, 2023 3:30 P.M.

Cassidy found her husband standing in the middle of her office, face flushed, hand gripping his phone, looking like he wanted to punch something. It alarmed her, as she rarely saw him angry. She rested her hand on his shoulder, saying his name twice before he turned to her. "You okay?" she asked.

"No. Not really. All of this…" He gestured toward the window; the press, the cops, the chaos lay beyond. "It's surreal."

"I keep waiting to wake up." She crossed her arms, hugging herself. "Piper asked about Daisy. I panicked and told her she's with my parents."

"Good." August lowered his voice. "If all goes well, this could be over in a few hours and then we'll have scared Piper for no reason."

If all goes well? "Did something happen while I was gone?"

His eyes shifted past her toward the police. "Not that I know of."

She swallowed. Normally, his eyes brought comfort. Maybe it was the dire circumstances. The nervous energy vibrating from his body. Her paranoia. Guilt. But something was up with him. She noticed it at Faith's house too. Was he doubting her? Did he think she hurt Daisy?

"You know how much I love Daisy, right?" Her question was saturated with self-loathing and insecurity. She never thought she'd have to make this case to anyone, let alone her husband. "Piper, too."

His face crumpled. "Stop—"

"No, listen—"

"I know you. Those girls are your world." He pressed his forehead against hers. "We're a team, remember?"

She wrapped her arms around him and buried her face in his neck. Relief that he loved her, didn't blame her, that they would get through this together, left her sobbing. He held her tight, so that if she let go, succumbed to the fear, she wouldn't fall.

"I'm scared," she said. He smelled of amber and sandalwood, a smell as near and dear to her as her babies.

He squeezed tighter. "We'll find her. I promise."

She pulled back, looking up at him. "Thank you for believing me. For keeping faith. I'd be a wreck without you." He pressed his lips softly against hers. They hadn't kissed passionately since a burst of exuberance took hold in the moments after Daisy emerged in the world. Sex, the two times since Daisy's birth, was rote. Between breastfeeding Daisy and Piper treating her body like a jungle gym, she enjoyed not being touched. But right now, his kiss was exactly what she needed.

"Can you two come into the living room?" She turned around. Detective Lewis stood in the doorway.

Cassidy followed him, passing two cops leaning against the spokes of the stairs. She sat on the opposite end of the couch from Detective Lewis. August sat next to her, resting his hand on her knee. Despite his warmth, she felt chilled. Fear, once again, flared in her belly.

"First, August, if I can get your signature." Detective Lewis handed August the consent to tap his phone and a pen. Cassidy watched as August signed and handed it back. She was annoyed he didn't sign it right away, but relieved it was done now.

"Did you take Daisy for a walk this morning?" Detective Lewis asked Cassidy.

The question threw her. "Yes. After dropping Piper off at school, we went for a walk in the woods. I go every morning."

"What time was this?"

"A little after nine."

"When did you return home?"

Cassidy thought about it. "Nine-forty-five-ish. I did some chores and then put Daisy down for her nap."

"We're trying to establish a timeline. A witness saw someone pushing a stroller this morning in the woods and we don't know whether it was you or someone else."

"If it was after ten, it wasn't me. Daisy was napping."

"Problem is," Detective Lewis said, "no one saw Daisy after you dropped Piper off at school."

August's hand tensed on her knee. "You have no basis to accuse her of lying."

His protectiveness worked like a ray of sun peeking through stormy clouds. She met his eyes and, in that one look, she felt loved. Supported. Understood.

But reality quickly came crashing down. He wasn't here to establish her alibi. Alibi! Insane. Cassidy squeezed his hand. "I'm here alone with the girls every day."

Other than the soft click of the ceiling fan, the room was silent, everyone thinking the same thing. Today was different. Today, one of her children was kidnapped.

"Second development." Detective Lewis held up a clear, plastic bag with a sea-green pacifier inside, one that had the hole in the front so that the baby could suck on your finger. "We found this on one of the trails. Does it look familiar?"

A surge of energy shot through Cassidy's body, similar to when she noticed the drapes were left partly open in Daisy's room. "Yes, it's Daisy's. Or at least the same brand. But she didn't have her pacifier when we went for a walk."

"You're sure?"

"Yes." Cassidy wished she could reach inside and hold the pacifier. Smell it. Anything to feel closer to Daisy. "I only give her the pacifier for naps."

"Good. If it's hers, it tells us the kidnapper most likely exited through the woods. We're in the process of running license plates on the surrounding streets—"

An officer came in the front door, walked over to Detective Lewis and whispered something in his ear. Cassidy gripped August's hand.

"Where's your stroller?" Detective Lewis asked. "The one you used for this morning's walk."

"In the—" She stopped. The stroller. It wasn't next to her car when she came back to the house earlier with Faith. She remembered passing her car, feeling like something was off, but then became preoccupied with the cops' arrival. "Garage."

As they walked to the garage, she already knew it wouldn't be there. Whoever had Daisy, had the stroller.

CHAPTER TWENTY-ONE

AUGUST
WEDNESDAY, SEPTEMBER 6, 2023 3:45 P.M.

August followed Cassidy, the detective, and two officers as they walked into the garage to search for the stroller. He kept thinking about the text on his phone. The picture of him and Maxi. How did it relate to Daisy? Or did he potentially put his marriage in jeopardy for nothing?

Inside the garage, August immediately started to sweat. The stress combined with the stuffiness of the room. They kept the garage door shut because of the press outside, which made the space dim and humid. Dust percolated in the air, highlighted by the rays of sun beaming through the upper windows. Cassidy stood in the empty spot where her car normally parked, turning slowly in a circle.

"It was here," Cassidy said. "Right beside my car."

"Can you describe the stroller?" the detective asked.

"It's black with light gray details. You click in the car seat. It has storage below…"

The detective handed Cassidy his phone. "Is this it?"

August peered over Cassidy's shoulder as she thumbed through four pictures, which showed a stroller flipped on its side in the woods.

"Yes!" Cassidy covered her mouth with her hand. "Oh my God, where is this?"

"A mile south, off Swan Road," the detective said. "We found a fingerprint—"

"Did you—" Cassidy inhaled sharply.

"Was there any sign of Daisy?" August finished for her.

"No. Only the stroller and car seat," the detective said. "The stroller handle and seatbelt were wiped clean, but my team found a fingerprint on the canopy. Might be one of yours—"

"No. I never close it." Cassidy shook her head. "She likes fresh air."

August didn't mess with anything when he used the stroller. Too complicated. "Not me."

"Good. If they're in the system, the fingerprint will match."

"And if they're not?" August asked.

"Then we'll use it when we prosecute them. Now, we also found footprints in the area, leading us to believe someone ditched the stroller and took Daisy in a vehicle."

Daisy could be anywhere. In a cold, dirty basement. A farmhouse in the middle of nowhere. A tricked-out nursery where some desperate couple planned to raise her as their own. He rubbed his eyes, trying to erase the images.

"They left the car seat," Cassidy said, pointing at the picture on the detective's phone. "Daisy can't ride in a car without it. It wouldn't be sa—" She stopped, likely realizing the kidnapper didn't care about Daisy's safety.

"About the footprints." The detective took his phone back from Cassidy. "Officers Ruiz and Kent would like to search the premises for size eight running shoes."

August laced his hands behind his head. "You gotta be kidding me."

Cassidy's eyes became owl-like, wide and unblinking. "I wear a size eight."

No one said anything. August looked down at the running shoes Cassidy was wearing.

"I swear," Cassidy hastily added, "Daisy came home with me. I put her to bed. She was fine."

"It's the size, but also the treads, the impression they make. We can get a warrant," the detective said with a touch more force, "but it would be faster if you consented to the search."

August walked over and wrapped his arm around Cassidy, pressing his lips to her ear. "I know you had nothing to do with this," he whispered. A small part of August, maybe due to being unsettled by the text message, maybe from having the detective's careful gaze on them, wanted to ask her if there was any reason to demand a warrant. Cassidy took Daisy for a walk this morning. Used the stroller. Was the last person to see her. It didn't look great.

"Go ahead," August said, wanting to rid himself of such disgusting thoughts. He watched Cassidy feed Daisy round the clock. Cuddle. Sing. Give every ounce of herself. Cassidy didn't have a dark side. "We've got nothing to hide."

The detective cleared his throat. "We need the shoes you're wearing."

Cassidy bent down and unlaced her shoes, pulling them off and handing them to one of the officers. He put them into a plastic evidence bag and both officers disappeared inside. To search August's house. Because they were suspects in the kidnapping of their daughter.

They passed horror and were deep into the realm of insanity.

"I'm going to lie down in my office," Cassidy said. Then she stopped. "Can I do that? I mean, while they're searching?"

The detective nodded. "Don't move anything."

She left the garage, her socked feet soundless on the cement, her shoulders hunched. Cassidy's defeated posture worked like an accelerant on his anger.

"What's the theory here?" August asked. "That Cassidy left the stroller behind and then what? Gave Daisy away? Kil—" He walked over to his car, resting both hands against the hood. He swallowed several times. Once calm, he faced the detective again. "She would never hurt Daisy. These kids are her world."

"What's Cassidy's mood been like since Daisy's birth?"

August bit his tongue as the detective moved around the garage, scrutinizing every corner, shelf, and drawer, aching to eviscerate him for wasting time. "Tired."

The detective pulled out a drawer where August kept random junk: duct tape, tools, nails. "Do you think she's depressed?"

August shoved his hands in his pockets, considering. Tired was different from depressed. "No."

The detective fingered the shovels hanging from the pegged wall, probably looking for fresh soil. "Does she seem different this time around? From when you had Piper?"

Yes, August admitted. More worn out. There was less videoing or taking pictures of Daisy, less savoring the moment, and more trying to get through the day. August thought she took on too much between the kids, blog, and podcast. No maternity leave when you're self-employed. "Nothing is easy with a newborn," August said. "It's pretty much impossible to feel like yourself without sleep."

"What about friends? A doctor? A therapist? Anyone we should talk to that might have a better gauge on her feelings?"

August ignored the veiled insult. The detective probably thought cheating made him a horrible husband. When, in fact, he was more attentive to Cassidy. "There's Faith, our neighbor. Her best friend, Kristin. A few others. But no, no doctor. If something's wrong, she talks to me."

"Is she on an anti-depressant?"

August's jaw ached from holding back his frustration. "No. Because she's not depressed."

"Do you ever feel uneasy leaving her with the kids?"

"No!" August raised his voice. It was stupid, probably playing into some cop trap, but goddammit, it felt good to let it out. "She would never hurt the kids. Neither of us would. Stop wasting time investigating us."

Heat filled the air between them. A mixture of adrenaline and testosterone and ego. Surprisingly, the detective backed down. "I wouldn't be doing my job if I didn't investigate all leads. To me, it seems she might suffer from postpartum depression."

"This is…" Insane. Absurd. Insulting. "You're wrong about her."

"I hope I am."

August asked, "Have you found out anything about the text?"

"Tech is working on it. Officers are interviewing Maxi," he said, turning to go inside. "Come on. We need your fingerprints."

"Give me a minute." August stood alone in the garage, unsettled by his helplessness. Admittedly, he was a control freak. With his affairs, he dictated the terms. Made clean breaks. Now, someone else had the upper hand. Knew his secrets. Possibly had Daisy.

The unknown scared him. What else was to come. August wished he could talk to this person. He was a great negotiator. Problem was, he didn't have that choice. He was quickly running out of choices.

CHAPTER TWENTY-TWO

VANESSA
WEDNESDAY, SEPTEMBER 6, 2023 3:53 P.M.

My phone sat mounted on the dashboard while I drove, the Twitter app opened to Sawyer Brinkley's account, a local gossip who I figured would report all the kidnapping details, both accurate and gritty. I leaned forward to read a new tweet. *Police investigating—*

The car veered onto the rubble on the side of the road, the tread of the tires screaming in protest. I jerked the steering wheel to the left, just in time to avoid plowing through a corn field.

Jesus!

Short of breath, heart thrashing, I pulled over and rested my head against the steering wheel. At this rate, I'd kill us before we arrived. I unbuckled my seatbelt and peered into the backseat, relieved to see my bad driving didn't wake Kiah. A small miracle she cried herself to sleep in the first place.

I grabbed my phone and scanned the tweet. *Source says police investigating parents re disappearance of #BabyDaisy.* Whoa. Whoa! WHOA! I pressed the phone to my mouth, a smile growing. Other than the hiccup with the stroller and the man in his truck, no one saw me. No one knew there was any connection between August and me.

After putting my phone back, I peeled out on the road, aching to read the comments. Get the inside scoop on why the police considered August and Cassidy suspects. Other than being terrible parents. Obviously. Tonight, I'd put Kiah to bed, drink wine, and watch this saga play out on Twitter like the latest Shonda Rhimes series.

I hit the steering wheel with my fist. This, right here, was the first step toward justice. For the baby August stole from me. The future he promised. His lies—

I passed a cop car.

Fuck.

Hidden next to a barn.

Fuck.

I looked at the speedometer. Seventeen miles over.

Fuuuuuuuuuuuuuck.

My eyes darted between the road and the rearview mirror. Maybe he wouldn't stop me.

Flashing lights.

I was trapped. Time slowed. My foot, which was pressed firmly against the accelerator, lost in the exhilaration of August's world crumbling, slowly eased off the pedal.

My hand trembled as I hit the blinker and pulled over. What could I say? What could I do? Was this the end?

How could I have been so stupid?

CHAPTER TWENTY-THREE

CASSIDY
WEDNESDAY, SEPTEMBER 6, 2023 4:15 P.M.

Cassidy lay on the chaise in her office, coming to grips with being a suspect in her daughter's kidnapping. Unbelievable. Unthinkable. Yet all evidence pointed to her. Was she being framed? Did that happen outside of the movies? Who had it out for Cassidy? Hated her enough to steal her child? She didn't have any enemies—

She grabbed her phone and pulled up her website, delving into the back matter, which held the comments, including the mean ones she wouldn't post. It was a long shot the kidnapper was a troll. But so was having a child kidnapped when you were at home.

As she scanned from the beginning, she felt heartened. Many, strike that, *most* were positive, thanking her for creating a supportive environment, being real about life with young children, making herself vulnerable so that other mothers didn't feel isolated.

She found her first negative comment from @Mama4life on October 14th of last year. *How will your kids feel when they grow up and listen to this? #unloved #unwanted #selfishmom* Proud, Cassidy hoped. That their mom was honest. That, despite her struggles, she showed up every day. Loved them fiercely.

The next day, an odd one from @LiveLaughLove2000. *Imagine having a gorgeous husband and telling the world you have no interest in having sex with him. What. Could. Happen? #divorce* Cassidy rolled her eyes. She assumed the rest of her listeners related to the feeling of having young kids and not always being up for it.

A couple weeks later, again from @Mama4life. *Using your kids as an ATM #Cha-ching! #shameless* An ATM? Really? This person had a warped understanding of how podcasts worked. The bigger ones could charge ad revenue, but she wasn't there yet.

Then in December of last year, a new troll, @luvmykids4ever. *Imagine waking up one day and your kids are gone. You're not a mom. You have nothing. Remember that during your next bitch session. #badmom* This one upset her and she told August about it. He hugged her, reminded her that these trolls were looking to feel better by bringing someone else down. They didn't know her, didn't see the thousands of ways she rained love down upon Piper.

Nothing for months and then in March of this year, @LiveLaughLove2000 again. *Prediction: you end up divorced and childless.* Cassidy screenshot it, heart thrashing at the "childless" comment. And why was this commenter obsessed with Cassidy getting divorced?

In June, the day she brought home Daisy from the hospital. @luvmykids4ever wrote, *I'm worried about the health and safety of your children. #CPS #knock-knock #byebyebaby*

Could @luvmykids4ever be the one? Or maybe @LiveLaughLove2000?

Cassidy jumped when she heard a knock on the door. "Yeah?"

Detective Lewis stepped inside, a laptop in one hand. "Can I sit?" He didn't wait for an answer before taking her desk chair.

She held out her phone. "Here are those comments on my website August mentioned."

He set his laptop on her desk and wheeled the chair close. He took her phone and flipped through, pressing his lips together as he read. "LiveLaughLove predicted you'd be childless."

"Right," she said. "And @luvmykids4ever wrote that weird bye-bye-baby comment on the day I brought Daisy home from the hospital."

"Did you notice anything else amiss that day?"

She thought back, but she was preoccupied with Daisy. Making sure Piper felt seen. And she hadn't slept for forty-eight hours. "Nothing stands out."

"I'm emailing my team. Although, my understanding is that if they used a public network, it's almost impossible to trace. But maybe they were dumb enough to do it at home."

She ran her hands through her hair, twisting the long strands. Alone with the detective, working together, she didn't feel like a suspect. "I'd never—" She paused to gather herself. "I'd never hurt Daisy. The person who took her is out there." She gestured toward the window. "Not in here."

He handed back her phone. "My gut says you're not involved. That you're a loving mother who's been dealt the world's worst day. But my gut's been wrong before. So, I follow the evidence. Bear with me, okay?" He opened his laptop on his knees. "I need to show you something difficult."

She held her breath and prepared for the worst. Daisy dead. Muzzled? Bruised? She couldn't see this alone. "Can I get August?"

"No," he said. "I'd like to get your opinion."

She flinched. Why did he want to separate them?

Before she could hypothesize, he turned the laptop to face her. "August was texted this picture today."

Expecting a picture of Daisy, Cassidy was too disoriented at first to understand what she was seeing. Two people kissing on a street. The woman's back pressed against the car, the man holding her hip with one hand, the other cupping her chin—

August.

She jerked back and pressed a hand to her cheek, her skin burning, as if the picture slapped her.

August kissing another woman.

Touching her.

Wanting her.

Maybe it wasn't him. Maybe it just looked like him.

She reached forward and magnified the picture, zeroing in on the hand cupping the woman's chin. And there it was. On the inside of his wrist. A tattoo of two small hearts. One for when he married Cassidy, the other when Piper was born.

Cassidy saw Detective Lewis's mouth move, but heard nothing.

Two hearts. Not three. This happened before Piper was born. When? How? *Why?*

August despised cheaters. Hated watching movies with cheating. Said it brought up bad memories from childhood. In whispered conversations, August promised he'd never hurt her that way. Promised to put her, their marriage, their family, first.

She flew out her chair, charging toward the door. "I'm going to find August."

She had questions. Problem was, if he cheated, how could she trust anything he said?

CHAPTER TWENTY-FOUR

VANESSA
WEDNESDAY, SEPTEMBER 6, 2023 4:33 P.M.

I sat inside my car on the side of the road, frozen with terror, watching the sheriff through my rearview mirror. Each minute waiting for him stretched like an hour. Months of planning. Sacrificing. Suffering. None of it mattered. I messed up as I took the final steps toward home plate. Speeding. Speeding! The stupidity of it, letting *my* emotions take over when it was finally *his* turn to hurt, was enough to make me smash my head into the steering wheel. Choose my own ending.

No time for that. I had a decision to make. Use the fake ID I bought with the name Mackenzie Roeper, or give him my real license, which put a record of my location in the system. Then again, my registration had my real name.

No good solutions.

The director settled into the passenger seat as the sheriff exited his car. Look at him, she said. He was short and stocky, with a handlebar mustache. Tug down your shirt, she said. Push up your breasts. Come on, hurry!

I did as I was told. The director always saved me.

"License and registration, please," the sheriff said in lieu of a greeting. I wished I could see his eyes. Determine whether they were kind. Honest. Trustworthy. His sunglasses made it impossible. Then again, I looked into August's eyes and bought every lie he sold.

I grabbed the registration from the glove compartment and put my real license on top, letting my fingertip brush his as I handed it to him.

Nothing. No indication he felt my touch. "I'll be back," he said.

I watched in my rearview mirror as he got in his car. Then I unbuckled and peeked over the seat, checking on Kiah. Asleep. How long would that last? Without the rhythmic movements of the car, she could wake any second.

I squeezed the headrest, frustrated that flirting didn't impress him. Time to change gears? Stressed out mother, the director said, snapping her fingers. Traveling with an infant isn't easy—

A car door slammed and I ducked back in my seat. A moment later, the sheriff handed me my driver's license and registration. "Do you know what the speed limit is here?"

The sign right in front of us proved helpful. "Forty-five."

"And how fast were you going?"

I looked at the dashboard. The real me wanted to point out that no one was around. Short of a deer or a stray cow, speeding didn't hurt anyone. Instead, I let my stress take over, the tremor in my voice real. "I'm—I'm not sure. Maybe fifty-five, sixty."

"Sixty-two."

"I'm sorry. I'm traveling with my daughter, Kiah…" I gestured toward the backseat, gazing in the rearview mirror at Kiah with love and affection. Any new mother couldn't help but smile when speaking of their baby. I was no exception. "She hates long car rides."

He peered into the back window. "Can you put down the window?"

"I don't want to wake her."

"I'll be quiet." His voice brokered no argument. As he looked her over, sweat dampened my armpits. Why was he inspecting her? Were they questioning anyone traveling with a baby?

"How old?" he asked.

"Four months."

His eyebrows furrowed. "She's tiny."

"I had preeclampsia. She was born eight-weeks early." The director gave a slow clap. I was in the zone now. An Oscar-worthy performance. "It was brutal. I might not be able to have another." I brushed away tears. Real tears. I *was* afraid that I might not be able to have another. That I cursed myself barren. That all the right-wingers were right. God would never forgive.

Fuck you, August!

Stop! Stop it. Right now. Focus. You're a loving mother, not a bitter mistress.

"I'm sorry to hear that." He returned to my window. "She's beautiful."

"Thank you." More tears fell. Tears of relief. Love. Frustration that I let myself get close to losing it all.

"You're lucky," he said, all stern. Very committed to his role too. "But let's keep it that way. Drive safely to your destination instead of quickly."

"Yes. Absolutely." I nodded eagerly. I could tell he believed I was a good mom. Devoted. And why wouldn't he? I was already better at this than Cassidy.

"But I can't let you go seventeen over with a warning," he said. "Even with a fussy baby."

He handed me a ticket for a loss of four points and a whopping fine of $268. I felt like snarling at him like a rabid dog. Instead, I thanked him and promised to drive safe.

I tossed the ticket at the director in the passenger seat—so much for her perfect record—before signaling and pulling back into the road. A little over an hour to my lake house.

The sheriff followed at a steady distance. Why? Was he waiting to see what I would do next?

The seatbelt felt like a blood pressure cuff, cutting off circulation to all my limbs. This was what my life would be like now. One eye over my shoulder. Guarded. Vigilant with every word, aware that one slip could ruin it all. Did I want to live like that? Could I live like that?

The close calls made me question everything. The brilliance of this plan. Whether I was clever enough, responsible, dedicated, to pull it off. I was so consumed with getting my baby, hurting August, that I didn't consider what would happen if something went wrong.

For the first time in my life, I couldn't bail. Kiah needed me.

A little late to have an existential crisis. Yesterday would've been the time to have a long think about the reality of this new life.

When I turned left at the next highway intersection, the sheriff drove straight. I was free.

For the moment.

CHAPTER TWENTY-FIVE

VANESSA
OCTOBER 2022

After discovering August was married, I didn't break up with him. Every time I thought about saying goodbye, my heart would race and I'd get this knot in my stomach, something between nausea and fear. Never see his smile again? Feel his arms around me? The rumble of his voice in my ear? Inhale the scent of sandalwood when I buried my face in his neck?

No. Impossible.

I started following Cassidy online and in person—not in a crazy-stalker way, but an altruistic-head-over-heels-in-love-with-August way. I'd do anything to understand him better. Bridge the gap between affair and exclusive relationship. What made Cassidy special? What hold did she have on him that he *couldn't* leave? Did she suspect he cheated?

Her social media painted an enviable picture. As creator of *Lost in Babyland*, a blog and podcast about parenting, selling her, August and Piper as #familygoals was key. And boy, did she sell. Whereas August's social media was business, advertising houses and sales and market updates, no mention of a wife or kid, Cassidy posted pictures of them at the beach, swinging Piper between them so her toes skirted the water; August and Cassidy gazing at Piper like she set the sun as she blew out candles for her third birthday; cuddling in front of the Trevi Fountain in Rome, *15 years with the man of my dreams. Loving every moment. #blessed* The perpetual kissing and cuddling and smiling would lead one to believe they never experienced something as taxing as a traffic jam. Blessed upon blessed on blessed.

Puke.

Except I knew better. As he came inside me, he'd grunt, *More* or *You're mine.* He wanted me. All of me. Not Cassidy.

Still, he continued lying to my face. I bit my tongue, trying not to go off on him. Long run, long run, long run, flashed in my head like the lights of a Broadway show. If I stuck to my plan—fuck him into oblivion, be cool, don't put pressure on him—he'd be mine.

This afternoon, I followed Cassidy to the grocery store. She grabbed a cart and hoisted Piper into the front. Then handed her a sucker. Sugar. Tsk-tsk. What would her listeners think?

Even in black leggings, an off the shoulder sweatshirt, and one of those messy buns twisted atop her head like a soft-serve ice cream cone, Cassidy looked beautiful. Beauty derived from confidence. The grace of privilege. Never left wanting.

I hated her.

At least I'm younger, I thought as I grabbed a basket for my groceries. Cassidy was in the midst of her dirty thirties. Botox and filler and cosmetic procedures her only recourse against decline— not that it appeared she'd taken that route. Yet. My skin glowed when hungover, wrinkles disappeared the second they formed, and my tits alone had the power to attract men.

Again, August, why is it taking you so long to leave her?

As I trailed Cassidy around the store, hanging back a comfortable distance, I listened to the latest episode of her podcast. She was discussing the phenomenon of never feeling like your body is your own after having a baby. *Piper is my shadow,* Cassidy said. *Crawling on me, kissing me. The kisses I love—obviously! But following me to the bathroom, watching me shower, do my makeup, not so much. And then when she goes to bed, my husband needs his time.* She gave a throaty laugh. *I know. I know. It's important to make intimacy a priority*...

Intimacy? Ugh! Way to take the sexiness out of sex. As if fucking August was a chore! Ungrateful bitch. No wonder he wanted me.

Cassidy turned down the toiletry aisle. I was maybe ten feet away, mulling the difference between super absorbent and extra absorbent tampons—surely both were a prescription for TSS?—when she picked up a pregnancy test. With her other hand, she made a phone call. "Guess where I am?" Cassidy said, her voice playful. "Buying a pregnancy test." She laughed at something the person said. "I'm actually late—"

No. No. Please. I gripped the shelf.

"Only by five hours, so don't get too excited. But honey—"

Honey? Honey was August. How sickeningly common.

"—I think it finally happened."

Horror engulfed my throat like flames, stealing my breath. Did he worship her body, hitting the same spots that gave me a meteor shower of pleasure? Did he whisper, *more*?

Yesterday, he said the thought of me with another man drove him mad. A sign he was getting closer to leaving Cassidy. But now, this. Was he fucking us both? What did *that* mean? I had no interest in starring in a *Sister Wives* redux.

"Alright. See you at home. Don't speed." She giggled and ended the call. Then she rested a hand on her stomach like the virgin fucking Mary.

Time to go. I didn't trust myself to stand here a second longer without losing it. If I blew up August's world, he wouldn't come running to me. Men liked to do things themselves.

I charged past Cassidy, accidentally banging her shoulder. Not enough to harm. Not nearly what she deserved.

"You could say excuse me," she said.

I turned around, stepping close enough to smell mint on her breath. "Oh, I'm sorry." I laughed. "Crazy how you can't see what's right in front of your face until it's too late."

She stood there, wide-eyed, mouth forming a perfect O. Perfect looks. Perfect husband. Perfect life. Perfect. Perfect. Perfect.

My hand flexed, ready to slap the metaphorical silver spoon out of her hands. Or, in this case, the goddamn pregnancy test.

"Are you…?" She lowered her voice, eyes skirting past me. "Do you need help?"

"Me?" I laughed harder and started walking backwards. "You think *I* need help?"

My laughter continued as I left the store. A sound I hoped would haunt her. My words a riddle that would nag, but she couldn't solve.

Later that night, with tequila swimming in my bloodstream, I got an idea of how to torture her until August got the balls to leave. I grabbed my phone, navigated to her website, and made up a fake name, @Mama4life. Taunting her worked at the grocery store. Doing it anonymously—the wireless supplied my entire apartment building, including the coffee shop downstairs, so nothing could blow back on me—would be even better. *How will your kids feel when they grow up and listen to this? #unloved #unwanted #selfishmom.*

Would it give her stomach-cramp-struggling-for-oxygen kind of shame? No. But it was a start.

The bigger problem was this baby. Perhaps Cassidy knew he was cheating. About to leave her. And she handcuffed his balls.

With more tequila, an epiphany struck. If she could scheme a pregnancy, why couldn't I? It wasn't a fair fight for August if I was handicapped. And he would definitely choose me. Our baby. On my life, that man had a foot out the door.

I rushed to the bathroom and pressed my birth control pills out of the foil, one by one, watching them sink to the bottom of the toilet. Then, with a flourish, I flushed.

Next step. Sabotage the condoms. Short of poking holes, which he might notice, a quick Google search proved that the easiest solution to make condoms less effective was to expose them to extreme heat or cold. Not wanting to freeze his cock off, I grabbed the condoms from my bedside drawer and laid them on the window frame, like plants I wanted to bloom. The sun sizzled this spot in the late-afternoon.

Game. Fucking. On.

Giddy with my plan, I messed with Cassidy one more time. I made up another handle, this time @LiveLaughLove2000. *Imagine having a gorgeous husband and telling the world you have no interest in having sex with him. What. Could. Happen? #divorce*

I hit post. With heavy limbs, a head swirling like a hurricane, I fell into bed.

Sat back up. Reread the post. Noooooooooo. What if she took it as a challenge? Spiced up their sex life? Ugh. Stupid me.

And now I felt wide awake. A drunken philosopher. Did I want to get pregnant? Was I risking too much, banking my future on a married man? Did I want to follow the conventional roadmap of marriage, babies, and soccer games? I was only twenty-two.

I love him. Our love story was no longer the romance I dreamed, but a second chance at love was also a great story line. Besides, all the lying and sneaking around would end once I got pregnant. He'd commit to me and we'd tell everyone we met after he separated from Cassidy.

Soothed, I drifted to sleep. Did I feel guilty for forcing August's hand? Hell no. With love, there were no rules.

CHAPTER TWENTY-SIX

CASSIDY
WEDNESDAY, SEPTEMBER 6, 2023 5:00 P.M.

Cassidy tried to leave her office to find August, but Detective Lewis stopped her. She crossed her arms, furious that Detective Lewis hadn't found Daisy. Furious she was a suspect. Furious he showed her this evidence—evidence of what? Cheating, clearly. But how far did it go? A kiss? Sex? A relationship? Was August planning on leaving her?—without considering that it would destroy the one thing keeping her sane. Her marriage.

"I know this is hard," Detective Lewis said, holding out the phone, "but, please, look. Do you recognize the woman?"

Cassidy glanced at the picture. The sight of August kissing this woman burned Cassidy's retinas. She couldn't unsee it. Someday, maybe, the pain would turn into a bruise instead of a flesh wound, but that day was far from today. "It's hard to tell. Her face is covered by my husband."

He clicked a link, bringing up a text. "This was sent with the picture. Does it mean anything to you?"

How many scars have you left behind? How will you atone for them?

Cassidy shivered, speechless. Scars? Atone? What did August do to this woman?

"Did you have any idea he was cheating?" Detective Lewis asked.

She shook her head. Her husband. Her kind, attentive, sexy husband. A cheater. Liar. Time thief.

Truthfully, she thought he loved her more. A horrible thought, yes. One she'd never admit out loud. But it was one of the reasons she fell in love with him. He adored her, embraced her faults, laughed off her neurosis, told her she was beautiful whenever she voiced an insecurity. As an only child, she expected that level of attention. And he provided it—without complaint.

"I don't believe in coincidences," Detective Lewis said. "August receiving this text today is very suspicious."

Cassidy peered closer at the picture. "You think this woman took Daisy?"

"I'm investigating it."

"I've never seen her before." Cheating. And she thought she had encyclopedic knowledge of August. "Can I talk to August now?"

"Just…" Detective Lewis gestured for her to stay calm. "Keep the big picture in mind. Finding Daisy."

She left her office and walked through the living room and kitchen. Unable to find August, she went upstairs to look in the girls' bedrooms. Each step she took felt like pressing a piano key, a haunting instrumental to accompany the memory of going to wake Daisy from her nap this morning.

She poked her head inside Piper's room first. Sunlight filtered through her window, highlighting the unmade bed, books shoved haphazardly into the bookshelf, the open toy chest with various princess dresses sticking out. No August.

The door to Daisy's room was closed. She knocked before entering, in case the police were inside, collecting evidence. Instead, she found August, sitting in Daisy's rocking chair, holding her favorite stuffed giraffe. He looked up, devastation and fear written in his eyes. For one second, the thunderous pulse of her blood slowed as she felt empathy—

August.

Kissing another woman.

Lusting.

Mouth hungry.

Hands greedy.

Time he should've been with her. Piper. Time he stole.

How could he grieve like a family man, knowing he cheated?

She closed the door behind her and yanked the giraffe from his hands, holding it to her heart. "Detective Lewis showed me a picture of you kissing another woman."

His head fell to his chest. She licked her front teeth, gearing up for a barrage of questions, but as she opened her mouth, she remembered Detective Lewis's advice. Only one question mattered. "Did she take Daisy?"

He looked up. "No." His blue eyes pleaded with her, asking for the same faith and understanding he gave her when she was interrogated earlier. He did not want to be accused of playing any part in this tragedy either. "She didn't know about Daisy."

"How can you be sure?"

"Because…" He ran his hands through his hair. "Because I never talked about my family. She didn't know you guys existed. It was just—" He took a deep breath. "Sex."

Sex. Hearing that word felt like being mauled by a pack of angry dogs, each paw heavy, the nails sharp, teeth razors, cutting fresh wounds. Sex. Not just a kiss. Sex. Did he love her? Sex. Was he downplaying the affair? Sex.

Admittedly, their sex life was more short and to the point, than sweat-fueled passion. With young children, exhaustion made sleep sexier than, well, sex. There wasn't time for romance, lust. But they had something better. Intimacy from building a family. Creating a safe nook to shield them from the chaos of the world. One day, when the kids were older, she figured the lust would return, a sexual renaissance.

Apparently, he couldn't wait.

"And that made it easier to cheat," she said. "Pretending we didn't exist?"

"It wasn't easy. Nothing about it was easy. I felt—" He winced. "I feel horrible."

"When did this happen?"

He tugged at the collar of his shirt. "Spring."

"As in a few months ago?" Fresh tears rose. "When I was pregnant with Daisy?"

He stood up, resting both hands on her shoulders. "I'm so sorry. It was an accident."

She stepped back, swatting his hands away. "An accident?"

"Sorry. A mistake. It was a mistake. A horrible mistake. I've been...lonely." He searched her eyes. "It feels like we're parents, in the trenches together, but there's no time for us. And you don't seem as...interested as before."

"You're pathetic. And weak. Like your father." She intended to maim. Still, the way he winced hurt her too. They didn't normally fight like this. Preying on each other's vulnerabilities. Going for the kill shot. "Was this the first time?"

"The first time what?"

"That you cheated, August," she snapped.

"Yes! Yes! Oh my God, yes." He reached out, again trying to hold her, but she stepped back. Did his emphatic response suggest truthfulness or that he was cementing his lie? She didn't know.

"Why would this woman text you this?" she asked.

"Maxi said—"

"Don't." She held up her hand, her voice sharp enough to clear-cut a forest. "Don't say her name in our baby's room. Don't you dare."

"She said she didn't send the text."

Cassidy flung her arms. "And you believe her?"

He ducked. "Officers are questioning her, but, honestly..." August rubbed his chin. "I thought maybe you found out I cheated—"

"Me?" She stepped toward him, hands crackling with energy, a fervent need to slap him. "And instead of confronting you, *leaving* you, I texted you—"

"You're right—"

"—today? When our daughter goes missing?" Cassidy paused as thoughts coalesced in her brain. "Assuming this woman isn't lying, then who took the picture?"

"That's what I'm trying to figure out."

She grabbed the phone from his hand, pulling up the text. "It sounds like blackmail. Like, if you don't atone, something bad will happen." Her head hurt. She didn't understand. Daisy kidnapped. August cheating. The threatening text. She hoped Detective Lewis was making headway. "But, if it's related to Daisy, then the bad thing happened before you got the text. You didn't have a chance to atone."

"Why would I atone?" He sighed, sounding annoyed. "It was barely even a thing."

Cassidy turned and left the room, slamming the door hard enough to shake the frame. He destroyed their trust, their love, their future. And for what? Sex. Barely even a thing. She took a step, maybe two, then braced herself against the wall. Fresh tears spilled from her eyes.

It was too much. No one could sustain the loss of a child and their marriage in one day.

She wanted her mom.

CHAPTER TWENTY-SEVEN

VANESSA
WEDNESDAY, SEPTEMBER 6, 2023 5:10 P.M.

By the time I arrived at Two Bear Place, a narrow, hilly road shaped like a horseshoe that skirted the perimeter of Hidden Lake, I had a snarling headache that wrapped around my skull like a python suffocating its prey. My eardrums felt permanently damaged from Kiah's screams, I hadn't eaten all day, and I sweat through my bra and shirt. Oh, and lest I forget the horrible sewer smell in the car that was not the great Wisconsin outdoors.

Thankfully, I prepared ahead of time, stocking the house with formula, diapers, and food. In the guest room, what would now be Kiah's room, I put fresh sheets on her bassinet, a changing table atop the dresser, and pushed the double bed to the side. Wasn't nearly as cute as the Pottery Barn Kids room Cassidy designed, but it would do. I also bought toys and books, a baby swing for the living room. We were set to weather the storm of her disappearance.

As I turned into my driveway, patches of blue-black lake flashed through the towering trees. The rear of my small, two-story house came into view. Gray shingle siding with a stone base. I'd kept it in good shape. Nothing leaked. Appliances and furnace dated, but workable. Dad would've been impressed—if he bothered to ask. After Mom died, he moved to Florida, where he worked as an accountant and golfed on the weekends. We talked a couple times a year. A biannual appointment, similar to the dentist. A sacrifice we both made in Mom's honor.

I pulled next to the detached garage, for once not worried about Kiah's screams. Things echoed on a lake, but the nearest house was a good hundred yards on either side and both neighbors already packed up for the season. A fact I knew because I'd be caretaking for those houses, along with several others, this winter. The job provided income and anonymity. Hopefully, by spring, Kiah's case would become cold, she would look different from her picture, and we could recapture our freedom. In time, everything was possible.

As I stepped out of the car, the scent of pine, wood, and leaves filled my lungs. I inhaled deeply. Best place on earth.

I opened Kiah's door and almost gagged, having located the sewer smell. Awesome. Her eyes were heavy with tears, her breathing labored with each cry, and her lower lip quivered. "You're okay," I said, unlatching the car seat and hauling her inside. I set her seat down in the kitchen and unstrapped her, surprised to find my arm wet beneath her butt. I twisted her around and screamed. The entire back of her beautiful new yellow onesie was stained a brownish-orange. "You've *got* to be kidding!"

She screamed louder, matching my outrage. I looked down at her seat, which looked glossy. With shit, of course. Would that come out? I couldn't afford to buy a new one.

Nestled next to my ear, her screams ensured I'd never hear properly again. Off the kitchen and to the left was the only full bath in the house. Beyond that was Mom's bedroom, her door closed. On bad nights I'd sleep in there, but otherwise I kept it closed, as if I could trap her spirit for when I needed her most.

I marched us into the bathroom, spread a towel on the floor, and lay Kiah on it. After starting the bath, I pulled off my shirt and scrubbed my arm.

When the water was warm, I put in the plug and dumped a capful of baby soap. Then I pulled her clothes off, chucking the onesie into the trash. Shit the color of rust had hardened against her back. I set her in the bath, only to watch in horror as she immediately tipped over. I caught her, but she kept slipping through my fingers. How did one bathe a baby? Why didn't I think about this before? I'd Google it later. In the end, I kneeled, holding her pressed up against the tub, one hand splayed against her chest and neck, the other scrubbing her clean.

It was horrible. I was soaked. The tile felt like kneeling on shards of glass. I might have a permanent hunchback from propping her up. And she screamed the entire ordeal.

But she was clean.

I set her on a new towel on the floor, stripped my clothes off and quickly showered. Much as I wanted to bask in the warm water, her cries persisted. I got out, toweled down, walked upstairs to my bedroom and put on a tank and loose pajama pants. Heaven. I stopped in Kiah's room for clothes before going back downstairs and dressing her. But being warm and cozy didn't stop her screams.

"What's. Your. Problem?" I looked into her blue eyes, which lost some of the dazzle from this morning. She was supposed to be happy, *grateful*, that I rescued her.

What if I started howling my frustration? I wanted two goddamn minutes of silence. Advil for my headache. Food—

Food. OMFG! Kiah was hungry. She was gnawing at her fist between screams.

I ran to the kitchen to mix a bottle and then Kiah and I settled onto my favorite reading chair facing the lake. She latched on. Silence caressed my bones like a deep-tissue massage. Later, I'd clean her car seat, but for now, I closed my eyes and enjoyed the peace.

Three-fourths of the way through the bottle, Kiah fell asleep with the nipple in her mouth. While cute, she looked nothing like my baby. My baby would've been dark. Dark hair. Dark eyes. Mysterious—

Kiah is your baby. Let. It. Go.

But I couldn't. August murdered my baby. Destroyed my dreams. My life. Without hesitation or consideration for what I wanted, what he promised me.

He had to suffer. In mind, body, and soul. I couldn't let Cassidy, the police, media, see him as a victim.

The high from the first text wore off. I needed another hit. I pulled out my phone and clicked on ViperByte.com. Then I drafted a disturbing, yet vague text, paid the hefty price which made me a believer in its encryption, and attached a picture.

Done.

Outside, a carpet of green grass ribboned down toward the small beach and then the lake. Hidden Lake. The water was inky, winking in the waning sunlight, as if teasing its secrets.

As I stared at the lake, I thought about August's secrets. The betrayals he hid from Cassidy. But secrets had a way of catching up with you. Everything hidden eventually becomes revealed. I would ensure as much.

I smiled. His nightmare was just beginning. Mine ended.

CHAPTER TWENTY-EIGHT

AUGUST
WEDNESDAY, SEPTEMBER 6, 2023 5:40 P.M.

August sat in Daisy's rocking chair, trying to answer the question both the detective and Cassidy posed. If not Maxi or Cassidy, who sent the text? Who else would care if he cheated? Her parents and friends, but none of them would text him anonymously. They would've told Cassidy or confronted him directly.

There were other women…other affairs. Should he have told Cassidy everything? No. Now definitely wasn't the time. She couldn't take any more bad news. As it was, her reaction to the one affair made him uneasy that she would ever forgive—

Screw the detective. Backstabbing prick. August flexed his hand, wanting to punch something. A certain someone. The detective gave his word and then showed Cassidy the text.

He'd deal with the detective later.

The other women. Think. Did one of them send the text? Doubtful. He had a routine for breakups; over the phone, ensuring no temptation for one last fuck. Some women were angry, others accepting, some begged, but he never changed his mind. Never spoke to them after. A clean and final ending.

He leaned his head back and stared at the ceiling, cracking his knuckles one by one. The room smelled of Daisy—fresh diapers, scented baby lotion, and an intangible warmth she carried everywhere.

They had to find her. He couldn't think about life without—

His phone buzzed. August sat up, seeing a text with a random string of numbers. He inhaled, a sharp knife that cut to his core, before opening it.

How many kids do you have, August?

August's body stiffened. A parting shot? Yes. Definitely. What other way could he interpret it? He had one child now. But did that mean Daisy was dead? Or that he would never see her again? What a horrible thought, his child, growing up a stranger.

The first message was ambiguous, but this one made it clear the texter was the kidnapper. August was the target.

Quickly, he tapped on the attached picture. Shot from a distance, August was pushing Piper on the swing at the park near their house. He recognized the picnic pavilion behind, the basketball and tennis courts to the right. Why include a picture of Piper when Daisy was kidnapped?

How many kids do you have, August?

Wait. Could this be a threat? The kidnapper was coming after Piper next?

He rushed out of the room. They needed police presence next door. Immediately.

August descended the stairs by two, finding the detective standing over the shoulder of a man working on a laptop at the kitchen table. "You saw the text?" August asked, breathless.

"Yes," the detective said, eyes never leaving the computer screen. "We're tracing it now."

"We need to get cops next door. In case this psycho comes after Piper."

"Police have been guarding Faith's house ever since Piper got home from school." The detective glanced at August. "She's fine. I promise."

August's heart wouldn't slow. He needed to show Cassidy the text. August checked her office first and then the bedroom. He found her sitting on the bed, her back propped up against pillows, knees tucked to her chest, crying into the phone.

He crawled onto the bed, resting a hand on her knee. She scooted over, putting a foot between them. He wasn't used to her rejection. Beyond menial stuff, he'd never tested Cassidy's tolerance for forgiveness.

"Mom—Mom, I have to go," Cassidy said.

Did she tell her mom about the cheating? Cassidy's mom had a sweet spot for him, from the first time they met during halftime of a college football game. The thought of her turning on August pained. The first of many cold fronts he'd experience when news of his infidelity got out.

"I'll text you with updates." Cassidy paused. "I know." Pause. "Love you too." Her voice caught on the word "love." After ending the call, she stared straight ahead, neither speaking to him nor bothering to wipe her tears. Now wasn't the moment to ask what she told her mom about him. Instead, he showed her the text and picture.

"What does that mean?" Cassidy asked. "She gone? Forever? Possibly dead?" She bit down on her fist as more tears fell.

He held her, pressing his lips to the crown of her head. This time, she let him. "We don't know what it means."

She turned to him. Tears clung to her lower lashes. "What do you think it means?"

"Clearly, I have a stalker." He didn't share his thoughts about Piper. Protecting Cassidy meant downplaying his fears.

"That's it? That's all you have to say? Someone is following you," she said, her voice rising, "taking pictures, playing some sick game, and you're just…whatever?"

Game. The word struck August. Were the texts clues? Clues to uncover the kidnapper, or perhaps clues to find Daisy? It had to be someone he knew. No one would select him, target his family, randomly.

"August," she pleaded, holding his hands. "Answer me."

He looked down at their intertwined hands. If he could solve this, bring Daisy home, she would forgive him. She would never find out about the others. And he would stop. Really stop this time. Individual therapy. Couples therapy. Whatever it took. He would never cheat again. This was more than a nightmare; it was Dante's *Inferno*. "I don't know—"

She groaned. "Stop saying you don't know. I can't take it."

"I'm sorry." He cupped her chin, but she pushed him away.

"Stop touching me!" Spit hit his face as she yelled. She closed her eyes and inhaled deeply through her nose. "How did things end with this woman?"

Maxi was a client. That short, intense burst of time searching for her first home propelled them into an affair. She was confident, teasing him with snippets of affection, enough that he needed more. But once she gave in, she was all in, wanting too much, too fast. "I" became "we." He backed off. Told her he wasn't feeling it anymore. An honest statement. The chase was over. The excitement gone. And Cassidy was about to give birth.

"I thought you loved me," Maxi said during the breakup call. He doubted he ever said love. Possibly in an orgasm haze. And if he said it, it wasn't a lie. Falling in love, to August, always felt possible at the beginning. But the high was as short-lived as a vacation. You enjoy the resort. The amenities. The food. The view. Great moments, great memories, but the end came. In August's case, he would always return home, to his family, to Cassidy. His true love.

"She was upset," he said now. "But not enough to do something like this."

"And you knew her well enough to know what she was capable of?" Cassidy's voice was pulled as taut as their bed sheets.

A trick question. If he admitted to knowing Maxi's capabilities, didn't that counter his defense that it was a fling? "She hasn't contacted me since *I* ended it." He stressed I, wanting Cassidy to know he choose her.

A knock at the door.

The detective stepped inside. "The texts are coming from an internet site called ViperByte. It sells encrypted communications, essentially making it untraceable for the average user," he said. "We've issued a subpoena to generate the account holder, but that may take a day or two—assuming the company doesn't challenge it. We've been running into privacy issues with some tech companies."

"Can't you make them understand our baby was kidnapped?" Cassidy's voice rose in hysteria. "A baby that needs her mom to eat, sleep—everything!"

"I promise, we're trying—"

Cassidy pressed her hands together in prayer. "Try harder."

"My officers interviewed Maxi," the detective said. August noticed how Cassidy winced at the name. "We've excluded her as a person of interest. She was at work all morning and also gave us access to her electronic devices to prove the texts didn't originate with her."

August stood up, needing to let out some energy before he exploded. He knew Maxi had nothing to do with this. Who would kidnap a child over a breakup? For this reason, he asked the detective to not involve Cassidy. And yet that prick went behind August's back, his promise as worthless as monopoly money. It didn't matter that the texts were now clearly part of the kidnapping. He should've given August the chance to break the news to Cassidy first.

"Someone is stalking August," Cassidy said. "Taking pictures of our children. Someone pissed off enough to take our daughter." She glared at August. "Who is it?"

As if he wouldn't tell her. Somehow, in her brain, the cheating made him responsible for the kidnapping too. A false equivalence. "It's not fair to pin this on me."

"Fair?" She jumped off the bed and charged toward him, getting in his face. "Are you seriously talking about fair?"

"Alright," the detective said, stepping between them. He touched Cassidy's elbow, gently leading her away. Wasn't hard to see whose side he was on. "Let's calm down."

That was the final straw. The detective, once again, telling them to be calm when their daughter was missing and his marriage was on life support—no thanks to him. "Calm down." August's jaw locked. "What's there to be calm about? Daisy's been gone for hours. And what do you have? A couple texts? A stroller? Shoe prints?" August crossed his arms. "What's the plan, Detective?"

"We need your cooperation." The detective matched August's hard tone. "I'm convinced you know more than you're saying."

"I don't," August said.

The detective's exacting stare suggested otherwise. "Why would someone photograph you with Piper? Make it make sense."

"I don't know."

"Why hasn't the kidnapper texted a ransom amount?" Cassidy asked.

August agreed. "Why not ask for the money and be done with it?"

The detective rubbed his chin, looking up at the ceiling fan. "My gut says this isn't about money."

Cassidy gasped. "You think they want to keep Daisy? Why her? Out of all the babies in the world?"

August rubbed his eyes, slotting unimaginable pieces together.

"August, give me something," the detective said.

August groaned and tugged his hair. Why was he asking August to do the hard yards for him? "I don't know. I don't know. I don't know! You guys can keep asking me, but I don't have a damn clue."

As Cassidy and the detective brainstormed, August pulled up each text, flicking back and forth between the pictures and the words. He wanted to find Daisy. Bring her home. Win back Cassidy's trust. Problem was, no matter how many times he reread the sinister texts, inspected the pictures, nothing made sense.

CHAPTER TWENTY-NINE

CASSIDY
WEDNESDAY, SEPTEMBER 6, 2023 6:33 P.M.

The house was too small, Cassidy thought as she walked laps through the kitchen, living and dining areas. To think she actually told August the house was too big when they first looked at it. The floor-to-ceiling windows, twenty-foot ceilings, and open plan made the space feel like a cathedral. Now, though, Cassidy felt claustrophobic. All the blinds were drawn. Police officers hovered wherever she went, like pawns in a chess game, ultimately useless. More police patrolled outside. Media prowled the street, ready to devour any detail like bloodhounds. Neighbors, well-wishers, people with no boundaries or personal lives, waited with bated breath.

And then there was August. He was in the bedroom, but his energy followed her like mall perfume. She didn't want to look at him, smell him, breathe the same air as him. He cheated! While she was pregnant! If Daisy wasn't missing, she'd kick him out. He felt neglected before? Not enough excitement with two young kids? Seeing his kids every other weekend would certainly free up time to recapture his youth.

Her cell phone lit up with calls and texts from her parents and friends, wanting updates, offering to help. She talked to Mom, but wouldn't let her come over. She couldn't; she'd fall apart. And her friends? No way. Seeing their relief that it wasn't them disguised as concern would make a horrific situation worse. She sent her closet friend, Kristin, a text saying she needed space and asking her to relay the message among their friends.

As she walked, Cassidy felt short of breath. A tightness in her lungs. An uncomfortable flush of heat on her skin. She gripped the kitchen island, knowing she had to leave. Before exiting through the patio doors, she told one of the cops she'd be next door.

Outside, she bent over, gorging on air. The sun was setting and the air cooled, which bathed her skin. While walking to Faith's, she heard the noise of the reporters, the click of cameras, but kept her head down. Refused to give them a clean shot.

She knocked on Faith's door. Unlike last time she stopped by, the blinds were down. A few seconds later, Faith's face peeked through the side of the blind and she opened the door. "Piper's sleeping," Faith said, leading Cassidy to the den. "We started watching *Frozen*, but she didn't last long."

Cassidy stepped inside the den, a small room off the kitchen with a couch and a TV opposite, framed by a built-in bookcase. The movie was paused on Anna dancing with Hans. Piper was curled up on the couch in a ball, her thumb tucked inside her mouth, a gentle sucking noise filling the room. Cassidy marveled at how small Piper looked, taking up less than a cushion. The moment Cassidy brought Daisy home from the hospital, Piper morphed into a giant. Her hands paws, her body a wrecking ball, her voice a megaphone. Without Daisy, Piper once again became her baby.

Kneeling before Piper, Cassidy kissed her cheek. She inhaled the scent of chocolate on Piper's warm breath. Let her sleep. The less she knows, the better.

Cassidy followed Faith back to the kitchen, accepting Faith's offer of coffee. She took a seat at the table, inspecting the pictures Piper colored. The top picture showed four stick figures standing in front of a square house with a triangle on top, a bright yellow sun, and a scribbling of green below. How would they ever explain it to Piper if their family of four became three?

"The phone has been ringing nonstop all afternoon," Faith said as she handed Cassidy her coffee and sat across from her. "I'm not sure if it's because I'm your neighbor, or someone in the media saw you coming over here, but I took it off the hook. Didn't want Piper hearing anything." She paused. "Have there been any updates?"

Cassidy looked into Faith's eyes. A warm brown framed by wrinkles that suggested a life spent smiling. James, her late husband, would no more have cheated on Faith than he would keep an extra ten cents a cashier accidentally gave him. Cassidy couldn't say the same for her husband.

"August got some texts today. Turns out he...ch-cheated." Cassidy ran her finger across her bottom lip, trying to compose herself. She felt humiliated. Her marriage, her life, based on a lie. August chose another woman when he vowed to choose her every day for the rest of his life. And she accepted the risk, didn't she? He was charming, handsome, smart. She saw how women looked at him. Not to mention the example his father set as a serial philanderer. Despite all this, until today, she thought their marriage was too solid for anyone to worm their way in. "They think the kidnapping might be personal."

Faith's hand covered hers. "I'm so sorry, Cassidy."

Cassidy looked around Faith's kitchen, kitschy with rooster decals, artwork with quotes about family, and pictures of her grandkids mussing up the fridge. Anywhere than at Faith.

"I think I saw him out with her," Faith said.

Cassidy snapped to attention. "What? When?"

"I didn't say anything, because I couldn't be sure. It felt...off." Faith sipped her coffee. "I was in the Third Ward with Molly, at this fancy bridal boutique. She was trying on a beautiful lace dress. It had a sweetheart neckline—"

"Tell me what happened." Cassidy loved Faith, but her habit of mentioning every exhausting detail was too much right now.

"I looked out the window and I saw August across the street. He was talking to a woman. I thought maybe she was a client." Faith shrugged. "Then she wrapped her arms around him and rested her head against his chest. He ran his fingers through her long, dark hair—"

"Wait." Cassidy pressed her hands against the table, dizzy from this new revelation. When was the last time she ate? A few bites of cereal this morning between brushing Piper's hair and teeth. "She had dark hair? You're positive?"

"Yes. Definitely." Faith frowned. "And young."

Cassidy thought back on the picture. The woman didn't have dark hair. Could she have dyed it? Possibly. Though the woman didn't strike Cassidy as young. Not that she saw her straight on. "How young?"

Faith looked away. "College-aged."

Cassidy flinched. The younger woman. Another cliché. "You went with Molly to try on dresses last winter, right?"

"Um-hmm. November 13th. I remember the date because…"

Cassidy tuned Faith out. August said the affair happened this past spring, when she was pregnant with Daisy. Had the affair lasted months? Months of sex wasn't a fling.

Or, or…the thought pressed to the forefront of her mind like a text begging to be read. There was more than one woman. He said this was the only time, but if he cheated once, he could've cheated twice. Or twenty times! He could be a pathological liar, like his father.

But she wasn't like August's mom. Turning a blind eye. She would've noticed any suspicious behavior. Unusual credit card charges. A secret phone. Not coming home on time. None of that was there.

Or was it? How often did he have impromptu showings? Open houses all Saturday? A deal that required late nights? Phone calls from clients he took in the other room, allegedly for professional reasons? She trusted August. Trusted he was working. Providing. Giving them the best life possible. He made enough money to substantiate it.

"I didn't tell you because there was nothing obvious like a kiss." Faith paused. "I'm from a different generation and we don't butt in—"

A knock at the door made Cassidy jump. Faith got up and pulled back the shade before opening the door. August. Cassidy turned her back as he stepped inside the kitchen.

"Hey, Faith." His voice was drawn. "Piper around?"

"She's sleeping in the den." Faith squeezed Cassidy's shoulder as she walked around the table. Then she grabbed her coffee. "I'll give you two some privacy."

August sat in the chair next to Cassidy. He ran his tongue across his front teeth. "I can't stop thinking about these texts, the photos, knowing that Daisy is relying on me." He briefly closed his eyes. "It's killing me."

Cassidy crossed her arms and looked straight ahead. "You lied to me."

"I know, and I apologized." He sounded nervous. "I promise, it will never happen again."

Slowly, she turned to face him. "You're still lying."

"Huh?" He had the audacity to look confused.

From the moment they met, August put her on a pedestal. She was the most beautiful woman he'd ever met. Smartest. Coolest. Best lover. Best mother. She felt this pressure to keep up, both in her looks and personality, be the woman he projected. All that effort.

And still, he cheated.

She lowered her voice and said, "In Daisy's bedroom, I asked you if there were any other women and you said no. You never cheated before. You lied to me." The pupils in his eyes contracted. She could almost see the gears turning in his head, the calculations he was making, how much to say, how to present the information to lessen the blow.

She held his eyes, wanting him to deny it. Wanting him to say it was one woman. The affair lasting for months was a problem she'd deal with later. He broke up with her, right? So, he must love Cassidy. When he said nothing, when the denial didn't come, she knew it wasn't one affair. "I'm asking, not because I care about our marriage—that's over." She relished the quick inhale of his breath. "But for Daisy's sake. How many more women have a vendetta against you?"

He ran his hands through his hair, the wrinkles on his forehead deepening like creases in a book. "It was never—" He rested a hand on her knee and she jerked her leg away, crossing it over the other. "I fell in love with you at that first Badger tailgate. Your smile lit me up; your lips stained red from the vodka-Kool-Aid. I did everything to keep you talking to me, remember?"

"I wish I didn't," Cassidy said. Why was he telling her this?

"You were my future," he continued, undeterred. "Everything I ever wanted." He shook his head. "Everything I still want." He pressed his lips together. "Yes, I've cheated. But it was only ever sex. I just, I need—I'm not proud." He hung his head. Was this a performance? "It wasn't—it's nothing like it is with us. I never loved any of them."

"You never—" She cut herself off, pressing a fist to her mouth to keep the words inside. Debating would be pointless. She thought she had a marriage built on trust and fidelity and communication. He thought he had a free agency contract so long as love wasn't involved.

She grabbed one of Piper's pictures and turned it over, slamming down a marker. She pushed it in front of August. "Make a list of names," she said. "Everyone you cheated with so the cops can interview them. Bring Daisy home."

August tilted his head, hand slowly approaching the paper and pen as if it was a nuclear device. Her marriage was based on a lie, but she was banking on his relationship with Daisy being true love.

CHAPTER THIRTY

VANESSA
DECEMBER 2022

PREGNANT! I clutched the test to my chest, hugging it with the same ferocity as I once hugged my teddy bear Belle. I, Vanessa Wren Jennings, had a baby inside me. Growing. Multiplying in cells. Needing me to give it life.

I giggled. Softly, at first, and then a full-on laughing fit, leaning against the bathroom vanity. Cooking the condoms worked! I waited an entire week to test, not wanting to waste money, because women acted like getting pregnant was nuclear fusion. But I, fertility goddess, did it with my man strapped. Must admit, I felt a blush of superiority rise on my cheeks. I'd never been the best.

Pregnant. Pregnant. Pregnant. Like hearing the word Christmas as a child or Happy Hour as an adult—excitement surged through me.

I lifted my T-shirt and pressed a hand to my belly, sending her love. My daughter. I'd make sure she felt important, safe, confident. A queen, living life by her own rules.

I ran to the bedroom, grabbed my phone, and called August. I bounced on my feet as it rang. Voicemail. Annoying. But maybe that was best. Telling him in person, seeing the surprise and joy, would make a better story.

After crawling into bed, I began a pregnancy deep-dive on my phone. Right now, my babe was the size of sweet pea. I pulled my index finger and thumb apart, trying to imagine. Crazy! The more I read, though, excitement switched to anxiety. Swelling. Cramping. Morning sickness. Miscarriage. Acne. What foods to eat. Which to avoid. Exercise. But not too much. No alcohol. *Spare me.* Shout the news or take a vow of silence? And for fuck's sake, girl, you should've started those prenatal vitamins months ago.

Ugh. My eyes traced cracks in the ceiling while thinking about Mom. Missing her something fierce. Whenever I was spiraling, she calmed me down. How would I do this without her? Since her death, I coasted. Stumbled through college. Hooked up with fuck boys. Tended bar. Little direction. Little desire. I felt little without her.

But this baby gave me purpose.

Over the next week, I felt more alive than ever. Hyperaware of my body—the tenderness of my breasts, the constant need to pee, tiredness, the zit blooming on my cheek. It all had meaning. I no longer felt alone. Wherever I went, my baby girl kept me company.

I couldn't wait to tell August.

Only problem? He canceled on me. Twice. We met a few days later to have sex between showings, which, I'm sorry, but no. A quick fuck with a clock hanging over our heads didn't feel momentous enough.

And then my cinematic moment appeared. August texted, saying he wanted to cook me dinner. That night, we shared a bottle of wine while he cooked pasta and I prepared a salad. He even held the spoon up to my mouth to have me taste-test the sauce. Adorable. After dinner, I kept the rom-com trope going by running us a bath. I lit candles around the edge, imagining how he'd hold me and wouldn't want to let go once I told him the good news.

We ended up fucking though. And then more fucking in bed. Fucking, fucking, fucking. You couldn't fake chemistry. We had it. Cue the curtains on his marriage.

When August started to doze, I got up and rinsed the dishes. Maybe the noise awoke him, because he came up behind me, tucking his hands inside my shirt, fondling my breasts. Kissing the back of my neck. He could never get enough of me. But I wanted to tell him before this turned from flirty to dirty. "Do my breasts feel bigger?" I said, all coy.

He groaned, pressing himself into me. "They feel amazing."

"They're only going to get bigger."

"N-o-o-o. Don't get implants."

I turned the water off. "What would you say if I told you I was pregnant?"

His fingertips clamped onto my nipples like garden shears. I bit my lip to keep from calling out. "I'd say you'd better be kidding."

My heart thudded. He'd never spoke in a curt tone with me. Never showed himself as anything other than kind, loving, seductive.

His hands darted to my hips and he twisted me around to face him. His blue eyes blazed, an animal trapped. And it hit me. He felt trapped. By me. By our baby. "Are you pregnant?"

"Yes," I said softly.

"Fuck." He stepped backward, hands pressed against his ears, mouth parted in a pantomime of shock. "How...? You're on the pill! We always use condoms!"

Best not to get caught up in the details. "It's a surprise, yes, but we love each other." I rested my hands on his chest. The rigidity of his body rattled me. As if he was tolerating my touch. "This was going to happen eventually, right?"

He said nothing. Several circuits in my brain flipped on, an assembly line of thoughts. Maybe I should've waited until I was showing, until he had visible proof of his child. Until he was ready to tell me about Cassidy. Maybe forcing him to choose was all wrong.

Wrong. Wrong. Wrong.

He turned and walked over to the window, resting his hands against the pane, his body forming a Y. "I can't have a baby."

I held my breath. Was he finally going to tell me the truth? The director gave my shoulder a reassuring squeeze and reminded me to play it cool. Be angry about the deception, she said, but ultimately forgiving.

"I already have a kid," he said, "and a baby on the way." He turned around. "This can't happen. Do you understand?"

Did I understand? No. He was giving me half-truths and expecting me to be satisfied. "You have a kid?" I asked.

"Yes." Deep breath. "A daughter."

I waited for more. Was I supposed to drag the truth out of him, fact by fact? Apparently. "Who's the mother?"

He ran both hands through his hair, inhaling until his cheekbones look sculpted. "I'm married."

I stomped my foot. Even now, he wouldn't say Cassidy's name. Give details. Why? Was he protecting her or me? "That's all you have to say, you're married? No apology. No explanation. No answers. We've been together for months."

He stared at the ground. "I can't believe you're—" He gestured at my stomach, unable to say the word, acknowledge his child.

"Pregnant," I said, helping him out. "With your baby."

He winced. "Are you sure—" He looked at the window and then back at me. "Are you sure it's mine?"

"Are you fucking kidding me?" I screamed. "Yes. It's yours. I haven't been with anyone else. Don't you remember saying the thought of me with another man drove you mad?" I waited until he nodded. An acknowledgement. These conversations happened. It wasn't my imagination. "I thought we were exclusive."

"Okay." He pushed down with his hands, giving me the universal sign to calm down. Infuriating. "I believe you. I had to be sure." His gaze slowly returned to my stomach. After a moment, he said, "How far along are you?"

"I don't know. I took the test a few days ago. So…"

A smile broke through. "Good."

Relief tasted like the first sip of a vodka martini; everything inside me loosened and warmed. He needed details. Something to humanize her. A few minutes to acclimate. I took a step toward him, eager for our celebration, when he said, "There's still time."

I froze. My heartbeat reverberated in my ears. "Time...for what?"

"To get an..." He averted his eyes. "An abortion."

I pressed my hands to my stomach, protecting my baby. "No." Shock turned to rage. Over his shoulder, I eyed the knives. I would make him regret every kiss, every lie, every minute with me. "No way. I love this baby. She's mine."

He closed the gap between us, wrapping me in a hug. I fought to get away, but he squeezed tighter. With his arms around me, arms that up to this point made me feel safe and hopeful, I started sobbing. Why was he doing this to me? To us?

I pulled back, hands cupping his cheeks. "I love you." His whiskers prickled my fingers. His beautiful face. Those eyes! I clocked warmth from the beginning. "Like, really fucking love you." Here I was, fighting for a man who put up zero fight for me. Pathetic. But I knew what we had, even if he was too stuck in his ways to admit it. "This is our baby." I took his hands and pressed them against my stomach. Saying goodbye to her—no. I couldn't. "I want you to leave your wife. For us to be a family."

He looked down at his hands. We were now connected— mother, father, child—by blood. He couldn't murder his own child, right?

He tucked my hair behind my ear with a gentleness that reminded me of Mom. "I could see us having a baby together," he said, his voice soft, mesmerizing. "Being a family."

I held onto his eyes, held onto hope. "Really? You? Me? The baby? You see it?"

He kissed me. "Yes. Absolutely." Another kiss. Two. Then three. "One day, I would love that." A longer kiss. "But now's not the right time."

I jerked away. "Why does Ca—" I almost said Cassidy. But the stupid jerk didn't tell me her name. I cleared my throat. "Tell your wife to get an abortion. Then we can keep *this* baby."

"She's further along," he said. "It's too late."

Was it too late? I wasn't up to date on abortion laws. Or was he choosing Cassidy over me? "You love her? Is that it? You'd rather have a baby with her than me?"

"No." He rubbed my shoulders. "Trust me, her pregnancy isn't ideal—" He groaned and turned away. "Obviously, we have issues. I wouldn't be here if we didn't have issues."

I enjoyed hearing his marriage was a sham, but I was sick of being his side piece. "I don't need your permission." My voice hitched, spoiling my bluff. "I could raise her on my own."

He turned around. Instead of arguing, he surprised me by saying, "You said you love me. Is that true? Or are they just words?" His voice was low, pained. "Something you say to men to get what you want?"

"No. No. No. I wouldn't." This was supposed to be the best day of our lives.

"You and me." He ran a finger across my collarbone, making me shiver. "Are we for real?"

"I love you." I sniffled. "More than anyone."

"Then what are we talking about?" He ran both hands down my arm, holding onto my wrists, and lowered himself so we were eye-to-eye. "Do you want us to be together or do you want this baby?"

"I want both."

He pulled away, looking around my studio apartment. "Are you going to raise this baby here? How will you work? Do you have insurance? Anyone to help?" His questions were gentle. No spite. No anger. Just the facts. "It could drive a person mad, being stuck all day with a crying baby."

I hated it when people made me feel stupid. "I could do it."

"Yeah, but honey, why would you want to?" He pressed a kiss on my forehead, lacing his fingers in my hair. He felt warm and safe, comforting against the chilly picture he painted. "Why not wait until we can do this together? The right way. Marriage. A home." He moved down to my lips, brushing them against mine as he spoke. A lullaby, promising a future I ached to live. "Both of us raising the baby. Doesn't she or he deserve to have two parents?" He kissed me, deeply, pulling back to say, "I love you, Vanessa." My breath hitched, relishing the first time he said those words other than during sex. "Trust me. Everything will come together for us."

For the moment, I agreed to think about it. Anything to get him to continue looking at me with adoration, saying words I longed to hear. Maybe now that everything about his marriage and kids was out in the open, he would tell Cassidy the truth too. Leave her. We could start building that future he talked about, one based on honesty and commitment.

CHAPTER THIRTY-ONE

AUGUST
WEDNESDAY, SEPTEMBER 6, 2023 7:00 P.M.

August sat at Faith's kitchen table, marker in hand, wondering how honest to be in confessing his affairs. In all the ways he imagined having this conversation, he never envisioned telling Cassidy everything. One woman. One time. One mistake. Difficult, yet manageable. As Cassidy warned, as soon as he wrote names on this paper, there would no longer be a marriage to fight for.

He wrote, "Maxi Anderson." Then he put the marker down. "Let me explain—"

"Write the list, August," Cassidy said. The woman that lit up when she saw him, treated every hurt with compassion, now rivaled the no-nonsense detective. "Now."

"I don't want to talk about this here." August pointed to the den where Piper slept. "Can we go home?"

Cassidy gave him a long look. "Fine."

"I'll say goodnight to Piper first." He walked into the den, bent down and rested a hand on her back.

She stirred awake, squinting. "Daddy," she whispered.

Her angelic voice made his heart contract. Regardless of what he wrote on that list, he would always be the girls' father. Every kiss, conversation, meal, and game, he infused with love. He adored them. They knew it too.

He was a good man. He was a flawed man.

"How it going sleepyhead?" He ran a hand through her hair. As soft as rose petals.

"Can I sleep in my bed?" she asked.

He wasn't expecting that. "Aren't you having fun? I heard you got cookies. In fact—" He swiped her lower lip with his finger. "There's still some chocolate left for me." He mimed eating it. "Thank you."

She grabbed his hand, giggling. "Mine."

"Now that I think about it, you should come home. I don't think you're old enough for sleepovers."

Her eyes widened. "I am."

"I should talk to Mommy about this."

"No. Don't ask Mommy." She held out her pinky. "Please. It'll be our secret."

He pinky swore and kissed her cheek. "Get some sleep."

As he stood, she grabbed his arm. "Daddy, will you bring me Millie? She'll be scared without me."

Millie. Her stuffed elephant. He cleared his throat, getting emotional imagining Daisy alone somewhere, with nothing familiar to calm her. "Yes, baby. I'll bring it right back."

In the kitchen, Cassidy stood by the door, holding out the sheet of paper for him. He took it, explaining that he'd finish after he brought Millie back for Piper.

Outside, the setting sun gave the grass a golden glow. His favorite time of the day. Work over. Bedtime for the kids. He could relax with Cassidy.

No one would relax tonight.

By the time he got Millie and returned to Faith's, Piper was asleep. He tucked Millie between her and the couch, grateful he could protect one of his daughters.

Back at home, he sat on a stool at the kitchen island and pulled out his phone. His exes—a generous term—were listed as contacts. Being a realtor gave him a built-in excuse, should Cassidy ever ask.

She didn't. Her trust, once a blessing, rubbed like salt in the wound, reminding him of everything he wasted.

A cop walked into the kitchen and grabbed an apple from the fruit bowl. He bit off a hunk, chewing like a horse. How was August supposed to think, remember, with all this commotion? One look at Cassidy, who was preparing food, told him she didn't care.

Aubree. For the first two years of marriage, he was faithful. Anything prior to taking vows he didn't consider cheating. Then he walked into his dentist appointment and met Aubree, his beautiful new hygienist. The sexual tension made it feel like he was going through puberty again, keeping his hands firmly on his lap in a dismal attempt to hide his erection. But she kept brushing her hand against his upper thigh, giving him lingering looks, letting him know she saw it and liked the attention. When she finished the cleaning, she wrote her number on the back of his appointment card.

He knew better than to call, but marriage with Cassidy hit a lull; the shine worn off. He wanted excitement, the feeling of not knowing what a night held. So, he called Aubree, thinking it'd be a one-off. Get her out of his system. His first of many mistakes. They had sex whenever possible, the excitement increasing with each risk he took. Living dual lives both thrilled and disgusted him. He wanted to stop. Couldn't stop. Second mistake, not wearing a condom. She was on the pill. A positive pregnancy test three months later debunked her fastidiousness. Third mistake, he thought he was the only one she was fucking. Didn't realize an ex took his share. August had to wait until Aubree was ten weeks pregnant to take a paternity test. An entire month where he gave himself a stress ulcer, thinking his marriage was over. But God granted him absolution, for he wasn't the father—

Wait. Did Aubree tell him the truth? He thought back on the clue, *How many kids do you have, August?* Aubree never showed him the paternity paperwork. She called and gave him the news and he changed dentists. Put her firmly in his rearview mirror.

Could the texts be from Aubree? Possible. But why wait years to seek revenge? And revenge for what? They both agreed she should be with her ex.

After Aubree, he was gun shy for the next year, but a New Year's triathlon resolution had him joining a cycling group where he met Savannah. She was cute, sporty, loved a challenge. He didn't mind being the challenge, the foreplay of will-they-won't-they sending him to the edge. Training for the triathlon made it easy to lie to Cassidy, telling her he was swimming at the gym or out cycling, neither of which made him accessible by phone. In reality, he went straight from cycling to Savannah's apartment.

After the triathlon, things fizzled—

Wait, no. That wasn't true. He rubbed his eyes. Remembering there was a pregnancy scare with Savannah too. Thankfully, she was only a few days late. Listening to her alternate between freaking out and planning the next eighteen years of their lives, though, terrified him. He ended it. Live and learn.

She was angry when he broke it off. Yelling that he was a liar. About what? He didn't ask. Didn't care. Thinking back now, Savannah may have seen him after the race, celebrating with Cassidy. But wouldn't Savannah have said cheater instead of liar? Not that he made a commitment to Savannah. And women weren't exactly known for logical thinking when upset.

Facts. Was it possible Savannah actually was pregnant? That she didn't want him involved with her child…because she saw him with another woman? Possible. But seeking revenge years later?

Again, unlikely, but worth mentioning to the detective.

Bobbi. A two-month fling. He met her at a promotional event at a wine bar downtown. Hot. Dirty. Uninhibited sex. A month later, she broke it off with him for someone else. A hit to his ego, but nothing to report.

Lauren. He met her at an out-of-town real estate conference. Both wanted sex and little conversation. They never exchanged numbers—

But. But, but, but! He tapped the pen against the table, wishing it was a sledgehammer. The condom broke one time. It was at the base, which didn't worry him. In her early forties, she assured him she wasn't fertile anymore. He took the statement at face value. He shook his head now, stupefied by his stupidity. Was it possible she got pregnant? Sure. Would it have killed him to follow up with her? No. But that would've required maturity, a level of awareness he wanted to leave behind during his affairs. Could she have found him via his website or social media to tell him the news? Yes. Did she? No. He doubted she got pregnant, but hell if he knew.

"Ahhh!" he yelled, cursing under his breath. If he thought long enough, he could make a case for nearly every woman.

Cassidy turned and looked at him from the fridge. "Everything okay?"

"Yep. Fantastic." He squeezed his eyes shut, calling up the next woman in line.

Natasha? Natalie? Nicole? Christ, he couldn't remember. She was an ecstasy-fueled one-night-stand in Vegas during a buddy's bachelor party. Was she worth including? No. No way she was involved. Though the sex was unbelievable. Nothing like sex on E. The warm sensations, intensity of every touch, an orgasm on steroids—

He watched Cassidy mix ingredients in a bowl. She'd be horrified to know he still dabbled with drugs. Definitely not writing Natasha's name.

After the bachelor party, his friend Troy got busted for his Vegas misdeeds. While August promised Cassidy he spent his time gambling, Cassidy's opinion that Troy's wife should kick him out made August risk-adverse. Better, but not cured.

A year later, maybe more, he met Vanessa and lost his goddamn mind. He noticed her at a client's wedding reception. The sway of her hips as she carried trays of food, her ass firm in horrible polyester pants, the pouty lower lip, eyes lined dark—he was obsessed at first glance. Then, she fell before him. Literally. Fell. He chatted her up later in the parking lot, away from prying eyes. She was beautiful, yet raw, sweet too, each conversational volley making him frantic to fuck her. Sex quickly became an addiction. Day or night, anywhere, any position, she was up for it. Sexual nirvana.

Being always up for it proved to be a problem though. She got pregnant too. Had this childish fantasy of him leaving Cassidy and starting a family together. She quickly agreed to the abortion when he presented a snapshot of her future; twenty-three, living in a studio apartment, a crying baby, barely scraping by. They broke up after and he hadn't heard from her since.

He should mention the pregnancy to the detective, but the abortion gave him pause. One, Cassidy was pro-life and might consider it to be his greatest sin. An unforgiveable one, whereas he hoped, someday soon, they'd move past the cheating. And it was clear the detective couldn't keep a secret. Second, Vanessa never had the baby and so the text—*how many kids do you have*—didn't apply. Honestly, Aubree was the only one for which that text made sense.

Okay. He'd group Savannah and Vanessa together, say both were late. Both could've lied. Enough to ensure the cops checked Vanessa out, but not dig his grave deeper.

Next, next. Who came next?

Emery. A grocery store pickup. He cut it off after a few times of lukewarm sex. Did she want revenge for ghosting her? Did he owe her a breakup phone call? *How many scars have you left behind?* Then again, if scars meant a breakup, or the ghosting afterwards, he could make an argument for every woman.

And then Maxi.

He put his head in his hands, no closer to the truth. But the names on this paper clearly forecasted the end of his marriage.

CHAPTER THIRTY-TWO

CASSIDY
WEDNESDAY, SEPTEMBER 6, 2023 8:30 P.M.

Cassidy moved in a triangle from the sink to the stove to the island, making pancakes for dinner. She needed comfort on this day where everything that could've gone horribly wrong did. August sat at the island, pen in his mouth, hand yanking his hair, staring at the paper as if the names might appear through osmosis. Each second that passed was an exercise in restraint. Cassidy wanted to scream. Throw the spatula at him. To be honest, the sizzling pan.

Their only lead was the text messages, someone with a vendetta against August. When Cassidy thought it was her fault, she immediately searched the comments on her website. Yet August dawdled. Was it possible he couldn't remember their names? Were there that many? Were they one-night stands where names weren't exchanged? Prostitutes? Where did one find a prostitute in Milwaukee? Or was his brain locked on damage control?

She had to get the list. At any cost. And the cost was kindness toward her cheating, narcissistic, reckless husband.

She slapped the final pancake onto a plate and yanked the burner switch off. Then she doused the stack with syrup and powdered sugar, no butter, the way August liked. "I know this is hard," she said, setting the pancakes before him. When he looked up, the demons waging war inside him were evident in the creases of his forehead. She gently brushed her thumb against his forehead, smoothing the lines. "And I know you're worried about us. But I need you to set that aside. For Daisy."

"Are you leaving me?" he asked, barely a whisper.

Yes. No. Maybe. Maybe it depended on how many women. How far the deception scaled. How many years she'd been living a lie. She wanted to reassure him she'd never leave, anything to get him to finish the list, but when she opened her mouth, honesty won out. "I don't know."

"Tell me you'll try." He squeezed her hand. Eyes wide and contrite. "We've built too much not to try."

She never cheated, but if she held her marriage up to a microscope, she'd probably find fault with herself too. Perhaps she wasn't, as August suggested, the most attentive wife since the kids were born. Then again, wasn't that parenting? Was she supposed to put his needs ahead of two dependent, helpless beings? She felt her blood pressure rise and forced herself to breathe. Be kind. "I can't think about anything but Daisy." She gestured at the sheet. Bit her lower lip, a move that usually softened him. "Please."

He picked up the pen and she walked back to the stove. "Thanks for dinner."

She flinched, then forced herself to say, "No problem." Nothing was a problem, so long as she didn't think.

After stacking three pancakes, she bathed them in butter and maple syrup, not caring about calories or fat grams or carbs. To think, this morning, getting toned after the pregnancy was an actual concern! Leaning against the cabinets, she ate while watching August. He'd take a bite, glance at his phone, stare into the air, sigh, tap his pen, groan and then write something. She let the warmth and sweetness of the pancakes soothe her frustrations. Evidence of his duplicity was at her fingertips and she never thought to check his phone.

Washing the dishes, her arm brushed up against her nipple. She winced and glanced at the clock. Past Daisy's bedtime. No wonder. She needed to pump. The thought brought more tears. She ached—

no, ached was too tame. She felt a desperate, rootless, dizzying sensation to feel the weight of Daisy in her arms, her mouth suckling on her nipple, the gentle splaying of her hand against Cassidy's breast, the endless lakes of her eyes staring back. Cassidy swallowed back sobs, noticing her shirt was now damp. Thoughts of Daisy caused her milk to let down.

"Here," August said, appearing at her side. She stared forward at the closed window blind, afraid that if she looked at him, whatever was tethering her together would rip at the seams. He set the list on the counter and wrapped his arms around her waist. Despite everything, she melted into him, let him hold her up.

"I'm sorry." His voice was ragged, his breath hot against her neck.

Closing her eyes, tiredness hit her body with the suddenness of a car accident. Her sleepless night caring for Daisy felt ages ago. She should've held her tighter. Kissed her more. Relished her warmth. Even the sound of her cry. You never knew when your last breath, your last moment with someone, was coming.

She opened her eyes and looked at the list. It was face down, as if August couldn't face, literally, that he cheated on her. Coward. Or, maybe he was presenting her a choice. She didn't have to read it. She could hand it directly to Detective Lewis. Naivety might be the only way to preserve her marriage. Reading the list would be like opening Pandora's box. Questions would follow. She would need dates, frequencies, choreography. An understanding of his feelings for the women. A never-ending nightmare.

No. A nightmare was when someone kidnaps your daughter. This was upsetting. Shocking. Sad. Regretful.

She stepped out of August's arms and picked up the list.

Maxi Rogers
Emery Stakofski
Vanessa Talbert
Lauren Pafford

Savannah Rhodes
Aubree Martinez

Six women. Seven years of marriage. Nearly a woman a year. How long did these affairs last? Did she ever have August to herself? Was he a sex addict? She didn't recognize any of the names. Only five phone numbers. Was it a one-night-stand? Numbers not exchanged? She swallowed her questions and forced an even tone as she did with Piper when acting up.

Her husband acted up. What an understatement. "Is this everyone?"

He nodded, hanging his head. "Yes."

To save Daisy, she believed he wouldn't hold back. She found Detective Lewis in the foyer, talking on the phone. She didn't wait for him to finish. "Find my baby."

He called over his officers, directing them to do a "deep dive" on each of these women—legal, employment, social media.

She walked to her bedroom, needing to pump. Pump and cry. Six women. She paused at the doorway, turning to look at him. He stood in the kitchen, hands covering his face. Depleted. Defeated. Or upset he got caught?

Cassidy didn't know. She wasn't sure she knew him at all.

CHAPTER THIRTY-THREE

VANESSA
WEDNESDAY, SEPTEMBER 6, 2023 9:00 P.M.

I woke with a start, unsure where I was. My arm screamed in pain, an aching, heavy numbness that felt like an elephant sleeping on it, but was actually Kiah. It was dark, the sun having set during our naps, making it impossible to see. A type of blackness you never get in the city. I waited a moment for my eyes to adjust and then slowly stood, feeling my way across the living room wall to the light switch.

I carried Kiah upstairs. There were two bedrooms upstairs, mine and the guest bedroom, which now served as Kiah's nursery, along with a half bath. I settled Kiah in her bassinet, tucking a fleece blanket—white with a miniature pink elephant décor—around her tiny waist. Then I stood and marveled. When not crying or pooping, she was beautiful.

The growl of my stomach interrupted the moment. I needed to eat. Clean. Get my butt to bed so I could do it all over again tomorrow.

Back downstairs, I wet paper towels with hot water and wiped off Kiah's car seat, trying not to gag. Then I grabbed an all-purpose cleaner and went to town, blasting any remaining fecal matter. Disgusting.

Surprisingly, it didn't deter my appetite.

Too tired to cook, I grabbed a loaf of bread and stood over the sink, shoving slice after slice into my mouth. Looking through the kitchen window, I couldn't see anything. Not the garage. Not a single tree. Blackness. It was both reassuring and scary. No one would find us. We were on a metaphorical island. But what if some madman living in the forest broke in? There was a phone. But who could I call? And how would I explain Kiah?

What a stupid thought. I'd been coming here my entire life and no one ever broke in.

Speaking of phones, I opened Twitter and scrolled between bites. #BabyDaisy was trending. I couldn't find more about the police suspecting Cassidy and August, but there were lots of comments on Sawyer Brinkley's tweet agreeing it must be the parents. Could the public see their selfishness? Or was it evidence of our hateful and judgmental society?

Initially, I was excited about August being a suspect. But now, I wondered if that could backfire. What if he had pictures of me saved on his phone? I knew he deleted our texts. *I'm OCD,* he explained. *Hate emails and texts clogging my phone.*

Ah, the excuses I lapped up from this man.

No. August was a professional cheater. Far too savvy to keep anything of me—

A screech sounded through the night air, high and keening.

I dropped to the floor, crouching beside the cabinets. What the hell was that? An animal? Then I heard it again. Without the shock, I immediately identified the source. Kiah.

What did she want? We had ten hours until morning.

I ate another piece of bread, hoping she would put herself back to sleep.

No luck. I walked upstairs with the same enthusiasm I greeted a pap smear. The closer I got to her room, the louder the cries. When I opened her door, I half expected to find a bat or demon spirit, something terrifying, attacking her.

Nothing. Just Kiah. In her bassinet. Fists squeezed in outrage. The headache from earlier came back with a vengeance. I picked

Kiah up and lay her on the bed to change her diaper. Pee, thank God. While cleaning her, I explained it was bedtime.

She didn't agree.

I carried her downstairs, where I made another bottle. She drank about two ounces before screaming and spitting the nipple out. Where was her pacifier? Lost it in the car. No way I'd find it in the dark.

I sang as I rocked her, but stopped when I realized that if I couldn't hear myself, there was no way she could hear me. Then I pressed my lips against her ear, shushing her, trying to create a white noise effect. No go. I wrapped her in a blanket. Decided she was too hot and took it off.

All while she screamed. And screamed. And screamed.

She was fed. Bathed. Cuddled. And I was bone tired. I put her back in her bassinet. In the moonlight, I could make out the cherry-red of her face. "I'm sorry," I said above her cries. I was close to crying myself. "I don't know what you need. But I need to sleep. I'm sorry." I repeated my apology as I backed out of the room.

After I closed the door, the decibel of her screams became a fraction softer. I padded past the half-bath, guilt ballooning with each step, a blimp by the time I reached my room on the other side. I had to take care of myself. *Practicing self-care as a new mom is vital,* Cassidy said on her podcast. *Your needs are important. Your mental health is imp—*

Jesus. Was I going to take advice from the woman I considered an unfit mother?

Yes. Yes, I was.

Crawling into bed, the ringing in my ears and pounding in my head crackled like low-grade static. Kiah's cries twisting the knob. I didn't understand. Kiah misbehaved with Cassidy, because she didn't get her time, love, and attention. But I gave Kiah everything today. What reason did she have for throwing a fit?

As she continued to cry, fear trickled into my belly. I could take one night of this. Maybe two. But what if it continued for weeks? I needed sleep. Sleep was the key to keeping the emotional dips at bay; the one bit of useful advice my otherwise useless therapist told me. Without sleep, that voice, the one that yelled I was stupid, second-guessed everything, bathed in paranoia, took hold.

I shoved my head beneath the pillow to muzzle the sound. Closed my eyes. Sleep, goddamnit, sleep.

CHAPTER THIRTY-FOUR

CASSIDY
WEDNESDAY, SEPTEMBER 6, 2023 9:55 P.M.

Cassidy paced the kitchen, listening as Detective Lewis questioned August about the women on his list. It amazed her how cavalier he was about these relationships, the risks he took. The first woman, Aubree—from their dentist's office!—pregnant. She was sleeping with her ex and August, presumably both without condoms. And Cassidy was drawn into this sick, what would it be, quadruple? All sharing the same…fluids? She felt dirty. Wanted a shower. If Daisy wasn't missing, she'd drive to the ER and demand an STD test.

Two other women with late periods. Possible early miscarriages? Another where the condom broke. Possibly pregnant? Did her husband have superhuman sperm? That wasn't Cassidy's experience. With both kids, they tried for nearly a year, having sex when she was ovulating, not doing it two days before ovulation so his sperm would be potent—

She stopped pacing and glared at him. He averted his eyes. Was he cheating while they were trying? Wasting his good sperm? Was that why it took so long to get pregnant? She got the leftovers? The lazy swimmers?

"As far as you know, you have not fathered any children other than Piper and Daisy?" Detective Lewis asked.

"No," August said. "Like I said, maybe Aubree lied because she was getting back with her ex and didn't want to deal with custody issues. But it's been years, so I highly doubt she came back now."

Cassidy zipped up her sweatshirt and then smoothed it out over the high waist of her yoga pants, trying to camouflage her postpartum roll. Aubree was curvy, wore tons of makeup, had cosmetic "help." Was that what August wanted? Injections, fillers, and breast augmentations? Were the rest of his women Kardashian worshipers?

"Did any of them take the breakup particularly hard?" Detective Lewis asked.

"None of them were happy." He paused. Difficult to organize his thoughts, she imagined, when he had a cheerleading squad of women to run through. "I don't know if they stayed upset for long, though. Once I broke up with them, that's it." August cut his hand through the air. "It's over. I don't let it get complicated."

Cassidy laughed. "I'm sorry…" Her laughing fit hit harder, making her stomach ache. She braced a hand against the island. "You cheat. On your wife. And children." The laughter abruptly stopped as she digested her words. "You live a double life. Isn't that the definition of complicated?"

"I meant—"

"Oh, I know what you meant," Cassidy said. Did he think sex was equivalent to a handshake? She gave herself to August exclusively. No flirtations, friendships, fantasies with other men. How did he cross the line, repeatedly, without feeling guilty?

"Let's focus," Detective Lewis said. Cassidy knew she shouldn't let herself get sidetracked, but it was difficult. "Not a single woman pushed you for more? Kept calling? Stands out as overly emotional? Perhaps threatened to tell Cassidy?"

August rubbed his forehead. "Maybe Savannah," he finally said. "She was emotional when she was late, half of her planning the baby's life, the other half terrified. Left me messages after we broke up, screaming at me for lying." August let out a long breath. "Same with Vanessa. She thought she was going to have a baby and then…didn't. The sudden change of plans left her…" He hemmed and hawed. "Angry. Women get attached to the idea of a baby.

Quickly, I guess." August shrugged, as if the concept eluded him. "Those two breakups stand out as more emotional than the rest."

August held Cassiddy each month she cried, depressed she had to wait longer for her dream to come true. He bought her spa days, poured baths, sent flowers. Was all the sweetness to throw her off track? Or was that real? Regardless, he must understand why the potential pregnancy made these women emotional. Then why was he talking about it from a distance, as if he had nothing to do with their predicament?

As Detective Lewis questioned August on where Savannah and Vanessa worked, their family, any friends he met, Cassidy witnessed August's lack of empathy firsthand. He didn't care. And with that realization, another came. From the moment they met, he probably cheated on Cassidy. Because his needs, his wants, came before anything else. His story about falling in love with Cassidy at first sight. Wanting her. Only her. Fiction he created to woo her. Fiction others didn't believe. She remembered her sorority sisters warning her August was one person around Cassidy and another with his boys. Cassidy chalked it up to jealousy. Her "sisters" were jealous about everything—boys, weight, grades, money.

To think, this could've been avoided if she listened.

She walked to the table and pulled out the chair, enjoying the harsh screech against the wood floor. Both August and Detective Lewis turned to her. "You've always cheated on me, haven't you?" she asked. "You've never been faithful."

"That's not true." He shook his head. "There's been months, sometimes years, I've gone without cheating. I've tried to stop—"

She leaned forward, her voice quiet, but intent. "You were reckless. Not only with my heart, but with my body." She put her fist to her mouth, pressing hard enough to bruise. "And now you've put Daisy in danger. You risked her life for your stupid affairs."

Heat crept up August's cheeks. "I never thought—"

"You're right," she cut him off, not wanting to hear another excuse. "You didn't think. About anyone but yourself. And now all we can do is wait and hope and pray. And even then—"

She closed her eyes, unable to finish. What was worse? August didn't care enough about them to stay faithful or he was conceited enough to believe he would never get caught? A sociopath or an egomaniac. Who did she marry?

CHAPTER THIRTY-FIVE

VANESSA
WEDNESDAY, SEPTEMBER 6, 2023 11:01 P.M.

I couldn't sleep through Kiah's screaming. Not one minute. How did Cassidy exist without sleep? Now, I understood all the coffee. Felt slightly less judgmental.

I can't do this. I can't do this. I can't do this.

I stretched my body to the brink, hands reaching to the sides of the mattress as if being nailed to a cross, feeling the taut agony in every muscle. My head pounded. Eyes burned. I needed to shut off, ideally ten hours of oblivion. I'd take six. How did Kiah not need the same?

I will not give in. She needed to learn how to put herself back to sleep. Otherwise, I'd be doing this every night.

I flipped on my side, squeezing the pillow against each ear.

Would Kiah sleep in tomorrow?

I feared I knew the answer.

Was something wrong with her? Like, *wrong*, with her? Did I get a defective baby? Cassidy's and August's embryo wasn't one I'd buy on the black market.

Do. Not. Give. In.

Back in my apartment, I'd lay awake, listening to a soundtrack of apartment doors slamming, footsteps pounding, car alarms, people shouting, music vibrating off the walls. It was less the noise though, and more August that kept me awake. Knowing his life was a short drive away. My baby on the Sunshine app. Cassidy's podcast a miniature reality show, filling in the gaps of their private world. I was obsessed. Couldn't stop. Hated myself for it.

Each sleepless night, I'd vow to move on. Find a man that loved me for me. Wouldn't lie. Manipulate me. Eventually I'd have another baby. Sometimes I'd get to noon not scratching the August itch, but then something triggered me—my period, a goddamn Pampers commercial, another #MeToo or cheating scandal in Hollywood. I would not, could not, let August get away with murdering my baby.

My baby. The one I was supposed to have. Not this crying, fussy, miserable baby. My baby would've slept at night.

Kiah screamed louder. How was that possible?

I kicked off the sheets and went downstairs to find my phone, giving Kiah's room the double finger as I passed. I paced in front of the picture window, the lake glistening like a black jewel under the gaze of the stars. What could I text August to mess with him, punish him, push his marriage to the brink? If I was suffering, he needed to suffer too. Them's the rules.

Creating content wasn't easy. Being evasive, yet haunting. Ensuring I orchestrated the demise of his life from the shadows.

Then it came to me. A test. A little fun in this madness. Well, fun for me. I logged into ViperByte and fired off the text, attached a photo for premium "fuck you" value, and smiled.

Sensing my momentary pleasure, Kiah let out a blood-curdling scream. The loudest of the night. One for a horror movie.

I stomped up to her room, much the way I stomped to my room as a teenager. How the tides have changed. I pushed open her door and picked her up, wishing I would've packed earplugs—

Shit. Everywhere. It seeped through her diaper and clothes, staining the sheets.

"Fuuuuuck!" I held her away from my body as I carried her downstairs for another bath, cursing my grandparents for never putting a full bath on the second floor.

Who was being punished more right now, me or August?

CHAPTER THIRTY-SIX

AUGUST
WEDNESDAY, SEPTEMBER 6, 2023 11:32 P.M.

August stared at the inside of the fridge, not particularly hungry, but wanting to rid the sour taste of guilt coating his tongue from writing the list of women. The taste became putrid after enduring the detective's questions and watching Cassidy's face shift from shock to disbelief and finally landing on anger.

He should've walked away the moment he met Cassidy. He knew it'd never last. But he was sunk. In love. She was a ten in mind, body, and soul. Was it a self-fulfilling prophecy that made him cheat? A way to take control over the inevitable demise? Make it hurt less?

If so, he was wrong. Nothing could blunt this pain. Handing her the list didn't feel inevitable, but rather an accumulation of mistakes, fears, and insecurities. A man that refused to grow up. Worst of all? He saw pain in her eyes, heard agony in her voice, and knew she loved him.

What if the first time he felt tempted to cheat, he admitted to Cassidy his fear that he didn't measure up, that he felt restless, the future preordained, instead of letting himself get distracted? Shared his demons in the hopes she could help? He never wanted to be like his father. And he was. Worse, probably, since Mom knew Dad cheated and stayed anyway. August fed the charade of perfection Cassidy believed in ardently.

A buzzing in his pocket made his stomach drop. He slammed the fridge door and pulled out his phone. Once again, he saw the random string of numbers. *Let's play a game*, the text said. *Truth: Did you want Daisy? Dare: Tell your wife.*

August squeezed the phone, wishing he could strangle this person. Yes, he wanted Daisy. He was ecstatic from the first moment. He remembered Cassidy calling from the grocery store, telling him she bought a test. He raced home, finding her in the bathroom. When the test was ready, she told him to look, holding her hands over her eyes. *If it's bad news, it'll be easier coming from you,* she said. He grabbed the test. *Open your eyes.* She could hear the smile in his voice and flung herself into his arms. She started jumping up and down and screaming, looking from the test to him and back to the test. Both were teary-eyed. After a year of trying, the moment felt sweeter for all the disappointments.

Dare: Tell your wife. Tell her what? How much he loved— loves—Daisy? Cassidy could question his devotion as a husband, but not as a father.

He clicked on the attached picture. Cassidy stood in a parking lot, one hand cradling her basketball-shaped baby bump. She wore sunglasses and a dress, her icy blonde hair shiny and wavy.

It was a beautiful picture, one he'd save—if it wasn't sent as a threat.

"Same website?" August heard the detective ask from the living room.

August went to Cassidy's office, where she retreated when the detective called a break in questioning to meet with his team. "There's another text," August said, after stepping inside.

She sprang from her desk chair and rushed to his side, reading the text. "What are you supposed to tell me?" Her eyebrows knotted as he flipped to the picture. "It's me. Why would someone…"

"I don't know." It exhausted him how little he understood. Daisy gone. August and Cassidy both being stalked. Cops sprinkled around his house like dust mites. His skeletons yanked from the closet.

"If you don't know, then who does?" Her gaze pierced, the blue a violent sea. "These messages—this person expects you to understand."

He said nothing, not wanting to repeat that awful phrase.

"Did you not want Daisy?" She bit her lower lip. "Were you tired of trying?"

He cupped her face, infusing every word with conviction. "I wanted Daisy. I love our family. This person is crazy." She remained stoic. Why should she believe him? He was a proven liar. He remembered reading Piper *The Boy Who Cried Wolf*, explaining why she had to stop lying. He was that boy. Years of trust, extinguished with a single text.

Detective Lewis cleared his throat. August turned, finding him in the doorway, leaning against the frame. "It traces to ViperByte," the detective said. "No word yet in response to the subpoena. What are you supposed to tell us, August?"

"He doesn't know," Cassidy snapped. "'I don't know. I don't know.'" She threw her hands up in the air, mimicking him. "That's all he says."

August groaned. They thought he was being purposefully obtuse. Their stares only made the blockage in his head grow.

"While you think," the detective said, "I'd like to discuss offering a reward for a tip that leads to Daisy's safe return. It sounds crass, but some people wait until there's money involved to help."

"People really wouldn't come forward if there wasn't money?" August asked.

The detective sighed. "Sometimes it's apathy, other times fear. Few people want to invite the police into their lives."

"Even to save a baby?" Cassidy asked.

"Even then."

"What amount would you suggest? It's one of those horrible moral dilemmas, putting a price on your child. Obviously," she said, gesturing around her, "we'd give up everything. But what will work?"

"Ten thousand," the detective said. "Shows the gravitas of the crime, will make people listen, scour their brains, but not so much that we'll get a hundred thousand false tips. Do you guys have ten thousand accessible to pay the reward?"

"Yes," Cassidy said, without consulting August. "Announce the reward."

August had to get away. He couldn't handle their skepticism, the dismissal of his pain and fear. Cassidy acting like they were no longer a team, like his opinion ceased to matter because he cheated. "I'm going for a walk. Fresh air will help me think."

"There's news vans out front," Cassidy said, as if he didn't have eyes.

August felt heat rise to his face, frustration getting the better of him. "I'll cut through everyone's backyard."

"Mind if I frisk you first?" the detective asked.

"Frisk me?" August belted a laugh.

"I'm wondering if you have a burner. Maybe this walk is an opportunity to call someone."

Still, *still*, the detective considered him a suspect. Why would he implicate himself with those texts? Destroy his marriage? It didn't make sense. His faith in the detective's ability to bring Daisy safely home dwindled.

"Is that true?" Cassidy stepped closer, grabbing his jaw. "Is there someone you need to talk to?"

"No. If I knew anything, I would tell you." Each word felt like chewing on screws, the resistance of Cassidy's hand, the struggle to keep his anger in check, painful. "I swear, on our children's lives."

Cassidy dropped her hand and flopped down on her desk chair, letting out a primal groan. August stretched his arms to the side.

Detective Lewis ran his hands up and down August's thighs and then patted down his chest before giving him the okay.

August walked into the bedroom and quickly changed into a pair of shorts, T-shirt, hoodie, and hat. Stepping outside onto their back patio, August breathed in the cool night air. It smelled of burning leaves. The moon was out; the stars, which normally he could see, were camouflaged by light pollution from the media vans.

Oh, to get high. Slow the spinning wheel of worries. Given that his house was swarming with cops, he started walking.

He cut through several neighbors' yards at a fast pace, trying to warm his blood against the chill in the air and release some frustration. Most of his neighbors' windows were dark, already tucked away for the night. At the next street over, he crossed into the Sawnee Conservatory.

As he walked, he zeroed in on the three pregnancy scares. Aubree, Savannah, Vanessa. He pulled out his phone and dug into Facebook, searching for Aubree. Something he never did. Once an ex, always an ex. Occasionally, he let himself indulge a fantasy, jerk off to a picture he hid on his phone, but nothing traceable.

Aubree's profile was public. Lots of pictures with her kids and husband. She wouldn't risk everything to take Daisy.

Next, he searched Savannah. She was married. No kids. Hmm. Maybe she changed her mind. Or maybe she blamed him and went after his child? A stretch, but this entire situation stretched the bounds of reasonableness.

"Ahhh!" He stepped on a large rock and nearly rolled his ankle. Walking in the woods at night was idiocy, but he needed the solitude.

Vanessa. She wasn't on Facebook. He searched Instagram. TikTok. Wasn't that Gen Z's thing, they were accessible 24/7? Why couldn't he find her?

Memories trickled in as he walked, snapshots of his time with Vanessa. Her smiling, teasing, kissing him, coming. Passionate and sexy, until it wasn't. Vanessa telling him she was pregnant. Crying. Yelling. Throwing a fit. Acting every bit her youth. Words and phrases from the conversation filtered into his consciousness, a novel with paragraphs torn out. A novel he never reread after their breakup—until now. Now, he remembered her asking why Cassidy couldn't abort. He told her Cassidy was further along. This didn't appease her. He tried another tactic—he was panicking!—saying he and Cassidy were having problems. She softened. He took it a step further, insinuating he wished Cassidy wasn't pregnant so he could have the baby with Vanessa.

He stopped up short.

He told her he wasn't happy Cassidy was pregnant. *Truth: Did you want Daisy? Dare: Tell your wife.* The rest of the texts clicked together like puzzle pieces. A scar—literal or metaphorical—from the abortion? Possible. *How many kids do you have, August?* Did an eight-week fetus count as a baby? According to some billboards.

Jesus fucking Christ.

He spun in circles, hands weaved behind his head. An owl hooted, sending a chill down his spine. Vanessa said she loved him. Loved the baby. Fought him to have it. And then he broke up with her and she never contacted him again. He was too grateful to question it.

The next thought took him out at the knees. He bent to a squat, covering his mouth with his hands, trying not to scream in frustration. Among the women, Vanessa was the only one that knew Cassidy was pregnant. What black hole did he put Vanessa in that he didn't remember this sooner?

He sprinted back to the house.

CHAPTER THIRTY-SEVEN

VANESSA
JANUARY 2023

Although I made the abortion appointment, I had no intention of keeping it. I scheduled it out a couple weeks, telling August we should take the holidays to think it over. He was going out of town with Cassidy anyway, and I wasn't getting an abortion on my own. Secretly, I hoped August would calm down, fall in love with our baby, realize our happily ever after started now. The family he wanted—not the one he felt obligated to return to at night. Nothing I did mattered though. Tears. Promises. Threats. He closed his ears, shielded his eyes, erected a steel barrier around his heart, refusing to love our baby.

It scared me, how quickly he shut down. If I went ahead with having our baby, would he shut me out too?

If I got the abortion, he would love me. That was the interwoven promise in every kiss, touch, and fuck.

The morning of the appointment, he came to my apartment to pick me up. He cupped my chin, his blue eyes never leaving mine. His touch, as always, triggered some chemical yearning inside me. A glass that emptied almost as soon as he filled it up. Would I ever get enough?

"You're so brave, Vanessa." He kissed me softly, then added, "I'll be here, whatever you need."

Knowing he'd be by my side made the nightmare bearable.

The clinic was located in the first floor of a three-story brick building. All the blinds were closed. Protecting the patients or shaming us?

After checking in, I peed into a cup. Congrats! I was pregnant. August held my hand as we made our way into the examination room. The doctor, a middle-aged Asian woman, soon joined us. I lay back on the examination table, the paper mat beneath me crinkling with each movement, spread my legs, and rested my feet in the stirrups. The doctor took what looked like a dildo, bathed it in lube, and shoved it inside of me.

A tremor ran down my legs. "I'm sorry," the doctor said. "It's cold." As if the temperature was the reason my body was convulsing.

My baby appeared on the screen to the right, a tadpole in a dark sea. "You're measuring about eight weeks," she said. "Which would make you due on…September sixth."

The flashlight of my baby's heart drew me closer to the screen. I reached out, my thumb caressing her tiny body. Clopping beats soon filled the room. Our baby. Wanting to live. Wanting a chance.

"August," I whispered, hoping the sight of the baby we made together would change his mind. Slowly, he glanced up from the floor and held my eyes. His lips parted and time stopped. This was the moment, the apex of every romance, where the man realized everything he ever wanted was right in front of him.

Without looking at our baby, he mouthed the word, "Please."

Stupid me. There would be no moment.

I could have August. Love. A future together.

I just had to kill my baby.

After the examination, the doctor went over my options—keep, adopt, abort. I could take a double dose of pills, which would allow me to have the abortion at home, or the vacuum at the clinic. August never said a word, but I knew my time was up. Him or the baby. Decide now.

How could I love this baby, who I didn't even know, more than him? I didn't. I couldn't.

We made an appointment to return the next morning for the pills.

Alone in my bed, I wasn't able to sleep that night. I caressed my tummy, asking the baby to speak to me. Nothing came through. Thoughts of August were too loud. Was he lying in bed, thinking about me? The baby? Was he holding Cassidy? Cupping her baby bump? I tossed and turned, a violent thrashing, as the unfairness of the situation boiled fresh rage. Why did he go home to her when he promised to be by my side?

When August arrived the next morning, the red vines running through his eyes belied a sleepless night. He rested his hands on my neck and pressed his forehead against mine. I felt the weight of his stress. It helped, knowing we were both suffering, but becoming stronger as a couple. "I know this is hard," he said.

I wanted him to say he loved me. That he wished he spent the night with me. That he wanted to spend every night with me. Was I being needy? Too bad. "You love me, right?"

"Yes." He kissed me. "With all my heart."

At the clinic, I took the first pill, the one that would stop my body from producing the pregnancy hormones. Essentially, starving my baby to death. The second pill would shred my baby apart. Expel her from my vagina like garbage. Eviscerating my heart along with it.

August dropped me off at my apartment, promising to be back tomorrow morning for the second pill, the tougher of the two days. Stupid me, thinking he'd stay with me *both* days.

I napped. Around five, I met a few friends for "happy hour." Though nothing was happy, getting drunk helped. And why shouldn't I? There was no baby left to protect.

I slept in a drunken haze, waking to the apartment door buzzing at nine the next morning. I had a foul taste in my mouth, last night's makeup giving me two black eyes, and hair as ratty as a bird's nest. "You look rough," August said, when I opened the door.

Just the greeting a girl wants to hear.

He got me a glass of water and watched as I swallowed the second pill. It scraped my throat as it went down. My body's final resistance. He drew me a bath and I crawled into the warm water, enjoying how he sat next to the tub, holding my hand and talking. Exactly the type of moment I envisioned us having when we lived together. After, we got into bed and streamed a show. I closed my eyes and rested my head on his chest, enjoying the delicate way he ran his fingers through my hair.

The first cramp hit me like an unexpected gunshot, piercing and precise. I felt a gush of blood and ran for the toilet. I sat there as cramps rippled through me, clots of blood the size of dates appearing on the toilet paper.

Not clots. Human tissue. My baby.

Up and down, alternatively collapsing in bed and sitting on the toilet with my head resting against the wall, was how I spent the day. Bleeding heavily. Horrific cramps. Exhaustion.

August gamely rubbed my back. Got me ibuprofen. Cooked food. We were a real couple.

Well, almost.

Cassidy kept calling. I need him today, I wanted to scream. You can't have him.

He waited until I was in the bathroom to return her call. Was this to protect me? Did he realize how much it hurt, hearing his hushed conversations? Or was he afraid I'd blow his cover? Fair point, I thought, as another cramp ripped through me. If I was out there, I'd snatch the phone from his hand, tell her everything, ruin her world, as she ruined mine.

But I was in too much pain to fight.

Later that night, as we lay in bed, Cassidy called again. With nowhere to go in my studio apartment, August apologized and took the call in the bathroom. I crept out of bed, listening by the door. I could hear her voice, loud and irate, but couldn't make out the words.

You know what made me irate? Recovering from an abortion while listening to August argue with his wife, the woman who got to keep her baby.

I crawled back into bed. "What did she want?" I asked when he came out of the bathroom.

"She—" He ran a hand through his hair. "I have to go home."

"I need you." I turned to face him, pressing my hands against my empty womb, remembering the flicker of the heartbeat. I couldn't be alone. Not the first night.

He sat on the bed next to me, leaning over to kiss my wet cheeks. Without realizing it, I was crying. I'd been crying all day. Maybe I'd never stop. "Please," I sobbed. "Just tonight."

"I want to. But I need time to sort this out." He brushed my tear away with his thumb. "Be patient."

Patient. I shivered, the word sounding like a threat. "You promised to stay with me."

"And I did. All day." He looked up at the ceiling, inhaling deeply. Was he annoyed? At me? No, it must be with Cassidy for dragging him home. "I'll check on you tomorrow." With one more kiss, this time on the forehead, as if today drained all the sexual chemistry between us, or possibly this argument, he left.

I cuddled my pillow, trying to block out the voices screaming at me that I chose wrong.

But that wasn't true. He told me to be patient. Said I was end game.

He promised, I recited. A bedtime prayer. He promised.

CHAPTER THIRTY-EIGHT

VANESSA
WEDNESDAY, SEPTEMBER 6, 2023 11:45 P.M.

As the bath water warmed, Kiah screamed, her pencil-thin ribs vibrating with each release. Her face was cherry red, a shade of lipstick I wore to the bars when I wanted attention. To think, I could be that girl right now. Instead, I spent ten minutes scrubbing shit off Kiah's back while she wriggled her body like a crocodile trying to escape capture. The shit was caked on like frosting; my efforts leaving the skin clean, but irritated.

I spread a towel on the ground and lay her on top. I turned to grab the lotion and heard a sound—half fart, half gushing water—that made my stomach drop. Kiah momentarily stopped screaming. Turning back, I saw a huge stain beneath her butt, the color and consistency of neon-green slime. "What. The. Hell!" I yelled. How much could one baby poop?

My outburst set her off again. I grabbed the wipes and began cleaning her butt. As I fastened a fresh diaper, I noticed her right arm was red and blotchy. I ran my fingertips over the skin. The bumps were raised. Was she having a reaction to the soap? Or was the water too warm? Since she was already crying, I couldn't get a read of whether it bothered her when I touched it. Cassidy never discussed whether her kids had sensitive skin.

Would she notice?

I carried Kiah upstairs to dress. Opening her bedroom door, the smell of shit, sour and pungent, reminded me I had to clean her sheets. That I couldn't go back to bed. I put pajamas on Kiah and placed her in the middle of the double bed.

She cried harder. What did she want? She was clean. Warm. Couldn't be hungry. She had an upset stomach.

Whatever. I stripped her dirty sheets and blanket from the bassinet, rolling them into a ball, before carrying them downstairs. Then I got the towels from the bathroom, ignoring the ring of shit around the edge of the tub—something else I'd have to clean. Past the kitchen, I entered the small utility room. I loaded everything and washed it on sanitary.

The washing machine thumped to life, but I could still hear Kiah's cries. It felt like a nail being hammered into the center of my skull. I slumped to the cement floor, feeling—could it be?—sympathy for Cassidy. No wonder she constantly complained about being tired, finding her purpose, needing August's help. This was a thankless job. Kiah didn't give a damn that I risked my life, my future, to rescue her.

Sleep deprivation was torture—

The Benadryl! I bolted off the ground and ran upstairs to my backpack where the dosage was tucked inside the front pouch. I kissed the vial. I could almost taste the sleep, the self-induced coma both of us would enjoy, as I walked down the hallway to her room.

I picked her up and held her like a football in the crook of my elbow, inserting the baby dropper into her mouth. She wiggled, using her tongue to shove the dropper away. The liquid dribbled out the side of her mouth, making her look like she ate a bloody steak. Did she swallow any? I didn't want to give her more and overdose her. So many unintentional ways a baby could die.

When the vial was empty, I carried her to my room, resigned to sharing a bed. This way, if she pooped again, I could change her before she ruined another outfit and bedding.

Laying on my side, I kissed Kiah's cheek and rubbed circles on her belly, something Mom did for me when I had a tummy ache. Kiah whimpered, but finally calmed, her eyes flickering shut, her breath becoming rhythmic.

I lay back and closed my eyes. Silence. The sweetest symphony.

CHAPTER THIRTY-NINE

CASSIDY
THURSDAY, SEPTEMBER 7, 2023 12:13 A.M.

Cassidy stood under the showerhead, letting the warm water run down her face, over her swollen breasts and sore nipples, thinking about the text message. *Did you want Daisy?* Was it a reference to them having another girl?

August wanted a boy. He entertained himself during her pregnancy with Daisy by researching old wives' tales. She remembered laying together in bed one night, both on their phones—Was he texting another woman?—when he yanked a thread from his shirt. He took off his wedding ring—Did he wear the ring when cheating?—tying it to the thread. *Pull up your shirt,* he said. She obliged, playing along. He dangled the ring over her bump—Was he secretly disgusted by her pregnant belly, wanting something young and taut?—his face lighting up as it swayed from side to side. *Yes!* He pumped his fist. *We're having a boy!* She laughed and accused him of doctoring it like a Ouija board.

When Daisy arrived, crystalline eyes, sinewy limbs, lungs fit for an opera singer, August cried tears of joy. He held Daisy to his chest, having taken off his shirt to maximize skin-to-skin contact, and kept saying how beautiful she was. He was in love. A total girl-dad.

Cassidy dug her nails into her scalp as she applied conditioner. Did a girl-dad cheat with six women? She did the hard lifting—baths, meals, school runs, doctor appointments—but, when he was home, he built forts, played chase, diapered Daisy, read bedtime stories. He was a deceitful husband, but she couldn't cast him as a neglectful father.

After rinsing her hair, she stepped out of the shower and toweled off. August bust through the door. Without knocking. She yanked the towel across her body, tying it shut. August's eyebrows crinkled and then he frowned slightly as understanding dawned. Too bad. Earlier, when she was pumping, she didn't want him to see her naked because she was embarrassed her body was stretched and swollen, functional rather than beautiful. Now, he didn't deserve to see her naked. Ever again.

"Come out to the kitchen," he said.

She crossed her arms, wincing as the towel brushed her raw nipples. "Why? Did something happen?"

"Yes—"

She stepped toward him, grabbing his wrists. "Tell me."

"I'll tell you and the detective at the same time," he said. "It's important we get the police on this ASAP, so hurry."

She pushed past him, pulling on yoga pants and a tank-top/sweatshirt combo. Could she stand another confession?

Yes. For Daisy, absolutely. She would steel her heart.

She followed August to the kitchen where Detective Lewis and another man he introduced as Dr. Fuentes, a psychological profiler with the FBI, sat at the kitchen table. Dr. Fuentes wore a light sweater and jeans, not the blue jacket with the yellow FBI logo she'd seen in movies. He shook her hand, giving a sincere apology for the circumstances. Hopefully, he would help, although she didn't know how.

August sat to her left, telling them he figured out who sent the texts. "This isn't easy to talk about." He looked at Cassidy. "Please know I did it because I love you and I love our family. I was trying to protect us."

Cassidy's stomach synched tighter. "Tell me."

August cleared his throat. "One of the women—" He took a deep breath, puffing his lips with the exhale. "She had an abortion."

Cassidy didn't move. Didn't so much as blink or breathe. It was a dead zone where time ceased to exist. Questions. So many questions. Which woman? Why didn't he say this when they were discussing the list? Did he try to convince her to keep the baby? How could he go through something so monumental and not tell Cassidy?

"Which woman had the abortion?" Detective Lewis asked, eyes scanning August's list.

"Vanessa."

"You said her period was late," Detective Lewis said.

Another deep breath. "I lied. I didn't think it mattered and I knew it would make things worse." He peeked at Cassidy. "With us."

Cassidy glared at him. He kept lying. With Daisy's life in jeopardy. How many lies did he tell each day? Dozens? Needing to physically restrain herself, she gripped the bottom of her seat.

"When was the abortion?" Detective Lewis asked.

"Last winter. January."

January. Cassidy searched her memory for signs he was distant. Preoccupied. Grieving. But she was pregnant and sick—

She covered her mouth with her hands. The depths of his deception; it held no bottom. She kept falling and falling with no end in sight, nothing to grip for understanding. What a horrible, displacing, disorienting feeling.

"And why do you think she's connected?" Detective Lewis asked.

"The messages." August pulled out his phone. "The first one, about scars. Maybe the abortion left a scar? Metaphorically? Asking me how many kids I have…that could refer to an abortion, right? If the baby went to term? If we're looking at an ex—"

Cassidy wanted to slap him for using the term ex. He said it was sex. Now she was an ex?

"—she makes the most sense. There's more, but…" August turned toward Detective Lewis, closing himself off to Cassidy. "Can

I talk to you alone?" he asked quietly. As if Cassidy wasn't a foot away. "About the specifics?"

He lied to her for years, and now he wanted to continue the charade? "No," Cassidy said. "Absolutely not."

August looked at Cassidy, his hands folded in prayer. "If you hear everything, you'll never forgive me. You know she took Daisy and why. Can't we leave it there? Try to save our marriage?"

"What marriage?" Cassidy surprised herself at the vitriol in her voice.

His face tightened. "Once you calm—"

"Everyone stays," Detective Lewis said with finality. "Now talk."

August glared at some indeterminate point in the ceiling. "I told Vanessa I was married. Already had a kid. That Cassidy was pregnant, too."

Did he love Vanessa? Consider leaving Cassidy? Maybe his decision to stay had nothing to do with Cassidy. Because if he loved her, he never would've cheated, right? Maybe he stayed for Piper. Or because Cassidy was pregnant. Or maybe he had a skewed sense of integrity. After all, his dad never left his mom, despite cheating.

"It clicked with the third message." August ran his tongue over his front teeth. "I may have let her believe Cassidy and I were having a hard time and—" He rubbed his eyes, though Cassidy didn't see any tears. "I wasn't happy Cassidy was pregnant. I didn't mean it. At all." His words tumbled over one another. "I said whatever I needed to get her to have the abortion. To protect our family."

Cassidy couldn't take her eyes off August. Who was this man that would rid himself of his child as easily as leftovers? It wasn't the man she married in no small part because of how much he loved children. They gravitated toward him, his silly demeanor and child-like joy matching their energy. The cheating blew her mind, but this, aborting his own child, made her question everything.

"And she agreed?" Detective Lewis asked. "To get the abortion?"

"Not at first. The pregnancy hormones were messing with her head—"

Cassidy pressed her fingers into her eyelids, her body shaking, ready to explode. "Oh my god," she muttered, "oh my God, oh my God."

"What?" August asked.

She hadn't felt rage like this—ever. "Having a man lie to her, treat her like his girlfriend, get her pregnant, and then demand she get an abortion." She leaned forward, wet hair pasted to her forehead, looking like a hot mess, and not caring one bit. "That could drive a woman crazy."

August's jaw flexed. "All I'm saying is she was young and romanticized having a baby."

"How young?" Dr. Fuentes asked.

"Twenty-two."

That must have been the woman Faith saw him with. "Do you have a picture of her?" Cassidy asked.

"A pic-picture?" August stuttered, letting Cassidy know she hit a tender spot. "I don't think so."

She grabbed his phone. "You do." He was trying to soften the blow. She didn't need anything softened. Everything was hitting a live nerve.

She found a file named V, how creative, which required a scan of August's face to open. She held the phone in front of him, allowing it to digest his image. Eleven pictures. The first, a sext. Vanessa kneeling on a bed, using the palms of her hands to push up her breasts for the camera, enhancing the cleavage. Not that she needed help. Her breasts were sexy. Youthful. High. Round. Pert nipples. No stretch marks from pregnancy.

He said he was attracted to Cassidy more after giving birth because she gave him everything he ever wanted. Another lie.

Drawn immediately to the nakedness, it took Cassidy a few seconds to take in her features. Dark, curly hair. Seductively wild. A mole on her cheek ala Cindy Crawford. Biting her lower lip. Her dark eyes were sleepy, yet mesmerizing. She looked familiar, though Cassidy couldn't say why.

"You don't need to study it," August said, reaching for the phone. She jerked away. He was nervous. Why? What else was he hiding?

"The rest?" she asked. "They're all sexts?"

"I—" He stopped. Slowly nodded.

"You still look at these?"

"It's—" He couldn't finish the sentence. The well of his excuses likely having run dry.

Cassidy texted herself the picture. If the eyes were the gateway to the soul, then Cassidy would study Vanessa's face for clues to find her daughter.

Before closing out, she hit the back button in the phone, laughing to herself as she noticed files named "S", "A," and "M." His trophies. Like a serial killer that couldn't walk away empty-handed.

She tossed the phone back at August. Chucked might be more apt. Detective Lewis intercepted it. He called over what Cassidy thought of as the "tech" officer. "Get an APB out on Vanessa Prescott," Detective Lewis said, "including a picture, description, and any car she has registered under her name. Use only her face—obviously."

Poor girl. Her naked selfies being viewed by every officer—

Cassidy would not feel bad for her.

"She drives a black Jetta," August said.

"August." She whispered his name, splaying a hand against her heart. "Remember how I felt like I was being followed by a black car? The store, the gym—"

"You never said it was a black Jetta," August said.

She rolled her eyes. "You know I can't recognize brands."

"Models," he corrected. "Not brands."

Cassidy crossed her arms. You would think now, more than ever, he would hand out support like a free flyer at the grocery store. "Whatever."

"When was this?" Detective Lewis asked. "That you started noticing the black car?"

Cassidy thought. "Last winter?"

"Did you get a license plate?"

"No, I…" Like the mean posts on her website, Cassidy dismissed it.

Detective Lewis dispelled an officer to do another round with the neighbors to ask if any noticed a black Jetta in the area. Another officer was assigned to rereview video footage for the car. "Ultimately, you convinced Vanessa to get the abortion?" Detective Lewis asked.

"Yes," August said.

"Then what happened?"

"We broke up."

"When was this?"

"January."

"So," Cassidy said, "you demanded she get an abortion, dumped her, all right after the holidays?"

"As if there's a good time to break it off." August's eyes bore into her. "I did what I thought was best. A clean break."

"Wow," Cassidy mumbled. "If that was your best…"

"Did she contact you after the breakup?" Detective Lewis, their referee, asked.

"No. At the time, I thought she agreed things got too serious."

"What made you think that?" Dr. Fuentes asked.

"It was over the phone, so I couldn't read her body language—"

"When did you call?" Cassidy asked, twisting her hair into a bun, squeezing it tight. This was absurd. To think he could treat people as inconveniences without any consequences. "How long did you give her to grieve her baby before you broke her heart all over again?"

August put his head in his hands. "The next day."

"The next day." Unbelievably, Cassidy felt herself tearing up for Vanessa. Then she remembered this woman stole Daisy right from her crib. The tears evaporated.

"As I said, she was upset," August said. "But when I never heard from her again, I assumed she moved on. Was relieved to be free of me. The baby. Everything."

"She wasn't relieved," Cassidy whispered. "She's a mother—"

"No, she's not." August's voice overpowered hers. "She doesn't have kids."

She looked at her husband. What an unbelievably glib asshole. "As soon as you become pregnant, you become a mother," Cassidy said. "For men, it becomes real once the baby is born, but with women, it's real from the positive pregnancy test. That's when the dream starts." Cassidy knew this truth down to her marrow. "Find this woman. She's the one."

With each word, Cassidy felt fresh terror rise inside her. The police underestimated their opponent. This psychotic, manipulative woman was a mother. Mothers will do anything to protect their children. And will avenge their death in equal measure.

CHAPTER FORTY

VANESSA
JANUARY 2023

The day after the abortion, I stayed in bed 'til noon, curled up with my phone, heavily bleeding, waiting for August come over. He promised to check on me. That meant in person, right? Although, I'd feed on a text right now. The intense cramps subsided in the middle of the night, but low-grade ripples amplified the emptiness. My baby was gone. There was nothing left, except for August.

I loved my baby. And I betrayed her. For a man. Mom never did that to me. During arguments between Dad and me—almost daily before I left for college—she'd tell him I needed love, not criticism. Freedom, not chains. She saw my emotion as passion. My dark days as evidence of an old soul. My inability to fit in a sign I broke the mold. I wanted to give my daughter that unconditional love. Instead, I killed—

Get up, the director said, trying to rip off the duvet. Take a shower to wash the blood away. Get some fresh air.

But what if August showed up while I was gone? I didn't want to miss him.

The director rolled her eyes.

I ducked beneath the pillow, blocking her out. Questions; incessant, unrelenting, strangling questions consumed me. Did I make a mistake, choosing August over our baby? How much longer would I have to put up with Cassidy? Why didn't he call?

The walls closed in on me. The air was stale. The metallic taste of blood filled my mouth—I'd bit my nails into bloody stumps—but it felt as if my broken heart bled internally. I grabbed my phone and typed, *WHERE ARE YOU?*

Delete. Delete. Delete.

I would not reach out first. Not today. He needed to make good on his word.

By seven that night, I hadn't heard from him and had to leave for work. I took an oxy for the lingering cramps and a Xanax to slow the merry-go-round of thoughts. Then I filled a water bottle with vodka. I planned to get make-horrible-life-altering-decisions drunk tonight.

Behind the bar, I watched myself take orders, mix drinks, make change through a foggy lens. My limbs were numb, but my body worked on cruise control. A few customers bitched about my lack of smile or personality or speed, but, post-holidays, it wasn't busy enough to matter. The director tried to help, instructing me to play a beautiful, broken-hearted girl. But nothing could blunt this pain. Not drugs. Not alcohol. Not pretending.

By eleven, my thoughts were drowning in a deep black ocean, barely coherent. My hand kept reaching for my water bottle, taking medicinal swallows of vodka. Each sip kept me from crying. I messed up my life, again, but this time, in a way I feared permanent.

My phone buzzed. I pulled it from my back pocket, holding the screen close to my eyes. The letters were fuzzy, like the bottom line of an eye exam, but I made out enough to know it was August. I told Crista, another bartender, I needed five and went out back to the alley.

The frigid January wind raced through my tank top, shorts and tights, alerting my brain I was cold, but it didn't pack a punch. I stood on the cement stoop, thumb hovered over August's name, debating whether to call him back. Apologies and explanations—did they matter? I needed him. And he abandoned me, broke his promise, calling minutes before midnight.

Maybe I should ignore him. Let him sweat it out.

I let my phone go to sleep and looked around the alleyway. It was narrow, stuck between two brick buildings, just wide enough for the garbage trucks. It reminded me of my first date with August. The Riverwalk. August pulling me into an alley, pushing me up against a similar brick building. Our first kiss. Followed by our first fuck. How did it come to this, a dead baby and a decimated heart, only months later? I was so sure about us.

My phone lit up with his call again. Anger, desperation, confusion, need—the onslaught of emotions had me tripping, literally, falling to my knees down the step. The phone tumbled, landing in the alleyway.

I answered it, resting my head against the railing. The cement ripped through my tights, scraping my knee. Blood oozed from the wound. I touched it with my finger, noting the wet red mark, but felt nothing. If only my heart could stop feeling.

"How are you?" he asked. I could hear wind whipping on his end, letting me know he too was outside. Avoiding Cassidy, like a coward.

"Where's Cassidy?" All spite. He deserved it.

He didn't answer right away. Did he ever say her name to me? Did I blow my cover?

I didn't care.

"She's sleeping," he eventually said. "Are you okay? You sound…strange."

Strange. What about hurt? Traumatized? Betrayed? "I'm upset about our baby. And you said you'd check on me today. I was all alone."

"Give it time. It'll get better."

Why did he sound as if he was commiserating with me about testing positive for COVID instead of mourning an abortion? Or was I paranoid? It always came down to this, didn't it? Could I trust my thoughts? My intuition? "It doesn't feel that way."

"Not right now," he said, "but think on the bright side. You have your freedom back."

"Freedom?" A reason he never mentioned when discussing the abortion. "Free to do what?"

"You're young. You're going to meet so many new people and this…this period—"

He still wouldn't acknowledge our baby.

"—will be like a bad dream."

I held my hand in front of my face, swatting away his words. "Yesterday, you said you loved me. That you saw a future together. Now you're talking about freedom and meeting new people. What. The. Fuck."

"Believe me," he said, "if things were different, I think we'd be happy together."

"Make it different." My stomach roiled. Saliva poured into my mouth. Burning, hot lava came up my throat. I swallowed. Hard. "Leave her. Be with me. Like you promised."

"She's pregnant, Vanessa."

"So was I, you fucking fuck!" My words echoed down the narrow alleyway. "And I got an abortion for you. Because you told me there'd be another baby in our future."

"I've been thinking about you, us, all day, trying to decide what to do. This was a huge wake-up call for me." August spoke faster now. Or maybe my brain wasn't able to keep up. "I need to be a better husband, a better father. Devote myself to Piper and Cassidy. I can't keep cheating…she's deserves better than that."

What about me? Didn't I deserve to be more than someone's mid-life crisis? Puke was seconds away, stopping me from voicing those questions. I kept swallowing, trying to keep it at bay, not wanting to end the conversation. I hated him, but the thought of never speaking to him again? I squeezed the phone tighter, my life raft.

"Listen, I really cared about you," he said with such finality, such apathy, that I gasped for air. Cared? As in past tense? "I feel lucky to have had you in my life. Brief as it was."

I couldn't hold on any longer. Nor could I give him the satisfaction of knowing he destroyed me. "Goodbye, August." I ended the call a second before I leaned over and puked.

The bile scalded my throat. Everything spun. August lied to me. Made me kill my baby. Then left me. He never loved me. I was alone. In an alleyway. Wasted. Oblivion was coming. But not fast enough to blot out one prevailing thought. Why did he get to walk away unharmed?

CHAPTER FORTY-ONE

VANESSA
THURSDAY, SEPTEMBER 7, 2023 2:11 A.M.

Even though Kiah was fast asleep next to me in bed, the questions kept coming. Was it normal for Kiah to have diarrhea three times in seven hours? Get a body rash? Was it stress? Could babies feel stress?

Or was it me? Had she already rejected me?

Babies pooped. It was nothing.

Right? *Right?*

One quick Google search to settle my mind.

I grabbed my phone and Googled diarrhea in babies. Heat rose to my face as I read that some babies are allergic to formula. It seemed obvious. People had food allergies. But why make a formula some babies couldn't drink? Epitome of stupidity.

Symptoms of allergies: Fussiness. Diarrhea or constipation. Fever. Skin rash. Sneezing. Swollen eyes. Weight loss.

Kiah had two symptoms, diarrhea and a small rash. Which could be my soap or lotion or sunburn from riding in the car. I rested my hand on her forehead, which was warm, but not scalding. I didn't have a thermometer, one of a hundred baby items I didn't buy.

Were two symptoms enough to diagnose an allergy? Was this life-threatening like a nut allergy or more like gluten, which made you sick? Was this Google trying to rachet up panic in new mothers?

Call your pediatrician with questions.

I didn't have a fucking pediatrician! Why did I never consider she might get sick? Develop a plan?

I watched Kiah, trying to decipher if she was uncomfortable. She was breathing steadily. Wasn't tossing and turning.

She was fine.

In the morning, I'd buy hypo-allergenic formula. Simple. Done. Issue resolved.

I set my phone down and closed my eyes.

Another problem quickly arose. What should I do with Kiah while I went to the store? I couldn't bring her out in public and it was dangerous to leave her in the car. I stocked up on baby supplies for this reason.

She had to stay home.

It wasn't like she could get into trouble.

She'd never know I was gone.

I exhaled. Once dawn broke, I'd run to the store.

Sleep. Now.

CHAPTER FORTY-TWO

AUGUST
THURSDAY, SEPTEMBER 7, 2023 2:35 A.M.

August sat at the kitchen table, enduring a round of questions from Dr. Fuentes about Vanessa, questions which delved into her behavior and personality more than the facts the detective pinned down, when a cop distracted him by carrying in a stack of pizzas. The aroma of cheese and fresh dough, the spice of pepperoni and sausage, made his stomach grumble. And he wasn't alone. Conversation ground to a halt. August stood up, grabbed a plate and two slices of pepperoni, before returning to the table. The crust held a buttery crunch, the sauce piping hot, and the cheese gooey. In the middle of his second bite, he felt Cassidy's eyes on him. She scowled, the two lines bracketing her mouth sinking deeper.

"Enjoying that?" Cassidy asked, speaking to him directly for the first time in a half-hour.

The detective piled four slices on his plate. Dr. Fuentes took two. "Am I supposed to not eat?"

She looked away. He was the bad guy. Irremediable. The abortion sentenced him in her eyes. Sitting through his discussion with Dr. Fuentes, hearing every detail of his relationship with Vanessa, sure didn't help either. The damn thing was, he honestly believed the abortion was the best choice for both women. Cassidy would've left him if he dared tell her the truth. There would've been no understanding that he made a mistake, that he struggled with demons, wanted to be better. And Vanessa? She lived in la-la land. When she asked him to leave Cassidy, be a family, she envisioned a chubby-cheeked Gerber baby; cheering the baby's first steps; foot rubs and bottles of wine after long days. She didn't see the sleepless nights; the never-ending crying, pooping, fevers and colds; the laundry, dishes, monstrous credit card statements; the sacrifices, compromises, arguments. He had affairs to live his fantasies so he could return to reality as his best self.

He loved fucking Vanessa, but he didn't love her. Cassidy was the only woman he ever loved.

"Vanessa no longer resides at the address you gave us," the detective said, reading from his phone with one hand, the other wiping his mouth with a napkin. The four pieces of pizza having disappeared in the time August ate one. "The building manager has no forwarding address. Phone number is no longer active. She has a P.O. Box downtown, but that's it. Officers spoke to her boss at Top Shelf, though she no longer works there. We're in the process of pulling legal and medical records." He set down his phone. "In the meantime, I'd like Dr. Fuentes to give his opinion on Vanessa. Then we'll discuss next steps."

"Right." Dr. Fuentes set a napkin atop his unfinished pizza and pushed his glasses up the bridge of his nose. "Having never treated her, I can't diagnose her. But based on your experience with her and what the police have independently uncovered—"

August wondered what they uncovered via her coworkers, friends, and family. He couldn't reconcile the Vanessa he knew— wild, dreamy, funny—would steal a child. What did he miss?

"—she is displaying signs of borderline personality disorder."

"What's that?" August and Cassidy asked at the same time. She winced, evidently not wanting to be associated with him.

"Borderline personality disorder is characterized by difficultly controlling emotions," Dr. Fuentes said. "Black and white thinking. Hot and cold. Highly sensitive. Impulsive. And, ultimately, self-destructive. A slight an emotionally adjusted person can shrug off would feel like the end of the world. In this case, Vanessa loved you, thought you were Prince Charming. When you disappointed her, she quickly transitioned to hate. Based on her decision to kidnap Daisy, she likely obsessed over how to destroy your life, as she perceived you destroyed hers."

August shook his head. "I was trying to help. She didn't understand the reality of having a baby."

"When people with BPD are on a high, there's no second guessing," the doctor said. "Or a low, as we're seeing now."

"I don't agree with your assessment. Our relationship—" August heard Cassidy's sigh. He shouldn't have said relationship. "It was casual. She was cool, laid back. Made it easy for me to come and go."

"It's possible you hadn't upset her until the abortion," Dr. Fuentes said. "Or, more likely, she shut down because she wanted you to think she was cool with it. People with BPD have an intense fear of abandonment, which leads to feelings of depression and worthlessness." He shrugged. "This is all conjecture. I won't be able to give a firm opinion until I speak with her."

"Which brings me to my plan," the detective said. "I want you to email her—with Dr. Fuentes' guidance—so we don't trigger any destructive behaviors."

"I don't have her email," August said. "We texted."

"We got it from her boss at Top Shelf," the detective said.

"If Daisy's her replacement baby, she wouldn't hurt her, right?" Cassidy asked Dr. Fuentes, her voice tilting up at the end.

"I'm afraid you're thinking too logically," Dr. Fuentes said. "People with BPD flip on a dime, going from rage to paranoia to self-loathing to ecstasy, all in a matter of minutes." He shifted his eyes down. "My concern is if this is driven more by revenge..."

"What?" Cassidy asked. "Say it. I can handle it."

"Tell us," August echoed.

Dr. Fuentes cleared his throat. "If she is motivated by revenge, there's no telling what she might do." He paused. "Even if she ends up getting hurt too."

Cassidy pushed her chair back and pulled her knees to her chest. Her head dipped between and she starting crying. August stood up and walked over, resting a hand on her shoulder. She jerked away, stumbling out of the chair. "Don't. Touch. Me."

"I'm trying—"

"Stop trying. Don't you get it? You've done enough." She tugged at her ponytail. "I'm going next door to sleep with Piper. I'll have my phone if anyone needs me."

"Cassidy, please stay—"

"After what you did—" She held up both hands before leaving through the patio door. He could finish the sentence for her. After what he did, she'd never sleep with him again.

Rage filled every cell of his body and he punched the wall, leaving a hole in the drywall next to Piper's painting of a princess. He regretted everything. Pursuing Vanessa. Demanding the abortion. Casting her aside. Who did he think he was? Brad Pitt? Tiger Woods? Why did he think he could get away with this?

"Let's email her," August said, flexing his hand as he sat down, willing to say and do whatever necessary to bring Daisy home.

CHAPTER FORTY-THREE

VANESSA
MARCH 2023

For weeks after our breakup, I waited for August's call, certain he'd realize his mistake. He would see how empty life was with Cassidy; how I brought excitement to each day.

While waiting, I listened to Cassidy's podcast, searching for signs her marriage was on the brink. Whenever she complained about her pregnancy—Fuck you! Fuck you! Fuck you!—I trolled her with comments about how she was too selfish to be a mother. That she looked fat, not pregnant. That pregnancy acne scarred. No matter how I taunted her, she never responded. Never even posted the messages on the site. Probably didn't want to know if others agreed.

Time passed. I had hookups, but starting over was impossible when my head was stuck in the past. I couldn't let go of my baby. Forgive myself for choosing wrong. Trusting August. Some days, the regret was unbearable. I never left bed. Drank myself sick. Imbibed pills until I was too numb to think. Other days, I believed he was suffering too. That Cassidy had him in chains. That our love was real. I would follow him, searching for glimpses of grief. Of the truth.

One Tuesday afternoon in March, I followed August to a ranch house in a northern suburb with a "For Sale" sign in the front yard. Parking a few houses away, I watched as he greeted a woman with a hug. While I couldn't make out his words, the low register of his voice worked like an ice bath. It hurt. It hurt. It hurt.

She laughed at something he said, throwing her head back. He wasn't funny! And then he pressed his hand to the small of her back as she stepped inside the house. My antenna rose.

What. The. Hell.

Would he dare cheat again?

Forever and a day later, they exited through the front door. As they walked across the street, he interlaced his hand with hers, as he did with me on the Riverwalk. That was his move! Hand-holding. Something romantic to make the woman fall, make her believe he wanted more than a quick lay.

Anyone could see them. He could get caught. Then again, he kissed me in public. He thought he was invincible—

Pictures. I grabbed my phone and started snapping photos. Maybe I'd send them anonymously to Cassidy. Let her know what a cheating asshole she married. Or maybe I'd blackmail August.

He pressed this woman up against the door of the car, hands on her hips, much as he once pressed me up against that alley brick wall. I was watching the movie of our romance, memorized the script, could choreograph each move, except I was no longer the star. He'd cup her chin. Kiss her. Press his thumb against the pulse point in her neck. Mutter how he'd never felt this way before. Go back to her place and fuck her. Twice for good measure. Make her come and come until she was begging him not to leave.

I bit my lip to keep from screaming. He was cheating. Again. After breaking up with me to be a better father. And I believed him. For the sake of his kids, I stayed silent. Stupid girl!

I was nothing but a pawn in his game. He pursued me, fucked me, manipulated me, and then forced me to murder my own child. Why? Because he could. I wasn't the first. Nor the last.

After August and this woman left, I plotted my revenge. No more sitting around being sad. First step, disappear. Move. New job. New phone number. No social media. No friends. On the off-chance August came looking for me, he needed to believe I was gone.

Second step, get my baby back. I started the car and headed toward August's house, eager to find Cassidy, see how my pregnancy was progressing.

Guess what, August? I liked games too. And I was pretty good at winning, once I understood the rules.

CHAPTER FORTY-FOUR

VANESSA
THURSDAY, SEPTEMBER 7, 2023 6:22 A.M.

Singing birds woke me early the next morning. Dawn hadn't quite broken and the air coming through the crack of the window was heavy with dew. As I pulled on a pair of leggings, a sweatshirt, and sneakers, every muscle ached with exhaustion. Four hours of restless sleep, stressed that Kiah pooped again, that I rolled over on her, that she was burning up, wasn't enough. But getting to the store before Kiah woke was essential.

Before leaving, I gently rested my hand against Kiah's forehead. Warm, but not sweaty. I pulled my hair into a bun and situated the blonde wig atop my head. Then I grabbed my backpack and tiptoed out of the house.

As I drove through the hilly roads, the sun rose, a collage of yellows and oranges with a hint of red flicking through the tree branches. But I was too stressed about leaving Kiah alone to enjoy the beauty. "Town" was twenty minutes away, plus time to find and buy the formula, and then twenty minutes back. Would I make it home before she woke?

A dozen cars were in the grocery store parking lot. After Labor Day, most seasonal residents were gone. All the better. I tugged on a plain black ball cap and made my way inside, searching several aisles before finding the baby one. I was ambushed by several types of formula. Gentle. Sensitive. Infant. Instant. Organic. Soy. Comfort.

I pressed my fingertips into my burning eyes. What in the actual fuck was the difference between hypoallergenic and organic sensitivity and gentle release? All claimed to help with fussiness, gas, spit-ups, tummy trouble. Shockingly, all boasted being the number one brand recommended by pediatricians. If I was rich, I'd buy all three. But I wasn't rich. And caring for houses this winter was a severe drop in income from bartending. I wanted to crumble to the ground and sob myself to sleep. It wouldn't be the first time a cool, hard tile floor served as a bed.

The article said hypoallergenic. I grabbed that one. Diaper cream too. And a pacifier. I never found the one I took from Kiah's crib. Maybe it'd improve her mood.

Since this town was stuck in 1992, I had to deal with an actual cashier. I tugged my hat down, shielding my eyes, set the formula, pacifier, and diaper cream on the belt, and pulled out two twenties to ensure an efficient exchange.

"How ya doing this morning?" the cashier asked. A woman. Middle-aged. Perm also circa 1992.

I smiled weakly. "Tired."

"I hear ya." She snapped her gum while scanning the items. "Thirty-eight-ninety-five."

I handed her the money, hoping she wouldn't notice the bills were sweaty. But money was gross. The germs. Changing of hands. Being held in pockets. Wallets. Nope. She wouldn't think anything of it. She wouldn't.

While preparing my change, she asked, "How old's your baby?"

My heart skittered to a stop. "Four months."

"Precious." She held the dollar in her hand, keeping the cashier drawer open, making no move to grab the five cents. "I remember when my kids were that age. Breastfeeding was all the rage." She tapped the formula with red lacquered nails. "You were a horrible mother if you used formula."

It reminded me of an episode of Cassidy's podcast where she discussed the breastfeeding versus formula "war." Weren't there more important things to stress about? Like getting a baby to stop shitting every two seconds?

"Not that I'm judging you," she continued. "Wish I would've used formula. Nursing ruins your breasts." She looked longingly at her breasts, like a lover that got away.

I wanted to rip the money out of her hand. Instead, I said, "You look great."

She smiled. "Aw, thanks, honey." Finally, finally, she handed me my change and the bag of items. "Now you get on home to that baby."

Mission accomplished, I walked to my car, scratching my arms, feeling like a colony of ants were crawling across my skin. So much for skating by unnoticed. Would I be able to do anything, go anywhere, without fearing exposure? Was I being paranoid or vigilant?

I didn't want to be "on" all the time. I couldn't. I would fail. It was only a matter of time.

Once inside my car, I looked in the rearview mirror. "You're fine." My jaw ached with the force it took to say the words. Believe them. "Everything is fine."

I started the car and left. The sky was robin's egg blue, the sun a golden sphere. I pulled on my sunglasses and focused on not tailgating. Why was he driving so slow?

A few minutes later, a train stopped traffic. Next, I'd probably run into a family of ducks crossing the road.

With a sigh, I put the car in park and grabbed my phone, scanning my email. AUGUST CHAPMAN. I shut my eyes, positive exhaustion made me hallucinate. I never gave him my email. But no, when I opened them, August's email waited. Holding my breath, I clicked it.

Hey babe,

Stopped by Top Shelf looking for you. Your manager gave me your email. Hoping we could catch up. Call me.

August

What. The. Fuck?

I reread the email, the tremble in my hand making the words jump. Why was he writing me, looking to hook up, in the middle of his child going missing?

He knew I had Kiah. But how? And why didn't he say that? Threaten to tell the police?

Or. Or. Or. I bit each nail, thumb to pinky, finding nothing but raw skin to gnaw. Perhaps he wanted me back.

Don't be stupid. He didn't care about me when I begged to keep my baby or dumped me like a prostitute that overstayed her welcome. And he didn't care about me now.

I pulled up Twitter, checking #BabyDaisy for updates. A moan escaped. *Police source reporting person of interest in kidnapping of #BabyDaisy.* Who? Why didn't they give a name? Was this person in custody?

Person of interest. A riddle. Why so goddamn vague? Why not say suspect? Or witness? For the hundredth time, I reran yesterday morning in my mind. Perhaps one of Cassidy's neighbors saw me push Kiah out of their garage, across the street, and into the woods. I wore my wig. Dark clothes like Cassidy. From far away, I doubted anyone could tell us apart. Doubtful, but possible. Perhaps Cassidy and August installed a camera without me knowing? Or maybe that sheriff recognized Kiah?

Or, and this thought made me want to nap on the train tracks, my texts backfired. Maybe August had a conscience. Maybe he bookmarked the abortion, revisited that day often, guilt plaguing him, and thus returned to thoughts of me.

No more texts.

The train finished and I slammed on the gas. Ten minutes later, I walked inside the house, greeted by frantic crying. I ran upstairs and found Kiah in the middle of my bed, sucking on her fist between

sobs. I unzipped her pajamas to change her diaper. "I have food—
"

The rash spread to her legs. How could I get it to stop spreading? Go away? I touched the raised bumps, trying not to gag, hoping it wasn't contagious.

Why was this happening to me?

CHAPTER FORTY-FIVE

CASSIDY
THURSDAY, SEPTEMBER 7, 2023 7:03 A.M.

Cassidy awoke with a start, unsure where she was or the time. Piper was curled into Cassidy's stomach like a kitten. Sunlight streamed through the edges of the windows, exposing the double bed, wooden dresser, and floral wallpaper. Faith's house. Daisy missing. August cheated. His mistress the kidnapper.

Exhaustion sunk into Cassidy's bones like feet into wet sand, tugging her deeper, but now that reality hit afresh, she'd never be able to fall back asleep. Her mouth felt coated with slime—she never brushed her teeth last night. Her breasts, again, begged for release. She couldn't go through another day like yesterday.

Cassidy grabbed her phone from the bedside table. No messages. More importantly, no Daisy.

Cassidy visualized Daisy safe, warm, fed. But Vanessa kept sneaking into the picture, turning it dark and sinister. Having once been pregnant, would Vanessa feel motherly, protective, toward Daisy? Or was this about revenge, as Dr. Fuentes feared? Vanessa lost her baby and now August would too?

Cassidy clicked on her texts, pulling up the picture she sent herself of Vanessa. With a little restorative sleep, a memory came, unbidden, the image put together like a painting, stroke by stroke, until Cassidy recognized it. The grocery store. Piper in the cart. Pregnancy test in hand. August on the phone. Almost a year of trying and Cassidy's period was actually late. Five hours late, but Cassidy couldn't wait another minute to test.

After ending her call with August, a woman banged into her shoulder. *You could say sorry,* Cassidy remembered mumbling. The woman laughed an apology, but her dark eyes blazed, her hands clenched as if physically restraining herself. Then she said something about not seeing what is right in front of you until it's too late.

Cassidy pressed a hand to her heart. Vanessa. Warning her. When Daisy was the size of a popcorn seed, her life was already in jeopardy. Was Vanessa pregnant that day? August never said how far along she was at the abortion.

Cassidy opened up August's email, curious what he wrote to Vanessa. As she read his words, blood rushed to her head. They didn't want to scare Vanessa, but his email sounded like a player who had a spot open in his rotation. Nothing suggested he understood how deeply he hurt Vanessa. That he regretted ending the life of his child.

She had to fix this.

Cassidy eased out of bed, gently closing the door behind her. Downstairs, she smelled coffee, but didn't see Faith in the kitchen. Cassidy poured herself a mug and went to the den, booting up Faith's desktop computer. Cassidy set up a new email address under her maiden name and started typing. Vanessa was a grieving mother—something none of the cops understood. Cassidy had to speak with compassion, mother to mother.

Vanessa,

August told me about your relationship. The baby you lost. I'm so sorry. As a mother, I know the dream starts as soon as you get the positive pregnancy test. You imagine every moment in their lives, from snuggling, holding their hand on their first day of school, kissing their boo-boos, cheering them on during games.

August took this from you. He was wrong. And deserves to be punished.

But please, don't punish Daisy. She is the sweetest, most loved baby. She and Piper are my world.

Please bring her home. I promise, you'll never hear from me again. For what it's worth, I'd like you to find love. Become a mother again.

Cassidy

Cassidy felt sick as she reread her words. Some of which she didn't mean; many which she did. She should run it by Detective Lewis. It was his case. He ran a tight ship and wouldn't appreciate anyone going rogue. Dr. Fuentes too. He was the expert. But none of them were mothers. And it was her daughter. If Vanessa wrote back, she would come clean. Until then, it would be her secret.

With a firm click, she hit send.

CHAPTER FORTY-SIX

VANESSA
THURSDAY, SEPTEMBER 7, 2023 7:45 A.M.

After feeding Kiah hypoallergenic formula, I settled us on the floor of the living room and flipped on the TV, thirsty for news on the "person of interest." No luck. Only local stations here, not cable, and they were preoccupied with the weather.

I handed Kiah a rattle, which looked like a hypnotizing wand with black and white swirled balls on each end and rainbow zig-zags between. Kiah shook it with all her might, invariably dropped it, and then looked around like it disappeared from the face of this earth. We played that game a few times before I got bored.

Wanting to reread August's email, I pulled it up on my phone. Perhaps there was a clue, some deeper, hidden meaning I missed—

I dropped my phone. It landed face up, displaying an email from CASSIDY CHAPMAN SCHULTZ.

This wasn't happening. This wasn't happening. This wasn't happening.

I rested my head between my knees and tried to breathe. August writing an email. Coincidence? Unlikely, but possible. An email from his wife? No. Fucking. Way.

I should've deactivated my email. Who would've thought my old boss would hand out personal information? Prick.

Then again, these emails were a blessing. Gave me a heads up. They knew I took Kiah. But so what? We were safe. Hidden. With the house held in trust, searching my name was a dead-end—even for the cops. They wouldn't think to look up any gifts Mom made upon her death. And no one else knew I was here—

Unless the cashier became suspicious when I bought formula. Copied my license plate and reported it to the police? And they somehow tracked me on street cams?

Unless the sheriff yesterday had another cop follow me in an unmarked car.

Unless a tracker app was attached to August's email.

Or Cassidy's email.

My heart banged harder and faster with each thought. I screamed, yanking my hair at the roots. Kiah let out a scream to match mine, her mouth tugged in an exaggerated frown.

I was spiraling, knew it, hated it, but there was no brake to hit.

With no choice but to face my fears, I read Cassidy's email.

"What the hell…" Why was she acting like we were friends? Moms in solidarity. Her compassion wasn't real. If I returned Kiah, nobody would let me walk away, especially Cassidy. She'd want me to pay, like I wanted August to pay for his sins against me.

Bottom line, Cassidy and August were trying to trick me. Both liars. Schemers. Takers.

Focus. I had to stay a step ahead.

In the kitchen I found a screwdriver and jogged to the lake. I stood at the edge of the water, the sun warming my face, the lake gently lapping against the sand. I unscrewed the back of my phone and pulled out the SIM card. Then the battery to deactivate the GPS. I sent the texts to August through ViperByte, but I used this phone to set up the account. I wasn't sure the extent of the police's powers, but, if you believed the republicans, the government was spying on everyone. Better safe than sorry.

I launched the SIM card, battery, and phone into the air. They disappeared into the lake with a plunking sound that reminded me of skipping rocks on summer nights. Happier times.

Don't think about that.

I ran back to the house and grabbed Mom's car keys before dashing toward the garage. I couldn't risk using my car anymore.

I couldn't risk a lot of things. The thought brought me to a standstill, gasping for air, even though I was standing outside, breathing the cleanest, least polluted air climate change offered. I crumpled to the grass, digging my fingers into the soil. What was I going to do? Live here forever? Become a hermit? I hoped by next spring, Kiah's story would die; she would look different enough that I could put her in daycare and get a job. But what if the story never died? What if August and Cassidy never stopped searching for me?

Move.

Panting now, I jumped up and opened the garage, driving Mom's 2012 Toyota Camry next to my car. Mom gifted her car to me. I told Dad I sold it for cash, but it smelled like her perfume and I couldn't let it go. I kept it here, driving it when I needed to feel close to her. She loved driving, windows down, music up, wind blowing her hair. Said it was her happy place.

Kiah's sudden scream reminded me I was at the polar opposite of my happy place. I went to check on her. Shit spilled out the sides of her diaper. What was the point of a diaper if it couldn't contain diarrhea?

I grabbed pillows, cushions, magazines, whatever I could find, and started trashing the room. The thoughts spun faster—What was I going to do? I was trapped!—each throw working as an accelerant instead of a release.

How was I supposed to make Kiah better? Why couldn't she be normal?

I took a cement paperweight off the bookshelf, manipulated the rough grooves in my hand, and threw it at one of the windows facing the lake. The glass shattered, spilling outside. Jagged edges framed the window.

Kiah stopped crying for a moment, before unleashing an unholy scream. I turned, heart thrashing and started sobbing. What if a piece of glass hit her? I swooped her up from the floor, whispering apologies into her neck, not caring that shit likely covered my clothes.

Kiah needed me. Needed my protection. A level head. I had to do better.

CHAPTER FORTY-SEVEN

AUGUST
THURSDAY, SEPTEMBER 7, 2023 7:55 A.M.

August awoke alone in bed, a thunderous headache from too little sleep, too much stress, and the great unknown—where Daisy was. He stared at the ceiling, growing frustrated as he listened to the buzz of cop conversation in the living room. If Daisy had so much as a bruise when they found her, he'd beat Vanessa to within an inch of her life, make her stay in a purgatory of ungodly pain, never letting her experience the pleasure of death. This wasn't an eye for an eye, it was pure evil.

He picked up his phone, first checking his email. Work emails, interview requests from media, friends and family, and junk. No response from Vanessa. He shot off a quick email to Charlene, his office manager, telling her to reschedule his appointments for the week, pass off his closing scheduled for tomorrow to Rick, one of the other agents, and to let August know if there were any major issues.

Next, the news. Daisy was one of the top stories on CNN and FOX. Good for her. More eyes and ears meant a greater chance of bringing her home. Bad for him. Soon everyone would know his darkest secrets. What he kept hidden for years would make headlines, become a cautionary tale for women, fodder for talk show hosts.

He wished Cassidy would've come to bed last night. He wanted to hold her, explain, let his guard down. He couldn't do that with the detective breathing down their necks. Cassidy fed off the detective's fear, doubled down on her anger. Seemed set on divorcing him.

Would she go through with it? He couldn't imagine a life without her. Once the shock and rage passed, she'd realize, he wasn't responsible for Vanessa's actions.

And if she did divorce him? He'd still have the kids. No matter how angry she was with him, he was their father.

Too frustrated to lay there, he showered, dressed, and went to get coffee. The living room blinds were closed and someone put tarps over the second-floor windows. The lack of natural light made it feel as if a storm was brewing.

He nodded at a few officers and found the detective at the kitchen table, working on his laptop. "Good, you're awake," the detective said. "I'll text Cassidy and we can talk."

After brewing a coffee pod, August sat across from the detective with his mug, eager to hear the update. But no words passed between them. August deflated. There was no update. Nothing big anyway.

Cassidy came in through the patio door. Her hair was pulled into a ponytail and her face was flushed. "Did something—" Cassidy cut herself off as she took in the hole he punched in the wall last night. She pursed her lips, refusing to look at him as she held onto the back of the chair settled between him and the detective. "This was you?"

"I'll fix it." And he would fix it. He'd fix everything, if she gave him the chance.

"Right. Anyway," Cassidy said, "I think I sort of met Vanessa last fall…"

August's stomach felt lined with antifreeze as he listened to the story of Vanessa confronting Cassidy at the grocery store.

"Do you think she was upset because we were both pregnant?" Cassidy asked.

"No. Vanessa wasn't pregnant yet," August said. "She was only eight weeks at the abortion. She must have…" He couldn't finish the sentence, each thought bleeding into the next. Was Vanessa's pregnancy an accident? Or was this planned? Only twenty-two, why would she choose to get pregnant?

"She must have what?" the detective asked. "Done this on purpose?"

August threw up his hands. "I can't imagine why, but yeah. What are the chances she accidentally gets pregnant after seeing Cassidy with the test?"

How did she do it? They used condoms. He thought she was on the pill. A lie.

"You're sure she saw the test?" the detective asked.

"I was standing in that section, holding it, when she ran into me," Cassidy said.

"The impulsiveness tracks with Dr. Fuentes' theory," the detective said.

"I think…wait…" Cassidy pulled out her phone, furrowing her eyebrows in the same way Piper did when concentrating. "Yes! I was right. The first two mean comments I received came within twenty-four hours of the grocery store incident." Cassidy read the comments. *How will your kids feel when they grow up and listen to this? #unloved #unwanted #selfishmom* and *Imagine having a gorgeous husband and telling the world you have no interest in having sex with him. What. Could. Happen? #divorce* "They're probably all from Vanessa, under different screen names."

"Good catch," the detective said. "Though tech has to trace it back to an IP address linked to her to prove it."

"It's her," Cassidy said with finality. "This is all her doing." She grilled August with her eyes. "And yours, of course. Can't forget your role."

"I—"

"Update," the detective said quickly, diverting them from another argument. "First, we've received a credible tip. Yesterday afternoon, in Calumet County, a man reportedly tried helping a woman he thought had car trouble. The woman got upset when he noticed a baby in the car and sped away." The detective held up his hands. "This guy has a record so I wouldn't take his word as gospel, but he gave an accurate physical description of Vanessa and her vehicle."

"So, what, we have to pay this guy now because he saw her?" August asked. Cassidy glared at him. He shrugged. It was a reasonable question.

"No," the detective said. "The tip has to lead to Daisy's recovery and this doesn't give us any idea where she is now. But it leads to my second piece of information. We sent out that APB on her car and got a hit."

August leaned closer. "Where?"

"Langlade county."

"That's further north," August said as Cassidy asked, "When was this?"

"Late yesterday afternoon. She was pulled over for going seventeen above—"

"Was Daisy in the car?" Cassidy asked. Her fingers were white from gripping the chair.

"The sheriff said a baby was sleeping in the back—"

Cassidy pushed the chair against the table. "She's being reckless."

"And stupid," August added. Why speed if you're trying to avoid the cops?

"When questioned," the detective continued, "Vanessa said the baby's name was Kiah and that she was four months—"

"Kiah?" Cassidy inhaled sharply. "That's not—she's lying. Obviously."

"The sheriff followed her until Highway Z, where she turned north."

"And he let her go?" August's voice rose. Anger, disgust, frustration swirled inside him like a shaken soda can, ready to explode.

The detective grimaced. "The sheriff thought it was a speeding ticket and nothing more."

"That was the point of the APB, right?" August asked. "So cops would be on the lookout?"

"Yes," the detective said.

August scalded his tongue on the coffee as a new thought hit him. "Highway Z leads to Canada."

Cassidy turned to look at him, her eyes growing with fear.

"We've considered that possibility," the detective said. "But she would need either a birth certificate or a passport for Daisy, and a letter from her co-parent authorizing the stay in Canada. If she didn't have proper documentation, she and the baby would be pulled aside and not allowed into the country."

"If, if, if," August said, losing patience with the detective's careful answers. "There's also a chance they wave her through without looking."

"And she could have forged papers," Cassidy said, her cheeks flushed, likely with the same frustration he felt. "She's clearly been planning this for months. Probably since the abortion."

"We've been in contact with border officials. They have Vanessa and Daisy's pictures and details, as well as the car information. Everyone is on high alert."

Cassidy walked over to the cabinet. "Why doesn't that make me feel better?"

August watched as she filled a cup with water at the fridge. "Because she already escaped the cops once."

"Final update," the detective said. "The print we lifted off the canopy of the stroller didn't match either of yours, but also wasn't in our database. And your shoes didn't match the impressions we found in the woods."

Cassidy didn't show any visible signs of relief. August knew she'd go to prison for a crime she didn't commit if it meant Daisy coming home safe. "We told you neither of us was involved," August said, pushing back his chair and going to stand by Cassidy. He tentatively rested a hand on her lower back, giving her the support he would've loved to have had last night. Cassidy looked down at her cup, but didn't move away. "Yet you continued to waste resources, investigating us when you could've used that time finding Daisy."

The detective stood up, facing them across the island. "We investigate everything."

"It's okay to admit you made a mistake," August said. "Hell, that's all I've been doing. Join the party."

Cassidy set her cup on the island with a thud. "Is that all?"

"For now," the detective said.

Without another word, Cassidy walked up the stairs. August ran his hands through his hair, avoiding the detective's gaze. There was nothing he could do beyond wait. As Vanessa intended. She wanted him to know what it was like to have someone else hold the power, dictate the terms of the relationship. Except when he was in control, it wasn't life or death—

The din of conversation drained to a buzz. The officers became shadowy shapes. She wouldn't take it that far, would she? Kill his daughter? To prove a point? No. If she was psychotic, he would've noticed.

The thought provided no comfort.

CHAPTER FORTY-EIGHT

VANESSA
JULY 2023

My baby was coming early. Two months early to be exact. Two months she'd spend with August and Cassidy, not getting proper love and attention, before I could take her home.

Alexa, define agony.

I parked facing the back of August's house, sandwiched between two other cars for camouflage, watching through my binocular glasses. Last time I saw Cassidy, she was fit to burst, one hand cupping the swell of her belly, the other her lower back. She had a full-on waddle as she walked, which, must admit, gave me a fair amount of pleasure to watch.

That was two days ago.

Yesterday, someone attached pink balloons to the lamp post in the front yard.

A girl.

My girl.

Fuck them both.

To distract myself, I pulled up the notes app on my phone and ran through the checklist. New last name? Check. The paperwork came through and I was officially Vanessa Jennings. It felt good to cut ties with Dad; Mom was the one that raised me, after all, so I should use her name. Fake ID as a fail-safe? Check. Mackenzie Roeper was at my disposal. New bartending job? Check. New phone? Visa gift cards? Eight-thousand in cash? Check. Check.

Check. Bassinet? Baby clothes? Swing? I went around to yard sales, throwing myself a baby shower.

I felt the sting of tears as I read the next item. *Stop texting/calling/seeing friends.* While I ghosted everyone, my lease wasn't up until the end of summer and my dick landlord wouldn't let me out early. Any of my "friends"—or August, if he actually loved me—could've come looking for me. But no. None of them cared. Not even a welfare check. What if I was dead inside my apartment? How long would I lay there decomposing? Bitches. All of 'em.

"I'm lonely," I admitted out loud, taken aback by the sound of my voice in the quiet car. Outside of work, I never socialized. Rarely spoke.

For the millionth time, I wondered whether my baby was worth it. Being a single parent, living at the lake house through the frigid winter, no dating prospects. Honestly, no life prospects. What would I do for money? Hadn't figured that one out yet.

I could go to jail. The plan was riddled with holes. With more surveillance, I'd learn Cassidy's new routine with two kids, but her podcast also taught me that nothing was routine with a newborn. And while I figured out the garage code, I had no plan for if the door was locked. If Cassidy heard me come in the house. If she was holding my baby. If, if, if—

I shivered. Too many ifs.

Mom would be disappointed. She didn't raise a criminal.

I rested my head against the steering wheel. Move. On. Let. This. Go. Call my friends. Get my old job back at Top Shelf. Be young, single, hot. I'd meet another guy, right? Someone better. Everyone had dating horror stories from their twenties. August would be Cassidy's problem. My daughter as distant as a dream.

As I turned the car on, Mom clasped her hands over mine. A warm rush of love filled me from the inside out. I was going to leave. And never come back. For real this time.

I looked up, checking the rearview mirror, about to pull out, when I saw August's car approaching. Immediately, I ducked, hoping he was too preoccupied to clock my car.

When I heard his car pass, I looked up, watching through my binocular glasses as he parked in the driveway. August went around to open Cassidy's door and then the rear door. Cassidy stepped out, back to her beautiful self. Hair glistening, skin glowing, legs lean in dark shorts, the slightest of tummy swell.

Fuck you.

August grabbed the detachable car seat. Cassidy rested her head against August's shoulder, both gazing down at my baby. I dug my nails into the seat, clawing at the leather so I wouldn't run after them, yank her from his arms, and scream, You never wanted her!

Cassidy said something and August brushed a kiss on her cheek, then whispered in her ear.

Fuck you. Fuck you. Fuck you.

He guided Cassidy inside, one hand holding the car seat, the other on the small of her back.

Such gentleness from a man who killed his own child. Who fucked other women as a game. Who lied and said he'd give me everything; baby, marriage, happiness.

No. No way was I moving on. I wanted my baby. And I would get my baby.

I grabbed my phone, pulling up Cassidy's website. In the comments section, I posted, *I'm worried about the health and safety of your children. #CPS #knock-knock #byebyebaby*

Would Cassidy leave him if she knew the truth? My fingers ached to confess everything, but it wouldn't get me what I wanted.

My baby. If only there was a way to do both, ruin August's life and take mine back. I had two months to fine-tune my plan.

After today, one thing was certain. No one would walk away unharmed.

CHAPTER FORTY-NINE

CASSIDY
THURSDAY, SEPTEMBER 7, 2023 9:40 A.M.

Cassidy stood by the windows in Piper's room, peeking through the side of the drapes to view the street. Police. Media vans. Reporters. Sympathizers. Curious people with nothing better to do. And then…could it be? A few of Cassidy's friends, women she specifically told not to come over, huddled in a small group across the street. She pressed her hand to the window pane, yearning for yesterday, where they'd discuss breastfeeding, cellulite on their thighs, difficulty finding time alone. Never again. Daisy's kidnapping drew them apart. A street separated them, but it could've been an ocean, a continent, a galaxy. Unwillingly, she joined a group—parents of kids with cancer, tragic accidents. She couldn't go back to "normal."

But she could protect Piper. Give her a sense of normalcy amid the chaos. Somewhere she'd be free. Able to play outside.

And away from the mess with her and August. Hearing August air his dirty laundry brought about a rollercoaster of emotions. She hated him for ruining their marriage. Putting their children in danger. Obliterating the trust she had in herself. Her faith in…the goodness of people. But then he'd stand up for her and she'd remember why she loved him. That he wasn't all bad. Then, he'd say something completely self-absorbed and thoughtless, like sarcastically baiting the detective into admitting he made a mistake. The depth of his narcissism and self-pity, the lack of awareness of the bigger picture, repulsed her.

Piper had to go.

Cassidy pulled out her phone and texted Mom. *Can Piper come stay with you? It's not healthy for her to be here.*

Yes! Mom texted. *Anything you need.*

No talking about Daisy. She doesn't know.

Mom texted a thumbs up and prayer emoji. *Hopefully we'll get good news soon.*

Cassidy pulled the princess suitcase from the closet and set it on Piper's bed. How long would she be gone? Cassidy grabbed three underwear. Three days without playing with Piper. Kissing her. Inhaling the fresh fruit of her skin. Hearing her giggle. But Piper would have her grandparents' love. And Cassidy? Who would take care of her?

It didn't matter. Right now, everything was about protecting Piper and rescuing Daisy.

"What are you doing?" August asked, appearing in the doorway.

Cassidy grabbed two of Piper's dresses from the closet. "I'm taking Piper to my parents. She'll go crazy if she spends another day inside."

"Agreed," August said. "But you rest. I'll take her."

"To my parents?" Cassidy shot him a look. "I don't think so."

He ran a hand over his mouth. "Did you…tell them about me?"

Cassidy turned around, selecting two nightgowns from the dresser. "No. But I will. It's not like we can keep it a secret."

"Please. Let me help." He rested his hands on her shoulders. "I'd like to spend some time with Piper."

She felt the tickle of his breath against the back of her neck. It gave her goosebumps. And not in a good way. "I need to get away." She didn't say, from you. It was implied when she walked over to Piper's stuffed animals, scattered in the corner by the bookshelf. She grabbed the monkey. Piper already had Millie, her stuffed elephant, but Cassidy knew her favorites changed by the hour.

Down deep, Cassidy feared Piper becoming a mean girl in high school, casting out friends with the same ruthlessness she did her stuffed animals. Cassidy almost laughed, remembering when Piper's behavior ten years from now was her biggest worry.

Cassidy struggled to zip the suitcase and August came over to finish the job. "What are we going to tell Piper?" August asked, gesturing outside.

Cassidy thought about it. "They're making a movie? That would explain the cameras and people."

August gave her a condescending half-smile. "She watches cartoons."

Cassidy threw her hands up. "What do you suggest?"

"How about a fraction of the truth?" He sat on Piper's bed. "The best lies have a bit of the truth."

"You would know," she said under her breath.

He gave her a wounded look. Too bad. He lied for years. If Daisy wasn't missing, she'd say more than a few sarcastic responses.

"Let's tell her a dog ran away and the police are looking for it." His face lit up. "She knows dogs run away from reading *Harry the Dirty Dog*."

Cassidy inspected her fingernail, hating his brilliance. "Fine. Let's go."

August trailed her as she walked downstairs. Detective Lewis leaned up against the kitchen island, fingers working his phone. "I'm going to take Piper to my parents," Cassidy said.

Detective Lewis stopped typing. "How long will you be gone?"

"It's a twenty-five minute drive. Faster with no traffic. I was going to stay for a bit. Unless you need me back?"

"Keep your phone on." He looked into the living room. "I'll get a couple officers to escort you."

"We're leaving from Faith's house since my car is there."

"I'll text you when they're ready."

With that, August and Cassidy exited through the patio door. Reporters positioned on the street to the right of the house started shouting questions. "Who's the person of interest? Do you have a statement for the kidnapper? Do you think Daisy's alive?"

August grabbed Cassidy's hand, pulling her along. Each question felt like bullying, kicking them when already down. How could these human beings, presumably with loved ones, not have any respect? Compassion?

At Faith's house, August walked in the back door without knocking. Faith and Piper were sitting at the kitchen table, playing Candy Land. "Mommy! Daddy!" Piper ran to hug them both.

"Hi, baby." Cassidy picked up Piper. She was too big to be held, but Cassidy wanted the weight of her child on her hip, legs and arms wrapped around her body, Piper's breath on her face. "I have a surprise for you." At the magic word "surprise," Piper's blue eyes grew large. "You're going to stay with Grandma and Grandpa."

"Grandma and Grandpa!" Piper shrieked, wriggling out of Cassidy's arms. "She'll probably let me have ice cream. She does that. Even when you tell her no."

"I'll have to talk with her," Cassidy said.

Faith winked. "It's a grandma's prerogative."

August ruffled Piper's hair. "You'll save some ice cream for me, right?"

Piper's smile widened, exposing every baby tooth. "Nope." Then her smile fell. "But what about school? It's Suzy's birthday tomorrow. She's bringing in rice crispy treats."

Did this child only think about sugar? "I'm sure Grandma will make rice crispy treats if you ask her extra nice."

"And Daisy can't have any because she's too young," Piper said.

"That's right," Cassidy said.

"They're all for me."

"Yup," August agreed.

"But I'll give her kisses to make up for it."

"Who?" Cassidy asked.

Piper rolled her eyes. "Daisy. When I get to Grandma's."

Cassidy blinked away a swear, having forgot her excuse yesterday. "I picked up Daisy from Grandma's this morning," August said, rescuing Cassidy. "And now it's your turn to stay, lucky girl."

"Why can't we both stay?" Piper asked.

"Remember," August said, "we talked about how Mommy needs extra time with Daisy, because she's a baby?"

Piper pouted. "Yeah."

"We'll have special time soon, just you and me," Cassidy promised, bending down to rub her thumb against Piper's cheek.

"Now," August said. "When you and Mommy drive to Grandma's it's going to be an adventure." He spoke as if starting a bedtime story. "Some police officers and neighbors are out on the street because a dog ran away."

Piper considered this. "Whose dog?"

Cassidy said, "I don't—"

"Remember that house, a couple blocks from here, with the friendly Golden Retriever?" August asked.

"Goldie," Piper said.

August snapped his fingers and pointed at Piper. "That's the one. I bet by the time you get back from Grandma's, they'll have found her."

"I think she's in the woods," Piper said. "It's easy to get lost in there."

"That's why you only go into the woods with Daddy or Mommy," August said.

"Wherever she is, they'll find her soon," Cassidy said. "It's their job."

Piper frowned. "Whose job?"

"The police."

"It's the police's job to find dogs?" Piper's voice was high, incredulous.

Cassidy momentarily forgot they weren't talking about Daisy. "The police help solve problems. So, yes."

Detective Lewis texted to say the officers were ready and waiting at the bottom of the driveway. She told August to move her car, which was parked in the driveway from when Faith picked up Piper from school, into the garage. That way they'd avoid further media exposure.

"Alright, let's go potty," Cassidy said. "It's a long drive."

Piper crossed her arms. "I don't have to go."

She guided Piper toward the bathroom. "Let's try."

Inside the bathroom, Piper sat on the toilet, humming until the pee came. After Piper finished, Cassidy hugged Faith and thanked her. "Stay strong," Faith whispered.

Inside the garage, August picked Piper up, blowing kisses on her tummy before buckling her into her seat. Cassidy massaged her temple, feeling dizzy. How could he cheat? Did he think of the girls? The example he was setting?

"Love you, Pipes," August said before closing Piper's door.

They faced each other. Cassidy said a quick goodbye, in case Piper was watching, and walked around to her seat. She then grabbed Piper's iPad from her suitcase, cued up *Encanto*, and handed it to her. Even though the officers were waiting, she didn't start the car. She wanted Piper to get into the movie so maybe she wouldn't notice the chaos outside.

A few minutes later, she took a deep breath and nodded at August to open the garage. She reversed the car, thinking they should've blindfolded Piper; made it a game.

Several cameras and hand-held phones were trained at her car as she pulled onto the street, sandwiched between the two cop cars. Cassidy watched Piper in the rearview mirror. Her eyebrows were scrunched together, her tongue poking out the corner of her mouth, as she took in the scene. "There's so many people!"

Cassidy gripped the steering wheel like she was hanging from the edge of a cliff, even though they were crawling along at five miles an hour. "Sure are."

"I hope they find Goldie."

"They will." Cassidy pushed her Audrey Hepburn sunglasses up the brim of her nose, ensuring no one would photograph the pain in her eyes. "They have to."

Once Cassidy drove past their block, Piper's attention returned to the movie. Cassidy saw people mowing their lawns, going for walks, toddlers playing in yards. The Starbucks line was several cars deep. The radio jockey reported another Hollywood divorce. Life carried on normally for everyone. Everyone except Cassidy, who felt Daisy's absence in the same way one would miss a limb or vital organ—unable to go a second without feeling the loss.

CHAPTER FIFTY

AUGUST
THURSDAY, SEPTEMBER 7, 2023 11:15 A.M.

August sat on his bed, TV tuned to CNN, watching a replay of Cassidy leaving Faith's house. Media vans lined both blocks of their corner lot, while reporters screamed at her car, giving her little leeway to navigate. Although sunglasses covered Cassidy's eyes, the tightness in her jaw gave away her stress. Piper, thankfully, was shielded in the back by tinted windows.

He rubbed his forehead. Surreal how fast this story steamrolled into the national consciousness. CNN, FOX, and CNBC ran sensational headlines. "Day Two of Search for Baby Daisy." "Police Investigating Person of Interest." "$10,000 Reward for Baby Daisy."

And surreal how slow the police were moving. They knew Vanessa was responsible, but couldn't find her. No clear plan *how* to locate her.

August checked his email again. Nothing from Vanessa. How could she hate him enough to kidnap his child? He went to the abortion with her, took care of her after, saved her from a life of single motherhood and poverty. Why didn't she run with this gift? Why act now, nine months later—

Oh, fuck.

He collapsed backward, staring at the ceiling fan. September 6th. Vanessa's due date. August ignored the date when the doctor said it, not wanting to hear anything that humanized it. A clump of cells.

Nothing like Piper or Daisy. He remembered leaning against the door while the doctor performed the exam, unwilling to hold Vanessa's hand, lest she construe it as support to continue the pregnancy. He looked out the window when the image came on the screen, convincing himself the thump of the heartbeat was traffic. The bass of a song. His own terrified heartbeat. He stayed silent while the doctor explained Vanessa's "options." Every fiber of his body ached to run, but when he met Vanessa's eyes, he saw she was terrified too.

Yes, he lied to Vanessa. Promised the sun and the moon, to get her to have the abortion. But what was he supposed to do? Let her continue with the pregnancy until she came to her senses? Until it was too late? No. He couldn't risk it. Unlike Aubree, this was his baby, his mistake, and he had to fix it. Should he have waited to break it off? Maybe. But the pregnancy held a mirror up to his life. It reflected how easily he could lose his marriage, the privilege of seeing his kids every day. He refused to let some cruel twist of fate ruin that.

A knock on the door. August groaned, but sat up and muted the TV. "Yeah?"

Detective Lewis stepped inside. "All the women on your list, other than Vanessa, have an alibi and are fully cooperating with police. None had accounts with ViperByte."

"Confirms what we already know."

The detective grunted his agreement. "More updates. Vanessa Jennings, née Prescott, legally changed her last name this past spring."

"How'd you find out?"

"My team did a deep dive on each woman, including legal," he said. "Vanessa Prescott has a small rap sheet. Drug possession—marijuana; unlawful possession of prescription drugs. Underage drinking. Nothing violent, for what it's worth. Dr. Fuentes thinks she probably used drugs and alcohol to self-medicate."

"She did like to party." Some of the hottest sex was when they were both high. He shook his head, erasing the thought. She better not be using around Daisy. She never struck him as an addict. Then again, she never struck him as mentally unstable.

"Cops are also interviewing her father in Florida. Hopefully, he'll have some idea of her whereabouts."

Given the way Vanessa spoke about her dad, August doubted he could help. "The due date for Vanessa's baby was yesterday."

The detective rubbed his chin. "Timing fits."

"Don't bullshit me," August said, taking the opportunity with Cassidy gone to voice his real fear. "If Vanessa's crazy enough to steal my baby to replace hers, what are the chances we get Daisy back?" He cleared his throat. "Alive?"

The detective met his eyes, his voice low, but firm. "The longer this goes on, the worse the odds."

August nodded. Although he would never forgive the detective for double-crossing him, he earned an ounce of respect back by giving August the truth. "Then go." August gestured toward the door. "Get back to work."

"Keep thinking. If Vanessa is taunting you with these texts, punishing you, perhaps you know where she took Daisy." He tapped his knuckles against the wall two times and left.

Did Vanessa want him to solve this? Come to her? Was the location buried in the recesses of his mind?

On autopilot, he walked into his closet, shut the door, and sat in the darkness, something he hadn't done since he lived with his parents. It started when he was young, probably kindergarten, trying to escape his parents' arguments. As a teenager, it became the place where he would smoke weed and think deep thoughts.

In eliminating the noise—Daisy's safety; Cassidy's anger; the cops; the media surrounding his house; the abrupt end of life as he knew it—he hoped to recover conversations with Vanessa, come up with a location.

CHAPTER FIFTY-ONE

VANESSA
THURSDAY, SEPTEMBER 7, 2023 11:20 A.M.

I paced in the kitchen with Kiah, doing everything to get her to stop crying. It felt like snuggling a heating pad. Did the fever get worse? Or was it the effort from hysterically crying? When I was upset, I felt like I was sunbathing on the equator.

Kiah wailed. I put the pacifier in her mouth, but she spit it out. None of the glass from the window cut her. I changed her diaper. She was fine. A little scared, but guess what? I was scared too.

How could I help Kiah feel better?

All at once, the solution came, so simple, I felt like an idiot for not thinking about it before. I couldn't take her to a hospital, but there had to be a chatroom or hotline for new parents. Bare minimum, a Reddit thread.

Except I had no cell phone. No internet access. A privilege, much like breathing, I took for granted until now. And I didn't want to call on the landline in case someone traced it.

Maybe a gas station employee would let me use their phone? But they might become suspicious when I tried to delete the search history. Too risky.

I carried Kiah into the living room and looked at the lake, chewing my lower lip until I tasted blood. I should stuff my pockets with rocks and take a nice long walk into the lake. End it all. That'd be one way to stop being a disaster. To stop people from taking advantage of me. To stop hurting.

I closed my eyes. No pain, ever again.

Kiah, perhaps sensing my desperation or giving into exhaustion, stopped crying and rested her head on my shoulder, her breath painting my neck. If I killed myself, Kiah would die too. No one would find her here.

I kissed the crown of her head as she fell asleep. "I'll protect you."

I needed to fix the window, but it wasn't like I could call a handyman. Maybe saran wrap and duct tape? A short-term solution.

I walked back toward the kitchen, but stopped short at Mom's bedroom door. If there was ever a time I needed her advice, it was right now. I opened the door, taking in the queen-sized bed, her end table with a small stack of books she was reading at the time of her death. I sat on her bed, fingering the titles. *28 Summers. The Seven Husbands of Evelyn Hugo. Things You Save in a Fire.* Mom loved romance. Must be where I got my unattainable ideas of love and men. I flipped open the top cover, seeing the bar code for the library—

I froze. The library. They had computers. And they used to have a payphone. Would it still be there? I had to try.

I set Kiah in the middle of Mom's bed, confident nothing bad could happen with Mom watching over her. Then I fastened my wig and rushed outside. Nothing less I wanted than to wear this itchy thing, especially on a warm day, but there would be witnesses at the library. Employees. Bored geriatrics with nothing better to do than people watch between *AARP* articles. Topped with my black baseball cap, I looked nothing like me.

But what if the police got footage of me leaving Cassidy's house and now they were looking for a blonde? Should I change my appearance? Maddening not knowing what the cops knew.

Twenty minutes later, I parked Mom's car at the library. It was an old red-brick building, one story, with windows arranged in a repeating rectangular pattern that reminded me of my high school.

And prison. Foreshadowing?

Stop it.

Once inside, I passed through the detectors and entered the open-spaced library. Save for the addition of computers in the middle of the room, nothing looked updated. From the towering wooden bookcases to the hutch desks to the occasional flicker in the lights above to the musty smell, I could have been walking through here as a girl, holding Mom's hand. I sat down and pulled up Chrome, typing "pediatric question hotline" in the search bar. Bingo. Halfway down the page, "Pediatric Injury and Emergency Care Hotline." I clicked the link. A chat box opened on the right with a nurse aviator asking, *How can I help?*

I typed, *Baby with diarrhea. Tried hypoallergenic formula but still sick. What should I do?* I clicked send with a smile. Getting advice would be easier than I thought. Elation lasted less than a second. A bright red exclamation appeared next to my message. Error. Message could not send. Try again.

I clicked it again, this time pressing my index finger on the enter key.

Same error message.

I wanted to bash the keyboard against the table. Why couldn't I catch a break?

Fine. Whatever. I'd call. I wrote the toll-free number on a scrap of paper and cleared my search. In the back of the library, a sign advertising restrooms, copies, and fax, hung above a wood door—like I remembered. I turned the door handle and looked to the right, seeing the payphone on the wall. I picked up the receiver, nearly weeping in relief when I heard a dial tone. I dialed. Then, from a menu of options, I chose infant care.

After a short wait, where I was serenaded by a symphony, a woman said, "Pediatric injury and emergency care hotline. This is Alice, how can I help?"

"Hi, yes, my daughter is two months—" Wait, I shouldn't give her real age! "Sorry, three months now, it goes fast, and she's having diarrhea whenever she feeds. I tried switching to a hypoallergenic formula, thinking that might be the issue, but she had diarrhea again."

"How long has this been going on?" Alice asked.

"Since yesterday."

"Does she have any other symptoms? Vomiting, blood in her stool, pain with touch, rash, fever, irritability, inconsolable when she cries."

I bit my lip, hating that some of them applied. "She has a rash, like, on her arms." I omitted that it spread. "It doesn't seem to hurt her when I touch it, though. She's hot, but not like fever hot." I was babbling, trying to get an answer while also minimizing Kiah's issues so Alice didn't call child protective services. Ironic if someone called CPS on me when I threatened Cassidy with the same. "And, yes, she's crying, but—" I thought about all the times I watched Kiah cry on the baby monitor. "She was born fussy."

"When did the rash start?"

"Yesterday." Did she need a hearing aid? I already said that. Was all this effort for nothing because I got an idiot answering my call?

"What's her temperature?"

An easy answer—if I took her temperature. What was normal? Ninety-seven? Ninety-eight? I needed something higher than normal, but not alarming. "A hundred."

"Did you give her any baby Tylenol?"

Stupid me, I bought Benadryl to keep her quiet. No Tylenol. Mother of the year here. "Not yet. Should I?"

"That will help with the fever," Alice said.

"How much should I give her?"

"How much does she weigh?"

Again, a good mother would know this offhand. I did not. She was definitely heavier than the ten-pound kettle ball at the gym. But the fifteen pound one? A stretch. "Umm…I think like thirteen or fourteen pounds."

"Okay. You can give her 2.5mL every four to six hours."

2.5, 2.5, 2.5, I repeated in my head, having no phone to record it in.

"Did you call her pediatrician?" Alice asked.

"No."

"They'd probably have a better idea, based on her history, what might be going on." Alice sounded impatient.

Why didn't you call her pediatrician, Vanessa? Hmm? "Sorry…I'm a little frazzled. We're out of town and I Googled the symptoms and found your hotline." I took a breath, trying to remain polite. Cassidy preached on her podcast about not judging moms. Hadn't Alice heard? Every mom was trying her best! Effort was all the rage. "Would you rather I called her pediatrician?" Please say no, please say no, please say no.

I could feel her hesitation, but Alice said, "Let's talk through it, but then you should follow up with your pediatrician. When did the diarrhea start?"

Yesterday—as far as I knew. Suddenly, it hit me. Maybe Kiah was sick when I took her. Maybe this wasn't my fault! Maybe Cassidy was to blame. "Yesterday morning. She cries for food, eats, but then it all comes out."

"And she's formula fed?"

"Yes, well, she just switched from breastmilk."

"When?"

I rolled my eyes. "Yesterday."

"How long did you wean her off?"

I rested my head against the wall. This conversation was exhausting. "What do you mean?"

"Generally, we recommend getting rid of one breastmilk feed a week, so it usually takes four to six weeks to transition from breastmilk to formula. This gives you, Mom—"

I blushed. She was the first person to recognize my role, that I was the most important person in Kiah's life.

"—a chance to stop breastfeeding without developing mastitis or other unpleasant side effects. It also gives the baby's stomach a chance to adjust. Formula tends to be thicker than breastmilk and initially harder to digest. Breastmilk is specifically designed for your baby, and given how young your daughter is, the abrupt change might have led to her upset stomach."

I stared at the white wall in front me, the tiny cracks symbolizing the crumbling facade of blaming this on Cassidy. My fault. Me. I sucked as a mom. I bought some clothes, diapers, formula, toys, read articles about sleep schedules and developmental milestones, listened to Cassidy's grating podcast, and thought I was prepared.

Stupid. Forever a mess.

"I'm going back to work next week." With another lie, sweat rose on my scalp, collecting at my hairline, making it feel like the wig was crawling with lice. "And I figured it'd be a good idea to start with the formula on vacation. You know, get her used to the idea."

"Try switching back to breastfeeding for a few days," Alice said. "Once her stomach has settled, mix in the formula gradually."

"I…I don't understand." I read about how it might be hard to go from breastfeeding to bottle, but nothing warned against the abrupt switch from breastmilk to formula. Formula and breastmilk were interchangeable, right? "Most babies drink formula. Is it possible she has an allergy?"

"Possible," Alice said. "But the first step is to wean her off the breastmilk. Then you would know if it was the formula making her sick and could try different options from there. You probably got a pamphlet about this at the hospital, when you gave birth."

I swallowed a dozen fuck yous. "Why is this happening to me?" I thought I said it in my head, but when Alice laughed, I realized I said it out loud.

"She'll adjust, but you have to give her time," Alice said. "Is this your first?"

My second. But I took an oath of silence regarding my first baby. "Yes."

"It won't be fun lugging the breast pump to work, but it's what needs to happen."

I said nothing. Breastmilk wasn't possible.

"And with the diarrhea," Alice continued, "I'm worried about dehydration. When she cries, does she produce tears?"

Was Kiah's face wet? I couldn't remember. The stabbing pitch of her cries made logical thought or observations impossible. "I think so."

"She has a fever, which is another sign of dehydration. Is she sleeping more or less than usual?"

This felt like taking a test for which I didn't study. "Umm…maybe a bit more."

"Another sign."

Wrong again. I banged the phone against my forehead. "Can I give her water? Wouldn't that help with dehydration?"

A pause. "It's not safe to give babies less than six months water," Alice said.

"Right, I forgot." I knew enough not to ask what would happen if I continued to give her formula, but wouldn't she adjust? Without breastmilk, my choices were limited.

"I'm sorry." Alice did not sound sorry. "I never got your name?"

Alarms fired inside my head. End the conversation. Hang up. Now. "Diane," I whispered.

"Okay, Diane, I think you should take her to the ER. It's probably the switch to formula, but if she's had diarrhea for twenty-four hours, along with a rash, fever, and is sleepy, it's best to get her checked out. Safe rather than sorry with these little ones, right?"

"Right."

"Can you give me your location?" Alice asked. "I can recommend the nearest hospital since you're not familiar with the area."

I slammed the phone into the receiver. Every emergency room in the state was on the lookout for a baby matching Kiah's description. I might as well march her into a police station.

What do I do? Save her or save myself?

As I walked through the library, a third option presented itself. I sat back down at the computers, navigated to ViperByte.com, and wrote an email asking for help.

CHAPTER FIFTY-TWO

CASSIDY
THURSDAY, SEPTEMBER 7, 2023 11:45 A.M.

Cassidy parked in the driveway of her childhood home, a four-bedroom ranch opposite a park, while the cops stayed on the street. Before opening Piper's door, Cassidy forced a smile. Her cheeks felt like moving cement. "We're here!"

Piper, for once, discarded her iPad without a fit, unbelted, and flew out of the car, letting herself in the side door that led directly to the kitchen. Cassidy followed, carrying Piper's suitcase.

Walking inside her childhood home, an unexpected swelling of guilt filled Cassidy's belly. At home, she felt claustrophobic, murderous spending time around August, but she was closer to Daisy. Being here felt like giving up. Moving on with life. Caring for Piper was necessary, but didn't ease her guilt. It anchored every breath.

Mom rushed over and hugged Cassidy. Cassidy bit the inside of her cheek to stop the tears. "Be normal for Piper," she grunted.

"Right." Mom stepped back and discreetly wiped her eyes. "Lunch. I'm sure you're both starved." Mom had a spread on the kitchen table—ham, cheese, croissants, watermelon and strawberries, chicken salad—fit for Easter Sunday. "Eat, eat," Mom said, pulling out a chair for Piper. Then she looked at Cassidy and added, "You need to keep up your energy."

Everything and nothing looked good. Cassidy was locked between thoughts of stuffing her face until she couldn't feel anything but aching fullness and puking from laying eyes on the food.

"Pipster!" Dad emerged in the kitchen doorway. Piper ran and jumped into his arms. "How's my favorite girl?"

After setting Piper down, he kissed Cassidy's cheek and whispered in her ear, "How's my most favorite girl?"

Cassidy shook her head, not trusting herself to speak, and took a seat at the table. Piper sat next to her, taking in the food with the scathing eyes of a Le Cordon Bleu chef eating at Taco Bell. "I want a hot dog," Piper said.

"I can make a hot dog!" Mom opened the fridge. Cassidy watched as her shoulders deflated. "Shoot. We don't have any. I'll pop out to the store."

"Mom. It's fine. Piper will eat a sandwich."

Piper shook her head. "No way."

"It's five minutes away." Mom grabbed her purse. "Be back in a jiff."

"I'm coming too," Piper said, her brain likely fixated on the candy aisle.

Dad took Piper's seat next to Cassidy and made a plate of food. "Let her buy hot dogs. She wants to help."

"Please don't buy—" Cassidy gave up. Who cared if Piper ate the entire candy section? She was alive, healthy, *here*. "Take my car. It has Piper's seat. And make an excuse for the P-O-L-I-C-E being outside."

"Right." Mom took Cassidy's car keys from the table. Cassidy quickly sent Detective Lewis a text, saying Piper was going to the store with her mom, but they were driving Cassidy's car. Best to keep him in the loop.

Piper skipped out of the house, shooting Cassidy a victorious smile before closing the door. Despite the cuteness, Cassidy immediately burst into tears. Everything she held in around August, Piper, the police, came out in messy sobs.

Dad wrapped his arms around her. She rested her head against his chest, inhaling the familiar smell of Old Spice. "They know who took her," Cassidy said. "It's a woman. She—"

Cassidy looked up at Dad. His raw concern and naiveté broke her heart. Did Dad ever cheat on Mom? He was good looking, for a man in his sixties. Full head of hair, though gray, kind blue eyes, a good smile, reasonably fit. He probably had opportunities, though Cassidy didn't trust her judgment anymore to say whether he seized them. Mom and Dad bickered, but most of the time, they seemed happy.

She didn't want to know. Today, she needed to believe in the goodness of her parents.

"August cheated," Cassidy said, watching as Dad's eyes widened. "Several times, I guess. Not that I had any idea." She hiccupped a sob and Dad rubbed her back. "But this woman, he got her pregnant. Made her get an abortion. The police think she's unstable and seeking revenge." Each sentence a domino, one knocking down the next, until there was nothing left but the inevitable conclusion that Daisy might never come home.

"I'm shocked. And frankly—" Dad's fist hit the table with a thud. "Pretty goddamn pissed off. To cheat on you? The gull."

Tears came faster with Dad's ardent support. August fooled everyone. Being one of many though, didn't dull her pain. "She stole Daisy from her crib." Cassidy grabbed a croissant, wanting a distraction. "Didn't care that she hurt me, Piper, you guys. All to punish August."

"What does August say?"

"It doesn't matter." She tore flakes off the roll. "All I care about is getting Daisy home."

He held both hands in tight fists. "Have they contacted this woman?"

Cassidy thought about the email she sent this morning. She set down the croissant. "She texted August. I'll tell you about it, but first, I need to use your computer."

"Okay." If he was thrown by the abrupt request, he didn't show it. As she walked away, he said, "I'd like to call August. Have a chat with him."

She stopped in the doorway, briefly closing her eyes, hearing the restrained anger in his tight voice. From teachers to coaches to friends, Dad was her hype man and muscle. But she didn't need more stress right now. "After, Dad, okay?" She didn't specify what after meant.

He opened his mouth, then pursed his lips and said, "Okay."

She walked down the hall to Dad's office, a bedroom they converted so he could check his IRA, watch YouTube videos, and set his fantasy football lineup. After sitting down, she looked outside. One police car was parked on the street; the other must have followed Mom to the grocery store. At the park, she saw moms pushing their kids on swings, chasing them, tickling their bellies as they went down the slides. Until yesterday, that was her life. Moments of joy between the rush of feeding, bathing, calming, running errands, and generally not losing her mind after being forced to repeat herself hundreds of times.

And she took it for granted. Never again.

She logged into her new email account, typing the password, DAISYISSAFE0702. A prayer. A premonition.

Spam. Sex toys and loans and insurance ads. Disappointment made her movements slow. She opened each email to be sure.

Does she have any food allergies? Skin sensitivity?

Cassidy flinched. She looked at the sender. A random string of numbers. Just like the texts. No subject line. No greeting or signature. No overt reference to Daisy. But it was Vanessa, alright. No one else had this email address.

Cassidy reread the email. Food allergies? Was Vanessa giving Daisy food? She couldn't chew! Her stomach couldn't process solids. Cassidy bit her knuckle, trying not to scream as she thought of Daisy choking. And skin sensitivity? Cassidy was going off the deep end now, imagining Vanessa putting perfume, sunscreen, oils, makeup on her baby.

A door slammed. "Mommy!" she heard Piper call in a sing-song voice. Likely eager to brag about the treats Grandma bought.

Much as she wanted to write Vanessa, demand her baby back, she refrained. She needed Detective Lewis's help. Time to go home.

Cassidy ran back to the kitchen to say goodbye to Piper and her parents. Once in the car, she'd call Detective Lewis and explain her reasons for emailing Vanessa, but she wouldn't apologize. When someone defied natural law, kidnapped your baby, all bets were off.

CHAPTER FIFTY-THREE

AUGUST
THURSDAY, SEPTEMBER 7, 2023 12:55 P.M.

August sat in his dark closet, thinking of places Vanessa might have taken Daisy, when his phone buzzed. He darted in his shorts' pocket, thinking it was another text from Vanessa, but it was Cassidy. *Go into kitchen.*

Bizarre. She was at her parents. Nonetheless, he left the closet, blinking rapidly as his eyes adjusted to the light. He found the detective at the kitchen table, sitting across from Dr. Fuentes, a phone positioned between them. "August's here," the detective said. August pulled out a chair and sat. "Tell me what's going on."

"I read August's email to Vanessa and thought it was…lacking." Cassidy's voice was scratchy from the phone connection. "I know you might be upset, but I opened a new account and emailed Vanessa—"

"Cassidy," the detective started.

"She wrote back."

August gripped the edge of the table. What did Vanessa say? What did Cassidy write that got her to respond? And why was he panicking at the thought of them talking? He already told Cassidy everything, right?

"Jack." The detective snapped his fingers, looking spry. "We need your help. What's the email address, Cassidy?"

Jack hurried over with his laptop, filling the last empty chair. He listened as Cassidy relayed the email address and password and then his hands flew across the keyboard, his eyes hyper focused behind his glasses. The detective read Cassidy's email aloud.

He was wrong. He deserves to be punished. The words echoed in August's head. Punished how? By leaving him? Or something worse? The email gave him little hope she'd allow him to repair their marriage.

"Smart, Cassidy," Dr. Fuentes said. "You established a relationship as mothers, but also as women wronged by August."

August glared at Dr. Fuentes. Not that he noticed. Everyone cast August as the villain, even though Vanessa broke the law.

The detective read Vanessa's reply and then asked, "Does she have any allergies?"

"I. Have. No. Idea." August could taste Cassidy's frustration, the way she chewed each word down to the marrow. "She's breastfed. It's made specifically for her—" Cassidy swore under her breath. "Someone cut me off."

"Can you please pull over?" August struggled to keep the edge out of his voice. "You're too upset to drive."

"I'm fine."

August rolled his eyes. His opinion was worth less to her than used toilet paper.

"Alright, let's take a second to focus on the positives," the detective said. "She's asking about allergies which means Daisy is alive."

"These questions also tell me she cares for Daisy," Dr. Fuentes added. "Or, at the very least, doesn't intend to harm her."

August didn't feel relieved. Vanessa never struck him as violent. It worried him more that she would keep Daisy forever. An eye for an eye.

"Let's craft a reply," the detective said. "Can you pull over to write this, Cassidy?"

"Sure."

Again, August rolled his eyes. She had no problem listening to the detective.

"Start by saying you're not aware of any allergies because she's breastfed," Dr. Fuentes said. "Ask her what she's feeding Daisy. We want to draw her out. Force her to engage, while subtly reminding her she's not Daisy's mom. She stole her. An act she knows is wrong."

"The email links to ViperByte.com, which pings off IP's all over the world," Jack, the computer guy, said. "We need the company's cooperation."

"That damn subpoena." The detective typed something on his phone and then said, "Any ideas about the skin question?"

"Maybe she put something on her—lotion or shampoo or perfume—and she got a rash." Cassidy groaned. "Or maybe stress made her skin flare. Or maybe she hurt her. I don't know. It's so vague!"

"Tell her we're not aware of any issues with food or her skin, but she should take Daisy to a doctor to make sure she's okay," August said, warming to the idea. It jived with Dr. Fuentes' plan to make her aware of reality. A doctor visit would sure as hell accomplish that. "Play up that we're concerned about her health—"

"We *are* concerned for her health." Cassidy slammed down on the word *are*.

"I know—"

"When you say 'play up,' it sounds like you think this is a game."

"I don't—"

"Stop. Both of you." The detective rapped his knuckles against the table. "If you write that, she might cut off communication, knowing any doctor would call the police."

"I agree," Dr. Fuentes said. "We don't want her to panic."

"What if I appealed to her as a mom again?" Cassidy asked. "How, as moms, we always put the kids first."

"I like that," Dr. Fuentes said. "Stress that you know she's taking great care of Daisy."

"I'll also reiterate that we won't press charges—"

"What?" August skidded his chair back. "No. We're pressing charges. She belongs in prison."

Cassidy huffed. "I don't care what happens to her—"

"I'm not letting her get away—"

The detective interrupted, "Pointless argument. It's up to the district attorney. Back to the skin issue, Cassidy. Tell her what kinds of soaps and lotions you use—"

August bristled. "To make things easier for her?"

"No." The detective narrowed his eyes at August. "To make things easier for your daughter."

"And it also has the byproduct of making her take active steps to care for Daisy," Dr. Fuentes said, looking at August. "It's harder to hurt someone you're emotionally invested in."

August stood and went to the window, peeking out the blinds at the chaos outside. Vanessa took away his daughter, ruined his marriage, handicapped his freedom. Were they even yet? Or did she have more in store?

"This is what I've got," Cassidy said, before reading the email.

August pressed his hand against the window as he listened to Cassidy, his fingers growing white with rage. Unlike Cassidy, he had no desire to let Vanessa walk away.

CHAPTER FIFTY-FOUR

VANESSA
THURSDAY, SEPTEMBER 7, 2023 1:10 P.M.

I sat at the computer in the library, tapping my foot, impatiently waiting for Cassidy's email. You'd think she'd jump at the chance to ensure Kiah was being taken care of properly. Nope. Too busy. Shocking.

I needed to get home to Kiah. Like, now.

She can't hurt herself.

Unless she was dehydrating.

I chewed on the inflamed stub of my thumbnail. The nurse was exaggerating. Kiah wouldn't be crying this much if she was dehydrated. She wouldn't have the energy.

After glancing around to ensure no one was watching, I searched #BabyDaisy. Pictures of Kiah, looking angelic with her big blue eyes and flawless skin. I skirted my finger over the constellation of zits that broke out on my chin today. Why do babies get pore-less, blemish-free skin? Total waste.

Another photo showed August's house. The blinds were shut and coverings fastened on the large, second-floor back windows. Once airy and alive, the house now appeared deaf, blind, and mute. Dead. Like no happiness existed there.

Good. Nothing less than August deserved.

Suddenly, rain pounded the library roof. I looked out the window; sunshine was replaced by dark clouds. It would take longer to drive home—

Oh no. The living room window I broke. Rain would come through. Flood the carpet.

Kiah would get cold in Mom's bedroom.

No. She'd be fine in her pajamas. They were cozy.

But. But. But. What if someone on the lake saw the broken window? Thought the house was abandoned and went to explore?

No one would be out boating in the rain.

Stop panicking.

I looked at the clock. Another ten minutes passed. I had to get home.

To distract myself, I continued reading articles. Nothing more on the "person of interest." If they know it's me, why haven't the police released my name? Were these emails from Cassidy and August a hunch? If so, I blew my cover by writing her back.

I had to write Cassidy. For Kiah.

I clicked on another article.

Apparently, the police were working with an FBI psychological profiler. Was this normal? Or should I take it personally? Someone tapping into my head. I didn't like it. It reminded me of when Dad forced me to see a therapist to control my "emotional outbursts." If Dad tried to understand me, support me, *love* me, maybe I wouldn't get so upset. Did he ever think of that? No one thought of love as a method of healing. Except for Mom.

And me, of course. I always led with love. I tried with August. My baby. And now I'd do the same with Kiah.

Would anyone ever love me—

Cassidy emailed! "Finally," I muttered before opening it.

Vanessa,

Thank you for writing back and for taking good care of Daisy. She's lucky to have you.

I don't know if Daisy has any food allergies, because I have exclusively breastfed her. Are you giving her formula? If so, what brand? There are formulas geared toward supplementing breastfeeding. That would be a good place to start.

We haven't had any skin issues. We use Johnson & Johnson for shampoo, soap, and lotion. We use Seventh Generation Free & Clear for laundry, because it is free of dyes, brighteners, or fragrances. These can be found at most grocery stores. It would comfort Daisy to use the same products from home.

If you have questions, feel free to call our pediatrician, Dr. Wilson. I've attached her contact information. Otherwise, I'm available by phone or email. As promised, I will keep conversations between us.

I know we both want what's best for Daisy. Please give her kisses from Mommy.

Cassidy.

I gripped the mouse, rereading the novel she sent. The subtle condescension. Thanking me for taking care of Kiah? Right, I'm sure she was ecstatic for this impromptu vacation. Dictating what brands of formula, lotions, and detergents to use, as if I was her nanny? Giving me her pediatrician's number, as if I was unaware of police traces? Asking me to give Daisy—I hated that name— kisses? Reminding me she was her mom?

Fuck. You. Cassidy.

I scratched my scalp, which sizzled like grease on a frying pan beneath this wig. I signed out of ViperByte, erased the search history, and stood. Nearly two hours away from Kiah, and to learn what? I needed to take her to a hospital? She had no known allergies? I was, in fact, the worst mom ever for not knowing you couldn't switch immediately from formula to breastmilk?

What a waste of time.

CHAPTER FIFTY-FIVE

CASSIDY
THURSDAY, SEPTEMBER 7, 2023 1:30 P.M.

Cassidy returned home to find another strategy meeting taking place in the kitchen. Detective Lewis, Dr. Fuentes, a man in a suit she didn't know, and August sat around the kitchen table, discussing whether to release Vanessa's information to the press.

Cassidy drank a glass of water at the sink and then stood next to Detective Lewis. A day ago, she would've greeted August with a kiss and stood behind him, resting her hand on his neck, running her fingers through his hair. Now, she didn't acknowledge him.

"She knows we're looking for her," Detective Lewis said, resting his eyes on each person. "The benefits of asking the public for help outweigh the dangers."

"Vanessa feels safe emailing Cassidy because we don't know where she is," Dr. Fuentes, said, "but if we publicize her name as a suspect—".

"She might panic and hurt Daisy," August finished.

"Or herself, which, in turn, would hurt Daisy," Dr. Fuentes said.

"But we don't know if Daisy's okay," Cassidy said, hugging herself, unable to get the coldness of Vanessa's email out of her head. "I don't think we should wait."

"Let's compromise." The detective turned to the suit man, who was typing notes on his iPhone. "Release Vanessa's name, picture, and stats. Call her a person of interest. Do not, at any point, say suspect. Ask people to come forward if they've seen Vanessa or have information on her whereabouts. Reiterate the reward for a tip that brings Daisy home safe."

"Got it." The man started a phone call as he left the room. Cassidy took his empty chair.

"How did things go with Piper?" August asked, cracking his knuckles.

August looked like her husband—blue eyes, Nike cap, stubble on his jaw—but it was an optical illusion. Everything he did and said was to mislead her from seeing his true self. "Fine. She feels special, getting my parents to herself, but that won't last forever."

"Agreed," August said.

She watched Dr. Fuentes' eyes ping-pong between them and felt tempted to ask him about August. Did he have a mental condition that made him a habitual liar? Was he a sex addict? Or just a selfish jerk?

Much as it appealed, she wanted his focus on Daisy. Afterwards, she'd find a therapist. Figure out why August felt compelled to seek—comfort? pleasure? excitement?—outside their marriage. Or not. She could have a clean break. Let the lawyers hammer out the divorce. Did she want that? She didn't know. Too many life-altering events in one day.

The urgency of Detective Lewis's voice drew her out of her thoughts. "What city?" He spoke into his phone. "Are the police there?" His eyes were rapt. "Let me know when you have more." He rested his phone on the table and said, "Good news. ViperByte complied with the subpoena. While the account was set up with a prepaid Visa card, the email traced to an IP address for the Medford Public Library. It's a small town in northern Wisconsin, close to Michigan. Vilas County. Police are on their way—"

"That-that-that—" August stood up, waving his hands like miniature windmills. "Her family has a house there."

"Officer Hastings!" Detective Lewis beckoned one of the cops from the living room. "Search property records for all of Vilas County. Last name Jennings or Prescott."

"Think, August." Cassidy stood and grabbed his hands, holding on tight, imploring him to remember. Hands that likely stroked Vanessa as she reminisced about summers at her vacation home. "What else did Vanessa tell you?"

Cassidy didn't care if August and Vanessa held their wedding there. If she got Daisy back, she'd buy them a wedding gift.

CHAPTER FIFTY-SIX

VANESSA
THURSDAY, SEPTEMBER 7, 2023 1:33 P.M.

Eager to get back to Kiah, I hurried out the library. Not quite a jog, but close. I barreled through the front entrance doors, knocking into someone trying to open it from the other side. I looked up—

Oh. Please. God. No.

A police officer. Was he here for me? No. Impossible. No one could've known I'd come here. I didn't know until a couple hours ago.

Unless…Were the police able to trace my email to Cassidy? Was that why it took her forever to write me back?

I never should've waited.

Check that. I never should've wrote her. Dumb and dumber.

The officer held the door open. "Coming?" he asked, gesturing with his free hand.

I forced myself to make eye contact and, fuck me sideways, he was gorgeous. Shiny blonde hair. Wavy. Brown eyes. Lips like a snack. Normally, I'd bask in a man like this not being able to take his eyes off me, but, right now, I wanted a brush off.

I walked through the doorway. One foot in front of the other. Yes. Just like that. The rain dwindled to a drizzle, dusting my skin.

"Your wig." His gaze rested slightly above my eyes. "It's…falling off."

Fuuuuuuuuuuuuuuuck. I touched my head and, sure enough, I could feel the webbing of the wig about an inch back from my hairline. Exposing my dark hair. Not Cassidy's blonde. Heat crept up my cheeks. I probably looked like a fresh picked tomato.

What could I say? "Healthier than dyeing it."

"Right," he said.

"Not as expensive as extensions."

"Okay." He smiled. The wind blew, a cool breeze that felt baptismal against my skin. I was saved. The smile said he wasn't here for me. He might think I was odd, but you couldn't arrest someone for being odd.

"Have we met before?" he asked. "You look familiar."

My heartbeat entered my throat. Was that a line? Or was my picture being shared among the police? If I was the person of interest, they probably had several photos of me circulating. "I used to summer here as a kid. Did you grow up here?"

He shook his head, studying my face as if it was a Picasso. "No. Green Bay."

"Hmm…must have one of those faces." I tried to smile. Probably looked like I had too much Botox since the muscles wouldn't move. "Well, see ya." I waved and walked to my car, feeling his eyes like two lasers on my back, hoping it was in the way a guy watches a girl he thinks is cute and not how a cop watches a perp, mentally cataloguing their suspicious behavior.

When I got to my car, he was still outside, messing on his phone. I sat, watching and sweating. What was he doing? Was he waiting for someone?

Finally, he went inside. I navigated out of the parking lot, pressing down too hard on the accelerator and slipping on the wet pavement. My car crawled up on the curb as I turned the corner. "Calm down!" I banged the steering wheel with my fist for good measure. I was panicking. Making horrible decisions. Getting distracted by hot cops.

Breathe. In. Out. Yes. That's it.

But breathing couldn't stop the swelling of thoughts, too fast and persistent to ignore. By emailing Cassidy, I confirmed my guilt.

The police were probably researching everything about me. Including my parents. While the house was held in trust, it was in Mom's name first. If there was a way to search the transfer of deeds, they could uncover the address of the lake house. Why did I tell the cop I summered here as a kid? Stupid. It gave the police another reason to look.

We couldn't stay there any longer. But where would we go?

My foot trembled as I pressed the gas pedal. Get Kiah. Leave. Figure out the rest later.

CHAPTER FIFTY-SEVEN

AUGUST
THURSDAY, SEPTEMBER 7, 2023 1:40 P.M.

August looked into Cassidy's pleading eyes, trying to resurrect the conversation where Vanessa talked about going up north. Here was his chance to save Daisy. Possibly save his marriage. And he couldn't remember a goddamn thing!

"Come on, baby," Cassidy whispered, the term of endearment feeling more tragic than sweet. "Think."

Was this part of Vanessa's cruel game, like the texts? Seeking revenge because she knew he was too preoccupied by sex to listen to her? Or was this a mistake? Did she not remember telling him?

He fell into his chair, resting his elbows on his knees and massaging his temples. A detail emerged. "It's on a lake," August said.

The detective told one of his officers to contact the police in Florida to ask Vanessa's father. Another officer said, "There's 1300 lakes in Vilas County."

The detective set the laptop before August. "Go through the list."

Any hope of playing superman drained as he scanned the names. They sounded generic—Beaver Lake, Goose Lake, Friendship Lake. Did she tell him the name? Would he recognize it? Or was this an exercise in futility? The names swam in his mind, blending together until he wasn't quite reading, but looking at clumps of indecipherable letters.

Cassidy came up behind him, resting a hand on his shoulder. A comfort and a surprise. "Do you need anything? Coffee? Something to eat?"

He knew her abrupt one-eighty from loathing to kindness was to help him remember. But did her intentions matter? Maybe she could fall back into the habit of caring about him. The love and trust, he'd have to earn through years of fidelity, accountability, and transparency—a task he wanted to believe he could meet. "Are you making something?"

"I ate at my parents." She paused. "But I can make you something."

He squeezed her hand. "A sandwich would be good. Whatever's easy." He turned back to the list, saying each name in his head, letting it resonate, before moving on. Cassidy delivered a ham and cheese sandwich with a side of Baked Lays. The rise in blood sugar helped him focus.

Hidden Lake. Like an old song coming on the radio, his brain supplied the lyrics without trying. *I hide away on Hidden Lake,* Vanessa said. Hidden Lake. Yes. Yes! That was it. Think. What else did she say? They were lying in bed, Vanessa with her head resting against his shoulder, running her fingertips through his chest hair, telling him how she and her mom spent summers at their lake house. Away from her dad, the kids at school. *I go there whenever I need to get away.*

He sprang out of his seat, cutting a fist pump through the air. "Hidden Lake!" The detective and Cassidy, talking by the island, turned to him. "Vanessa had this saying, 'I hide away on Hidden Lake.' The house is her safe haven."

"Hidden Lake," the detective repeated to the officer researching property deeds.

Cassidy covered her mouth with her hand. Tears were in her eyes as she closed the gap and threw herself into his arms. The smell of her shampoo worked like a dopamine hit. "Thank you," she whispered in his ear, the tease of her lips making it tingle. "Thank you."

A glow exploded inside August's heart, warming his body. Daisy would come home. Cassidy would forgive him. He'd get a second chance.

CHAPTER FIFTY-EIGHT

VANESSA
THURSDAY, SEPTEMBER 7, 2023 1:47 P.M.

Rattled by the police officer at the library, I thought my mind was playing tricks when the radio DJ said my name. Paranoia run rampant. The second time, every nerve in my body pinged to attention. "Vanessa Jennings or Vanessa Prescott. She goes by both," the DJ said. "Police named her a 'person of interest' in the kidnapping of baby Daisy. Twenty-three years old. Milwaukee resident. Drives a black Jetta. License plate QXB-447. Our social media feeds have a current photo. If you have knowledge of her whereabouts…"

I felt a wave of vertigo. Instead of hitting the brake, pulling over, I floored the gas. They knew I changed my name. What else did they know? Were they at the lake house, waiting for me?

Much as I wanted to leave, I had to get Kiah. I couldn't leave her there in case I was wrong.

And go where, Vanessa? Why didn't you develop a plan B?

Canada was out. Couldn't use my passport. Michigan, a short drive away, was the obvious choice. But I'd do the opposite. Drive across the state, four hours or so, to Minnesota. Keep the police guessing. Then I'd find a cheap motel. Somewhere that took cash. Didn't care if you were mainlining heroin or had a baby as long as you paid.

If the public had my picture, that cop at the library definitely did too. Did he make the connection? Was thirty seconds enough to tattoo my features in his mind?

"Bitch!" I screamed, pressing the gas, flying twenty miles over the limit. So much for Cassidy's promise not to involve the police. Fake as a Kardashian! I never should've written her back. But I was being a good mom.

And I got screwed. Maybe I should get that as a tattoo. Always getting screwed. In cursive. Fancy like.

Towering trees whipped past me on both sides of the road, making it feel like I was riding a roller coaster, the track getting narrower and narrower.

I lifted my foot off the gas. I couldn't help Kiah if I got pulled over again.

My life as Vanessa? Gone. But Mackenzie Roeper had options. Along with the fake ID, I had eight-thousand in cash, and four prepaid $500 VISA gift cards.

This wasn't over.

Dad. Did the police contact him? My heart embarked on another sprint. Yes. Absolutely. And Dad would help. He was rule-following, law-abiding, meticulous; an accountant to his core. That was why I drove him nuts. I hated rules. His especially. He'd gleefully direct them to the lake house.

Slow. Down. Somehow I was going twenty over. I rubbed my thigh, trying to loosen the muscle.

Then again, if the police were asking the public for help, maybe Dad didn't sell me out. Maybe he protected me. A gift in Mom's memory.

And. And. And! He didn't know I was using Mom's car. He thought I sold it. The license plate they gave on the radio was my Jetta. I was a step ahead.

Unless cameras at the library clocked Mom's license plate.

I sped through a stop sign. Excellent work, Vanessa.

The library was an old building. Maybe no cameras. And the officer went inside before I left. Could I be that lucky?

Recent history suggested otherwise. Kiah and I should've been cuddling, napping, playing. Instead, there were endless crying fits. Diarrhea. Rash. Fever. No smiles. Kisses. Love. And now, running from the law. I felt like I was on a never-ending merry-go-round ride, too dizzy to think clearly.

I drove past my house, scanning the trees for cops, anything suspicious. Satisfied everything looked normal, I did a Y-turn, pulled into the driveway, and parked the car.

As soon as I entered the house, I heard Kiah crying. She lay on Mom's bed, arms and legs stretched to the brink, as if she was nailed to the cross. Fingers and toes curled. It looked… uncomfortable.

I pressed a kiss to her forehead. Hot. Despite her cries, there were no tears. Dehydration.

I sprinted upstairs, shoveling necessities—underwear, pants, shirts, a couple sweatshirts, onesies and pajamas for Kiah—into my backpack. There wasn't room to take much. Back downstairs, I grabbed toiletries from the bathroom. I took the large box of diapers and stacked the formula and bottles atop, leaving the old formula behind. A grocery bag with bottled water, cereal, and protein bars. Whatever was close.

Three trips and sixty seconds later, the car was packed. Though, the kitchen was a mess. Bathroom too. Clothes in the dryer. Garbage full. What was a little more evidence at this point?

I picked up Kiah and turned to leave. At the last second, I grabbed *28 Summers*, wanting to have the book Mom last held.

Outside, I fastened Kiah in her seat. She cried, but didn't fight me like yesterday. "I'll feed you soon," I promised, thinking of the formula. Her stomach would adjust eventually, right?

I opened my car door, taking one last look at the lake. Dark as the night sky, glittering like a crown jewel. A movie montage played in my mind—a toddler, dipping my toes into the cold water and squealing; at seven, strong enough to swim to the raft; twelve, trying to look sexy in my bikini; fifteen, skinny dipping with my summer boyfriend; twenty-one, tucking blankets around Mom as she shivered on the beach, bald and pale, our last summer together.

As I drove away, I cried, lowering the windows to inhale my last breath of Hidden Lake air. I would miss this place. But after losing Mom and my baby, I would survive this pain too.

CHAPTER FIFTY-NINE

CASSIDY
THURSDAY, SEPTEMBER 7, 2023 2:15 P.M.

Cassidy sat next to August at the kitchen table as Detective Lewis updated them on the situation in Vilas County. After August identified Hidden Lake, the police uncovered a property deed previously owned by Elizabeth Jennings and now held in trust, presumably for Vanessa. Problem was, the police force in Vilas County was not equipped to handle this situation. Wisconsin had eight regional SWAT teams; the closest one in Green Bay. It would take time for them to arrive. Time they didn't have.

"Not all bad news, though," Detective Lewis said. "The road that leads to her house only has two exits." He turned his laptop around so they could see the house on Google Maps. Cassidy leaned forward, searching, as if it was a live feed. A gray shingled house with white framing. Two stories. Narrow. Two-car garage located to the right. The lawn led down to the lake. Nothing fancy.

"Right now, local officers are heading there to set up a blockade. They'll search every car that comes through." Detective Lewis pulled back the image to show how the road looped around the lake like a horseshoe. "If Vanessa leaves, we'll get her."

"What about a side road?" August asked. "Perhaps a road not noted on a map. Something manmade?"

Detective Lewis shook his head. "I've been told these are the only two exits. Lots of places to hide, of course, but she wouldn't get far on foot with a baby."

"What if she's coming home, not leaving?" Cassidy asked. "She'll keep on driving if she sees the police."

"Possible," Detective Lewis said. "But where will she go? Her belongings are there. We have her car details. Every officer in the state is on the lookout. She won't get far."

Cassidy landed on another catastrophe. "What if she sees the police and doesn't pull over? Swerves around it? I don't want this to end in a high-speed chase, where Daisy dies in a car accident." Did Vanessa know how to properly strap an infant into a car seat? That the straps needed to be tight over her shoulders, the harness in the middle of her chest? Cassidy's body went rigid at the thought of Daisy propelling out of her seat, her precious face smashed against the windshield. "She didn't come this far to hand Daisy over."

"She's not going to risk her life for this," August said.

"Dr. Fuentes said she might." Cassidy squeezed her eyes shut. So many things could go wrong, she didn't see how it could go right.

"The police know what's at stake," Detective Lewis said, "and will be careful."

"Careful." Cassidy often said the word to Piper. "Be careful." How careful could the police be when carrying guns? Guns were the antithesis to carefulness. "Let's go. I want to be there the moment they find Daisy." Cassidy's breasts hardened at the thought. "She needs to feed."

"We can't interfere with the operation," Detective Lewis said. "I promise, we'll leave the second we get confirmation."

"She could be back with us before dark," August said quietly, worrying his hands. She appreciated him using the word "could." If she wanted false optimism, she would've called Mom or gone to see Faith. August understood how nothing was certain until Daisy was in their arms.

Detective Lewis's phone buzzed. After reading something, he said, "Vanessa's father confirmed the address and ownership of the lake house. He emphasized that while Vanessa is emotional and somewhat erratic, she's never been violent."

"I can't do this. I cannot sit here for another second." Cassidy pushed away from the table and walked to the sink. She filled a glass of water, gulping it down. Not violent. Anyone could be violent if pushed too far. If Vanessa was here, Cassidy would strangle her, despite her ardent pro-life and anti-death penalty opinions.

"Why don't you rest?" Detective Lewis said. "It'll be awhile before the SWAT team arrives."

"I can't sleep." She stared at the dark shade over the window, hating how closed in the house felt. "I can't..."

August walked to her. "Come with me." She let him guide her through the living room and into the bedroom. The room was dim, just the rectangular outlines of daylight coming from the windows. She looked at the bed. The softness of the sheets, the cool breeze from the fan above, her sleepless nights, pulled her in. There was nothing she could do. No way to bring Daisy home. Best to rest, regain energy.

She lay on the bed, listening to the rustle of sheets as August climbed in behind her. At first, he didn't touch her, but after a few minutes, he tentatively draped an arm over her hip, tracing the length of her fingers with his. Tears prickled her eyes.

Hate held her heart hostage. August was a liar, a cheater, most of all, a stranger. But in this moment, she realized he could be all those things and be her husband. His horrible behavior didn't have to negate years where he acted with love, kindness, generosity. Should she erase all the kisses? The whispered conversations? The amazing father he was to her children?

Drifting to sleep, Cassidy realized the search and recovery process for her marriage wouldn't be black and white. However big the mistakes, right now, she needed him. She was too tired to care whether that made her weak. It just was.

CHAPTER SIXTY

VANESSA
THURSDAY, SEPTEMBER 7, 2023 2:18 P.M.

Minutes after leaving the house, out on Highway Z, a cop car zoomed past me. I pushed my sunglasses up my nose, reminding myself not to speed. One cop. NBD. This was America. Cops were everywhere. But up north? In a small town?

Stop being paranoid. I never noticed the cops before because I wasn't running from them.

Momentarily satisfied, I reached back and held Kiah's hand, trying to comfort her. She was miserable, wailing between frantic sucks on her pacifier. Clearly hungry, but there was no time to feed her.

Two more cop cars passed me, headed in the direction of my lake house. I gripped the wheel tighter. None of them had their lights on. If it was an emergency, they'd use the sirens.

Keep driving. Minnesota was only a few hours away. I wasn't sure why I thought Minnesota was the holy grail, that it would bless me with eternal safety, but right now, a different state felt like a different country. Minnesota or bust.

Eventually, Kiah quieted, which was good for my eardrums, bad for the paranoid thoughts fighting for attention. Were the police headed to my house? How could I protect us without internet? Access to the outside world?

AM radio. Dad used to listen to post-game shows on Packer Sundays and Mark Belling during the week. I found a station, but they were droning on about inflation. Thanks for nothing.

When an hour passed with no cop cars, my shoulders unhinged. The lack of imminent danger worked like a Xanax. Come to think of it, a real Xanax would work even better. I had some in my backpack—

Kiah's sudden scream reminded me why I needed to keep a clear head. "We'll be there soon," I said. Kiah ramped up the volume, seeing through my lie. Or maybe she detected fear in my voice. Were babies like dogs, senses more attuned because they couldn't speak?

Her cries sounded violent. Like the blood vessels in her face might blow. What if it wasn't hunger? Or poop? But something serious?

A few miles later, I saw a logging road and turned onto it. The gravel crackled beneath my tires, while the unevenness felt like riding in a canoe. The road looked abandoned with weeds growing between the gravel. Tall trees abutted each side, blocking the sun and making the car dim even though it was afternoon. I locked the doors and crawled into the backseat, wanting to make this fast. Didn't want another fruit stand incident.

I unbuckled Kiah and checked her diaper. Dry. Another unwelcome surprise. I mixed a bottle of formula and pulled her close. Her eyes widened upon the first taste and she sucked furiously.

"Kiah." I sang her name and brushed my fingertips across her cheek, but her gaze stayed focused on some indeterminable point in the ceiling. "Kiah." I was risking my life to keep her safe. Yet, she treated me like the help. Like mother, like daughter—

No. She was my daughter.

When she finished the bottle, she whimpered, but we didn't have time for more. I patted her on the back, trying to encourage a burp. No luck. After buckling her into her seat, I crawled up front and pulled back onto the road.

A mile later the gas light came on. Why didn't I notice I was low?

The ulcer in my stomach grew as each mile marker passed without a gas station. If I ran out of gas, I was finished. I'd be reliant on a good Samaritan. A cop. Or another psycho like the guy at the fruit stand.

"Please, please, please," I whispered, almost hyperventilating.

Like magic, I came upon a small town. Three bars in two blocks. One liquor store. Wisconsinites. All alcoholics. Then, at the end of the third block, a general store/gas station. "Yes!" I half-screeched, half-cried.

Two cars were pumping gas when I pulled in. Wary of cameras, I parked at the furthest pump. After checking to make sure Kiah was sleeping, I pulled out two twenties, walked inside, and asked the older man at the register to put $40 on pump eight for me.

While the car was filling up, I caught my reflection in the window. Long, platinum blonde hair. It had to go. The library cop probably already reported the wig.

Did they sell hair dye here?

Back inside the store, I choose a light brown, far enough away from my own dark hair and nothing like Cassidy's platinum. Could I dye Kiah's hair too? Could a baby's hair withstand dye? Then again, if it fell out, that would be beneficial.

I'd decide later.

I grabbed a Red Bull from the fridge and walked to the register, searching for the phones. Cigarettes. Alcohol. Chewing tobacco—

"Can I help you?" the man asked, eyeing me quizzically. Or maybe not. I couldn't tell.

"Do you sell phones? I can't find—"

He pointed behind him.

"Oh. Thanks. I need your cheapest phone." Tell him you're poor, Vanessa. Desperate. Alone. Running from the police. Hell, why not offer to blow him for it? The endeavor would last thirty seconds and save money.

Stop!

He pulled a box from the shelf, which showed a picture of an old flip phone. "This is twenty-five dollars. Let's you text and call. This one though—" He grabbed another, which looked like an outdated smart phone. "It has Wi-Fi technology and costs sixty-nine dollars. With either, you buy a prepaid phone card for data and minutes."

With internet, I could check on the case. Stay one step ahead. "I'll take the one with Wi-Fi." I set the hair dye and Red Bull on the counter. "And a prepaid phone card. Fifty dollars."

He held the phone box. "You ever use one of these before?"

I shook my head. He'd definitely remember me. The girl that bought hair dye and a burner and was an idiot about technology.

"If you want to stay anonymous, turn off the Wi-Fi, location, and GPS when you text or call." He rubbed his beard. "Otherwise, you've defeated the purpose of a burner."

"Th-thank you." I briefly met his eyes, wondering why he was helping me. What did he see? A young girl on the run. Probably thought it was from an abusive man. And he wouldn't be wrong. "How much?"

"138.21."

I opened my backpack, sorting through a fat stack of twenties, suddenly aware he could see I was carrying a large amount of cash. Maybe the nice-guy act was exactly that, an act. He knew I was vulnerable. He probably had a gun. What stopped him from using it to threaten me? It wasn't like I could go to the cops.

Only one way forward.

I handed him seven twenties. He took the money, opened the cash register, and gave me my change. Once outside, I ran to the car. I lost touch with where my paranoia started and reality began, but I was trusting my gut here.

And my gut said get back on the road. Continue driving west.

Half-hour later, I saw a stone carving of the state of Minnesota on the side of the road. "Minnesota Welcomes You."

Tears streamed down my cheeks. I made it.

CHAPTER SIXTY-ONE

AUGUST
THURSDAY, SEPTEMBER 7, 2023 5:40 P.M.

August woke from a bout of fitful sleep when someone knocked on the bedroom door. Cassidy's body went rigid and then she bolted out of his arms to open the door. He was left with the minty smell of her hair and a prayer their nightmare ended.

"She's gone," the detective said, his words clipped. August stood, getting a head rush. "The SWAT team found dirty diapers, baby clothes, formula, but no Daisy."

"You said she'd be there!" Cassidy reached out as if she wanted to shake the detective. "How can she be gone?"

"She's a goddamn college kid, not some criminal mastermind," August yelled. What was Vanessa's plan? Run from the law forever? He forced himself to lower his voice. "Do you have any leads?"

The detective ran a hand across his mouth, drawing it down. "Vanessa's vehicle was at the property. We're trying to determine her mode of transportation. Did they leave on foot? Are they hiding in another house? Is a third party involved? There was a broken window at the scene. We're canvasing the area and going door-to-door."

"Why would she leave the car? The formula? Clothes? Everything she needs? Unless—" Cassidy hiccupped a sob. "Maybe she killed them both. Maybe they're in that lake. Maybe the broken window is a sign she went crazy."

August's throat closed up. A murder-suicide. "No." He steadied himself against the dresser. No way an affair could lead to his daughter's death. "No. She wouldn't."

"We're looking into all possibilities," the detective said quietly.

Tears ran down Cassidy's face as she asked, "Are you searching the water?"

The detective nodded. "Yes."

August's legs gave out and he slipped to the ground, not hiding his sobs. Until now, he thought Daisy would come home. Back at square one, with no idea where Vanessa and Daisy were, he ventured alongside Cassidy to the dark place. Daisy dead. Her last feeling on this earth terror. Abandonment.

He'd never forgive himself. A lifetime of self-loathing wasn't enough to pay for his selfishness, greediness, entitlement.

It wasn't enough.

CHAPTER SIXTY-TWO

VANESSA
THURSDAY, SEPTEMBER 7, 2023 7:07 P.M.

As I drove through Minnesota, the sun set, and my eyes and body begged for a reprieve. A nap. Although I passed several motels, nowhere felt safe. Problem was, I needed to pee. Urgently. Not wanting to risk another gas station, I waited, feeling like there was a watermelon pressing against my bladder, until I saw a rest stop.

Eight cars were parked in the lot. I parked at the far end, several spots away from the closest car. There might be cameras, but it wouldn't be showing a live feed. I adjusted my wig—

Wait. I should dye my hair now. I shoved the hair dye, phone, formula, and bottle inside my backpack. Given Kiah's quietness, I assumed she was sleeping, but when I went to grab her, she was staring straight ahead. I snapped my fingers in front of her eyes. She blinked, but didn't look at me. Why wasn't she more alert? Food. That would perk her up.

I unlatched her car seat, put down the canopy, and walked inside. There was a giant map of Minnesota in the entrance, but before I could study it, a toilet flushed and I stepped inside the family restroom.

A toilet, sink, and changing table. No shower. The smell of urine as potent as a teenage boy's cologne. After opening the canopy and setting the car seat down, I flew to the toilet, sighing in satisfaction as my bladder released.

Since Kiah wasn't fussing, I started the hair dye so it could set while I fed her. I grabbed my manicure scissors, all I had, eying my long, dark hair in the mirror. Shiny. Thick. My best feature.

Get a grip. It's hair. I pulled it into a ponytail, bent over the garbage and hacked through my hair just beyond the elastic. I looked in the mirror and tried not to cry. Jagged layers landed above my collarbone. A hipster look, if I was being generous; ugly, if I was being honest.

Oh, well. I wasn't looking to get laid. Sex caused this disaster. Besides, ugly was the best disguise.

I opened the hair dye and read the directions. Leave on for thirty minutes, checking every five for your desired outcome. A recipe for beauty. I mixed the dye, wincing at the toxic smell, and then wrapped my neck and shoulders with paper towels. After applying the dye, I used more paper towels to clean my hair line, inside my earlobes, and the sink and mirror.

With slick, wet hair piled atop my head and an astringent smell filling my nostrils, I made Kiah's formula. I held her in the crook of my arm, teasing her lower lip with the nipple. She pursed her lips. "Come on," I said. "You have to eat." It didn't matter. Even when I shoved the nipple in her mouth, she refused to suck.

"Fine. Whatever. You do you." I set her back in the car seat and opened my phone, charging it in the socket next to the sink. Then I input the prepaid phone card and searched for updates on the case, clicking on the first link: CNN. "You're big time, girl."

She didn't care.

Side-by-side photos. One of Cassidy holding Kiah and Piper, August with his arms around all three, a protective papa bear. Puke. Then me, looking like I was auditioning for *Love Island* with a low-cut crop top, a pouty kiss, and blood-shot eyes. One of my stupid "friends" must have supplied it.

The happy family versus the homewrecker. How original.

I clicked on a video, watching an aerial shot of cops combing the grounds of my lake house. "Jennings took Daisy to this lake house in northern Wisconsin…" the voiceover said loudly. I slammed the button to lower the volume, in case someone passed by in the lobby. "Police are asking the public to be vigilant, as Jennings is considered unstable and potentially violent…"

Icy drips of water from my hair slid down my spine. I shivered. Five minutes earlier, the cops would've caught me.

I didn't want to go to prison.

I was innocent. August used me. Manipulated me. Killed our baby. And they had the audacity to call me unstable? Any woman in my position would've done the same.

The media should ask why. Why a woman without a criminal record would take a baby? Why pick that couple? That baby? What was the connection?

No. Nobody cared. August would get away with it. Again.

I picked up Kiah, kissing her forehead. Her skin was warm, a reminder of her fever. I would never hurt her. I wanted to be her savior. Her mother. Everything.

I tried feeding her again. No go. "Please eat, baby. You have to get better."

Twenty-four hours and she was on death's door. Probably a good thing I got the abortion. At least she died before she could feel pain.

Stop it.

I rocked Kiah, while chewing on my cuticles and brainstorming solutions.

A hospital? I didn't have insurance, but I could use my fake ID. They'd have to treat her. Would they ask for a birth certificate? Unlikely. Who carried that around? But maybe a bulletin went out to hospitals nationwide, requiring ID checks on infants.

Identification wasn't the biggest problem either. You show up with a sick baby, there would be questions. Question I couldn't answer—namely why I switched to formula. Could they check to see if I had been breastfeeding? I wouldn't let them.

A hospital was out.

The metallic taste of blood filled my mouth. Looking down, I saw I tore the cuticle up to the first ridge on my index finger. I started chewing on the next finger, unable to feel the pain.

So, what? What should I do? Hope and pray Kiah gets better? It wasn't trending that way. I never thought I'd miss her crying, but I wanted her to scream. Fight. Instead, she was shutting down.

I was in over my head. Options dwindling like a reality star's followers.

There was another option, one I'd been ignoring until now.

Give her back?

I kissed Kiah's cheek. With a fake ID, gift cards, and cash, I had a fighting chance at escaping. With a sick baby, it was a matter of time before I got caught.

I buckled Kiah in her seat, dipped my head in the sink, and rinsed the dye. After, I squeezed out the moisture, leaving it to air dry.

Hair littered the floor. I drenched a paper towel and wiped the floor, not wanting to leave DNA, but, without a broom, it was impossible. Whatever. Like a janitor would see hair and call the police.

Outside, the sky turned a deathly black, but the twinkling stars made me think of Mom. My guiding light. Mom would want me to put Kiah's health first.

With that thought, I latched Kiah in her seat and sat up front. Inside my backpack was my journal with Cassidy's number. I pulled out the burner, shutting off the Wi-Fi, location, and GPS. How could I protect Kiah if I wasn't with her? Ensure August wouldn't hurt her? At once, I knew. Hurting him too was a bonus. After sending the text, I shut off the phone and drove.

Now, where should I leave Kiah so she'd get help and I could still get away?

CHAPTER SIXTY-THREE

CASSIDY
THURSDAY, SEPTEMBER 7, 2023 8:11 P.M.

Cassidy was pumping in her office while listening to an oldies station on Pandora. She needed something that would drown out the whoosh-whoosh of the pump and wouldn't trigger memories of Daisy. Oldies worked. Neil Diamond was singing "Sweet Caroline" when she received a text. A random string of numbers. She jolted, one pump falling off her breast and dribbling milk down her stomach. For once, she didn't care. The only thing more precious than breastmilk was finding the baby the milk belonged to.

If you want Kiah back, you need to leave August. Refuse him custody. Visitation. Promise me and I'll tell you where she is. And no tricks. I'll be watching.

Cassidy screamed. She pulled the left pump off her breast, setting both bottles on her desk. Then she snapped her nursing bra, tugged on her shirt, and raced out the door.

Detective Lewis walked toward her. "Don't text back. Let the trace go through first."

"I can't promise her custody," Cassidy said, her breath skittish. Didn't Vanessa understand basic family court laws? No. Of course not. This woman, more like *girl*, understood nothing of the world except bending it to get what she wanted. "Courts decide custody."

"Don't worry about that," Detective Lewis said as August appeared at the bedroom door. "We'll get Daisy and then arrest Vanessa."

"What's going on?" August asked.

"I am worried!" Cassidy stood in front of Detective Lewis. The happy ending where he was the hero and justice was served grew less believable by the minute. "She took Daisy once; she could do it again."

"Someone tell me what's happening," August said.

"Vanessa texted me." She held up her phone, watching as his eyes widened in shock, softened in relief, and ultimately how his entire face shut down when he understood they were being blackmailed.

"She doesn't get to decide this." His voice a finely sharpened blade, his eyes electric. "This family is everything to me."

"No, it's not." She said it softly, sadly, but it held the same impact as screaming. He wasn't negotiating. But neither was she. "You made that clear every time you cheated."

"And I always came back to you—"

"It traces to a prepaid phone card," Jack, the tech guy, interrupted from the living room. "We can use the serial number to find out where it was purchased, but that'll take—"

"Time," Detective Lewis finished, cursing under his breath.

Silence filled the room. Cassidy tugged at her ponytail, wrapping it around her hand. So close and yet so far away.

"Here's your out," August said, his voice flat.

"My out?" Cassidy didn't understand.

He crossed his arms. "You can leave me and no one will say you're the bad guy."

Daisy was missing. And he was playing the victim. With dozens of reasons to leave him, she didn't need an "out." "I'm not discussing this—" Her phone buzzed. "It's her!" Detective Lewis and August stepped closer, reading over her shoulder.

Time's ticking. Daisy's sick. What's your answer?

Without permission, Cassidy texted back, *YES! Tell me where she is.*

She looked up at August. "I get it," he said, squaring his shoulders, jutting out his chin and slowly nodding. "I'd say or do anything to save Daisy too. I just wish you weren't so goddamn eager about it." He turned and left. She heard the basement door close gently behind him. The silence pierced, as if he was reminding her of what it would be like when he was gone.

She stared at her phone, waiting for a text, noticing the tremble in her hand. For Cassidy, it wasn't a choice. Love was love was love didn't account for the love between a mother and child. That was primal, paramount. Everything else secondary. Regardless of the circumstances, the ethics, the legality, her kids would come first. And she wasn't going to apologize to August for that. Not now. Not ever.

CHAPTER SIXTY-FOUR

VANESSA
THURSDAY, SEPTEMBER 7, 2023 9:10 P.M.

I was fifty miles outside Fargo when I exited the highway. For safety reasons, I couldn't drive much longer. If the library had cameras, the cops probably already had Mom's license plate. Or Dad gave it to them as a longshot when my car was at the lake house. Two questions pressed. Where to flee? And where to leave Kiah?

Needing time to plan, I parked on a quiet residential street. Better camouflage than a store parking lot. Some houses were dark, but most had lights on. The blue glow of TV's radiated from front windows. Here, if someone came outside, they'd assume I was visiting.

I switched on my phone. Cassidy texted, *YES! Tell me where she is.*

She agreed to kick August to the curb. Shocking. I never believed she loved him, not the way I did. She listened to August's sins and, instead of granting absolution, she turned on him. I could only hope she kept her word. Protected Kiah. Ensured his hell continued long after I disappeared.

Content to make Cassidy wait—warranted after that condescending email she wrote—I navigated to lastmintix.com. I put Fargo as my departure city, needing something early tomorrow morning. The further the better.

The options were ick, bad, and worse. Midwest cities were too close. Florida? No way would I live in the same state as Dad again.

California? Too expensive. East coast? Littered with cops and governmental officials. No thanks.

Near the bottom of the list, Fargo to Dallas to LA to Honolulu for five-hundred-and-seventy-five dollars. A steal. It departed at 5:15 a.m. Good. Fewer people to spot me. Or perhaps worse? People might look at me more closely?

Ugh. Stop catastrophizing. Every option had pitfalls.

With changeovers and no delays, I'd be in Hawaii by tomorrow night. Hope rose in my chest. I could get away. Start a new life.

Quickly, I pulled out two Visa gift cards and my fake ID. Although the name was Mackenzie Roeper, it had my real picture. Similar to the image shared on TV and the internet. Another snag. I looked different now with my short, dyed hair, but some diligent TSA agent might make the biggest catch of his life. But what TSA agent was diligent at 5 a.m.? I was carrying on my luggage, so I only had to show the ID when passing through security.

One person. One time.

Stay and be arrested? Gamble for freedom?

I booked the ticket.

Seven hours until my flight. The clock started ticking.

Now, where to take Kiah?

I drove, chewing on my cuticles as I passed houses, a grocery store, pharmacy, gas station. I couldn't drop her at a hospital or urgent care. Too many cameras. Witnesses. I'd never get away.

Searching, searching. Where was safe? And helpful?

"Bingo," I muttered as I saw a sign advertising Bright Smiles Dental, Rainbow Pediatrics, and Focus Physical Therapy. Corner lot. Two stories. Pulling to a stop in the back parking lot, I noticed a cement landing in front of a glass door, all three business names stenciled on it. A camera high in the corner. So much easier to be a criminal thirty years ago.

I found a receipt in the glove compartment from 2009 for gas and M&M's. Mom had a sweet tooth; needed chocolate on her "just in case." In case of what? I remembered asking. Mom laughed.

This is Kiah, I wrote. *She's sick. Fever, rash, diarrhea for past two days. Contact Cassidy with questions.*

I wrote Cassidy's number below and tucked the note in my pocket.

While I didn't think leaving Kiah would be the moment I'd get caught, my stomach was tied in fishing knots. I pulled on my cap, tucking my short hair inside so nothing showed. Then I tugged it low over my eyes and zipped my jacket until it covered my chin, refusing to make identification easy on the police.

Kiah was asleep. I wiped down the handle and buckle of her car seat with bleach wipes. Then I unlatched it and carried her to the door, using the sleeve of my shirt to avoid fingerprints. I squatted, wishing I had a blanket to give her. I didn't want her to catch a chill. Was that even a thing? A good mom would know.

I went to the trunk and got her clothes from my bag, tucking them around her body. Better than nothing. Besides, I had to get rid of them before the airport.

Time to go.

I bit my lip, debating the wisdom of this plan. I'd text Cassidy before the plane departed to give her the location. They would send an ambulance. Worst-case scenario, one of the doctors would be in by seven, right? And if Kiah woke up crying, maybe somebody would hear her.

Ever so gently, I brushed my finger against Kiah's warm cheek. She was tiny. And innocent. Caught up in this mess. "I tried my best." My throat swelled with each word. "I thought I could make things better for you. For both of us. But you're going to be okay. I've made sure your daddy will never hurt you."

The imaginary clock ticked louder. As I turned to leave, a squirrel scampered by. What if an animal attacked her? Mauled her face? Her fingers? She'd be defenseless.

What do I do? I turned her car seat to face the glass door instead of the parking lot. Then I closed the canopy; maybe the lack of eye contact would keep her safe. An extra barrier. Maybe a janitor would see her.

I have no choice.

Not true. What do babies need to travel? I could bring her with me.

No. She's sick. I can't help her.

I squeezed my hands into fists. Time. Was. Running. Out.

I love her.

Bringing her would be suicide.

I promised to take care of her and now I was leaving her sick, vulnerable to the elements, animals, time. What kind of mother am I? What kind of person am I?

A survivor, that's who. Move!

I left, watching the car seat in my rearview mirror until I turned the corner.

I was alone. Again.

CHAPTER SIXTY-FIVE

AUGUST
THURSDAY, SEPTEMBER 7, 2023 10:45 P.M.

August stood in the unfinished basement, lifting free weights. Unlike most men, he hated weightlifting. He enjoyed moving. Running. Biking. Tossing a football. Lifting weights was exacting in its painfulness, but he couldn't leave the house and he had nervous energy to burn while waiting for Vanessa to text a location.

He pulled the dumbbell toward his chest, grunting with exertion. Why text them and then leave them hanging? Daisy was sick? With what? Was Vanessa messing with them?

August set the weight down on the rack with a bang and grabbed a towel, burying his face in it. Vanessa's vagueness mixed with her control over Daisy's life and personal instability drove him to the brink.

He heard footsteps on the wood stairs and turned to see Cassidy round the corner. She rested against a cement pillar, staying ten or so feet away.

"I understand why you agreed," he said, repeating what he said upstairs, but wanting to remind her they had the same goal. "I'd do anything to get Daisy back, too."

"But…" she prompted.

"It's so goddamn frustrating." He tossed the towel on the weights. "We have no power. We're negotiating with a crazy person. And you…" He held out his hand, asking for time, needing to choose the *right* words. Cassidy sharpened his words and threw them back at him like daggers. "It feels like—I'm not saying it's true—like you saw her threat as an opportunity. No hesitation. No discussion about different ways we could respond. No acknowledgment that we're married. We took vows, Cassidy. For better or for worse."

Cassidy rubbed her fingers against her temples. "This is too much for me, August. This constant you, you, you mentality while our daughter is missing."

"It's actually us, our marriage. But I'll set that aside for now." Get Daisy. Arrest Vanessa. Then, grovel, promise, work to become the man Cassidy deserved, the father Daisy and Piper needed. Be present with both his time and mind. "Promise me I'll be part of the kids' lives. That Vanessa doesn't get a say in our family's decisions."

She crossed her arms. "Wo-o-o-o-w."

Frustration took over with her sarcastic response to his genuine concern. "I've tried, through this whole hellish ordeal, to be your teammate. All I want right now is a little support—"

She gasped. "Teammate? Support?"

"Yeah." He pointed at her. "When the cops were all over you, I defended you."

She narrowed her eyes. "Were you acting part of this team when you cheated?"

"Ahh!" August groaned. "You're missing the point."

"I'm missing the point? Me?" Cassidy threw her hands up. "Daisy went missing because of you! How do you still not get that? She might not come home, August. Who knows what Vanessa is planning next. Not me. Certainly not you."

"It's my fault! I get it. Jesus! Do you need me to say the words?" He could make all the excuses in the world—Vanessa was crazy, the abortion was the best choice, cheating wasn't a crime—but it was his fault. By bringing another woman into his life, check that, several women, he put his kids in danger. Daisy might die, because of him. "I literally despise myself—"

His throat was raw from the guttural yelling. Every harm Daisy endured, both physical and psychological, was his fault. And there was nothing he could do to change that.

"You're a good father." She directed her words to the ground, not him. "Even now, I don't question your love for them. But the problem is, and I didn't see it until this happened, is you love you more."

He wanted to defend himself, but everything he said was wrong. Did he put himself first? At times, yes. But not over the kids. Not knowingly.

With no response, she turned and left, her footsteps creaking on the wood stairs. He wrung out his fists, pacing the damp basement. What she was asking—the "she" being applicable to both Cassidy and Vanessa—required him to sacrifice everything he cared about in this world. To never see his kids again. Hold them. Kiss them. Hear them laugh. Watch them grow.

That wasn't fair.

Then again, maybe he didn't deserve fair.

CHAPTER SIXTY-SIX

VANESSA
THURSDAY, SEPTEMBER 7, 2023 11:40 P.M.

About ten miles before the airport, I exited the expressway, driving through unfamiliar city streets. I didn't want to leave my car at the airport, tipping the police off to search the surveillance cameras and find out where I went. Without the car, though, how would I get to the airport? Buses didn't run this late. An Uber was possible, but did I want another witness?

No.

I passed a coffee shop, laundromat, McDonald's—I called a quick audible and joined the drive-thru, ordering a quarter pounder, fries, and a coke. I parked on the street instead of the lot, not realizing how hungry I was until the juices of the burger met my taste buds.

A couple walked past, hand in hand, but instead of getting jealous, I smiled. Walking. I could park in a neighborhood close to the airport and hoof it there on foot. Someone would eventually find the car, maybe tomorrow, maybe several days later. How could I make sure it wasn't linked to me?

Remove the license plate. Simple, yet obvious. Throw away every scrap of paper inside. Clean the surfaces to eliminate prints.

With that thought, I drove to the Walmart I passed. On the way, I thought of Kiah. Was she okay? Did someone find her? Or was she still waiting? More than an hour passed since I left her. Not knowing was agony.

Walmart was busy. After parking, I cleaned out the glove box. Receipts. Insurance. A map. Candy wrappers. I found lipstick beneath the driver's seat. Pale pink. Not my color, but I put some on. Mom's way of aiding my disguise. Studiously, I removed everything, including the base of Kiah's car seat, and put it in the trash bin.

The wind whipped against my naked neck, making me shiver. Or maybe I was terrified of going inside. The cameras. Nosy people. Making a mistake.

Go. Quick. Get it done.

I walked past the greeter—at midnight? For real?—with a wave. While I didn't know where to find a screwdriver, I wasn't asking. Up and down each aisle, until I found it by electrical tools. I grabbed a screwdriver set, not knowing which kind I needed. Up front, I went through the self-checkout.

I started walking out when I heard someone say, "Ms."

My stomach dropped. Should I continue walking? Pretend I hadn't heard? But I already paused. I turned around. A woman wearing the trademark blue Walmart vest held out a pacifier. "This fell out of your pocket."

Of course, it did. I meant to rest it by Kiah's mouth in case she woke up and needed comfort. But I forgot. Because I was a terrible mother. And a terrible criminal. Leaving a trail of breadcrumbs for the police.

"Thanks." I shoved it in my pocket with the smallest of smiles.

I walked into the parking lot, shaking my head, amazed at my stupidity. And bad luck.

As I started the car, I glanced in the rearview mirror to check on Kiah before remembering she wasn't there. I felt a pang, missing her something fierce. Close to two hours without her and it wasn't getting any easier. Even though she cried relentlessly, I wanted her.

I followed the signs to the airport. Once I reached it, I looped around to the nearest neighborhood. I repeated my steps, trying to memorize the route. It shouldn't be hard, but my brain felt like scrambled eggs, too little sleep, too much stress.

Satisfied I wouldn't get lost, I found a dead-end street, four houses on each side, that abutted a large soccer field. None of the houses had lights on. A dead-end would ensure less traffic, but also might cause more nosiness about a stray car from the residents.

Too bad. Every decision carried risks. And time was running out.

After parking in front of the second to last house, I started cleaning the inside with bleach wipes—steering wheel, radio, vents, heat controls, seatbelts, and glove compartment—shoving the dirty wipes into the Walmart bag. Then I took off my sweatshirt and hat, trading them for a long-sleeved blue shirt and gray hat— in case the police got footage from the pediatrician's security cam and sent out a still.

I wiped off the key and left it in the ignition before getting out of the car. Maybe someone would find it, think it was their lucky day, and it would never be connected to me. We could both escape to a new life.

After wiping the door handles, I set down my backpack and kneeled in front of the car. The screws were dirty and rusted. I grabbed the screwdriver and turned. Nothing happened. I sat on my butt and used all my strength to twist. I grunted with effort. Loudly. I froze, glancing around to see if any lights came on.

Nope.

I let out a slow breath. Back to work.

Finally, finally, one side came undone. And the other. The same with the license plate in the back. I was sweaty and out of breath when I finished.

Before leaving, I looked through the windshield of the car. I saw a thousand memories of Mom singing, dancing, laughing. That was how I would remember her. Free and happy.

I started walking. At the first garbage can, I dumped the bag of soiled wipes. Then shoved the license plates, screwdriver kit, and

Kiah's pacifier down a sewer grate. Much as I wanted the last item as a keepsake, dumping it was smart. Especially going through security at the airport.

I should've felt lighter, freer, but my hands gripped the straps of my backpack, pulling it tight, hyperaware all my money and possessions were on me. If I got mugged, what would I do?

Keep walking.

Don't think.

A pair of headlights appeared in the distance. I ducked behind a nearby bush, waiting for the lights to pass.

Breathe.

Breathe.

Breathe.

When I could no longer hear the motor or see the lights, I started walking. The neighborhood felt abandoned and alive at the same time. Like everyone was inside, cataloguing my moves from behind a curtain, waiting to pounce. An animal they would trap and torture.

The police would do worse if they caught me. Inmates in prison—

I stopped and leaned against a mailbox, doing a quick 4-7-8 breathing exercise. In for four, hold for seven, out for eight. My chest tightened instead of loosening. I experienced a similar sensation in the woods after taking Kiah. How did I get the panic to go away?

One step at a time, the director said, resting a hand on my backpack. She pushed me forward. I stumbled, but it got me walking.

The residential area turned commercial and then there were blocks with nothing. The airport was only three miles away. Why was it taking so long? I looked around. Did I take a wrong turn? Was I lost?

No. If I kept going, I'd find it.

My shoulders ached from the heavy backpack.

I felt a blister forming on my right heel.

Even though I was sweating, I was cold. The wind like an icy shower—

Was it…?

Could it be true…?

I saw a sign for the airport. Bright yellow. "Hector Airport EST 1925." The terminal was another half-mile. I wanted to sprint, while also fall to the ground.

I pulled out my burner phone, ensuring the location and GPS were still off. I texted Cassidy, *Rainbow Pediatrics*, along with the address. A moment later, I texted her again, *Remember our deal.*

I shut off the phone and took a few steps before wondering whether I was stupid to text Cassidy from the airport.

The gas station guy said it was untraceable.

Yeah, because he was a secret tech giant, working at a gas station for kicks.

I'm leaving soon. The police will be preoccupied with Daisy's rescue. It'll be fine.

I kept walking.

Nothing felt fine.

CHAPTER SIXTY-SEVEN

CASSIDY
FRIDAY, SEPTEMBER 8, 2023 3:00 A.M.

Cassidy, August, and Detective Lewis stood around the kitchen island, listening to Detective Lewis's phone on speaker as an officer or police liaison in North Dakota—Cassidy didn't have room for extraneous details—relayed the recovery mission. Apparently, there was protocol to ensure the site was secure before they could move into the area.

Cassidy clenched her jaw until it felt like it was wired shut, the muscles running through her face and neck screaming. With each passing second, she prayed. Please let Daisy be there. Please let her be safe. Healthy. Unharmed. I will give anything. Do anything. Any penance or punishment you want.

"Object identified by the door," Cassidy heard the man on the phone say. "Officers approaching." She imagined them with guns at the ready and swallowed her screams. "It's an infant car seat." Her nerves skittered like a game of pinball. "A baby. Can confirm a baby!"

"Yes!" August shouted.

Cassidy stayed rigid. "Is she okay? Tell me she's okay!"

A gush of static. "Alert and breathing," the man said. "Paramedics will assess her en route to the hospital."

"Can someone ride along and FaceTime us?" Cassidy asked, her words jumbling. "Let us see her? Let her hear my voice?"

"The paramedics need to work without interruption," the man said.

"We'll get an update as soon as they have one," Detective Lewis said.

Not good enough. "But—"

"There's a note," the man said. "It says, 'This is Kiah. She's sick. Fever, rash, diarrhea for past forty-eight hours. Please help her. Contact Cassidy with questions.'"

"It's Daisy!" August pumped a fist. "Vanessa calls her Kiah."

Cassidy gripped the counter, feeling lightheaded. A fever and diarrhea? They could fix that. All the ways she imagined Vanessa might have hurt her and none of them came to fruition.

"Take a picture!" Cassidy needed more proof. "Please!"

There was an audible jumble of the phone and some shouting, but too many people were talking to understand. Cassidy heard sirens roar and eventually fade.

"Sending now," the man said.

Cassidy and August leaned forward, heads tilted together as Detective Lewis clicked on the photo.

Daisy! Cassidy moaned, fingers brushing the picture, caressing what she could of her baby girl. Daisy had a fist stuffed inside her mouth. "She's hungry," Cassidy said as her breasts hardened. "I need to feed her."

"She's alive." August wrapped his arm around Cassidy, pressing his lips to the top of her head.

Detective Lewis pulled the phone to his ear, his voice grim, his mouth drawn. Fear spiraled from her stomach. "What's wrong?" She tugged August's arm, needing answers. "What aren't they telling us?"

August pulled away, his eyebrows furrowed. "I don't know."

Detective Lewis said little more than, "uh-huh" and "I see." What? What did he see?

A lifetime later, he ended the call. He looked at them with steely eyes. "At this point, we don't have any leads on Vanessa's whereabouts. The police are reviewing security footage from the building, as well as the surrounding streets."

August swore under his breath and turned away, walking to the sink.

Vanessa tricked August. Outmaneuvered the police. Media. Crossed state lines, evading detection at every turn. But she gave Daisy back. In this moment, that was enough. "Can we leave?" Cassidy said, pleading. "Now? Please."

"There's a six-ten flight," Detective Lewis said.

"Fine." Cassidy grabbed her purse from the cabinet on the side of the fridge, ready to go. Daisy was all she needed. Anything else could be bought in North Dakota.

"Wait," August said. "I need to change."

She set her purse on the island. "You're coming?"

He tilted his head. "Cassidy."

"What if Vanessa sees you at the hospital?" Cassidy brought a fist to her mouth as tears of frustration spiked. "*Remember our deal*, she texted. She's watching!"

"She can't get near the room," Detective Lewis said. "There's security."

How many times had Detective Lewis been wrong about Vanessa capabilities? Cassidy walked to August, pressing her hands to his heart. "There'll be media everywhere," she said. "Vanessa will see you on TV."

"Isn't there a separate entrance I could use?" August asked Detective Lewis. "Cassidy could go in the front, let the media get footage. No one will know I'm inside."

Detective Lewis pressed his lips together. "We'll find a way."

"Why risk it?" She kept her breath steady, even as her blood pressure rose. "Go get Piper. Take care of her while I help Daisy. Both of our daughters need us."

"I need to see Daisy," he said quietly. "For the same reasons you do."

Cassidy saw pain in his eyes. She also saw determination. Selfish determination. He wanted to hold Daisy to assure himself she was safe and healthy, but also that he was absolved. He wasn't capable of loving unconditionally, of sacrificing for the greater good, because he couldn't see past his own needs.

"Fine," she said, knowing the discussion had the same usefulness as banging her head against a wall.

Losing Daisy didn't change him. Nothing ever would. In many ways, that made her decision about their future easier.

CHAPTER SIXTY-EIGHT

VANESSA
FRIDAY, SEPTEMBER 8, 2023 3:05 A.M.

When I arrived at the airport, the doors were locked. It didn't open until 3:30 a.m. No one was around. A ghost town. I took a seat on a bench, pulled my knees to my chest, and rested my head against them. Almost immediately, my eyes closed. I jerked awake a second later.

The way my luck was running, I'd fall asleep and miss my flight. Or be awakened by a security officer. I had to stay vigilant. Why didn't I buy coffee at McDonalds? The coke was doing jack—

I snapped awake. This torture reminded me of high school, where they put on a movie, turned off the lights, and expected you to complete a worksheet.

A car approached from my left. I pulled out my phone, pretending to be transfixed, while watching out of the corner of my eye as a man exited the vehicle, grabbed his suitcase from the trunk, and kissed a woman goodbye. She got in the driver's seat and drove away.

Soon after, I heard the terminal doors open behind me. I wanted to run. Get on the plane. Fly far, far away. Where the sand massaged my feet, the water aqua pools, the sun a warm hug, people unsuspecting and, best of all, strangers. Instead, I took a deep breath, pulled my hat low, and walked through the automatic door.

Less than two hours until my flight.

I went to the portal, imported my booking number, and printed my boarding pass. A few others did the same. Other than the sound of suitcases rolling on the floor, the room was quiet.

Not good. With so few people, everyone would scrutinize each other. Or was it like riding in an elevator? Avoid eye contact at all cost?

I walked toward security, passing a restaurant with a TV tuned to FOX news. My picture on the screen. Me with a wide smile and a graduation cap. The headline, "College Grad to Baby 'Napper: What Went Wrong"

Great question! Why don't you do some goddamn investigating.

Stop it. August was the past. Vanessa gone. I was Mackenzie Roeper. Learn it. Live it. Love it.

As I approached security, only a few people were in line. I felt tired, thirsty, terrified I would get arrested. I took several long pulls from a drinking fountain and then ducked inside the bathroom to wait for security to get busier. I wanted to be another faceless part of the mass.

On the toilet, I put my head in my hands, trying to stop the verbal assaults that screamed to leave the airport. Buy a shitty car. Drive west. But that plan had pitfalls too. Namely, lack of vehicle and money. Any way I went about it, I could get caught. A thought that didn't help the tremble in my legs or the sprint of my heart.

At the sink, I nearly laughed when I saw my reflection. Short, uneven hair that reminded me of my dolls after I gave them haircuts—

Doll. I thought I was clever, leaving that doll in Kiah's crib. I remember the elation of first holding Kiah, becoming a mother—

I bit my lip. Don't think about that.

I leaned toward the mirror, peering at my bloodshot eyes, the dark bags beneath, the cold sore by my lower lip, the zits sprinkled on my chin. Wasn't going to win any beauty pageants.

Good. No resemblance to that smiling girl on the news.

"You can do this," I whispered to myself.

I pushed off the sink, needing momentum to move. Outside, twenty or so people were lined up at security. One roadblock. One gigantic, life-altering obstacle.

Someone bumped my shoulder from behind, mumbling an apology as they passed. Probably shouldn't stand in the middle of the hallway, Vanessa. You'll draw attention to yourself.

And yet, I couldn't move.

The director clasped her hand inside mine. It was warm, a guiding light. As we approached security, she whispered in my ear, You're a recent college grad. Going on a solo trip. To Fiji or New Zealand or Australia. Passing through Hawaii. You're nervous. But excited.

Go!

As I got closer, I studied the security officer. Mid-twenties. Dark red hair. Pale skin. Patches of facial hair. Stocky. Was he the type to watch the news? Be a hero?

Fifteen people.

Was it in my favor that we were of similar age? Or would that pique his interest?

Too delirious to tell.

Ten people.

I had my ticket and ID ready. Like any other passenger. Except I wasn't any other passenger. I was a fugitive. My picture everywhere.

Five people.

I'd be running the rest of my life. Never able to trust. Let down my guard. Be me.

Never.

Never.

Never.

"Ms.?" The TSA agent waved me forward. "Ticket and ID, please."

I handed him both, willing my hand not to shake. He didn't smile, but he could be bored. Or tired. It was early. Maybe he hated his job. That would be a plus. He wouldn't scrutinize me. Or maybe smiling was forbidden.

"Take off the hat," he said.

I complied, not daring to breathe.

"Look at me." I looked him straight in the eye. Not blinking. Barely existing. I should've bought glasses. Or drawn on freckles. Something, other than the hair, to distract.

Another mistake.

He looked between me and the ID. Twice. Was this normal? Was I a walking red flag? "I'm going to Fiji," I said.

"Uh-huh." He held up a flashlight to the ID.

I felt lightheaded. About to pass out. I paid good money for the ID. Was told it was valid. What if he lied to me? All men lie.

"College graduation trip." I reached forward to stabilize myself against his podium at the same moment he handed me back my documents.

"Enjoy your trip," he said.

I nearly wept.

The rest happened like a dream. Taking my shoes off. Loading my backpack on the conveyer belt. Walking through the metal detector. Getting a bagel at Starbucks. Boarding the plane. Buckling. Listening to the flight attendant's directions.

Up, up, up in the air we went. High above the clouds. My heart soaring along with it.

Free. I was finally free.

CHAPTER SIXTY-NINE

CASSIDY
FRIDAY, SEPTEMBER 8, 2023 6:10 A.M.

From the moment Cassidy boarded the plane, she sat in her seat with her hands tucked between her thighs, back rigid, mouth cemented shut, her feet firmly planted on the floor as if pressing the accelerator on the plane. August didn't speak either. He sat next to her with his eyes closed, letting the drone of the engines lull him to sleep.

For an hour-and-a-half, she didn't move. Didn't eat or drink or speak or sleep. Every ounce of energy left, she saved for Daisy. She used the maroon stain on the seatback as a focal point. It looked like an irregular mole against the tan leather, but was probably a swipe of lipstick or ketchup or blood. She imagined snuggling Daisy, the soft tug of her lips as it clasped around Cassidy's nipple, Daisy's blue eyes searching for answers, comfort, love. Cassidy would give it all. And more.

The plane descended. Detective Lewis led them off first. Cassidy strode through the airport, inhaling the scent of coffee and fried food. Her breasts were heavy, engorged to the point of pain. But she endured it to feed Daisy.

On the curb outside, a police SUV waited to take them to the hospital. Cassidy and August got in the back, while Detective Lewis took the front next to the driver, Officer Packard. Traffic was thin, but the twenty-minute ride proved excruciating. Cassidy again found a focal point and prayed. Please, please, please. As they pulled into the circular drive of the hospital, a dozen reporters stood waiting. Men and women with cameras, microphones, and phones ready.

She hated the media for making a spectacle. Profiting off their pain. Daisy's trauma. Cassidy pushed her sunglasses tight against the brim of her nose as the SUV stopped. The blacked-out windows meant she could see them, but they couldn't see her.

"I'll open your door and we'll walk in together," Detective Lewis said, turning back to face her. "Officer Packard will drive August to the delivery entrance and he'll be up soon."

The plan made her nervous. She didn't want August near the hospital. There was bound to be a leak. Vanessa would find out.

"It'll be fine." August squeezed her rigid hand, nearly crushing the bones.

She unlatched her hand. "Sit back so they don't see you when I get out."

When Detective Lewis opened the door, she immediately heard shouting—*Is Daisy okay? How do you know Vanessa Jennings? How do you feel?*

Get inside. Hold Daisy. Feed her.

More questions as she stepped out of the car. Detective Lewis put a protective arm around her shoulders, leading her into the building. As she walked through the automatic doors, her ears rang. It felt like those reporters had megaphones.

A woman in a long white jacket approached, introducing herself as Dr. Rhodes. She wore an N95 mask, which covered everything but her eyes. Dark brown, almost black. Detective Lewis handed Cassidy a paper mask—an item she no longer carried in her purse—before putting on one himself.

"Is Daisy okay?" Cassidy asked.

"Yes," Dr. Rhodes said, gesturing for them to follow. "I'll tell you everything when we get to her room."

They went up one elevator, down a hallway, and up two floors on another elevator, not walking fast enough for Cassidy. Dr.

Rhodes used her key pass to let them through two locked doors, which lowered Cassidy's anxiety. Vanessa would not get in here.

Dr. Rhodes picked up what looked like an iPad from the nurse's station, scanning through it with her finger as she walked. Down the hallway, she paused outside a door. "Daisy was severely dehydrated when she came to us this morning," she said, her voice hushed. "We used an IV to increase her fluids. Good news is, her numbers are up—"

"Can we talk while I hold her?" Cassidy's voice broke. Each second without Daisy was torturous. "Please."

"Absolutely." Dr. Rhodes opened the door.

"I'll wait here," Detective Lewis said.

The room was bright with sunlight, yet small. A bassinet sat in the middle. Cassidy peered down at Daisy and immediately sobbed. Daisy's head turned, her gaze lighting on Cassidy. She smiled, her cheeks rising to her eyes, her tongue poking through the gums.

"Oh!" Cassidy picked Daisy up, careful to not move the IV inserted in her tiny leg. Red bumps covered her leg, but Cassidy would ask the doctor about that later.

She embraced Daisy. The powdery scent, the warmth of her skin, the downy blonde hair, the weight of her. Or lack thereof! Cassidy swore she felt lighter.

Bliss. Pure, unadulterated bliss.

Daisy burrowed her face into Cassidy's chest, trying to reach the milk. Cassidy's breasts tingled and tightened, begging for release. She carried Daisy to the tan reclining chair in the corner, wheeling along the bag of fluid. After sitting, she lifted her shirt, unclasped her bra cup, and teased Daisy's lower lip with the nipple. She latched on with a ferocious tug, drinking deeply and quickly. "Mommy's here," Cassidy said, as the milk in her other breast let down, soaking her bra. "I'm never leaving you again. I promise."

While Daisy fed, Dr. Rhodes explained the dehydration, diarrhea, and rash was due to the formula. "Perhaps her stomach couldn't handle the sudden change to formula. She might also have had problems feeding from the bottle, or maybe she's allergic to the brand…"

Dr. Rhodes discussed slowly weaning Daisy off breastmilk when Cassidy was ready, testing formulas, and getting an allergy test when Daisy was six months. Cassidy never took her eyes off Daisy. The deep blue iris struck her as resilient, precocious, calm. As if she was saying, *I'm okay, Mommy. Stop worrying.*

Cassidy would never stop worrying. Not with Vanessa free.

"Her fever is down to ninety-nine-point-seven," Dr. Rhodes continued. "Physically, she should make a full recovery."

Daisy splayed a hand on Cassidy's breast, searching, perhaps, for Cassidy's heart. Her home. Cassidy swallowed. Daisy would forgive Cassidy, but would she ever forget? "What about emotionally?" Cassidy stroked the rash on Daisy's arm, wishing her touch could heal. "Will she remember anything? Could the feeling of being scared or abandoned stick with her?"

"It's possible, yes," Dr. Rhodes said. "Infants can remember trauma even though they don't have language to process it. We don't know what happened over the past two days, but given her health, we can assume it wasn't the level of attention, love, and care she was used to."

Daisy is safe, Cassidy reminded herself. Anything else, we can fix.

"But it's equally possible she has no emotional scars," Dr. Rhodes went on. "Babies are resilient. Many spend time away from their parents. The situation here is different, but this was two days, not two months."

"If she has issues, what would it look like?" Cassidy wanted to be prepared.

"Separation anxiety—"

"Crying when I leave?" Cassidy asked.

"Yes, but it can manifest in other ways. A zoned-out, shocked look, less smiling, cooing—"

Cassidy couldn't help herself. "She smiled when she saw me." Who was she trying to convince, herself or the doctor?

"That's great. There could be a loss of eye contact or eating skills, though that doesn't seem to be a problem either. Breastfeeding is the best thing for her right now, both physically and emotionally." Dr. Rhodes gazed at Daisy, her eyes crinkling in what Cassidy swore was a smile beneath the mask. "As she develops, she might be slower to meet the sitting, crawling, and walking guideposts." Dr. Rhodes shrugged. "Even then, you can't be sure it's not her normal development."

"What can we do?" Cassidy switched Daisy to the other breast. "It's not like we can take her to a therapist."

"You could see a pediatric psychiatrist," Dr. Rhodes said. "But the biggest thing right now is to understand her signs of stress. Certain noises, smells might trigger her. Spend time with her. Reestablish routines so she can predict what's next. It will make her feel safe."

Cassidy half-laughed, half-cried. "I love routines."

August walked into the room, distractedly greeting the doctor. He squatted in front of Cassidy's chair, palming the crown of Daisy's head. She looked at him through the corner of her eyes, but didn't stop eating. When he ran his hand down to hers, she wrapped her fist around his pinky and didn't let go. August let out a sob.

"I'll give you some time," Dr. Rhodes said before leaving.

"She's dehydrated," Cassidy said. "That's why she has this IV. But her fever is down."

"She'll be okay?" His voice was slow, thick with emotion.

"Yes." She rested her hand on August's, the one Daisy held too. A team—of sorts. "She missed you."

He lowered his head and pressed a kiss on Cassidy's hand. "I'm sorry," he whispered, his chin quivering against her hand. "I'm so, so sorry."

"I know." There was nothing else to say. Nor did Cassidy want to have another discussion. She wanted to enjoy feeding Daisy, nourishing her back to health. The gentle suck, the way Daisy's curious eyes searched the room, the whisper of breath against Cassidy's breast, the slight pauses she took between swallows. I love you, Cassidy kept saying, both in her head and out loud. She couldn't stop saying it. Cheek-to-cheek, she burped Daisy and then, all too soon, she handed her to August. Even a foot away, Cassidy missed her.

She fixed her bra and shirt, watching as August tucked Daisy in his arm, eyes glinting with tears. He whispered something in her ear. Probably telling her he loved her. Or maybe apologizing. Seeing him with Daisy, she understood why he needed to come. Perhaps was too hard on him earlier.

He was a good father. Was that enough?

No. She couldn't stay in a marriage without trust. Without respect. Love.

Nor could she keep her end of the deal with Vanessa to deny August custody. Piper and Daisy would suffer if she shunned August from their lives. And everything had to be about keeping them safe and healthy. How would Daisy ever feel safe emotionally if people kept disappearing on her? How would Piper grapple with the sudden disappearance of her dad? Despite Vanessa's threat to return, Cassidy would agree to joint custody. The more love and attention they could shine down upon both girls, the better.

As far as keeping Daisy physically safe, Cassidy would enter a self-imposed witness protection program until Vanessa was caught. End her podcast. Her blog. Sell the house. The moment Daisy was taken, the truths that came out in the aftermath, made it impossible to go backwards, reclaim what was lost. And with Vanessa knowing the address, August couldn't keep the house either. She wouldn't let the children spend time there. She and the girls would move in with her parents until she got sorted. And

August would move…somewhere else. Hopefully not too far, but far enough for her to start over.

A divorce.

She would be a single mother. Alone. She'd never been alone before. She lived with her parents. Then her sorority sisters. Then August.

Another emotional adjustment, not just for herself, but for the kids.

She would likely spend months mourning her marriage, doing a crash reconstruction about how he cheated for years without her knowledge, but right now, her only thought was her girls. Meeting their needs. She grabbed her phone and texted Mom, telling her Daisy was okay and asking Piper to FaceTime. While Piper didn't know about the kidnapping, she missed her baby sister. And Cassidy wanted to share this happy moment with both her daughters. August too. She wanted one last moment as a family.

EPILOGUE

VANESSA
ONE YEAR LATER

Favorite thing about living in Maui and working at a five-star resort? The gorgeous men. Today's candidate sat on a low cream sofa, bracketed by tiki lamps, the flames glowing a violent orange to match the sun setting over the ocean behind him. Bare ankle crossed over his knee, hand absently stroking the back of his neck, eyes transfixed by his phone. Everything about him screamed class, sexiness, confidence. Was it the Rolex? The Italian loafers? The Gucci aviators tucked into the dip of his v-neck? The bronze skin, glowing in the waning light? The ease with which he occupied prime seating without ordering a drink, as if his presence was enough?

While mixing drinks behind the bar, I couldn't stop checking him out. I should've been immune to this level of beauty by now. Genetically blessed, successful, gym-hardened men featured on magazine covers and Page Six jetted over for long weekends. No covers for this guy, but he had an aura. Much as I tried to resist, I felt Vanessa, the girl I buried, come alive.

Anticipation. Passion. Love—

Don't do it.

I wanted this man. Wanted him to want—

Not worth it.

Looking wasn't enough tonight. I started thinking. Lusting. Hoping.

"Excuse me, Ms." An old man with gray hair and a strawberry tinted nose from a lifetime of imbibing waved. I walked to the other end of the bar. "We'd like a bottle of Dom. We're celebrating our fiftieth wedding anniversary."

After congratulating them and popping the bottle, I asked, "What's the secret?" In other words, how do you get someone to love you and not leave?

"Never fall out of love at the same time," the man said, squeezing his wife's shoulder.

She laughed. "Forgive, forgive, forgive."

I poured two glasses and put the bottle in an ice bucket. "I'll keep that in mind." Always pleasant, but I never lingered. Avoided giving away personal details. Kept busy, preventing customers from getting a good look at my face.

A year passed since I arrived in Honolulu, stressed, starved, and skittish. First, I found a cheap hostel and slept for three days, waking only to pee and drink water. Then I searched for a job. With no references and little documentation, all I could scrounge up was a cocktail server at Strip'n'Sin, where the manager was "morally flexible" and tips were decent.

The job led me to Rico. A businessman cum opportunist. Whatever you needed—ID's, drugs, girls, passports—Rico could get it. No questions asked—for a price. Five thousand bought me a new identity; birth certificate, social security card, and permanent resident card. Almost two-thirds of my money gone, but necessary. I couldn't get a good job or apartment without it.

I quit the strip club and got a bartending gig at a resort in Maui. Hopping islands had the added benefit of erasing the final tie to Vanessa and Mackenzie. With a steady income, I polished my transformation. My hair was now brown with honey and golden lowlights. Mascara, subtle lipstick. No sexy clothes. Flats. My formerly thick eyebrows were threaded to give my face a different shape. Topped off with cat-eyed black glasses, I looked understated. Underwhelming. Unfuckable.

And I made peace with that. Vanessa was gone. The excitement, the highs, the sex. Gone. Gone. Gone.

Or not.

Watching Hot Guy strum his lower lip with his finger, my groin tightened into a pleasurable fist. Oh, to be that finger!

It's safer this way, I reminded myself, busying my eager hands with washing a glass. Vanessa was still on the authorities' minds. The FBI vowed to "bring Daisy's kidnapper to justice." Turned out, when I crossed state lines, it became a federal crime. Who knew? Not me.

Honestly, their persistence pissed me off. Let. It. Go. I gave her back, didn't I? No one got hurt. Everyone moved on. Cassidy ended her podcast, disabled her website, deleted her social media. They sold the house. Got divorced. Refused to give interviews.

And yet, the media was relentless. They dug their claws in, giving us the soap opera treatment—the affair, abortion, Kiah's "near death" experience. They dubbed me mentally unstable, hell-bent on having a baby. August a sex addict. Anointed Cassidy a saint; a beautiful and loving mother devoted to raising her children.

Wrong. Wrong. Wrong.

Everyone ignored Cassidy's constant bitching about motherhood on her podcast. How she was asleep, on the job, when I took Kiah. How August promised me a future together, a family, in exchange for aborting my baby. How I was trying to give Kiah a better life. Save her from August's manipulative ways. Kiah getting sick wasn't my fault. Who could've predicted she couldn't digest formula? Ultimately, I got her help. I *saved* her.

No one wanted to print a story about that, though.

The only time I regretted disappearing was listening to my father's interview. He argued August was to blame; that I never would've gotten an abortion and kidnapped his baby if he hadn't manipulated me. I cried. Dad never defended me. Did he say this to honor Mom's legacy? Or did he truly believe in my goodness? I was tempted to reach out, but caught myself. His words of support were so unlike him, it must have been a ploy by the FBI to trap me.

I didn't need his love. The public's understanding. To become a media darling. Just one man to love me. See me. Accept all of me.

Speaking of, Hot Guy got up from the couch and made his way toward the bar. His body formed a V, the wide shoulders coming down to narrow, defined hips. Closer, closer, he came, his long legs walking with purpose. Me? A girl could hope.

He pushed a stool to the side, leaning against the bar and grabbing the leather drink folder. He gave me a closed-mouth smile as I walked over. Part cocky, part mischievous. He knew how to have a good time—and make sure the woman did too.

I tucked a stray hair behind my ear and smiled. "What can I get you?"

"Jameson. On the rocks."

I glanced at the menu. Mocking. "Needed the menu to decide that?"

He laughed, his entire face lighting up, transforming from hot to I-need-to-fuck-this-guy-against-the-bar-tonight irresistible. "I might order food."

"Then you'll need this one." I handed him a bigger leather folder from behind the bar. "Kitchen closes in a half-hour though."

Much to my delight, he took a seat. "What's good here?"

"Sushi. Crab cakes. Lobster tail." I gestured toward the ocean behind him. "Anything fresh."

"What would you choose?"

"Me?" I pointed to my chest. Nothing here on my budget. "I'm easy to please. A burger and fries girl."

He gave me a wry smile. "Few women are easy to please."

This was my opening. Don't blow it. I softened my voice and said, "You've never met anyone like me."

The way his eyes danced with mine suggested he was no longer thinking of food. "What's your name?"

I held up a finger as I helped another customer. Much needed time. I got nervous introducing myself as Crystal. As I made a couple Mai Tai's, Hot Guy watched me, which both turned me on and terrified me. Was he an undercover cop?

Always the fear of being caught.

No. He asked my name. The world's most commonly asked question.

Stop. Being. Paranoid.

Oh, how lovely it would be to let go. Fall into his arms. Be held. Feel the warmth and safety of his embrace. The rise and fall of his chest. The tease of his lips brushing—

Focus. You can't lose your job over this guy.

I cashed out the customer, mouthing "sorry" to Hot Guy. He winked, as if we already had a shorthand. My heart rate spiked.

"Decide on anything?" I tapped his menu, thinking, did you decide on me?

"How can I decide when I don't know your name?" Pushy? Or flirty? Impossible to tell when he looked this good. Maybe I should cut my losses.

But I felt something palpable running through my veins, hitching my breath, energizing my soul. Maybe he was my soul mate.

Stop being dumb. He's not your soulmate. He's a man. He'll lie to you, use you, and spit you out, damaged and depressed. Just like the rest. Move on. Serve someone else.

But what if…

"Crystal." I pulled off my glasses, letting the tip of the temple rest on my lower lip. Turned out, I still wanted to be sexy. "And your name, sir?"

"Sir." He laughed. "Harrison Wright. But you can call me Henry."

"Not Hank?"

"Definitely not Hank." He held out his hand. I dared to meet it with mine. Warm. Inviting. Undiscovered terrain, yet familiar. Can a handshake be intimate? This one was. I saw our future in that split-second. He did too. I swear. "So, Crystal, what's your story? How'd you end up in Hawaii?"

I let go of his hand and put my glasses back on, wanting the safety of my disguise. His persistent questions made me nervous. "How do you know I'm not from here?"

He paused. "The accent. Sounds Midwest."

I brought my hand to my mouth, wishing I could gnaw on my fingernail. I was breaking all my rules, but his gravitational pull made it impossible to think. "Lifestyle, the ocean, sunshine...shirtless men." I stuck my tongue out at him. "What about you? Where are you vacationing from?"

"L.A."

Obviously. "What's in L.A.?"

"Work." He paused, his gaze penetrating. "I'm an agent."

My gut seized. Federal? Or the movies? Was he messing with me? I filled a glass with ice-cold water and took a sip, ensuring my voice didn't shake when I spoke. "Sounds exciting."

He raised his eyebrows. "You'd be surprised how dull it is."

I doubted that. "More exciting than working in a bar."

A small smile. "I'm hoping tonight is a bit more exciting for you than usual."

He wasn't wearing a ring. Nor was there a tan line. But some men don't wear rings. August didn't. I brushed my finger against his, grazing the area where a ring might lie, knowing it was too forward, but the past requiring me to ask, "Wife?"

He closed the gap between us. "Haven't found the one."

His breath smelled like whiskey. I wanted to run my tongue over his lips. Reluctantly, I pulled my hand away. "It's Hawaii. Never know, maybe your luck will change."

"I have a feeling it might." He drew out each word.

We both laughed, the sexual tension a tightrope between our eyes, both of us struggling to stay upright.

"Fancy a drink after work?" he asked.

Loved the way he said "fancy." "Yeah."

"When does your shift end?"

I glanced at the clock. "An hour."

"I can wait." His smile grew. "Something tells me you're worth waiting for."

This, right here, was fate. A moment. *The* moment. The real start of my life. Every false start, mistake, heartbreak, disaster, running from the law—all brought me to Hawaii to meet the man of my dreams.

Henry.

Henry and Vanessa—

No. Henry and Crystal. Must not make that mistake in front of him.

I bit my tongue to keep from giggling while I went back to work.

An hour later, Henry held my hand as we walked down to the beach. I thought of how August held my hand on the Riverwalk on our first date. The sweetness I intuited from the gesture.

Don't think of August. He was evil. Henry is nothing like August.

I turned around and winked at the director, knowing exactly how she would shoot the scene. First, she'd get close, filming us walking and talking, occasionally stumbling into each other with laughter, the lingering looks of two people yet to fuck. Then the director would fall behind, panning out for a wide shot, the moon a spotlight. We'd get smaller and smaller until all that was left was our footprints in the sand, the ocean creeping forward, lapping them up. Everyone would leave the theater, asking their boyfriend or husband or gay BFF, Was it a trap? Or was it love? Was the erasing of the footprints a metaphor? That she would pay for her crimes, cease to meaningfully exist? Or that she would escape? Again?

Ah, cinema.

Henry worried me. But he intrigued me more. A girl had to live, right?

I let go of his hand and ran toward the water, splashing with my feet. I turned around and yelled, "Come and get me!"

THE END

About the Author

Marisa Rae Dondlinger is the author of *Gray Lines*, *Open*, and *Scenes From a Bar*. She lives in Wisconsin with her husband and two young daughters. A graduate of the University of Wisconsin Law School, Marisa practiced law for several years before devoting herself to writing fiction. When not writing, she enjoys reading, being in nature, and watching her daughters play sports.

Note from Marisa Rae Dondlinger

Word-of-mouth is crucial for any author to succeed. If you enjoyed *Come and Get Me*, please leave a review online—anywhere you are able. Even if it's just a sentence or two. It would make all the difference and would be very much appreciated.

Thanks!
Marisa Rae Dondlinger

We hope you enjoyed reading this title from:

Subscribe to our mailing list – *The Rosevine* – and receive **FREE** books, daily deals, and stay current with news about upcoming releases and our hottest authors.
Scan the QR code below to sign up.

Already a subscriber? Please accept a sincere thank you for being a fan of Black Rose Writing authors.

Made in the USA
Monee, IL
16 May 2024